SWEET LIKE POISON

SAVAGE U

J. WOLF

Copyright © 2022 by J. Wolf

Little Bird Publishing LLC

All rights reserved.

No portion of this book may be reproduced in any form without written permission from the publisher or author, except as permitted by U.S. copyright law.

Editor: Word Nerd Editing—Monica Black

Proofreading: My Brother's Editor

Cover Design: Kate Farlow

Cover Photo: Regina Wamba

This book is for every girl who was called bossy and every woman who has been labelled difficult. You're perfect.

Author's Note

Dear lovely reader,

Sweet Like Poison is a dark (ish) new adult college romance intended for mature readers. Although this story isn't as dark as others in the Savage River universe, it does explore topics and situations that might make some readers uncomfortable.

Inside these pages, you will find detailed mentions of past sexual assault and the aftermath of that trauma.

This story also contains mentions of depression, mental health treatment, and multiple pregnancy losses for a side character.

Please treat yourself kindly when choosing whether or not to read this story.

xoxo,

Julia

Prologue

Elena

Freshman Year

ALL I WANTED WAS a milkshake.

A thick, strawberry milkshake with piles of whipped cream on top. And a cherry. There had to be a cherry. Why else bother?

This would be my first one in...I couldn't remember the last time I had one. All I could think about were the milkshakes I used to get at the *T* when I was a kid. I couldn't get them out of my mind.

I'd be back in Berkeley tomorrow. Thank Prada. This had been a hell of a trip back to Savage River for Thanksgiving. My mom wasn't good, and my dad was too busy to really notice. He *did* notice the scratch on the Porsche and my abysmal showing at midterms. Threats flew like paper airplanes. There was no room for mistakes or failure in the Sanderson household. At least, not from me. Dad didn't stop to ask *why* my grades were shitty or the bags under my eyes could use their own luggage cart. It was all too much.

Hence, my burning desire for a milkshake and an excuse to escape my house.

The *T* had been *the* hangout post-football games in high school. As I stepped inside the old-fashioned diner and glanced around, I could almost see the ghost of my former self, queen bee-ing it in my skimpy cheerleader uniform.

Raucous laughter drew my attention to a booth on the far side of the restaurant. A group of skater boys and a couple girls were crowded into a corner booth, shooting spitballs or whatever those types did. I recognized one of them. Helen Ortega's red lips gave her away. It was sad a girl like her was going to be stuck in this town forever.

I shrugged.

The counter was mostly empty. I took a seat near the cash register, away from the random old guys farther down. The menu trembled in my hands. Or maybe that was my hands trembling.

This trip needed to be over. I loved my family, but they weren't easy. Berkeley wasn't a walk in the park, but compared to this? I put the menu down and caught the waitress's eye. I *really* needed that milkshake.

"Hello, honey. What'll it be?" The waitress was older, silver-blonde, wearing an impeccable white button-down. I respected that she was able to keep her clothing stain-free.

"Strawberry milkshake, please. I'm trying to suck away my problems, so the thicker, the better."

She winked. "That's what she said, baby doll. I'll be right back with your shake."

I must have been out of my mind because I snickered at her played-out joke. I mean, really, I'd walked into that one. How could she not go with it?

Sitting at the counter alone was strange. I never did anything by myself. I could have called someone to join me—Annika most likely wasn't going back to USC until tomorrow—but I had every intention of drinking this entire milkshake. I could picture her face now, counting the calories I was ingesting, gloating internally that it would land on my ass. Besides, it would be strange for me to call Annika. I hadn't returned any of her texts or Snaps since we went our separate ways for college, why start now?

The waitress came back with my shake before I was forced into too much introspection. I did enough of that in therapy. *Shudder.* She winked at me again. I decided I liked a woman who winked unabashedly. Especially one who kept her white shirts crisp, even in the face of adversity.

The first hit of milky strawberry sent my eyes rolling back in my head. Yes. This was exactly what I needed. I had to suck so hard on my straw, there was no room in my body for thoughts or worries. My concentration went to the goal of transferring shake to mouth.

Halfway drained, I took a break to catch my breath. My stomach was churning. It wasn't used to being full, much less with full-fat dairy.

Chewing on the end of my straw, I spun on my stool, idly scanning the diner. The skaters were still there. I accidentally caught Helen's eye. She flipped me off. I made two of my fingers into a *V* and waggled my tongue between them. She rolled her eyes and gave me the back of her head.

Good. The last thing I wanted was to spend time looking at a Savage River nobody.

There were a few people on the other side of the diner. An older couple, a family, a group of friends—

Oh.

I'd know the shape of Nate Bergen's head anywhere, even from the back. I'd spent my high school years crazy in love with him—emphasis on crazy—and mortally terrified of him. He'd ruined me in every way. Or maybe he'd just activated the poison that had always festered inside me.

He was with a girl. I could see her face from my angle. She was young. Had to still be in high school. Her cheeks were rosy as she smiled at him. I recognized that look. Nate could be charming and funny. He was uncommonly good-looking—and he used that as a weapon. Once you were his, so fully under his spell, you had no chance of recovering, he'd reveal his true self.

Nate was a monster.

The girl he was with had no idea. She must not have heard the rumors about him. The reason he was expelled from our high school. The money his father had paid out to multiple families to keep his misdeeds hush-hush.

The shake in my stomach curdled. I was off my stool before I knew what I was doing, my feet carrying me across the diner to their table.

They stopped talking abruptly, both looking up at me. The girl smiled. Nate's face flashed from friendly to contemptuous back to friendly again.

"Hi, Nate." My fingers curled around the thick glass in my hands. Oh yeah, I still had my milkshake. I didn't remember walking over here, much less bringing it with me.

"Hey, El. What are you doing here?" Affable. Like we were old friends. Like he hadn't pinned me down over the summer and—

I gnashed my teeth together, grinning at him. My first love. My first hate.

"Are you on a date?"

He lowered his chin, and that same flash of contempt lingered a little longer.

"Uh, yeah. This is Sera. Sera, this is Elena. We went to high school together."

If we'd been alone, Nate would have wrapped his hand around my throat and reminded me to behave. As it was, he had the edge of the table in a death grip.

The girl shot me a smile a little shaky at the edges. She was pretty, with freckles sprinkled across her nose, and thick, dark-red hair. Nate didn't have a type looks-wise. As long as a girl was emotionally vulnerable and physically weaker, he got hard as a rock.

"Hi," Sera said brightly. "It's nice to meet you."

Nate cleared his throat. "We were just having dinner. We'll catch up later."

I shook my head. "Oh, right. Silly me. I just have one more thing to say, then I'll go."

I focused on Sera. Her sunny demeanor. Her wide smile, even in the awkward situation. I didn't know her. I'd probably never see her again. But I knew when someone was whole and when they were broken. Sera was still whole. My mouth was moving before my mind was made up to say something.

"Just so you're aware, Nate has a bad habit of misinterpreting the words 'no' as 'yes.' If I were you, I'd get up and walk away and block his number. He'll only hurt you. I know I might sound like a bitter ex—and I *am* bitter. Though, not because he broke up with me. That was a relief. I'm bitter because this man hurt me just like he's hurt a lot of other girls. Nate is a rapist, and even though they don't say it, everyone in this town knows it."

Sera's rosy cheeks paled. Her eyes darted back and forth from Nate to me.

"Elena," Nate gritted out. "That's enough. Walk the other way."

I turned to him. "I'm not scared of you anymore. You've done your worst." Then I took my beloved milkshake and dumped the entire contents in his lap. "Fuck you, Nate."

He jolted out of his seat, swiping the shake off his pants. "You fucking cunt," he hissed. "You're dead, bitch."

I met his date's wide eyes and parted lips. I hoped she'd listen. Get out. Go. I'd really hate for her to deal with an angry Nate. From the boiling red going on beneath his skin, he was raging.

"Run, Sera."

Taking my own advice, I spun on my toes and scurried to the exit. It had started to rain while I was inside. It never rained around here, so I hadn't been prepared, but my car was parked close, illuminated by one of the few parking lot lights. I flung myself inside, slamming my hand on the ignition switch. Creamy bile rose in my throat.

I didn't have the chance to think or wrap my head around what I'd just done. Nate exploded out of the diner doors, looking for blood.

My dad had taught me to park in well-lit spots in parking lots. For my safety. So no dangers could snatch me up in the shadows. I could use some shadows right about now. I might as well have been under a spotlight. Nate found me on his first sweep of the lot, storming to the hood of my car.

His fists slammed down on my cherry-red paint, sending raindrops flying. "Get your ass out of that car, cunt. You owe me."

A maniacal laugh burst out of me. That was so rich. "I owe you nothing, psycho!"

"Get out of the car, Elena. Then we'll talk about all you owe me."

I shook my head, watching the froth gathering at the corner of his lips. God, this dude had been watching too much *Cujo*.

That left-field thought snapped me out of my inertia. I gave Nate a finger wave as I shifted into reverse and backed out of my spot as quickly as I dared. I was already going to have to explain the Nate-shaped dents on the hood, I didn't need broken taillights or a messed-up bumper on top of that.

In my rearview mirror, Nate was running through the lot. If sheer hatred gave him speed, he'd have caught my Porsche in his bare feet. Luckily, he had to contend with gravity like the rest of us. I gunned it out of there, swerving onto Main Street and away from my own personal monster.

My hands shook as I drove a little too fast toward home. I couldn't convince my foot to lighten up on the accelerator. I should have known better than to go into town. I'd stayed holed up with my family all break for good reason.

I was going fast. Too fast for the wet roads and relentless pulsing in my ears. Plus, I was a terrible driver. On my best days, I couldn't remember to check my mirrors or signal before changing lanes. This wasn't one of my best days. My hands were vibrating on the wheel. My breath was coming in uneven pants.

I wondered if this was a panic attack. I didn't *have* panic attacks. That was my mother's thing. I wasn't fragile. I didn't break. But this...seeing Nate, speaking to him, my reaction—oh god, it felt like an unraveling.

Bright lights filled my rearview mirror. The jackass coming up behind me had his high beams on. The road *was* dark, but he was too close, practically blinding me.

What was he doing?

The beams lowered, and he backed off, still riding too close, but not in danger of hitting me.

I glanced in my mirror, making out a little white sports car. I couldn't tell the make, not in the dark and the rain. Possibly a BMW, but it could have been a Tesla.

The car accelerated again, nearly scraping my bumper. I checked the rearview mirror. Through the reflection distorted by the rain, I made out the shape of a man. He was tall, his head practically hitting the ceiling. He must have seen me looking at him. One arm swung wildly, gesturing to the side of the road.

I couldn't make out his face, but I had no doubt Nate was the one tailing me. Had he lost his mind? As if I'd pull over on a dark road, in the rain, no one around, while my milkshake was still damp on his pants.

There was nowhere to pull over anyway. One side of the road was all craggy boulders and a metal guardrail. The other was dried-out underbrush and trees, broken occasionally by small, residential streets. No shoulders or bike lanes. Not even a sidewalk.

My foot went heavy on the gas. My focus centered on the damp, two-lane road. I'd be home soon. Nate was brazen, but not enough to harass me in my own driveway. I just had to get there. Then everything would be okay.

My mind was scrambling, a million thoughts attempting to rise to the surface. And my hands...they wouldn't stop trembling.

Wipers swished back and forth in a hypnotic pattern. The rain was light, coating the thirsty ground, slicking the road.

His high beams were back, momentarily disorienting me. My foot hit the gas in a wave of panic. Metal scraped metal as Nate's car nudged mine. I was jarred forward, breath squeezing from my lungs as my seat belt held me in place, and all I could think about was how my dad was going to kill me if I came home with a scratch.

Not exactly rational, but there wasn't time for rationality.

I slammed my foot down, my sole focus on getting away without my car suffering any more damage. Tomorrow, I'd be gone, back to Berkeley, and Nate would crawl back into his hole.

I wasn't thinking straight. I should have slowed down at the sign for Larson's Nursery. Since I was a kid, that was the landmark I always used to know I was almost home. Tonight, frazzled and afraid, I missed it. The turn for my neighborhood came up unexpectedly, and I sailed by it before it even registered.

Shit.

Nate wasn't backing off. I knew what I'd do. I'd keep driving. In a few miles, there was a shopping center with a twenty-four-hour grocery store. I just had to make it there. There would be lights. People. He might follow me, but surely he'd give up. And if he didn't, I'd call my dad. No way Nate would want to face off with Gil Sanderson.

I squeezed the wheel and sucked in a deep breath. I could do this. Three or four more miles and this would be over. I just had to make it there, make it to the lights. My dad would give Nate Bergen a piece of his mind.

High beams flashed on again, and Nate's car nudged mine a little harder than the first time. I didn't recognize the scream that filled the cabin of my car, but it had to be mine. I was alone, screaming, while my ex-boyfriend terrorized me.

All I'd wanted was a milkshake.

I was paying better attention this time. A deep curve was coming up in the road. Despite Nate's unrelenting presence on my ass, I let up on the gas, slowing as much as I dared. My tires hit a slick patch, skidding a foot, maybe two, before they found traction, taking the rest of the curve easily.

I could barely breathe. My heart was lodged in my throat. It was only by sheer will I was staying present and not floating outside my body. I sure as hell didn't want to be here, experiencing this.

Just make it around the curve. Get to the lights. Then it will be over.

From behind, Nate's tires squealed on the pavement, in the same spot mine had. Instead of finding traction, he kept slipping.

It happened quickly. One second, he was behind me, close, close, breathing down my neck. The next, he was spinning out of control. And the next, he was careening into the guardrail and over it.

And then he was out of my sight. I'd made it around the curve. Nate was gone.

Oh shit.

My throat closed like there was a hand squeezing it. He wasn't just gone. He'd crashed. That little car against those big boulders.

Oh god, what had I done? Did I have to go back? What if he needed help?

Of course he needed help. He'd just gone head-on with an immovable force. But someone else could help him. It didn't have to be me. He wouldn't even want my help.

What if no one else passed? The last thing I wanted was guilt over Nate Bergen. I'd slowed to a crawl, hoping against hope someone would drive in the opposite direction. Though it wasn't very late, the road was empty. I guessed the rain was keeping people home.

That hand squeezed tighter around my throat, leaving me no choice. As carefully as I could, I made a U-turn in the road, retracing my path. I hadn't driven very far from the curve. My chest was knotted tight as I came closer to where Nate had disappeared.

Nate's little white car was crumpled against a boulder. Only his rear wheels were on the ground. The front two hung over the guardrail.

He wasn't alone. Someone in a pickup truck had pulled over. Their door opened. They were getting out. Relief surged through my veins. I didn't have to stop. Nate had help. This stranger would help him. I'd go back to Berkeley and forget this happened.

I slammed my hands down on the wheel as I drove past the accident. I had to make better choices. I'd never let my emotions get the better of me again.

And no more milkshakes.

Chapter One

Elena

I was bored, antsy, and a little uncomfortable—a combination that had proven to be dangerous for me. It meant I was likely to go looking for trouble. I raked my eyes over my roommate in the seat in front of me. She had on cute little biker shorts and a crop top.

"Where's this party again? A gymnasium?"

Helen turned her head, shooting me a dry look from beneath her lashes, then continued applying her signature red lipstick without the help of a mirror. She didn't reply, but to be fair, my question had pretty much been bait to entertain myself. Helen just didn't want to play.

"It's casual." Theo, her sparkly eyed boyfriend, glanced at me in his rearview mirror.

"Pffft. You *would* say that. You're so in love with her."

He chuckled. "You got me there."

Third wheeling it with my roommate and her beloved boyfriend wasn't how I'd expected to spend the last days of summer before buckling down for my junior year at Savage U. But since Helen, Zadie, and I had moved in to a house off campus together last month, I'd quickly come to realize how much quality time they spent with their respective men, which meant *I* had to spend time with them.

Fortunately, both Theo and Zadie's boyfriend, Amir, were tolerable. Even better, Theo often volunteered to be the designated driver.

Not one to turn down a free ride, I'd scrunched my long legs in the back of his Toyota more times than I could count.

"No one told you to dress like a high-end escort," Helen said.

"I *always* dress like a high-end escort. No one has to tell me to do it," I replied.

Oooh, so we were going to spar. Fun times. Since Zadie was back home in Oregon with Amir for the week, no one was here to step between us. Double fun.

She tossed a tube of lipstick into the back seat. "Put some on. You forgot to reapply after your last client."

I uncapped it, checking out the color. It was a pinkish nude, not her shade at all. "No trampy red?"

She huffed. "You don't need any more help looking like a harlot." Turning around in her seat again, she shot me a crooked grin. "That's yours. You made me hold it last time we went out."

Oh, right. I remembered now. The bonfire on the beach a couple weeks ago. The upside to Helen's unerring habit of wearing jeans or cutoffs was she always had pockets for me to stash things.

"Because you're the only woman I hang with who insists on dressing like a twelve-year-old boy."

She made tomboy look sexy. Bitch.

Helen arched a brow. "Sorry, floozy, no pockets on me tonight. Carry your own shit."

"Floozy? That's rich. I haven't had sex in months, yet we're running late because you and golden boy just had to bang it out."

The blackest part of my heart was jealous of their relationship. Once upon a time, I would have eaten that jealousy for breakfast and spat out cruel vitriol to soothe the burn. Instead, I let it pass through me, feeling it and moving on. It wasn't like I wanted Theo, or even someone Theo-like. I just wanted…something. Hating on the happy couple wouldn't get me anywhere or anything.

She tossed her long, brown hair behind her shoulder and reached over to squeeze the back of Theo's neck. "I'm sure you can find some poor, unsuspecting fool eager for you to suck his soul out of his dick tonight."

I moved my legs—or tried to, at least. Apparently, being five-nine put me over the height limit for Theo's sensible, family sedan. My knees were going to look like I'd spent some time on them when I got out of here.

"Is that what I'm supposed to be sucking out of dicks?" I snapped my fingers. "Damn, I've been doing it wrong this whole time."

Theo laughed again. Helen's smile went soft and gooey as she slid her fingers into the back of his hair. My stomach nose-dived.

Gross.

Love was really, really gross.

·········

The party was at a random off-campus house. Since it was still officially summer break, it wasn't as packed with bodies as it would have been if school were in session. Still, there were all the usual suspects—the dealers, the stoners, the table dancers, the vomit-in-a-houseplant girl. I really only knew Helen and Theo, but since I was trying not to be a stage-five clinger, I'd been mingling and drinking since we arrived.

And watching the table dancer wistfully. That used to be me once upon a time. Why wasn't it me anymore?

I made my way to the stone patio that led out to dead grass. The music wasn't quite so loud out here, and there was a slight breeze in the night air.

Helen snuck up beside me and passed me a lit joint. "You need this. You look all uptight."

I took it gladly. "That's because I am. Thanks."

"Me too." Clicking her lighter, she lit her own joint between her red lips. "I still can't believe I agreed to go camping with Theo."

That made me smirk. I would have found it harder to believe if she hadn't agreed, that was how far gone she was for her boy. "He has a way with you."

"That he does. He sparkles those eyes at me, and I get stupid. I am not built for the outdoors unless it's paved and I can ride my skateboard."

Smoke drifted from my mouth. "You'll have fun."

"Luc will, at least. I'm looking forward to watching her experience it all. The downside of taking my little sister with us is I'll have to stare at Theo every damn day and not be able to touch because the camper we're staying in has absolutely no privacy. So, I'm going to be in nature *and* horny."

My mouth twitched. It was crazy to think I didn't *know* Helen a year ago. I'd walked by her a thousand times and had never given her a second thought. Now, I knew intimate, personal details of her life—details she shared with me openly. We'd been thrown together by fate...or the university housing randomizer, but that wasn't what had drawn us closer. *That* was something neither of us really spoke about but understood intimately. Bad, bad men.

"Make sure you bring your journal so you can write down all your big, beautiful, horny feelings," I quipped.

Her eyes rolled skyward, but she was grinning. "Yeah, I'll do that." She glanced at the other groups around the patio. "You know, you've been lurking in the shadows all night. I could introduce you around."

I choked out a cloud of smoke. "I don't lurk, Helen."

"Fine, you don't lurk, even though you were definitely lurking. Do you want me to introduce you to people?"

My hackles rose for no real reason, except I wasn't used to being the one who had to be introduced to people. *I* had always been the one people introduced themselves to. *I* had never lurked in shadows—yes, lurking, dammit. *My* phone had always been blowing up with invitations to parties and yacht weekends and impromptu trips to Ibiza.

I'd stepped away from that, but it wasn't easy going from being the center of it all to hanging on the edges. When things weren't easy or I got uncomfortable, I lashed out.

I pointed to the joint. "Let me finish this before I meet Theo's scrubby mechanic friends."

Helen had known me forever—not that we'd been friends forever or anything. Far from it. But now that we were, she saw right through me and didn't react to my snobbery outside of a soft huff. Her man may have been a part-time mechanic for campus maintenance, but he was so far from scrubby, it wasn't even funny. She knew that too.

A throat cleared behind us. "Helen."

We whirled around at the same time. My heart stuttered in my chest, just like it did every time Lachlan Kelly towered over me. And tower, he did. I wasn't short by any means, but Lachlan had to be six and a half feet. Not just tall, but broad and dense. The span of his shoulders seemed to go on forever, eclipsing everything around him.

He was Helen's friend. Helen and Theo's, really. He was around a lot, and when he was, he actively ignored me. More than ignored me, he avoided looking at me. And when he was forced to interact with me, he did so in a way that conveyed how much it pained him. No one else seemed to see it. To them, he was Lock, affable, laid back, sweet, if not gruff and somewhat brooding. I saw that too, which was why his complete disregard for me drove me up the wall.

"Hey, dude." Helen punched Lachlan's tree trunk bicep, giving it a good thwap. He didn't even flinch. "Did you just get here?"

"I did. Worked late. I had to scrub my hands extra hard before I came."

Helen snickered. "Oh, you scrubby mechanic, you. Why don't you have a drink in your hand?"

He raked his fingers through his shaggy brown hair. "Just got here. I'll make my way inside, grab a bottle." He nodded toward the beer bottle hanging between Helen's fingers. "You good? Want me to get you something?"

"Nah, I'm good. El and I are sliding into relaxation mode out here." Helen bumped her shoulder into mine. "Want?" She held up her *J*.

His overgrown hair flopped back into his face. "Not my thing."

Lachlan paused for a beat, the tendons in his thick neck flexing, then nodded again and tromped off in his heavy work boots. Not even a flicker of recognition had come my way.

Helen's brow pinched. "That was strange. Did you go invisible for a minute?"

"That must be it." I held my joint up to my lips. "Or Lachlan is a snob."

She sputtered, smoke coming out with her laughter. "You think Lock is a snob? Are we talking about the same Lock who just walked away? The salt-of-the-earth, nice-guy mechanic? That Lock?"

Lock. Right. Everyone called him that. To me, it was too small of a name for someone like him. In my mind, he was Lachlan, which reminded me of a treacherous pass over rough, deadly terrain.

"Oh, the Lachlan Pass? I traversed it back in '02. Half my crew died, but I conquered the Lachlan. Hoo-ah."

Yes. Lachlan suited the overgrown asshole much better.

"That's the Lock I'm talking about. The one who never addresses me, rarely looks at me, and can't even remember my name. That Lock."

Helen's eyes flared. "Whoa, dude. I never noticed, but now that you say it, you're right. Lock really doesn't like you. What'd you do to him?"

I shot her the middle finger. "Eat a dick, Helen. You watch me like a hawk around your friends. You know I've been nothing but a lady."

Something in her softened. Before we spent our sophomore year sharing a dorm, she'd had a lot of reasons to hate me, but I thought I'd more than proved I deserved the benefit of the doubt. Guessed not.

She started to reach out to me, but let her hand drop midway. That was well and good. We both would have been embarrassed if she got mushy with me.

She shuffled her Vans against the patio stone. "I don't watch you so much like a hawk anymore."

"Thanks, buddy." I stamped out the tail end of my joint. Any calming effects from the THC in my bloodstream were being overpowered by the foul mood Lachlan Kelly had put me in. "Thanks for trusting me around your precious friends. Maybe you should start watching *them* instead. I'm going to go find a quiet corner to practice my incantations."

If I *could* summon a demon, it would be to curse Lachlan with the inability to look away from me. If he did, he'd feel like a million beetles were walking all over him, their little, sticky, clawed tarsi pricking his skin with each step they took.

I went inside the house, tacitly avoiding the kitchen where the alcohol was—where Lachlan probably was. The trouble was, I desperately needed something to drink to bring me back into party mode.

I saw a guy. Cute, but as Helen called guys like him, Medium. Everything about him was right in the middle. A perfect target.

I bumped into him, grabbing his shoulders to brace myself. "Oh, I'm so sorry."

His smile was extra wide and white, standing out on his otherwise forgettable face. "No worries. Are you steady now?"

I held on to him, giving his shoulders a squeeze. He was dressed nicely. I thought I recognized his untucked button-down as Eton—the brand my mom bought my dad when she was trying to "hip him up." Could one really be hip if they paid two-hundred-dollars for a dress shirt, though? Not that my dad had any hope.

"I'm steady, thanks to you." I bit my bottom lip. "I'm Elena."

"Trevor. Excellent to meet you, even if by accident." He crossed his arms over his chest, tilting his upper body toward me. "What year are you?"

I fluttered my eyelashes in a way that came so naturally to me, I barely thought about it. "Junior. You?"

"Senior." His navy-blue eyes raked over my short dress and long legs. "How have I never seen you before?"

SWEET LIKE POISON

"I don't know." I wrapped the ends of my blonde waves around a couple fingers. "I haven't seen you either. I guess we've both been wasting time."

He brought his drink up to his mouth then stopped. "Something's not right here. A beautiful girl, but her hands are empty. Can I get you a drink, Elena?"

I gasped, like his offer was completely unexpected and not the reason I'd stumbled into him in the first place.

"Would you? That would be amazing." I pointed to the ground in front of me. "I'll save your spot."

He beelined it to the kitchen with my drink order. Through the open entryway, I spotted Lachlan, Helen, and Theo laughing. Helen and Theo would welcome me into their group if I wanted to join them, but why would I? I wasn't a girl who stayed at the edge of the crowd. The center was my happy place. So, Lachlan could go die with whatever bug had crawled up his ass. I wasn't going to keep putting myself in a position to be ignored.

··········

Three drinks later, Trevor had coaxed me into playing Truth or Dare with a big group that had taken over the living room. Most of the dares had involved taking articles of clothing off. Nobody had even attempted to tell the truth.

A girl across from me, Trevor's medium counterpart, had been eyeing me since we sat down together. During her dare, she'd taken off her shorts and wiggled her thong-split ass in Trevor's direction. He'd been so busy staring at my tits, he hadn't noticed. Medium Girl had, though. And when it was her turn to pick someone to go next, she looked straight at me.

"Truth or dare?" she asked.

"Hmmm..." I tapped my chin, which was just a little numb from all the vodka and weed I'd consumed. "I think I'll go with truth to mix things up a little."

Her eyes narrowed, and I wondered if I was supposed to be intimidated. I'd eaten jealous little chickadees like her for breakfast. I did *not* get intimidated.

"What's the worst thing you've ever done?"

Her lips tipped into a smug, smarmy smile, like she actually knew the answer. Since Nate was the only one who knew and he was dead, it was impossible.

"Too many to count."

Trevor slung his arm around my shoulders. "I find it hard to believe you've ever done anything bad."

"Oh, Trevor, you have no idea. I was an absolute monster in high school." I faced down my newly appointed nemesis. I was just drunk enough to name the first thing that popped into my mind. "I'd say it was leaking a girl's half-naked pics that I stole from my friend's phone. That was pretty shitty."

The girl's mouth turned down in dismay. "That's awful. Why'd you do that?"

I shrugged. "I was a bored teenager who thought I was a lot more clever than I was." Leaning forward, I grabbed one of the shots of tequila lining the coffee table and tossed it back. "Who's next?"

I turned my head to pick the next victim, and my eyes caught on Lachlan standing just outside the group, his thick arms crossed as he leaned a shoulder against a wall. No doubt he'd heard what I said. At least now he had a legitimate reason for looking down on me.

I took another shot. A few more, and Lachlan Kelly's face would be so fuzzy, I'd forget he existed.

Trevor took off his shirt and swung it in a circle over his head while gyrating his hips. He did this while standing in front of me, his knees pressed against mine.

His dare had been to strip for me. It was a good thing he was in college. If he took up stripping for a living, his clientele would be severely disappointed at his concave chest.

"Truth or dare, beautiful," he slurred, falling down beside me.

I'd lost track of the shots I'd thrown back, but I knew I'd had three really strong drinks. Or maybe it was four. I never slurred, no matter how toasted I got.

"Dare."

He tucked in his chin and wagged his eyebrows. "Hmmm...what am I going to do with you? Should I have some fun or be nice?"

I shrugged. "Do your worst, bucko."

His brows went wild again. Medium Girl probably dug that move. To me, it looked like he had a pair of deranged caterpillars attached to his head.

His grin went crooked. A few guys jeered at him, yelling for him to dare me to streak or skinny dip. One even suggested a blow job. Trevor paused on that suggestion, but in the end, he shouted out his own very clever idea.

"Take off your bra."

Oh, balls.

Well, a dare was a dare. I'd never back down from one. But after this, I was out. Hopefully Helen and Theo were ready to go because this party had grown stale.

My feet only wobbled slightly as I stood. Yeah, I probably shouldn't have had that last shot. I raised my head, finding *him* still watching. His massive shoulders were tight, a bull poised to charge. Why was he watching if he hated me so much?

If he wanted to watch, I'd put on a show for him. One foot at a time, I climbed onto the coffee table. I swayed, listing sideways, but found my center and raised my hands over my head to celebrate.

Lock shook his head while everyone else cheered for me.

Averting my eyes, I reached behind me. My fingers fumbled to tug down my dress and find the clasp of my bra. Finally snagging it, my next task was to get it unhooked.

I squeezed my eyes to concentrate. That was why I didn't see him coming. I really should have been paying attention.

Then again, how could I have predicted Lachlan Kelly would scoop me up and haul me out of the party over his shoulder?

Chapter Two

Lock

I'd had enough.

No more games. No more foolishness. And no fucking way was I standing there while she took her bra off. If she'd managed to do it without cracking her head open.

Ridiculous woman.

She squirmed and hissed over my shoulder, threatening to bite me, hit me, vomit on me. I charged out of the house without a single person trying to stop me because most of them were selfish idiots, and headed directly to my truck.

Swinging the passenger door open, I did my best to be gentle with the writhing bag of snakes in my arms while I lowered her into the seat. As soon as I did, she tried to spring up and out of my truck.

Placing a firm hand on her belly, I pushed her down, and leaned across her to buckle her in. She shoved my shoulders, making kitten growls in my ear.

"Stay still, Elsa," I barked.

"There's no way you can possibly think my name is Elsa." She slapped at my hands. "Why are you buckling me into this death trap? I'm not going anywhere with you."

As soon as I straightened, she had herself unbuckled. I'd been impatient watching over her at the party, but now I was done.

"You are." I cuffed her throat, drawing her attention. "I'm not letting you strip in front of the entire campus. Because that's what will happen. You take your tits out, you think it'll end in there? Don't tell me you're that naive. I saw at least three phones out, recording your show. You wouldn't be able to walk to class without some dickhead looking at you, knowing exactly what you have underneath your clothes. I'm not letting that happen."

She rolled her eyes, but the rest of her had gone still. "Drama king," she whispered, but that was the last of her protest.

I let go of her and gave her head a pat. "Good girl. Don't move an inch."

By the time I got into my seat, she'd kicked her heels off, tucked her legs under her, and curled into a ball, facing my way. Reaching into the back, I grabbed a hoodie off the seat and draped it over her shoulders. Her fingers darted around the fabric, gathering it under her chin.

Cute. Never thought the ice queen could pull off cute, but she managed.

The drive back home was mostly silent, but the glare to the side of my head was resounding.

"Where are Helen and Theo?" she asked.

"They went home. I told them I'd drive you."

"They left me with you?"

My fingers drummed the wheel. "They were ready to go. I wasn't. You weren't either."

She hmphed. "Pretty sure Helen broke girl code. Hos before bros, man."

"She knew I'd get you home safe."

Her mouth opened in a wide yawn. "I guess she's missed all the times you've looked at me with murder eyes."

"I don't."

"Mmmhmm." She brought the hoodie up to her nose and sniffed. "This smells like motor oil and the outdoors."

I glanced at her, her blonde head barely peeking out from under the hoodie. "Toss it in the back seat if you don't like it."

She reeled back, clutching it tighter. "I didn't say that. Don't be a hoodie thief, Lachlan. It's not a good look."

"I'll remember that."

I could still feel her glare as I turned into my driveway. I parked, came around to her side of the car, and unbuckled her. She uncurled, looking up at me. Her nose was crinkled, but her eyes were drowsy, half-open.

I held a hand out. "Come on. Time for you to go home, sleep it off."

Ignoring my offer, she grabbed her heels and hopped out of the truck on her own. Only, she must've misjudged the height—or misjudged how drunk she was. She'd started flailing, as graceless as I'd ever seen her, and would have gone down if I hadn't caught her and scooped her up bridal style.

I expected to get kicked and clawed again, but she barely protested. With a groan, she went limp, her head falling back, her long hair swinging freely, as I carried her dead weight to her house next door.

Right. Next. Door.

I climbed up her porch steps, stopping at her door. "Gonna put you down now."

She gave my arm a slap. "No, horsey. I don't want to walk. My feet are broken. Carry me to my bed."

"Nope." I tipped her body so she was perpendicular to the ground and set her on her feet. She stumbled into me, catching herself in my arms. "You have your keys?"

She slowly lifted her head, blowing her hair off her face. Attempting to, at least. The silvery-blonde strands only lifted the slightest then fell back down.

"Probably. But I think I'll just sleep out here."

She started for the Adirondack chair next to the door, but I caught her around the shoulders, steering her back to the door.

"I don't care if you sleep in your bed, but you're going inside. Curl up on the kitchen floor if that sounds comfortable. All I promised was to get you home in one piece."

Her eyes narrowed. "I'm home. You can go now."

"Where are your keys?"

"Wouldn't you like to know?"

I blew out a heavy breath. I was way too fuckin' sober to be dealing with drunk-girl logic.

"Yeah, Elsa, I want to know, that's why I asked."

She stomped her foot on the porch floor and dug her hand into the bodice of her dress. Her hand emerged, clutching a single key.

"See? I told you you'd want to know." She waved it in my face. "This is a tit key, Lachlan. It's warm from being snuggled up to my boob all night."

My patience was pretty much endless, but I didn't know if I had it in me to deal with this. I needed to get her inside before I lost my head.

Plucking the hot key from her hand, I unlocked the door and swung it open. "In."

She took the key back from me, dropping it into her dress again, then stumbled into the house. "You should stop calling me Elsa. It's rude."

Nothing to say to that, I lifted a shoulder. "Go to bed."

A soft sigh fell from her parted lips, and she leaned against the doorjamb. The house behind her was dark. The light above me flickered, not doing a very good job of illuminating the porch. It'd been bothering me for a while now. I'd have to come back over and switch out the bulb, see if that fixed it.

"Why do you hate me?" she asked.

My brow dropped. It was late, and this was the last thing I'd expected to come from her. I crossed my arms over my chest, moving my jaw back and forth.

"Never said I did."

"Pffft. It's pretty obvious." She flicked her fingers carelessly. "I'm used to people hating me—but for valid reasons. I've never done anything to you, so your disdain confuses me."

I waited for another question. It never came. So I tipped my chin. "Go inside. Lock up. Drink some water. You'll be thankful you did in the morning."

Even in the dark, I could see her eyes darting between mine. Finally, her head fell against the jamb and she sighed.

"It's a good thing I don't give a damn if you like me, Lachlan. If I did, I'd be really annoyed right now. *Really* annoyed."

Patience snapped, my fingers curled into my palms.

"You're lucky I *do* give a damn. If I ever catch you accepting open drinks from a guy you don't know like you did tonight, I'll make good on the promise I made last semester and redden your stupid ass. Now, *go inside*."

With a huff, she swiveled on the ball of her foot, took a step inside, and slammed the door behind her. I stayed until I heard the lock click, then I took the too-short walk home.

···········

There was a ruckus next door. Two guys were ripping out the rotted boards of the deck, tossing them into the yard. It was barely eight, too early for the kind of noise they were making in a college neighborhood, but it wasn't my problem. I was always up with the sun.

Leaning against the counter, I chugged coffee and watched their sloppy work through the window, wondering if the ice queen was supervising or if she'd shelled out her father's money and left them to their work. She wasn't on her porch reading her newspaper like she did every morning. Hadn't seen her out there since the party a couple days ago.

I shrugged. Not my business.

Theo came strolling in, Helen trailing behind him.

"All ready?" I asked.

Helen headed straight for the coffee pot. "I will be when I've consumed a gallon of this." She grabbed an oversized mug from a cabinet. "When I agreed to go camping, I didn't realize that meant I'd be waking up at the crack of dawn."

Theo chuckled and kissed the side of her head. "It's eight, baby."

"Too early," she grumbled.

"You're going to love it."

She leaned her head against his. "Luc will love it. She's practically frothing to get into the wilderness."

I set my mug down. "You have to come to Wyoming with me, see some real wilderness."

Helen's head popped up. "Dude, I can barely handle glamping with my boyfriend and little sister. Do you think I'd survive being surrounded by trees and bison or whatever the hell's in Wyoming?"

"I think you're gonna come visit," I said.

"Maybe." She threw back more coffee. "But only if you teach Theo to chop wood and I get to watch."

"That could be arranged."

Helen shot me a wry look. "Let me survive this camping trip, then we'll discuss future travel plans to Wyoming."

I grinned at her. "Yeah, you'll visit."

When I'd arrived at Savage U two years ago, I'd had no intention of making connections beyond surface level. I had four years of college, then I'd be moving to Wyoming to help my dad run our family ranch. That would be my focus for the foreseeable future. I didn't see room for friendships or relationships—not when I'd be gone in a few years and never look back.

I made it a year, then Helen happened. With her came Theo. A year of friendship, and now Theo and I shared a house with another guy, Julien, while Helen lived next door, and I'd resolved myself to the fact that I wasn't leaving California clear of connections. It was too late for that.

After Theo and Helen left for their trip, I got back to watching the guys destroy the deck. When I'd killed enough time, I knocked on Julien's door. He took a full minute to open it, and he did so without a word. I stepped aside, giving him space for his chair. He wheeled toward the front door, pausing for me to open it, then rolled down the ramp in front of our house.

I grabbed his crutches and headed out to meet him at my truck. By the time I got there, he was no longer alone.

"Elsa." I tipped my chin at her and laid Julien's crutches across his armrests.

The two of them couldn't have looked more different. She was tall, lithe, the picture of health. Julien had been broken, scarred, and couldn't get it up to smile more than once or twice a week—and those were always fleeting and pained. And yet, I caught El shooting the shit with him on a regular basis.

Instead of returning my shitty greeting, El picked up the crutches and pretended to examine them. "Come on, Phantom. Hasn't it been like four months since you were hit by a car? I think you've milked the injury enough. Hop up."

Julien stared up at her, the good side of his mouth twitching. "Fuck you."

She rolled her eyes. "You'd have to catch me first, and that's not going to happen while you're faking it in that chair. Get off your lazy ass, then I'll consider it."

"You're not my type," he grumbled.

She flipped her hair behind her shoulder. "Too pretty, huh? Yeah, I could see how you'd be intimidated." Then she ruffled his shaggy hair. "Get a haircut while you're out, Phantom."

"I'll think about it."

"Good. I want to see that gorgeous face." She winked at him, then sashayed down the sidewalk, waving over her shoulder.

I stood there, watching her go in disbelief. Julien wasn't as stunned. He pushed himself up on his crutches and swung into the passenger seat of my truck. His low groan as he tried to get his legs in snapped me to attention. I moved the seat back as far as it would go and helped him get situated—a thing he hated but silently accepted.

It was hard to be pissed for Julien when he didn't seem to give a shit about the way he'd just been treated. Maybe that was why I was pissed. The guy was so beat down, he didn't even care about being mocked and talked down to.

I squeezed the steering wheel until it squeaked under my palms. Julien turned, and in my periphery, raised an eyebrow.

"You good?" he asked.

"Yeah. You?"

He scoffed. "Better than ever. Obviously."

Like I'd done twice a week all summer, I parked in front of the physical rehabilitation facility, helped Julien into his chair, and told him I'd see him in an hour. Then I pulled into a spot and waited.

It was supposed to be just Theo and me in the house. But our place had a first-floor bedroom, and the house Julien had been living in prior to his accident had too many stairs, so I built a ramp leading up to the porch, and he became our third roommate. He kept to himself. I got the feeling he was in a good amount of pain, but he didn't like people fussing over him. I wasn't one to fuss anyway.

So, I drove him because I had the time and he was in need. We did it in silence. He always came out of his physical therapy sessions looking like death warmed over. I never asked how it went. He never offered.

Today, he was shaking, his face red, T-shirt stuck to the sweat on his body. All I could fucking think about was the shit El gave him. Shit he didn't need or deserve.

I didn't get that girl. Didn't know that I wanted to get her. Not when she could be so casually cruel. She reminded me of girls I knew growing up. Girls I never wanted to see again. I'd dismissed her the first time I saw her. Put her in that vapid, rich, pampered category and erased her from my mind. Except she kept showing up when I was around, and sometimes, the things she said gave me whiplash. Things that made her seem human, and maybe even kind.

"You wanna stop anywhere before we go back home?" I asked.

He grunted. "You have better things to do than chauffeur me around."

"I really don't."

I did. My hours working campus maintenance were close to full time, and I still had responsibilities for the family business I completed remotely. I had a pile of shit to do back home, but I'd gladly ignore it if it meant Julien went somewhere outside of home and rehab.

Silence followed. Always silence. I didn't mind that, except I could practically hear him screaming on the inside.

"Think we could grab something to eat?" he asked as we drove down Main Street.

"Hell yes. Something in Savage River, or you want to drive?"

He turned his head, eyeing me. "You good with driving for a while?"

"I am."

His head fell back on the rest. "Let's drive then."

We ended up at a dive on the beach, one I'd discovered freshman year on an aimless drive. I got the sense Julien didn't like being seen in his chair, but he'd had another surgery last month, and his leg couldn't take any weight at all right now. Plus, his shoulder was jacked, so his crutches weren't easy for him to manipulate. Luckily, the deck was basically empty, and it had a ramp, so we were golden.

We ate our sandwiches to the soundtrack of the waves beating into the sand.

"Are you ready for classes next week?" I asked, wiping my mouth with my napkin.

"Not really." He put down his sandwich, looked out at the waves. "You?"

"Mmmhmm. That's why I'm here."

His head cocked in my direction. "Not for the parties and the girls?"

"There are parties and girls back home."

"No ice queens, though."

It took me a beat to get that he was referencing our next-door neighbor. I chuckled. "Nah, there are plenty of ice queens back home. Plenty just like her."

He hummed, shifted in his chair, and laid his clasped hands on his stomach. "I thought you grew up on a ranch or something. You have fancy women on every fence post?"

I shook my head. "I grew up in Northern California. Plenty of money and icy blondes around there. The ranch belonged to my granddad. My father didn't take over until I was in high school. Spent all my summers there, though."

"Not this summer."

"I was working, couldn't get back there for more than a couple weeks. I'll be on the ranch full time when I graduate."

He nodded. "That must be something, to know exactly where you'll be, what you'll be doing."

"It's something, for sure."

We sat there listening to the waves for a while before heading back home. The workers were gone, quiet restored, but the mess next door remained.

Chapter Three

Elena

I HAD NO IDEA what I was doing, but I wasn't going to let that stop me. Not when the alternative was so unthinkable.

I brought the hammer down on the first nail of…oh, five thousand or so.

And missed.

But that was okay. Someone with less determination might call this a bad omen, but not me. I'd watched two hours of YouTube videos last night. I was armed, skilled—in my mind—and ready to work. This deck was going to be my bitch.

Maybe I should have listened to the guy at the hardware store and rented a nail gun. If he'd been less of an overbearing, smug, misogynist, I might have taken his advice. There was no way in hell I was going back now.

I had less than a week to get this done before Zadie came back from Oregon, Helen emerged from her trip to the wilderness, and classes started. I could hammer five thousand nails in six days.

·········

By noon, I wanted to die. The sun beat down on the back of my neck, and my fingers had gone numb from being hit so many times.

Who knew a bent nail would finally break me?

Tossing my head back, I let loose a scream of pure frustration. Defeat beat down on me just as heavily as the sun. I was sweaty, sore, exhausted, and had made next to no progress. The one board I'd laid and hammered into place was crooked. I'd have to pull it up and start over. The idea of starting over from scratch was so sickening, I had to swallow it down.

I flopped onto my butt, rubbing my face with my filthy, sore hands.

"You okay?"

My head shot up. Lachlan was walking across my backyard, either frowning at me or the mess surrounding me. Most likely both.

"I'm fine." I waved my hands in front of my face so he wouldn't see the tears welling. "You can go back inside. Nothing to see here."

"Are you hurt?" He towered over me, blissfully blocking out the sun. "Where's the crew?"

"Not here. Obviously."

His hands went to his hips. "Why not?"

My pride had already taken a serious beating. I needed him to walk away. "Honestly, I'm good. I appreciate your neighborly concern, but I've got this."

With that, he crouched down in front of me. Except, when Lachlan crouched, he went from mountain to boulder, still looming over me like an unmovable force of nature.

"I've spent the morning listening to you spit and curse between manually hammering in nails. Are you going to tell me where the hell the guys who've been tearing up your deck the past couple days are?"

"I fired them."

He blinked, his brow dipping in the middle. "Okay."

"They were assholes, all right? They dipped out with my money, so now I'm building my own deck. Everything's fine."

"What the hell?" he grumbled.

"You can go."

He fell back on his butt and scanned the yard, then me, stopping on my ravaged hands.

"Why'd you fire your crew?"

"I told you, they were assholes."

He cocked his head. "Did they play their music too loud? Make eye contact with you?"

Something sharp, like barbed wire, snarled inside my chest. He really thought the worst of me. To think, he didn't even know a fraction of the things I'd done.

"No." I shot to my feet and picked up the hammer I'd discarded in the grass. "It's no concern of yours anyway. Let me get on with it."

He climbed to his feet too, exhaling heavily through his nose. His shaggy brown hair fell forward as he looked down on me.

"Why don't you hire another crew?"

"I'm doing it myself. It'll be fine, like I said." I marched to the pile of wood planks I had to figure out how to cut to the correct length and dragged one toward the deck.

I wasn't delusional. The chances of me actually completing this job on my own were fairly dismal. But the idea of tucking tail and explaining to my dad what'd gone down kept me clinging to the minuscule hope I might succeed.

Lachlan wrapped his fingers around my wrist. "You don't even have the right tools. You're going to really hurt yourself."

"It's fine, Lachlan. You don't need to worry about me." I tugged my arm, but he had a firm hold on me. "Really."

For a breathless moment, he swept me with his gaze. Lachlan's eyes were the only thing pretty about him. Long, curled lashes surrounded chocolate-brown irises lightened with gold rings. They dragged over my face and down to where he held me. My fingers twitched.

Finally, he dropped his hand and shook his head before striding away, back to his house. As soon as he was out of sight, I dropped the wood and groaned.

My father owned this house, as well as the one next door, and two more a couple blocks over. I'd whined and begged until he'd agreed to let me oversee the renovations, with the caveat that if it became too difficult for me, he'd take it all away from me. I knew what that meant. The moment I asked him for help, I'd no longer be the project manager and someone else would be put in charge.

I'd spent the summer managing plumbers and handymen and electricians completing small jobs in the four houses. Our deck was the final project. I'd been down to the last of the money my dad had fronted me. All of that was gone now, along with the crew.

I could tell him what happened. Explain the circumstances. He'd pay for someone else to come in and finish the job. I'd be off the hook.

Except that wasn't the kind of daughter I was. The weight of being the only child in the Sanderson family was nearly unbearable. Every hope and dream my parents would have spread around to multiple children had been draped on my shoulders from a very early age. No one had ever said, "You have to be perfect, Elena," but the ghosts of my siblings who would never be spoke loudly enough.

I wouldn't go to my dad with this.

I'd figure this out, even if it killed me—which was looking more and more likely.

Just as I opened my mouth to shriek like a banshee, Lachlan reappeared, carrying a toolbox and...oh, a nail gun too. He'd changed into a white T-shirt stained with paint and oil. It stretched tight over his arms and chest and hugged his middle—the only place on his body that looked soft. His shorts were meant for basketball players, which was probably why they were long enough for his towering frame, skimming his knees. On his feet were Timberland work boots, the laces loose and hanging open. They were just as scuffed up and stained as his T-shirt, a testament to the fact that he used them for what they were meant for: work.

Nothing about his clothes, his soft belly, his labor-honed muscles, unruly hair, or scruffy jaw should have attracted me. I'd always found myself on the arms of guys destined for yachts, charity galas, and boardrooms—like my father. Lachlan Kelly was none of those things, and that might have been his greatest asset.

He set his tools down in the grass. With his mouth in a flat line, he stared at me.

"Tell me why you fired the crew and I'll build the deck for you."

My lips parted, but no sound came out. That wasn't what I'd expected him to say. It wasn't often people surprised me.

He shifted closer, bending his neck so he could hold my gaze. Then he dropped his voice into something slightly above a whisper. "Tell me, Ellie."

"They were talking about me. About my tits, my ass, whatever. I ignored it because I don't care what anyone says about me. Then I found one of them in Zadie's bedroom yesterday. He had her underwear in his fist. I saw it, clear as day. I told the head of the crew, and instead of reprimanding the perv, he had the audacity to laugh. I made them leave. At the time, I was so pissed he'd violated Zadie's space and things, I didn't even consider demanding a refund."

I wiped the back of my hand across my forehead.

"That's it. I don't let panty-stealing pervs hang around my house. Word to the wise, if that's your thing."

His shoulders seemed to grow three sizes while contracting into spiny rocks.

"They came into the house without permission?" His brown eyes bored into mine, as serious as I'd ever seen him.

"They did."

His nostrils flickered. "You did the right thing, firing them. Next time something like that happens, though, come get me. I'll get your refund and make sure they know what will happen the next time they consider entering a house uninvited."

"Why would you do that?"

His head barely tilted. "It's the right thing to do."

As simple as that. That was Lachlan Kelly. He wouldn't protect me because he liked me or cared about me. He did the right thing because it was the right thing. Black and white—no gray.

"Is that why you're going to help me rebuild the deck?"

He straightened, surveying my chaotic work area. "Nah. That's because I'm ready for some peace and quiet. Can't take days and days of you hammering and getting nowhere."

"What a coincidence, I can't take it either." I kicked a plank. "Where should we start?"

"You start by going inside. Then you stay out of my way. It's not a big deck. I can knock it out in my off-hours and be done in a few days."

Insulted, I stepped into his space. "Stay out of your way? I'm perfectly capable of doing the work with some direction."

"That's the thing—" he tugged the end of my braid, "—I don't want to give direction. It'll go faster if I'm on my own."

My eyes narrowed on him. "Instinct tells me to fight you."

A reluctant half smile escaped before he hardened his jaw. "But you won't because you're smarter than that. Fighting me won't change things, and it really won't get your deck built."

"I can't pay you."

"I wouldn't take it if you could."

Steeling my spine, I clicked my heels together and saluted him. "Aye, aye. Your wish is my command, captain."

He bent to pick up the nail gun and glanced at me over his shoulder. "Don't think that's how that goes, Elsa."

"I know you know that's not my name."

"Do I?" He didn't spare me a look as he unwound the cord from the gun. Since I wasn't one to overstay my welcome—the very idea of doing so gave me hives—I took my damn leave.

If he wanted to build my deck on his own, he could have all the fun in the world doing it. I had more important things to do. I didn't know what they were yet, but I'd find something infinitely better than baking in the sun next to a sweaty, growling beast of a man.

I went inside, hopped up on the kitchen counter, and drank a big glass of water. So what if I now had a perfect view of the backyard? I *always* supervised my work crew.

··········

Two days later, the deck was more than halfway done. I'd examined it when Lachlan wasn't around, and of course, his workmanship appeared meticulous. He was back at it again, having come straight from work on campus to my backyard.

I poked my head out the sliding door. "Do you need a drink?"

He shook his head, marking the place on a board he intended to cut. "I'm good."

"All right. I'll be around."

His head stayed bent, like it always did when I was around. It drove me crazy. At this point, I wasn't sure if I wanted Lachlan's attention because I liked him or because he didn't give it to me. I wasn't a girl who was used to being ignored. After a year of being casually dismissed by him, I was close to grabbing onto his massive shoulders and demanding he look at me.

I wasn't there yet, though.

I snagged a bag from the fridge and tromped back outside. "Is your door unlocked?" I asked.

His fingers flexed on his level. "The sliding door is. Why?"

"I have something for Julien."

His head turned sharply in my direction. "What?"

"That's between him and me." Flipping my ponytail, I crossed my yard and his, and stepped into his cool house, feeling Lachlan's glare on my back the whole way.

"Phantom," I called. "Get your lazy ass out here."

His bedroom door—which was under the stairs—swung open, and he wheeled out. "Breaking and entering now?"

"Only entering. The beast working on my deck told me I could come in." A stretch of the truth, but who was keeping tabs? "Still milking the wheelchair for all it's worth, huh?"

He came to a stop in front of me, the constant grimace on his scarred face deepening the pit of worry in my belly.

Julien had started as Zadie's boyfriend's friend. I hadn't even met him until right before he'd moved into this house at the beginning of summer, and even then, he'd hid himself away most of the time. Zadie fussed over him. Amir was constantly stopping by and leaving not long after, looking like someone had kicked his puppy—which was saying something since he could be a scary monster in his own right. One day, I found myself in the same place as Julien. He caught me staring at his scars, which covered almost half his face.

He'd snarled. I'd snarled back and told him he didn't get to be a little bitch to me simply because he was stupid enough to get hit by a car. I thought he'd murder me. He'd laughed.

So, we were friends now, or as friendly as one could be with a man whose life had been upended in a hideous, violent fashion. Julien didn't want pity, though, and he hated being fussed over.

"What's in the bag?" he asked.

I help up the plastic grocery bag. "Well, I did some reading about food that helps with inflammation and—"

He cut me off with a growl. Right. Reading about how to help his pain qualified as fussing. I should have known.

Rolling my eyes, I dropped the bag in his lap and knelt in front of him so we were closer to eye level.

"Okay, how about this, Phantom? It's been so long since you've had sex—because, you know, you're so hideous, you're now a born-again virgin. To celebrate, I bought you cherries. Get it? Cherries for your cherry."

His scarred mouth curled as he opened the bag. I would have gotten a smile out of him if not for the grumble that came from behind me.

I peered over my shoulder. Lachlan stood inside the sliding door, his expression a storm cloud. I guessed he didn't appreciate my joke as much as Julien had.

"Get out of my house." His command was low, but there was nothing subtle about it.

"What—?" I spun on my knees. "You're kidding."

He threw his arm out, pointing to the door. "Get the fuck out, Elena. You're not welcome here."

"Man, she—" Julien tried to speak, but Lachlan slammed his palm into the wall, rattling the glass door beside it.

"Get. Out," he seethed. "Right now."

I scrambled to my feet. Julien reached out for my hand, but I tore away from his grasp. My fight-or-flight instinct had been activated by

Lachlan's rage, and flight was winning by a landslide. I ran past him, back to my house, and locked the door behind me, shaking from adrenaline and anger.

I hadn't found my bearings before my phone started to vibrate. My mother's name flashed on the screen, and I answered it automatically, like I always did when she called.

"Hi, Mom."

"Angel, you sound out of breath. Did I catch you at a bad time?"

The worst time. But honestly, talking to her was better than pacing the halls, seething at Lachlan.

"No, I just ran to the phone. Any time is a good time to speak to my precious mother."

She giggled, and the fist inside my chest unclenched slightly. Giggling was good. This kind, at least. Not the manic, high-pitched, inappropriate laughs always followed by bouts of keening wails. Those laughs sent shivers down my spine.

"I don't feel so precious when you haven't stopped by to see me in over a week," she chided.

"I know, and I'm sorry. I promise to come home before school starts again."

"Good. And bring your roommates. I'd love to cook for all of you."

"I'll see if they're free. You know, they both have boyfriends. They're always busy being loved up and doing couple-y things."

My mother had been enchanted by Helen and Zadie each time she met them. But then, it wasn't hard to earn my mother's love, not on her good days. She had the softest heart of anyone I knew, which might have been her downfall.

"What about you?" she asked. "You haven't mentioned if you're seeing anyone."

"No, I'm not." I shuddered. The last boy I'd dated at the behest of my parents had been a monster. Not on Nate Bergen's level. Then again, not many were.

"Well, I was talking to my friend, Daphne Clymer, at the Heart and Art Banquet and—"

I knew what was coming. What always came when my mother talked to a friend at a banquet or an acquaintance at tennis. Eligible sons, who'd love to wine and dine a girl like me, were often thrust at my mother. A sacrifice, to earn her friendship, or my father's favor in business. Because everyone wanted to be friends with Diedre Sanderson or do business with Gil Sanderson. That's just how it was.

By the end of the call, I'd agreed to giving my phone number to the son of a friend of a friend. My mother had sounded so excited about the potential match, I couldn't have possibly said no and listened to that excitement slip away.

To my parents, I was the perfect daughter. Their angel. To Lachlan Kelly, I was a girl who'd kick a man when he was down. A monster.

The truth was somewhere in between.

Chapter Four

Elena

Every morning, I read the newspaper on my porch. Every morning, I watched Lachlan, dressed in work clothes, walk out of his house, climb into his beat-up truck, and drive away.

This morning started the normal way. I had my paper. My feet were kicked up and resting on the porch railing. Lachlan emerged from his house, his booted footsteps heavy. But he didn't head to his truck. Instead, he rounded it to the sidewalk and strode to my porch and up the stairs.

I'd dropped my paper by then and had gotten to my feet. He looked me up and down, his eyes flaring as he took in my pajamas. I didn't give two thoughts about sitting outside in my silky slip. All the important parts were covered. But when he raked his gaze over me, I'd never felt more exposed.

"What?" I forced impatience into my tone.

"You call him Phantom. After *Phantom of the Opera*."

I crossed my arms over my chest to hide my pebbled nipples. "I'm aware."

"He thinks it's 'funny as hell.' That's a direct quote."

"I'm aware of that too."

Lachlan rubbed the back of his neck, scowling. "You brought him cherries to help with inflammation."

"Why are you telling me things I already know?"

"I yelled at you."

"Again, with the things I know."

"I made a mistake."

I sighed. "Yeah, you did. I hope you feel like a big asshole."

"I do."

"Good. Now, can I read my newspaper in peace?"

His hand shot out to loop a finger in the spaghetti strap of my slip. "You can't sit outside wearing this."

"I can't? It seems like I am. I do every morning."

"Dammit, Ellie. I can't deal with this. I have to go to work." He gave my shoulder a shove, directing me toward the front door. "Get inside."

"Are you kidding me? No."

"Fine." He turned and stomped down the stairs, eschewing the sidewalk to flatten the grass with his big feet. Ignoring his truck again, he disappeared into his house. When he didn't reemerge after a minute or two, I took my seat and picked up my newspaper.

Of course, that was when the asshole decided to show up again. Only, this time, he wasn't alone. Poor Julien had gotten roped into Lachlan's insanity. They both came to a stop at the base of my steps.

"I'm here to guard you," Julien announced, rubbing his heavy-lidded eyes.

A puff of air expelled from my lungs. "You woke him up?"

Lachlan's lips tipped into a smirk. "You want him to go back to bed? Go inside. Otherwise, Julien's going to stand guard until you do."

I tossed my newspaper aside, my morning ritual thoroughly spoiled. "You know what, Phantom? I thought you were better than this."

He looked at my pajamas and then at Lachlan. "I see your point. She can't wear that outside."

I jabbed my finger at them both. "You're both idiots. I wear much, *much* less clothing to the beach, and neither of you chase me around with a towel to cover up."

Lachlan grumbled. "Maybe someone should. You need a keeper, Elsa."

Julien raised his hand. "I'll do it, if you want to prance around in front of me in your bikini."

Pressing my lips together to stop from laughing, I swept my gaze to Lock, and my amusement faded. His genuine irritation at my choice of clothing rankled me down to my bones. The fact that he'd pulled Julien into this mess had only made it worse.

Then, he had the audacity to growl at Julien, and I was absolutely done with this conversation.

"I'm sorry you're unable to control yourself at the sight of me in my pajamas, Lachlan, but that sounds like a *you* problem."

I stormed inside, slamming the door shut behind me. As I watched Lachlan and Julien head back to their house, I smacked my palm against the window.

I'd done exactly what Lachlan had wanted.

•••••••••

That evening, he came back and got to work like he hadn't yelled at me and bossed me around. Perhaps that was par for the course for a man like Lachlan Kelly. I couldn't say I knew him very well. It definitely wasn't par for the course for me.

I opened the sliding glass door wearing his hoodie and what appeared to be nothing else but was actually a tank and cheer shorts.

"You know, you never apologized to me."

His head dipped lower as he shot a nail into a plank. "I didn't?"

"No, but I think you're aware of that."

He grunted, continuing on his task. For any other girl, Lachlan building my deck for free would have been enough of an apology. It certainly would have earned him some leniency. I'd never been any other girl, though, and he *still* hadn't looked at me.

"Do they pass out the knowledge to manhandle wood when you reach six feet?" I asked.

"About then," he answered.

"Interesting. My dad's a tall, strapping Scandinavian. I'll have to ask why he's never picked up an axe around me."

He chuckled low, under his breath, laughing at me. Little embers of embarrassment sizzled on my nape.

"If you're thinking about why my dad never chopped my head off or something—"

He dropped his nail gun like it had scorched him and whipped around to face me. He was on the ground, and I was still in the house, a few feet above him, but he didn't feel that much lower.

"Why the fuck would that ever cross my mind, Elsa?"

Because Nate would have said it. It was exactly what he would have said.

I shrugged off my ghosts-of-terrible-boyfriends past. "Just a joke. What were you laughing at, anyway?"

He stared at me, his hands on his hips and forehead crinkled with fury. That broad chest of his rose and fell like a great tsunami.

"Who's been saying shit like that to you?" he demanded.

"No one has. I just couldn't imagine what you thought was so funny about my dad wielding an axe."

He rubbed the back of his neck, his eyes flicking up to mine, then down to my stolen hoodie and bare legs. I crossed one ankle over the other, which made him jerk his eyes upward again.

"I was thinking if your dad is anything like you, him trying to use an axe would be quite the picture."

"Like me?"

He hummed in assent, as if that was a good enough answer.

"What do you mean, like me?" I pressed.

But I'd lost his attention. He picked up his nail gun and wrapped his fingers tightly around the handle.

"I mean, you're a princess. Your pajamas are silk and lace. Nothing's ever out of place on you. Bet your dad is a lot like you."

"He doesn't wear silk and lace."

His shoulders popped then lowered. "My point stands."

"I'm not afraid of working hard. I tried to help you with the deck and you refused, remember? As for my dad, no, he doesn't get his hands dirty with manual labor, but that doesn't make him less of a hard worker."

"Never said that. You asked why I laughed, I told you."

I stood there, dismissed. Lachlan went back to work. If he would just look at me, I wouldn't have been so bothered by his disinterest. It wasn't as if I was interested in him. He was too big, too broody, too rough. I had no idea what wilderness he'd emerged from, or who his parents were, or what his plans postgraduation were. I didn't want to *know* this man—but why the hell didn't he want to know me?

"You still haven't apologized."

"Yeah." He tucked a lock of unruly hair behind his ear. Of course, it slipped right back out. "I misjudged the situation, so I apologize."

"Thank you."

He peered up at me, sweeping over my bare legs again before landing on my face. "Gonna give me my hoodie back?"

I tugged on the strings hanging in front. "I'll consider it."

"I'm building you a deck for free, Elsa. Think that warrants the return of my favorite hoodie."

I hugged my arms around my middle. "But I washed it, so it doesn't even smell like you anymore." *Lies.* "And it's so soft and comfy."

He groused under his breath while he worked methodically, shooting nails and double-checking his work with his level. I had no idea how long I stood there watching. Probably an embarrassingly long time. But it wasn't as if Lachlan noticed anyway.

· · · · · • • · • · ·

He finished the deck the next evening with two days to spare. I stepped out onto it with my bare feet while he swept up random nails and sawdust.

"It looks good."

He grunted. "Yeah, it's all right."

"Thank you." He turned my way, stopping short to take in my teal cotton and lace chemise that stopped midthigh. I held out one of the beers in my hands. "You saved me."

He leaned his broom against the new rail and carefully approached, accepting the beer. He took a long, long pull. His throat worked, bobbing with each swallow. Stubble trailed down to his Adam's apple. When he opened his eyes, he caught me looking.

I took a sip of my beer, hoping the cool liquid would calm some of the heat stoking in my belly. Not that it was a bad feeling, but it was foreign. I couldn't remember the last time I'd been truly attracted to a guy, much less squirming on the inside from his presence.

Thank Prada for vibrators when I was alone and warming lube when I had to spread my legs for one of my parents' friends' sons.

I didn't think I'd need lube for Lachlan. He could slide right in and—

"Thanks for the beer." He held up his empty bottle.

"Of course. Consider it payment rendered." I reached for the sliding door. "Want another one? You deserve at least one more for all the work you did."

Not waiting for his answer, I went to the kitchen and grabbed a cold bottle from the fridge. When I turned around, Lachlan was *right there*. He accepted the beer, then placed it on the counter beside him.

My breath caught in my throat. His gaze scraped me raw, from my toes all the way to the top of my head. I'd worn this chemise to dig under his skin. But maybe it was more than that. Maybe I was still trying to capture his attention.

I had it now.

His nostrils flared. The sinews in his powerful forearms rippled as he curled his fingers into his palms.

"Fuck it."

His hand shot out, fisting the back of my hair and twisting until my head slanted to the side and his mouth came down on mine. My gasp opened me to him, letting his tongue sweep in, tasting the beer I'd had to drink and licking it away to get to *me*.

There was nothing imprecise about the way Lachlan Kelly kissed me. He went hard, but that was no surprise. His kiss was greedy and domineering, taking exactly what he wanted but giving too.

Pressing myself deep into his body, I shoved my hands under his T-shirt, ripping it out of my way to get to his skin. He was sun warmed and smooth, so big, I spread my fingers as wide as they would go, and it still wasn't enough. There was so much of him, so much to touch and lick.

I should have been questioning why this was happening, what it meant, what it *would* mean, but I gave no thought to that. I handed myself over to the heat Lachlan was stoking in me, heat I thought had been permanently extinguished.

He ripped his mouth off mine, moving down the side of my neck, nipping and sucking. I leaned into him farther, giving him all my weight, and he took it. One arm banded below my ass, lifting me off my feet. He held me against him, pulling my bottom lip between his and nipping at it.

"You want me to stop, tell me to stop," he rumbled, gaze locking on mine.

The shake of my head was short, but definite. "Don't stop."

Without warning, he walked us out of the kitchen and into the living room, dropping me to my feet again. Running his big hands along my shoulders, he tangled his fingers in the straps of my chemise and dragged them down my arms to my elbows. Rough palms kneaded my breasts, bringing them together so he could trail long, wet licks along both, then cover one nipple, then the other with his mouth.

I scratched his back as I worked his T-shirt up, trying hard to get it over his head. All that skin needed to be against mine, right this minute. Finally, he obliged, tearing himself away from my breasts to reach behind his head and tug his shirt off. I only got a glimpse of his torso before he was on me, lowering me to the sectional couch and yanking my chemise and underwear.

I reached for him at the same time he lowered himself over me. His mouth and hands and teeth were all over me, and I wanted it. I was there, completely present, a live wire, sparking against everything I came into contact with.

My mouth was on him too, kissing his ruddy cheeks, sucking on his ears and neck, nipping at his jaw. He tasted like the outdoors and sweat and Lachlan. So much Lachlan. He gave, and I took. But I gave back, more, more, I kept giving, emptying all that was before this moment so I could fill myself with this newfound aching desire.

My legs wrapped around Lachlan's thick waist, locking together in the back. He pressed his erection to my core, and I had no doubt I'd be leaving a wet spot on his shorts. I didn't give a damn. I was *wet*. I was turned on. Even if I didn't come, I'd have this. I'd know it was possible. I wasn't dead, I'd just been asleep for so many moons, I'd forgotten what this could be like.

And then, he reached between my legs, and my entire body went taut. He drew a line down my center, teasing my entrance, then ventured back to my clit. There, he didn't tease. The calloused pad of his finger pressed down hard and rubbed in circles while he sucked on my lips and throat.

I grabbed onto his hair, fisting and tugging the same way he'd done to me, until his nose was on mine.

"Fuck me, Lachlan."

"Planning on it." He squeezed his eyes shut. "Condom."

Reality fizzled at the edges of this encounter. If we stopped for too long, it would creep in and ruin everything. I couldn't lose this, not now that it was building.

"I'm on the pill, and I've been tested." I nudged his back with my heel, drawing him closer. "Come on."

His brows drew together, like he was warring with himself inside his head. "I'm clear too. But I—"

I tunneled my arm down in the space he'd created between us, palming his thick erection. He rocked his hips into my hand, and I could have sworn there was a direct line from my palm to my clit because I *felt* him there.

"Now. *Please*."

"Yeah," he gruffed, releasing a ragged breath. "You're gonna get it, Ellie."

He stopped rubbing my clit to push his shorts down. His bare skin slid through my wetness, the tip of his cock finding my opening. My foot trailed down to his ass, nudging him forward, while I slung my other leg over the back of the couch, giving him all the room he needed to maneuver.

That was when the world ended.

Lachlan drove in deep. Air left my lungs as he filled me. My hands flew to his shoulders, and I anchored myself to him with my nails.

"You like that." His nose brushed mine. "Ready for more?"

"Yes. Make it hard."

Lachlan was nothing if not a good listener. He trailed his big hands down my sides, gripping my hips and lifting them so he could plant himself even deeper inside me. I gasped at the fullness, at his weight pressing me into the couch, at just how fucking *good* having Lachlan Kelly inside me felt.

He moved over me, driving in hard, rough, relentless. His mouth kept finding mine, giving me bruising kisses as he pounded into me.

It was a lot, bordering on too much, yet I found myself panting, "More."

"Bossy." He bit down on my jaw and fucked me into oblivion. "Gonna give you more. You'll take it."

The pressure in my belly came out of nowhere. It took me by surprise. My head arched back, and my mouth fell open. Was this happening? Was I…?

Lachlan rotated his hips and ground his pelvis against mine. It was exactly what I needed, where I needed it. I mewled, desperate to keep building this, to not let it slip away. He read me, keeping at that spot that made me climb and climb.

There was a boom inside me. A catastrophic bomb rearranging all the broken pieces of me from the last two years, righting them into something different but whole. The dried-out husk of my insides flooded with pleasure, until I was lush, softened, alive.

And then, I was coming. Coming harder than I ever had. I cried out Lachlan's name, clawed at his shoulders, so stunned, I couldn't do anything except let my body succumb to what he was giving me.

My limbs were shaking, trying to hold on as he rode me through wave after wave.

He powered into me as my shaking subsided, and all I could do was cling to him. His grunts in my ear curled my toes, then his mouth was on mine, giving me a deep, wet kiss. He was there, his lips on mine. His thrusts became erratic, harder, more frantic, then his forehead rolled against mine. The sound he made as he came, low and pained, yet immensely and totally satisfied, carved its way into my chest.

Lachlan shoved his face in my neck, panting heavily, warming my skin. I twisted my fingers in the back of his hair, buzzing everywhere. My brain was fuzzy from coming. Coming with Lachlan. Coming so hard, I could live off that one orgasm for months.

He lifted his head, then his body, moving off the couch. It happened so suddenly, I didn't notice him leaving until he was already gone. I had tears in my eyes, and Lachlan was tucking his dick away, looking for an escape route.

"That was good," he gruffed.

I rolled to my side, covering my breasts with my arms. The fuzz in my brain was clearing, but it still coated my thoughts, slowing them down. Lachlan was bent over, picking up his T-shirt from the floor, and I hadn't moved.

He tugged the shirt over his head then raked his fingers through his hair. His eyes traveled over me, then his knuckles grazed my shoulder.

"That was good, Elsa. I'm gonna go if you're okay."

"You can go," I replied, unthinking.

I probably wasn't okay, but there was not a chance I would admit that to him.

He nodded, dipping his head, sending his hair right back in his face. "All right, then. Good night."

Rolling onto my back, I watched his swift exit from the room, and listened to the back door slide open and closed. Just like that, he was gone.

I stared up at the ceiling and squeezed my thighs together. The raw ache that seeped all the way to my belly told me that had been real. I hadn't dreamed it, even if Lachlan had faded as quickly as one.

Another tear slipped from my eye, trailing down my temple and into my hair. But I didn't cry because I was sad. I was *relieved*.

I came.

I actually came.

Tossing my head back, I released a laugh that emanated from the most broken part of me. The part *he* broke, severing my attachment to my body, my feelings, my pleasure. And holy shit, all it took was one massive mountain of a man, fucking me like he couldn't go another minute without it, kissing me like he'd never stop, to reattach me.

Lachlan Kelly made me come. I couldn't be angry that he walked out on me directly after, that he'd planned on such a quick getaway, he hadn't even taken off his shorts and boots. I couldn't.

I cupped myself between my legs and giggled, something warm spreading across my chest.

I'm not broken.

CHAPTER FIVE

LOCK

EVER SINCE I WAS a kid, my hands had to be busy fixing things or I was a grumpy motherfucker. Didn't matter what it was, my brain liked to figure out what made it tick, and my hands liked to put the broken pieces back together.

Now that the deck next door was finished, I was working on my truck. It'd belonged to my granddad. On the outside, the age showed, but I'd restored all the inner workings myself. It was a constant work in progress, but I liked that.

My head was under the hood when I heard footsteps on the stained concrete garage floor. Expecting a pissed-off ice queen, I moved with wariness, dropping the hood and wiping my hands on a nearby rag.

Elena Sanderson was in my garage, checking out my tool bench. She dragged her manicured fingers over the shiny metal and picked up a wrench like she was checking the weight. Her back was to me, and if I hadn't been on alert for her inevitable attack, I would have admired the hell out of her long, smooth legs showing under her tiny skirt. It'd been less than a day since those legs had been wrapped around me, and I hadn't forgotten for a second how they'd felt.

"Need something?"

"Yes."

She glanced at me over her shoulder, then turned the rest of the way around. There was no anger in her expression. No ice queen.

Her plush lips were soft. Her tongue darted out to wet the bottom one.

"What's that?" I asked.

Closing the distance, her hands met my chest and slid up to hook around my neck. Her long fingers dug into the hair at my nape, pulling herself closer.

"More," she breathed.

Her blue eyes were on fire, and not with anger. Elena was wanting, and she'd come to me to slake her need. Her fingers were demanding, trying to yank me down to her mouth. That wasn't how I worked, though. I didn't give in to the demands of spoiled little princesses.

"You want more of my cock?"

She nodded, breathless already. "I do."

"Ask."

Her pink lips parted, and a rush of sweet breath brushed across my chin. "*Please.*"

It was barely a whisper, but the ache behind that one word was a direct hit to my cock. That ache was mine, and I was gonna make it better.

"C'mere."

She jumped at the same time I grabbed her, lifting her into my arms. Her legs wound around me, and her hungry mouth fastened to mine. I walked her to the nearest wall, pressing her back into it, my erection against her hot little cunt. I could feel her, the heat between her legs seeping through the cotton of my shorts.

Skirt around her waist, I reached beneath her, pushing her panties aside. Bare, slick skin met mine. Her folds were soaking. Her clit was already throbbing. She'd worked herself up before she'd gotten here, had built herself into a frenzy.

Her mouth was busy on mine, sweet and demanding, that tongue plundering, tasting, battling. I let her have her way, gave her control of the kiss, since she'd been so sweet, asking for what she wanted.

My finger slid into her, deep as I could get it. She moaned against my lips, tugging harder on my hair. I gave her little ass a smack and slammed my finger into her, twisting and curling. Her legs trembled around me, then tightened, her heels digging into my back. I kept going, working her up. And she liked it, mewling so sweetly. This was a side of her I'd never seen. A side she never showed. My seat was front row now, and I couldn't stop watching.

"Lachlan...fuck me." Her words were thick with need. Her pussy was dripping down my fingers. Hottest thing ever, this difficult woman begging for what she wanted. What only I was capable of giving her.

We didn't need to talk. She told me what she wanted, and I was more than willing to give it. In my mind, yesterday had been a one-off, a period at the end of a week of battling and flirtation. Now that she was here, asking for more, I realized I wasn't done with her yet either.

I unsnapped my shorts and tugged down the zipper, freeing my cock. If I were smart, I'd go inside and grab a condom. But I had a hot pussy begging for me, fluttering for what I could give her, and there was no amount of logic that would take me away from that.

Her head fell back against the wall, watching me from under heavy-lidded eyes. So fucking pretty, so damn hot, this girl. I never let myself look at her. Now would be the only time I'd indulge in studying the heart shape of her face, the spray of freckles across her nose, the way her lips formed a perfect little rosebud. More than pretty, Elena was gorgeous and sexy.

My tip lined up with her addictive heat. She tilted her hips forward, and it was all the invitation I needed. One rough jerk, and I slammed home. She squealed at the intrusion and grappled with her hands on my shoulders.

"Oh fuck," she moaned. "Oh shit."

"That's right, Ellie. You're in trouble now. Gonna get what you came for, girl."

"Hard, Lachlan."

"You'll get that. Not a chance I'm not gonna give that to you."

And then I was moving, slamming into her over and over. Her mouth found mine again, and we were tangling up. Pulling hair, nipping, sucking, messy, desperate. Elena knew exactly how to drive me out of my mind, so it should have been no surprise that extended to when we were fucking. Her little sounds, claws digging into my skin, chants for more, harder, faster, were all like kerosene on an open flame.

She slid her hands under my shirt, pressing into my skin like she was trying to absorb it. Her nails raked along my chest, around my nipples, then down to my belly. She was everywhere, touching me like she'd never touched a man before.

This girl was so damn hungry. Her mouth latched onto my neck, sucking and biting. Teeth nibbled on my earlobe, and her pants warmed my jaw. I let her go, explore, conquer her hunger while I watched where we were joined. My cock had her stretched around me, so pink and slick, taking me and sucking me back in every time I retreated. Her cunt was just as hungry as the rest of her.

I pressed my thumb to her clit, digging the rest of my fingers into her thigh, and she gasped, almost going still. After a pause, where she barely breathed, one of her hands wrapped around my wrist.

"Don't stop," she implored.

"Never. Need to see you lose it. Let me have it. Let me see it."

Her neck arched, and the back of her head rested on the wall while I rubbed her, fucked her, watched myself disappear inside her. Having this power over her, this girl who never showed her cards and walked around like she either owned the world or had plans to, was addictive. So intoxicating, I couldn't see straight.

"Oh fuck. Oh god, Lachlan." The hand around my wrist tightened, and her eyes found mine. They were wide, pleading. "Don't stop."

"I won't."

She clung to me while she trembled, tightening everywhere, bringing me close, so damn close. But I held on, giving her what she needed, rocking into her to hit that spot that kept her shaking, panting, squeezing me.

Mouth open, she released a silent scream. Letting go of my wrist, her arms banded around my neck. I pressed her so hard into the wall, if it had cracked, I wouldn't have been surprised. And then I went at her, giving her the hard she asked for, the rough I had to have. Her heat, her mouth on my throat, the sweet, floral scent on her skin, drove me higher and higher, until my vision narrowed and blackened at the edges. All that existed was the silvery blonde in my arms and the place where our bodies connected.

Planting myself as far as I could, I spilled inside her, grunting my pleasure. My teeth clamped down on her shoulder, muffling the sounds she was tearing out of me.

My heart jackhammering in my ears, I stilled when Elena dug her fingers into my shoulders and made a strangled sob. At least, I thought that was what it was, until I lifted my eyes and found her, her head tilted back, her eyes squeezed shut, giggling softly to herself. It was beautiful and perplexing, seeing her so light and free. And soft. She'd gone soft all over, the ice on her surface melting away.

When she felt me looking at her, she sucked in a breath, composing her expression. I pulled out of her, letting her feet drop to the floor, holding on to her waist until she was steady, then I stepped back. I turned to tuck my soaking cock away and give myself a second to get my head on straight. As I ran my fingers through my hair, inhaling the scents of sex, motor oil, and wildflowers, Elena darted by, heading for the wide-open garage door.

Shit. I hadn't even thought about closing it. Once Elena asked for more, that'd been the end of everything outside of giving it to her.

My arm shot out, catching her around the middle, and dragged her backward until she hit my chest.

I pushed her hair away from her neck and lowered my mouth to her ear. "You're in a hurry, Elsa."

She tilted her head to the side. "Mmm. We both got off. Time to go."

"Is that happening again?"

"Do you want it to?"

"I haven't gotten to taste you yet. So, yeah, let's do that again. Maybe try a bed out next time."

Goose bumps spread along the column of her throat and down her shoulders.

"We'll see."

I nipped at her ear. "Yeah. We'll see. You have my number. You know where I live. If you want more of that, let me know."

"I'll think about it."

She sounded cool, but I didn't think she was playing. This happened again between us or not, she'd live. I liked that. It made me want her in my bed even more. I got the feeling I could have her and it wouldn't get complicated. We could both get off then get away.

"You do that, Elsa." I pressed my half-hard dick against her back. "Don't take too long, though."

· · · • · • • • · ·

The moon glinted off her silvery hair as she knelt between my legs and lowered her mouth over me, taking me deep. Her hands roamed over my thighs, my stomach, cupping my balls, squeezing my shaft. I grabbed another pillow to shove under my head so I could keep watching her head move up and down over me.

She'd come back to me last night. And again tonight. Last night, we only made it as far as my kitchen. This was the first time I had Elena in bed, but she'd jumped on me, determined to take me into her mouth before I could do it to her.

Every encounter I'd had with her after the first had started with the same fiery determination. Like she was showing up for a job she was committed to seeing all the way through. If she didn't get off so damn hard at the end of it, I'd question it. And maybe I *was* questioning it in the far recesses of my mind.

But the wet drag of Elena's lips was at the forefront, blocking every other thing out. She hummed around me, her eyes flicking up, like she was checking in. I brushed her hair away from her face and cupped her cheek.

"Jesus, Ellie. Get your cunt on my face. I need to taste you before I come."

She paused with just the tip of me between her curling lips. Little devil dove back down, keeping eye contact the whole time she ignored me. Like she was punishing me by sucking me off.

Truth was, it was a punishment. I wanted her how I wanted her, and I didn't like being defied.

My hand trailed from her cheek to her throat, cupping her there. "Get up here, El. If you want me to feel good and get off, you'll give me what I'm asking for."

Her lips popped off me, and she crawled up my torso, rubbing her breasts along my stomach and chest, until I caught one in my mouth, giving her a nice, long suck.

Leaving a peck on my mouth, she swung herself around, straddling my face backward. I yanked her down and went to work, while she leaned forward, recapturing as much of me as she could. She wasn't going hard, only toying with my tip. I'd get mine later. Right now, her sweet flavor was hitting my tongue for the first time, and it was all I could think about.

She rocked back, whimpering as my tongue delved deep and my fingers rolled her greedy little clit. It was swollen, looking for attention. Her skin was perfectly smooth and felt expensive, so soft and refined, like she bathed in rose petals daily.

"Lachlan," she breathed. "Please, *please.*"

She probably did. Long baths, filled with imported water and sacrificial petals. I'd never felt a softer woman, like licking the top layer of cream. And her taste...god, it was her. Spicy, tangy, with a surprising sweetness that had me coming back for more and more, until she was burying her face in my stomach to muffle her long, yearning moans.

She lay limp like that, while I lapped her up. Slow licks over her slick folds. She exhaled a long breath, then kissed the head of my cock and petted it softly. That move—unexpected, innocent, and so damn sweet—had me jerking, no doubt leaking too.

"Turn around, El." My fingers stroked her outer thighs. "Give me that mouth."

Scooting down to my chest, she peered at me over her shoulder. "Just my mouth?"

"Start there. Then give me the rest." I swatted her ass, enjoying the slight ripple of her flesh.

Elena moved like a cat back down my body until she straddled me the other way. Cupping the sides of her head, I brought her mouth to mine, kissing her puffy lips hard. While I did, she settled over my erection, guiding it inside her.

I had time, and so did she, so we took it, stretching this out as far as it would go. She rode me for a long time, and I gritted my jaw through another one of her orgasms. I rolled us to our sides, me behind her, her leg draped over my arm. She reached above her to grip the headboard and ground her ass into me. The long line of her spine was graceful and sexy. The skin on her back was so unmarked, I wouldn't have believed it was real had I not been holding her in my arms.

Rolling her clit under the pad of my finger made her moan and her head fall back on my shoulder.

"Lock, I don't think I can come again."

"You can." I caught her earlobe with my teeth.

"I can't. I just—" Breaking off, she moaned again, and her ass pressed into me. "Maybe."

"Yeah, Ellie. Maybe."

Maybe turned to yes as she gave herself over to it. The feel of her clamping down around me, so hot and slick, was the end of me. Banding my arm to keep her fastened against me, I pumped in and out hard, rough, until I found my own release. I jerked her tight in my arms, burying myself deep, keeping her in place while I spilled all over her fluttering walls.

She reached back, digging her fingers in the scruff at my nape, sighing as I panted into her neck. Didn't seem right how well she fit against me. It didn't make any sense, but I guessed it didn't matter.

Everyone was coming back tomorrow. School was starting the next day. Life was going to get back to normal really soon.

I regretted pulling out of her as soon as I did. Leaving her perfect heat wasn't easy. She whined at my absence, turning her head to scowl at me. Laughing, I flopped onto my back. She took the pillow next to mine, stretching out her long legs.

"Comfortable?" I asked.

"Mmmhmm. I'll leave in a minute or two."

"No rush."

She snorted softly. "What a gentleman. You have your way with me then allow me to stay in your bed for a few minutes after. Chivalry isn't dead after all."

Unable to resist the call of her skin, I laid my palm on her stomach, my fingers stretched between her hip bones and down to her mound.

"There was a lot of you having your way with me tonight," I said.

"True." She slid her hand over mine, lining up her fingers on top of mine. "God, Lachlan, you're so damn big. Two of my fingers make up one of yours."

Lifting my eyes from our hands to her face, I found an amused, sleepy expression. She caught me looking, but the amusement didn't fade.

"Are you tired?" she asked, sucking her bottom lip between her teeth.

"Not really."

"So, if I stayed a little while, do you think that huge, beautiful cock of yours could get hard again?"

Her hand still on top of mine, I cupped her between her thighs. "You seemed to think you'd met your coming quota. Do you still think that?"

Still watching me, she shook her head. "I want to go again. I want you to make me come again. You're really good at it."

"Yeah?" I had a feeling this girl didn't give out compliments often. Though this one was sexual, it still shot warmth to my chest—which was crazy. I still hadn't decided if I liked this girl or not.

"Shut up, you know you are."

My finger dipped a little lower, sweeping over her slit. She shuddered, scissoring her legs.

"Yeah."

●●●●●●●●●●

It hadn't been my intention—then again, none of this had—but we went all night like that, getting each other off again and again. Each time, it seemed like we were done, then one or the other would touch, or give a look, and we'd be at it again.

My eyes cracked open. The sun had just about risen. Elena was sprawled across my chest, thoroughly fucked and passed out. She'd probably hate knowing I was seeing her like this, lips hanging open, hair an unruly mess, naked as the day she was born. The thing was, even in the stark light of day, she had next to no flaws on her body and face.

My breathing must've changed when I woke up. It didn't take Elena long to stir. She yawned first, then snuggled closer, her leg slinging across me. It wouldn't have taken much for me to lift it a little higher and slide inside, but from the pounding I gave her, she was probably sore. To tell the truth, even *I* needed a break.

"What time is it?" she mumbled.

"Morning," I answered.

"I slept here all night?" She hadn't opened her eyes yet. Or shifted away from me.

"There wasn't much sleeping going on."

"Hmmm. I should go home."

"That's a good idea."

The change in her was subtle. If we hadn't been pressed so tightly together, I wouldn't have noticed. Her breath hitched, fingers curled inward, leg shifted on mine.

"Okay." She rolled off me, swinging her legs over her side of the bed. "Thanks for the good time."

She pulled her little nightgown over her head and hopped up, running her hand over the back of her tangled hair. I didn't really want to send her out in the broad light of day like that.

"Grab one of my shirts, El. Put it over your pajamas."

She glanced at me over her shoulder. "I'm just going next door. It's not a big deal."

I jackknifed into a sitting position and pointed to the dresser in the corner. "Take one. Top drawer. We don't need to argue about it."

She stomped to the dresser, but instead of grabbing the first thing on top, she riffled through my T-shirts until she was satisfied. The black Savage U shirt was like a beach cover-up on her, swimming to midthigh. It covered the silky nightgown, but she looked like she didn't have anything underneath the shirt. I wasn't sure this was much better. It *definitely* wasn't better for me.

Pressing on my hardening cock, I locked eyes with her. She had her hair draped over one shoulder, somehow tamed in the short time since she'd gotten out of bed.

"I'll bring it back tonight." She plucked at the hem of the shirt, and I was tempted to agree. Really fucking tempted.

"Don't worry about it. If you want to return it, just leave it in my truck bed. I'll get it."

"In your truck bed?"

"Yeah. Everyone's coming back today. I don't think either of us want to answer questions about why you have my shirt."

Her fingers dug into the ends of her hair. "Questions would be terrible. Though it's not anyone's business."

She was saying the right things, but something was off. I didn't know her well, but even I could see that.

"We're on the same page, then?"

Her forehead was taut and smooth. When her eyebrows drew together, it barely crinkled. "What page are we on?"

"That this is done."

She took a retreating step. "Done?"

Her surprise took me aback. We hadn't said we were just hooking up temporarily, but it had been so clear in my head, I didn't even question if it was clear in hers too.

"Done. I've got a lot going on. I had fun with you, but don't—"

She ripped my T-shirt off her body and tossed it at me. "Here. Take your shirt. Our friends might talk if they see it in my possession, even for a minute. I wouldn't want that." Calm and level, she walked to my door, opening it carefully.

"Elena—"

Peering over her shoulder, she arched an imperious brow. "Yes?"

I had nothing to say. I didn't owe her anything. We weren't ending a relationship. We'd had some really fucking amazing sex, but that was where it started and ended. That was where it always ended for me. I had a hard time believing the ice queen would ever want anything more from me anyway. Something about this didn't feel right, but it wasn't because it was ending. Maybe I was doing it wrong. I hadn't really anticipated needing to do it in the first place.

"Wear my fucking shirt." I stalked across the room and tugged the cotton material over her head. "Throw it in the garbage when you get home if you want. I'm not letting you walk out of here without it on."

Her long fingers pinched the material at her shoulder. "Thanks, Lachlan. I'll leave it in your truck. And I guess we're even now."

I followed her into the hall, my toes at her heels as she headed toward the stairs. "What does that mean?"

"You built my deck, I sat on your dick a few times." At the bottom of the steps, she used the balustrade to spin herself around. "I think we both got a pretty good deal out of this."

She tossed her hair behind her shoulders and sauntered out of my house like she didn't have a care in the world. And maybe she didn't. Maybe that was all real and she wasn't going to bite my head off the next time we ran into each other.

Despite being unsettled, I had no regrets. She was right. We had fun. We both got something out of the past week, and now it was done. If Elena iced me out after this, we'd be right back to where we began. No harm done.

Chapter Six

Elena

No one bothered to tell me junior year of college was when things got real. The first two years were spent knocking out core requirements and dipping my toes into business management courses.

With the exception of my Spanish class, all my other courses were for my major. The one I was most anticipating was New Venture Research, Design, and Implementation. The name of the class could use a makeover, but from everything I'd heard, it was going to be an adventure.

Despite being my last class of the day, I walked in fresh as a daisy. I was ready to throw myself into this course, get my creativity flowing, and hone my business acumen—especially after the incredibly dry hour I'd just spent in quantitative analytics. Surely someone could present the information without making me want to saw my own ears off. Dr. Chen had not been that person. The only thing keeping me awake was the fact that I'd been running late and had to take a seat in the very front row. No surreptitious napping for me.

New Ventures was a smaller class with only twenty-five students. Rows of long tables were built on risers. I took a spot smack in the middle. I was early, so as students arrived, I checked everyone out. Some I vaguely recognized from other business classes. Some were new faces.

A group entered together. The first two blondes were Kayleigh and Abby, friends from last year. I used the term friend loosely. I hadn't hung out with either of them since Kayleigh disrespected Zadie and I slapped the shit out of her. I'd been done with that crowd at that point anyway. The slap had just punctuated my exit.

Some forethought on my part would have been nice, though. Considering we shared a major, I'd be seeing those girls for the next two years whether I liked it or not. From the glare the two of them shot me, they did *not* like it.

Which made sense, considering a handful of guys from Pi Sig followed them into class. I should have said formerly, since the frat lost its charter last semester. I'd had a helping hand in making that happen, so they probably weren't going to enjoy sharing a class with me either.

Wow, I was racking up enemies left and right. It was like high school all over again, except I didn't have a posse of sycophants and a psycho boyfriend to insulate me from them.

If nothing else, this semester would be interesting.

The group took up the row behind me. I could practically feel them boring holes in the back of my head. My lips curved at the corners, amused. A lot of people might've disliked being hated, but I found power in it—especially since these people hated me for calling them out. They might not have seen it that way, but I knew the truth.

··········

New Ventures was everything I'd hoped it would be. Professor Seavers was more than I'd expected. My mind was going a mile a minute, which was why I wasn't paying attention as I walked down the aisle to the steps. If I'd been paying attention, I would have noticed the foot sticking out from the aisle above mine. And then I would have dodged it instead of walking right into it. If I'd been paying attention, even if I'd tripped on that fucking foot, I would have been able to catch myself before I went down.

None of those things happened. The errant foot caught me in the shin, and since I had my laptop under one arm while digging through my messenger bag, I had no way to brace myself. The tumble seemed to take forever. It was as if I could count the carpet fibers individually in the time it took for my face and shoulder to collide with the ground. And then, time stood still.

I lay there, hoping to sink into the carpet and disappear. I hadn't felt the pain yet, but from the way my head had bounced off the floor, I knew it was coming. When I didn't disappear, I resolved myself to dying in this spot.

Unfortunately, some hero stuck his hand out to me, helping me off the ground.

"Oh my lord, are you okay? You just went down flat."

The guy winced as he looked me over. He looked to be about twelve, maybe thirteen if I was pushing it. Several inches shorter than me, and undoubtedly several pounds lighter, he was a small guy with black hair that stuck up all over, wearing a neatly pressed pair of khakis. In high school, I would have dismissed him as a nerd. Now, I knew better. He'd probably be the next Bill Gates or something.

I pressed a hand to my head and whipped around to the aisle above mine. Kayleigh was slack-jawed. Abby was a little less stunned. One of the guys they were with leaned over the desk to peer down at me.

"Are you okay?" he asked.

"Do you care?" I retorted. "You didn't when you stuck your big boat of a foot in my path."

He held his hands up. "That wasn't me. You just tripped. We all saw it."

I narrowed my eyes at him, willing the tears pricking at the backs of them to stay away. My head really hurt, dammit.

But I was Elena Sanderson. I didn't let the bitches get me down.

"I recognize you." He was handsome, in a generic way that did nothing for me, much like the guys my parents were always setting me up with. "Your name starts with a *D*. Don't tell me...is it David? No, that's not it. Devon?"

He shook his head, cocky smirk engaged. "Nope."

I snapped my fingers. "That's right. It's Dickweed. How could I forget that? So catchy."

Smirk fading, he stood to his full height, no longer pretending to be concerned. I turned my back on all of them, facing the guy who'd helped me up. He was holding my bag and computer out to me.

"Thank you for helping me," I said with as much sincerity as I could muster.

"Sure, sure." He pointed to his forehead, then mine. "You might want to get some ice on that. It looks like it's going to swell."

I let out a sardonic laugh. "It feels like it too. What's your name, by the way?"

"Sal. Um, Salvatore," he answered, skittering backward. "I have to go. Be careful."

Oh, yeah, I'd be careful. I wouldn't be letting my guard down in this class ever again.

••••••••••

Zadie, Amir, and I shared an accounting class on Tuesdays and Thursdays. I'd made sure to enroll in the same section since she was an accounting major and knew her stuff. I would never say I didn't know my stuff, but...well, numbers. If I needed help, I could just walk down the hall at home to ask her.

Amir was a senior. He probably didn't need this class and only took it to be near Zadie—which was completely fair, in my opinion.

I arrived first, but they walked in a few minutes later. Zadie was carrying a cup, Amir had two.

"For you." She set the cup and straw in front of me before sitting down in her chair. Amir handed her one of the coffees he was carrying before he sat down on her other side.

"What did I do to deserve this?" I picked up the condensation-covered plastic cup and poked the paper straw into the lid. Without even tasting it, I knew she had my order exactly right. That was just how Zadie was. Conscientious of others, she paid close attention, noticing little things like coffee orders, and bigger things like sour moods and hideous bruises on her roommate's forehead.

"Did you think I'd buy coffee for myself and not bring you anything?"

I gave her a look. "Really?"

"Really." She opened her laptop and sighed. "Well, obviously I'm concerned about you. You spent yesterday evening vacillating between kicking furniture and icing the nasty bump on your forehead—which you claim is from tripping, but you don't trip. So, I thought if I sweetened you up with a latte, you might confide in what's really going on. Maybe you'd even let me hug you."

I patted the top of her head. "You're very sweet, but I'm fine. I appreciate the coffee, though. I'll make sure to look like a sad sack on a regular basis so I can have a repeat."

Amir put his arm around Zadie and pulled her back into his chest. His deep, dark eyes met mine. I didn't scare easily, but Amir made me quake on the inside. He wasn't like Nate, and I knew for a fact he'd never hurt Zadie, but my inner prey instinct screamed *run* when we were in close quarters.

"You need me to take care of something, I will," he murmured.

She turned her head to look up at him. "Nonviolently, of course."

He lifted the hand resting on her shoulder. "Hey, mama, I've gone straight. That doesn't mean I can't have a talk with someone who's bothering your girl."

I shook my head. "No one's bothering me. If I do run into trouble, I'll remember your offer."

And I would. But one little foot in the aisle by some D-named douche canoe wasn't going to send me running scared. The Pi Sig boys might have something else up their sleeves, and if they did, they could bring it. I'd faced down way bigger bads than overgrown, overprivileged mama's boys who couldn't find a clitoris if it were sixty feet tall with neon arrows pointing to it.

After class ended, Amir, Zadie, and I walked out of the building together. They were headed home, but I had one more class left. I started off in the opposite direction, only taking two steps before Amir said my name.

"Yes?"

He cleared his throat. "You've been hanging with my boy some, right?"

"Julien?"

He nodded. Of course he meant Julien.

"We talk. Banter. We're neighbors, after all."

His hand came up to rub the stubble on his chin. He had Zadie tucked in close to his side. Her head was tipped, looking up at him.

"How do you think he's doing?" he asked.

"Well..."

His hand fell away from his face. "The kid won't talk to me. I didn't want him to move out of my house, but it made more sense to live where he is now. I'm thinking it was the wrong move, though. He's withdrawing, and I can't get a read on him."

"Look—" I was going to have to lay out some truth that might have been uncomfortable. I very much didn't want to, but there was no getting out of Amir's question. "—I obviously didn't know Julien before his injury. To me, he's my grumpy, reclusive neighbor. There's no baggage between us. No guilt. No pity. None of that stuff. If he's an asshole to me, I don't hesitate to be an asshole back. I know he's dealing with pain, and he's frustrated with his physical limitations. I don't think he's anywhere close to wheeling himself off a cliff, if that's what you're worried about."

They both winced at my bluntness, but why beat around the bush and waste time?

"Fuck. He won't even let me help him with anything." Amir tugged at his short hair, frustration seeping out of his pores.

"At least he still lets me cook for him," Zadie said.

"Anyone would let you cook for them, mama." Amir locked eyes with me. "I get what you're saying. I try not to lay my guilt on him, but no doubt he smells it rolling off me."

Shifting, I hiked my messenger bag higher on my shoulder. "He's pretty astute that way."

Amir released a long exhale. "Let me know if you get worried about him."

"Of course."

We parted ways after a few more promises from me to alert Amir to any worrisome changes in Julien. It might have annoyed Julien if he found out about the arrangement, but he wouldn't be hearing it from me. The guy had enough of his own inner turmoil. He didn't need to deal with his best friend's too.

My forehead was throbbing by the time I'd crossed campus to my final class of the day—Spanish for business. My shoulder wasn't faring any better. I'd live, though. Maybe after this, I'd go visit Julien and allow him to scoff at my injuries so I'd feel better about myself and he could relieve some of his pent-up anger.

I was smiling to myself at the idea when I entered the classroom. Around twenty or twenty-five desks were arranged in a semicircle. I slid into an empty desk on one end of the open circle, dropped my bag to the floor, and cupped my forehead.

Class was about to begin, and all the desks were filled except the one beside me. I guessed my scowl warded off my classmates. And that was fine, since I wasn't in the mood to socialize. I'd be better next time. Maybe.

Someone pushed into the room at the last minute, and in my periphery, I saw him coming my way. There was no mistaking that mountainous frame and slow, precise gait.

Lachlan took the desk beside me, barely fitting his big body in the seat. His long legs stretched out in front of him, breaching the empty interior of the semicircle.

I glanced over at him. He lifted his chin, then his eyes narrowed, and he leaned toward me. Undoubtedly, he was looking at my face, but I didn't need or want his concern. I shifted in my chair, taking away his view of my face.

Throughout the lecture, I felt his eyes on me. Not the whole time, but his gaze was heavy, so I caught it when it landed. He made it impossible to concentrate on what the professor was saying. By the time the lecture concluded, I was pretty pissed.

I stuffed my laptop into my bag and swung it over my good shoulder. Lachlan rose in front of me, blocking me like a brick wall.

"What happened to your forehead?" he demanded.

"None of your business." I swerved around him, but he was faster than he had any right to be, staying on my heels out of the classroom and into the hallway.

"Are you okay?"

He looked down at me as I walked, determined to get away from this man. God, I couldn't believe I'd have to spend all semester in a small classroom with him. I'd transfer sections if there was another available, but I already knew this was it. I was stuck with Lachlan Kelly.

"I'm fine, thanks." Chin up, I focused on the exit ahead of me.

"What happened?" he pressed.

"Ran into a door."

His scowl was so deep, it carved a divot in my periphery. "Someone didn't do that to you, did they?"

"Oh yes, you caught me. I'm in a fight club. Oops, shit, I forgot I wasn't supposed to talk about fight club. That's, like, the number one rule." I rolled my eyes as I pushed outside. Lachlan reached around me to hold the door open for me. Ducking under his arm, I picked up my pace, coming to an abrupt stop when his thick fingers curled around my bicep.

Memories of those calloused hands holding me and touching me and delving into my body in an entirely different way blasted through me. I didn't want to look at this man. The last time I had, he'd tossed me aside like an old, dirty condom—which he hadn't even bothered to use.

It wasn't like I'd been in love with him, but I hadn't expected to be dismissed that way. We'd had fun. More than fun, we'd had some extremely hot sex. The hottest of my life—which wasn't saying much considering my previous partners' paltry effort toward getting me off, but still. I hadn't been ready to stop hooking up with him. There were still things I wanted to try, positions and...activities we hadn't gotten to. Orgasms that should have been had—on both sides.

I'd assumed it had been on both sides, but I guessed not. Inside my own head, I could admit his rejection had cut me to the quick.

"What?" I bit out.

"I'm talking to you. You can look at me like a person due a modicum of respect."

My eyes flicked to his. It cost me, but I held his gaze as steady as I would have anyone else's.

"Is there anything else you need, Lachlan?" I asked sweetly.

He dipped his face, closing in on my forehead. "This looks bad."

"Why, thanks. You say the sweetest things." I shook my arm. "How about you let go now? That'd be great."

His hold loosened, but instead of letting go, his thumb stroked the inside of my bicep.

"You didn't mind me holding on to you a couple days ago."

"I didn't?" I would have tugged my arm away from him, but he'd caught the sore one, so I was at his mercy, and right now, the way he was looking at me was pretty merciless. "You didn't mind me taking your dick in my mouth. But times change, don't they? Our friends are back, and now we don't touch. Go back to being the guy who leaves the room when I enter and—"

"You'll be the ice queen. I don't think you ever stopped unless you were naked."

Pain be damned, I *did* tug my arm out of his grasp then. "Wow, Lock. You know me so well." My tough girl act would have sold better if I wasn't breathless from the shooting jabs of agony in my shoulder. Making it worse, I automatically clutched it, drawing Lachlan's attention.

"What the fuck?" He moved into me, easily pushing my hand out of the way to gather the V-neck of my shirt in his fist, revealing my bruise-mottled shoulder and arm. "Don't tell me this is nothing."

"It isn't nothing. It hurts like hell. But the thing is, my body is not your business, and I truly don't appreciate you shoving my clothes aside like you have any sort of rights to me."

This time when he grabbed me, he did it gently, but otherwise, he ignored all I'd just said. "Are you going home?"

"I'd like to, yes."

He tipped his head to the side. "Come on. I have my truck. I'll drive you."

"No thanks." I would not be spending another minute with this man. My house was nearly a mile away, and I didn't have a problem walking that distance.

As always, Lachlan didn't listen. "You'll ride with me." Then he started walking, and unless I wanted to be dragged by my already injured arm, I had no choice but to go with him.

"You really shouldn't touch women who tell you not to," I said.

He grunted but didn't slow or let go of me. "I'm giving a clearly injured and delirious woman a ride home. Don't make it out to be anything other than what it is."

The double meaning was heavily implied. He thought I'd made the sex into something more than it was. And maybe I had. Not that I'd fallen for Lachlan, not even close. He'd given me something without meaning to, and I wanted more of it.

Logically, I knew it wasn't Lachlan's fault he was the first man to ever make me come while inside me. I knew it wasn't his fault sex with him didn't feel like an exchange of services. Most of all, I knew it wasn't his fault he'd been the one to awaken nerves that had been numb since Nate raped me.

God, I hated that word so much, but adding "date" didn't pretty it up.

So, no, I wasn't in danger of falling in love with Lachlan. But I was pissed he'd taken away the one thing I thought would be impossible for me to ever have. All because...what? I was an embarrassment to him? He'd die if our friends knew he'd stooped so damn low?

He practically threw me into the front seat of his truck, buckling me in like the first time he gave me a ride. I caught a whiff of his scent. Obviously, he smelled good. Why wouldn't he? Everything about him was good except his personality.

We rode in silence through campus until traffic came to a crawl. Everyone was leaving at the same time, and no one knew how to drive. So, I was stuck in a truck with a fuming lumberjack in stifling silence.

"I don't know you," I said.

His head turned my way. "No, you don't."

"Is this your MO?"

"What do you mean?"

I looked at him, then away. I didn't like his face right now. "I mean, do you regularly hit it and quit it? Bang and run? Is that your thing? I guess I should have found out before…except you were the one who tore my clothes off. There wasn't much time for talking."

His chest made a rumbling sound. "You came to me the other three times."

"Well, you're good at sex. Interpersonal relationships, I'm not so sure."

His huff was low and humorless. "I didn't think I had to explain what it was. That was my mistake."

"I'm not some desperate chick begging you to love me, Lachlan. I was never going to turn into that girl. Not with you. But the fact is, you didn't use a condom with me, so I need to know how often you do this kind of thing. Should I be concerned?"

"Not with me," he muttered, repeating my words.

"Oh, don't be insulted because you're not my type. I'm obviously not your type either."

His hands tightened on the wheel. "You don't need to be concerned."

"Why not?"

"I always wear a condom. I don't know why I didn't with you. That was also a mistake. But you don't need to be concerned."

The truck inched forward in traffic. My head was pulsing. This conversation annoyed me. So, I unbuckled my seat belt, unlocked my door, and started to open it. Lachlan stretched across the truck, slamming the lock down.

"What the hell are you doing?" he barked lowly.

"I would have been home by now if you hadn't stuffed me into this heap of a truck."

"Heap of a truck," he muttered. "The traffic is clearing. I'll have you home in a few minutes. You're not jumping into traffic because your ego is bruised."

"My ego?" I snarled.

He buckled me back in one-handed. "Yeah, Elsa, your ego. You're not interested in me. The only reason you're mad is because I was the one who walked away, not you. If it makes your pride feel better, you can insult my truck, my personality, everything about me. That bounces off me. But I'm not going to let you hurt yourself out of spite—especially not when you're already hurt."

"Okay, Lachlan. If it makes you feel better to play the hero, I'll sit here like a good girl. We're not having a repeat of this on Thursday, though."

"I know."

Surprised he didn't argue with me, I sighed and turned toward the window. "Swell."

"I'm working Thursday, so I can't drive you home. I'll drive you after Tuesday classes."

"You'll have to kidnap me."

He worked his hands on the steering wheel, squeezing and sliding like he was trying to reshape it. "Don't be difficult for the sake of it."

I'd never been one to back down from an argument, but my head was killing me, and something told me Lachlan wouldn't take no for an answer on this subject. Thankfully, he seemed to be finished arguing too and stayed quiet the rest of the trip. As soon as he pulled into his driveway, I threw my door open, escaping.

Lachlan called my name, but I held up my hand, giving him a beauty queen wave as I walked across the grass to my house.

All he wanted from me was some ass, he could take a good look at it as I walked away.

Chapter Seven

Lock

When my sister called, I knew I was in for a long conversation. Her name appeared on my screen just as I walked into the house from work. The last thing I wanted was to engage in family drama, but when Saoirse called, I answered.

"Hey, baby girl. Let me grab a beer and get settled in. One minute."

She laughed softly. "You need a beer to talk to me?"

I pulled open the fridge. "Don't I?"

"Oh, probably. I could use one."

I growled. "No beer."

"Relax, father. If I drink alcohol, do you think I'd tell you?"

"Saoirse," I barked. "You're seventeen. Cut that shit out."

I could practically hear her eye roll. "Oh, please, dude. As if you weren't drinking at my age."

I sat down on one of the rickety chairs on the deck, and the metal creaked under my weight. I'd be pissed if I ended up on my ass.

"You know things are different for me and you."

Saoirse took after our mother. Tall and willowy, she was a delicate blonde who screamed innocence—even though she could out cuss a sailor. That, she got from our dad.

"Because men look at me and see a damsel?" she asked.

"I know you're no damsel, but that's what others see. You can't let your guard down. Getting drunk in a field with your stupid friends—"

"Hey, Lock? This isn't why I called."

I scrubbed my hand over my face, flicking my eyes next door. The lights were on. The drapes were wide open. All three girls were sitting down at the table in their kitchen, eating dinner. They were laughing about something, even the ice queen.

Good. That meant she was feeling better. I'd seen her in class today, and it'd looked like the swelling had gone down on her forehead, but she wouldn't tell me how her shoulder felt. Actually, she refrained from speaking to me at all.

"What's up, kid?" I tipped my beer into my mouth, letting the cool liquid slide down my throat.

She groaned, long and pained. I'd gotten enough calls from my little sister to tell the difference between dire and dramatic. That groan sounded somewhere close to dramatic. Either way, I wouldn't blow her off.

"Since we have a long weekend coming up, Mom said she would take me on a couple college visits. Obviously, I told Dad the plan, and he wants to come too. I couldn't say no. I mean, I didn't want to, he's my *dad*. But Mom's flipping her shit. She doesn't want to see *Connell*. *Connell* will have too many opinions. *Connell* will try to convince me to go to college in Wyoming—as fucking if. She hasn't calmed down since I told her last night."

I blew out a long exhale. I'd spent the last decade on the Connell and Lily Kelly merry-go-round. Thankfully, they finally divorced five years ago, but the fights between my parents hadn't slowed. I'd been out of the house long enough not to get caught in the middle anymore, but Saoirse was still in the thick of it for another year. The kicker was, our dad didn't even live in the same state as our mom, but they still found a way to drive each other to madness.

"Ignore her," I said. "She'll get over it."

"Easy for you to say. She's on a rampage. I've had to listen to her tell at least ten friends the same story over and over. And you know all her friends are bitter divorcées who hate their exes as much as Mom does, so they're all egging her on. Like, honestly, what's so bad about them both taking me to see colleges? They don't even have to talk to each other."

I shook my head. "You got me, kid. I'd say they should have never gotten married, but then you wouldn't exist."

"Awww, that was pretty sweet."

"Feel better?"

She sighed. "Not really. I have to tell Mom something else."

"What?"

"Well…"

I pictured her sitting on her bed, picking at a torn spot on her jeans, surrounded by pink and frills. It was a little girl's room, and while Saoirse wasn't really a little girl anymore, it mollified me that she hadn't made over her room. At least part of her wasn't ready to grow up.

"Dad convinced me to look at colleges in Colorado, not just California. He knows I won't move to Wyoming, but—"

"You go to school in Boulder, you'll only be a couple hours from Dad."

"Yeah. And I like Boulder. It would be really different, but I've lived in California my whole life."

The idea was a good one. Saoirse was the kind of girl who needed to be able to spread her wings knowing she had backup nearby. I would have pulled for her to come to Savage U, but by the time she got here next fall, I'd have one foot out the door, and then she'd be on her own on the other end of the state.

"Is this call about me breaking the news to Mom?" I asked, already knowing the answer.

"Um…would you? No decisions have been made or anything. I haven't even set foot on UC Boulder's campus. But, like, I've looked at the programs and checked out some student forums. I think I might like it. It's just…Mom, well, she'll be pissed. She'll accuse me of abandoning her and choosing Dad over her."

The wobble in her voice at the end did me in.

"I'll talk to her."

"Really?" she squeaked. "You promise?"

"Yeah, baby girl. I promise. Doesn't mean it'll go smooth, though. You know that."

"I know. Nothing with Mom is smooth. I don't know how Dad ever put up with her."

I set my beer down on the deck and rubbed my face again. "Don't do that. Dad's far from perfect. Don't make her the villain, Saoirse."

She giggled. "Lachlan Kelly, protector of women, even when they don't deserve it."

"Shut it if you want me to talk to Mom for you."

That quieted her down. "I do, I do. Just maybe do it when I'm going to be out of the house for a few hours so she has time to cool down before I have to see her."

"You got it, kid."

We talked for a while about a little bit of nothing before hanging up. I leaned back in my creaking chair, staring through the dark at the lit-up window next door. Saoirse would probably like Elena. They were a lot alike—both brats with mouths on them. Either that, or they'd be at each other's throats since they were too much alike.

I shook the thought off. They wouldn't be meeting or making friends with each other, so it really didn't matter if they got along in my head. I didn't even know why I'd pondered it.

Elena's eyes flicked to the window in my direction. I was pretty sure she couldn't see me, but even so, the mirth in her face drained, leaving her with barely a smile.

I'd screwed up with her. I shouldn't have gone there, not with a girl I had to see every day. Not without an up-front conversation first. I regretted that. Regretted hurting her if I had—and really fucking regretted having to live next to her, go to class with her, hear her laugh, see her smile at other people, knowing just how damn good she felt from the inside. How silky smooth her skin was. The sounds she made when she let go of her attitude and gave herself over to me.

Jesus. I pushed on my hardening dick, adjusting it behind my zipper.

This line of thinking would get me nowhere fast. Elena Sanderson needed to be out of my head for good.

Chapter Eight

Elena

When I walked into New Ventures, I was handed an iPad by the TA. She passed one out to everyone entering, telling us what we were doing would be explained to all of us at once.

I took a seat in the front row, like I had the second day of class. I'd thought I could avoid the Pi Sig douche-canoes with the change of seating, but they'd piled right into the row directly behind me—and today was no different.

Assholes.

I didn't give one damn what they hissed about me during class. Their opinions of me had exactly zero impact on my self-esteem. What did bother me was how distracting they were. I'd been looking forward to this class for a while and having to put up with baby bullies while trying to pay attention to Professor Seavers was headache inducing.

As I tapped around on the borrowed iPad, the two seats on either side of me became occupied. I didn't even have to look to know who had just sat down. The heavy floral perfume mixed with fake tanner told me all I needed to know.

"Hi, Elena," Kayleigh cooed from my right.

"Your forehead's looking a little less gnarly," Abby said from my left. "It looked *so bad* the last time I saw you. Like, incredibly awful."

I nodded, not lifting my eyes from the tablet. "Must have been the blood of virgins I bathed in last night. It's hard to come by, but really healing for the skin."

Kayleigh sputtered. "What virgin did you find on campus? Your little nerd boyfriend?"

That had me peering up. "I don't know what that means, dear."

She pointed to the lone soul at the end of the aisle. "You two seemed cozy on the first day of class. I just thought…"

Salvatore, the kid who'd helped me off the floor when I'd gone splat, was pretending not to be listening. From the flame in his cheeks, he'd heard at least some of what was said.

The irony of the situation was, a few years ago, I would have been Kayleigh, laughing at the scrawny kid with thick glasses, as if I was better simply because of hitting the genetic lottery. I'd been trying so hard to hold on to *something,* it hadn't mattered who I'd trampled to keep my reins.

I'd still trample bitches like Kayleigh and Abby without any qualms. Guys like Salvatore? Nope. Not unless he gave me a reason, then it was *on*.

"No, Salvatore actually doesn't qualify. When I was riding his huge cock after class on Monday, he didn't say whether it was his first time or not, but from the way he got me off *three* times before he got his, I'm thinking not." I fanned my face at the fake memories and winked at Sal before he bowed his head. "Skinny guys always have horse cocks, I swear. It's a scientific fact."

Abby scrunched her face up in disgust. "I hope you're kidding."

I drew a heart on the iPad with my finger. "I don't kiss and tell."

"But…but…" Kayleigh's mouth gaped like a fish. "You just…"

I shrugged. "Honestly, it's rude you keep trying to pry details out of me about my personal sex life with Salvatore. If you really must know, he had to let me down easy because one night with him, and I was a goner. Sal is a rolling stone, you know? He was a sweetheart about it, but I'm still a little brokenhearted."

Abby leaned in, examining my face. "I actually can't tell if you're serious."

"I'd never lie about something so personal." I tossed my hair behind my shoulder. "Don't tell anyone, okay? I wouldn't want to ruin Salvatore's reputation."

"What do you mean?" Kayleigh whispered. "Who *is* he?"

I laughed, like she'd just told an amazing joke. "You're so funny, oh my god." I shook my head, muttering, "Who is he?" while Kayleigh and Abby stared holes into the side of my head.

The professor started class, explaining she'd be sharing slides to our iPads of start-ups we'd be analyzing together. Despite sitting between the Blonde Terrors, I got so involved with the lesson, I tuned out their existence.

A message popped up on my screen, alerting me that a device nearby wanted to AirDrop a file to me. Thinking nothing of it, I clicked accept.

The file wasn't from Professor Seavers, like I had assumed.

And from the giggles and gasps going around the class, I wasn't the only one who'd received it.

Displayed on my iPad screen, and everyone's around me, was a picture of me from Monday, laid flat out on the ground. Whoever had taken it had captured me from the side, getting my shocked, derpy expression. They'd made a meme out of me too. Stamped across the bottom were the words, "Diving for dicks: right spirit, wrong execution."

Clever.

So fucking clever.

I swiveled in my seat to look up at the sniveling band of hyenas behind me. The lead D-named dickweed grinned at me as he lounged back in his chair, the picture of innocence and a boy who breastfed until middle school.

Professor Seavers slammed something hard on her desk. I spun back around, finding her holding a thick book and scanning the class. Her eyes landed on me, and she shook her head, then shifted her attention to the boys behind me.

"How embarrassing," Abby whispered.

Kayleigh leaned into my side. "Oh my god, are you dying?"

I kept my face relaxed and unaffected, but on the inside, I was seething. Not because I especially cared about the meme. I didn't. Tripping me and then taking a picture of me when I was down was child's play. Literally, I'd done things like that when I was ten years old with my first iPhone.

It was the fact that these idiots felt comfortable enough to do it to *me*. I'd helped take down their fraternity. My father was one of the biggest benefactors to this university and owned half this town. Plus...well, I did not play. If they insisted on striking at me, I'd strike back, and it wouldn't be with a fucking meme.

"Am I teaching a bunch of children?" Professor Seavers had steely-gray hair, her fashion style was no nonsense, and her expression said she was D-O-N-E. "What kind of adults come into my classroom and take the opportunity to not only disrespect me during my lesson, but also one of their fellow classmates?"

Her attention laid square on the guys behind me. She wasn't saying their names, but she was calling them out.

I knew I loved this woman.

"I'm not blind. I saw what led to this picture on Monday. I didn't intervene because I'm not running a daycare. You're adults. Handle your issues like adults. If you pulled a stunt like this at a job, you'd be fired immediately." She hadn't taken her eyes off the Pi Sig boys for a second. "I will not tolerate this in my class. If you can't control yourselves, withdraw now. I'm only interested in sharing space with future professionals, not toddlers. I got tired of two-year-olds when I turned three. Anyone who still has an issue may leave now."

No one moved. This class was coveted and difficult to get into. The boys behind me were stupid, but not *that* stupid.

"All right." She looked at me and lifted her chin. "Let's carry on."

⋯⋯•••••⋯

As I'd promised, I was heading to my parents' house after classes were finished for the week. On the drive there, I called my cousin Penelope. Besides the therapist I had started seeing my senior year of high school, Pen was the only person in the world who knew absolutely everything about me. From my worst to my...even worse. Actually, her boyfriend, Gabe, probably knew most of it too. I'd accepted that she didn't keep anything from him, and while he was chaos incarnate, he loved her dearly and would never betray her confidence, and in turn, mine.

But I didn't ask, and she didn't tell. It worked for us.

"Hi."

"Hey, El. What's up?"

"Driving to the parentals. You?"

"Gabe has a game tonight, so I'm hanging out until it's time to go cheer for him."

Gabe and Pen had been together since high school. They went to college a couple hours away from Savage River. I saw Pen often, but not often enough. My jealousy over Gabe taking my beloved cousin from me had made it difficult for me to tolerate him in the beginning. It took a year of them being together for me to get over it, since it was obvious they were a packaged deal now. I'd even gone to several of Gabe's soccer games, though painting my face his school's colors was where I drew a very hard line. Never happening.

"Tell him to break a leg for me."

Pen snorted a laugh. "I would, except I know you mean that literally."

I gasped. "I'd never wish a broken bone on Gabriel. Now, broken vocal cords..."

"One day, you're going to admit you like him."

"Never."

"You will. I'll wait. Now, what's up with Diedre and Gil?"

"Who knows? My mother guilted me into staying over for the night. You know her," I answered. "Something happened in class this week, and specifically today, that I want to run by you."

I told her about the trip, the whispers, and finally the meme. Pen was silent throughout. Even when I finished.

"So, I think I'm being bullied," I added. "How should I destroy these cretins?"

She sucked in a sharp breath. "You should report them. They physically assaulted you."

"The trip was only bad because I didn't have free hands."

She spoke carefully, as one did with a scared animal or a child. "You don't have to be tough all the time, Elena."

"Of course I do."

"Not with me, you don't. You know that."

I did. Pen and I were two peas. We'd gone different directions in school—she had a brain for science while mine was more tuned in to world domination—but outside of school, we always retreated to our cousin pod. Pen knew about the monster that dwelled inside me—the jealousy that drove me to many of the destructive decisions I'd made. She was the first one I'd told about Nate, the rape, and the night he died. She'd held me through both. I didn't hide my ugly from her. I couldn't.

At Larson's Nursery, I slowed and flicked on my turn signal. A moment later, I turned into my neighborhood and pulled over against the curb.

"My head ached for three straight days after that idiot tripped me. I wondered if I had a concussion, but I never went to get checked. My shoulder still isn't right, but it's getting better. I won't report the idiot because he doesn't get to have any power over me. If I report him and nothing happens, he'll have permission to keep doing it...and you and I both know nothing will happen to him."

I took in a deep swallow of air, and Penelope blew it out on the other end of the line.

"Something might," she said.

"It won't. It doesn't matter. Our professor shut it down today. I'll be surprised if they continue. It's just—" I clamped down on my bottom lip.

"What? It's what?"

"I'm getting a big taste of my own medicine. The bully gets bullied. Maybe there really is such a thing as karmic justice. Remember when I shoved Grace's face into her locker?"

Pen hissed. "Uh, no. You never told me you did that."

I tapped my steering wheel, thinking back to my senior year of high school and all the awful, unforgivable stunts I pulled. And most had been in the name of keeping my man. What a fucking joke *that* had turned out to be.

"I guess I probably didn't think twice about it at the time. But the second I hit the floor and came up with a goose egg, I thought of her."

"You're not the same person you were back then. You were in an abusive relationship, going through trauma at home, and you lashed out. You lashed out a lot."

"You don't have to excuse what I did."

"I'm not, El. There really isn't an excuse, but there are reasons. I'm also reminding you, if you truly believe the universe expects you to pay for the misdeeds you carried out, then you've already settled up your bill *and* left a big tip."

"You're the sweetest," I said. And I meant it.

"No, you."

I scoffed. "That's the biggest lie you ever told."

"You're sweet to me, and I know everything about you. Shouldn't my opinion count the most?"

"*Because* I'm sweet, I won't be responding to that."

She laughed. "All right, fine. Tell me what's happening with your hot neighbor."

"Who knows?" I flicked my fingers through the air. "He's probably wrecking some other lucky girl's pussy. Definitely not mine."

The green-eyed monster inside me reared its twisted head. It did not like that idea.

"Well, he's stupid."

"Hmph." I laid my head down on my steering wheel. "I wish that was true."

"I know, El. At least now you know you're not broken. You know it for sure. Maybe he was the key, and now that you're unlocked, you don't need him. He got you off, and that's amazing, but that's *your* body. He doesn't own the orgasms he gave you."

Everything she said was true, but it didn't lessen the sting of rejection. And I had absolutely no desire to go experimenting with other guys to find out if I was only unbroken with Lachlan.

We talked a little while longer, until Penelope had to leave for Gabe's soccer game and I couldn't put off going to my parents' house any longer. I promised to visit her soon, and she did the same. Then I pulled away from the curb and drove home.

Chapter Nine

Elena

My mother was the woman everyone wanted to befriend. She was elegant and kind, friendly and whip-smart. Her acquaintances were as widespread as her admirers. She didn't have any friends, though. Only my father and I knew her beneath her surface. That was where the cracks were, and there were many.

My mother was as fragile as she was beautiful. She was a tragedy in motion, one word of bad news away from falling apart.

I loved her and hated her, but I was always careful with her. That was my duty as the only surviving Sanderson child, after all.

My visit home was as normal as they got around here. Dad had worked late, returning home at ten p.m. while Mom and I were watching a movie. He joined us until he received a call, then he was off.

So typical.

I spent the night in my childhood bedroom. It was as large as the entire top floor of my current house with a four-poster king-size bed, a seating area, desk, vanity, and a closet filled with so much designer clothing and shoes, it could have fed a small country for a year.

In the morning, Dad tapped on my bedroom door then pushed inside. He was dressed in a suit, straightening his tie as he strode in. I rarely saw him out of a suit, even on the weekends. He never stopped working, hence always being in work attire. If he owned pajamas, they were a mystery to me. It used to shock me when I'd spend the night at Pen's and see her parents hanging out in their pajamas in the mornings. It was like a foreign planet to me.

I was in my bed, barely awake. My phone told me it was only half past the crack of dawn.

Dad shook his head. "You're developing bad habits in college, Elena."

I suppressed the urge to roll my eyes. "It's barely seven, and Mom and I were up late watching movies. I need my beauty rest. Would you really begrudge me that?"

He chuckled, perching on the opposite side of my massive bed. "If you get any more beautiful, I'll have to buy a gun. Do you really want me owning a gun?"

I burst out laughing. "Absolutely not. You'll wind up shooting the delivery guy for leaving a speck of an oil stain on the driveway."

Dad lowered his chin and wagged a finger at me. "When you spend a fortune to get the exact right color of concrete poured, only to have a goddamn stain on it the next day, you'll understand my fury. It hadn't even been twenty-four hours."

"It's the driveway."

He folded his hands in his lap, his gaze drifting to the window. "It made your mom happy."

That was all he'd needed to say. Despite his workaholism, he absolutely adored my mother and was hopelessly in love with her. Her happiness was his ultimate goal. The way he went about it was sometimes backward—like working long hours so he could give her the world, which conversely took away the one thing in the world that would have made her the happiest: him.

I let out a long yawn. "I'll get up soon. Promise."

He reached across the bed and patted my leg. "Don't hurry back to campus. Spend some time with your mom."

You spend time with your wife!

"I will. I'm in no rush to leave."

He exhaled through his nose and checked his phone. "How are things going with the houses? You're managing well?"

I nodded. "Things are quiet. I drive by the two houses on Lambert Ave on a regular basis. They haven't needed anything from me since school started and the work on the houses was completed." I held up my crossed fingers. "So far, so good."

Our two other houses were rented by student athletes. *Not* the football team. I was hoping that meant less partying and more responsibility, but time would tell. Since Dad had made me the property manager, I was keeping a keen eye on my rentals.

He slipped his phone into his pocket. "That's what I like to hear." His eyes snagged mine. "I'm proud of how you handled the remodels this summer. I have to admit, I assumed you'd run out of money and ask for more. You surprised me in a good way when you didn't."

Warmth spread across my chest and down my limbs. My father didn't hand out compliments freely. They had to be earned. He wouldn't be saying this if he knew about the near disaster of my deck project. Thank Prada I would never have to tell him.

"Thanks, Daddy."

He rose from the bed, giving me an indulgent smile. "Have a good day with your mom, angel. Don't be a stranger here. She needs you."

Later, I found my mother in the kitchen. She was cheerful. The kind of cheerful that made my skin crawl because it wasn't quite real. I knew this mood. It almost always came before a violent swing in the other direction. I crossed my fingers this would be one of the few times it didn't.

She kissed me on top of the head, then curled her arm around me, giving me a squeeze.

"How long can you stay today? Please say a while."

Smiling at her, I nodded. "I don't have anywhere to be."

She let go of me and clapped her hands. "Oh, brilliant. Now, I made these muffins I found the recipe for in an old cookbook. You're my guinea pig since Dad refuses to eat anything that might possibly be healthy. He's lucky he's got those hearty Scandinavian genes. All he has to do is drink some vodka and all his ailments are cured."

She rambled on for a solid five minutes about that subject, even after the timer on the oven went off. I finally got up, put on a pair of oven mitts, and removed the pan from the oven. Mom didn't stop talking or really watch what I was doing as I plated each of us a muffin.

I guided her by the shoulders to a stool, pushed her down on it, then took the seat beside her.

Maybe it was the smell of the cinnamon wafting up from the steam, but she snapped out of her monologue and turned to me.

"Do you need new clothing, honey? Should we go shopping?" she asked.

"No. If you can believe it, I don't. At least not until the next Prada sample sale."

She sputtered a laugh. "Since when do you care about sales?"

I threw back my shoulders. "I think it's a sign of maturing." I popped a piece of muffin into my mouth. "I'd rather just bum around the house with you anyway."

"I have never seen you bum around anywhere." She gently elbowed me. "Tell me about Helen and Zadie. Oh, and the boys next door. How is Julien doing? Is he healing? And that tall one with all the scruff? What's his name?"

"That's Lachlan—well, Lock. Everyone calls him that. And he's...I don't think he likes me."

She scoffed. "Oh, I doubt that. My gorgeous girl could wind that big man around her pinkie finger with absolutely no effort. But I'm sure you don't want to. He's not your type."

"No, he isn't my type. I don't think I'm his either." I shrugged. "Julien is doing okay. He's grumpy, but—"

"Understandable. That poor boy. I can't imagine how hard it is for him to attend class while he's trying to heal. Tell me if there's anything I can do for him. Does he need a referral to a new doctor? I'm sure I know one who could give him another opinion on how he's healing. Or does he need—"

"Mom." I laid my hand on her arm. "Julien doesn't really like anyone to fuss over him, but I'll pay extra attention. If there's anything I think you could help with, I'll let you know."

"Oh, Elena." She leaned into me. "You are my sweet, sweet girl. Do you think any other mother is lucky enough to have a daughter like you? I really don't think so."

I hooked my arm through hers. "I doubt there's any other daughter lucky enough to have a mother as sweet as you."

She started monologuing again, and I tried really hard not to fully tune her out. My dad was mad about his wife, but he didn't listen to her, not when she was like this. He never noticed the warning signs of a spiral coming. It was always me, questioning her meds, calling her therapist, pulling her back when she went off course.

Thankfully, by lunchtime, her mania had ebbed. She was still bright and chipper, but the glazed-over look in her eyes had receded.

She pressed her palms together as she peered out the patio door. "It's beautiful out. Shall we walk the gardens and check on my babies?"

I'd rather dig up Nate and fuck his rotting corpse.

"Sure, Mom. Let's go for a walk."

The grounds our house sat on were expansive. We had a large patio and pool directly outside the rear of the house, and beyond that was a wide stretch of lush grass leading to my mother's garden. We passed under a little ivy-covered archway to enter it, strolling along the path made by precisely trimmed hedges.

In the center of the garden was a fountain surrounded by a circle of bricks and two stone benches. On the edges of the circle were my mother's babies: her rose bushes.

She greeted them each by name, stopped to sniff them, pet the petals, coo at them. An outsider might view this behavior as unhinged, and maybe it was, but I was so used to it, I didn't blink. Each rose bush represented a pregnancy my mom had lost. It had been her way of coping, and I suppose it still was.

I was The One Who Lived. The only one. It wasn't easy carrying that mantle and the expectations that came along with it. *Ask Harry Potter.*

My mother sat next to me on one of the benches. She wasn't crying, so this really was a good day. With my hand in hers, we sat there for a while, letting the sun shine down and the peace of the garden seep in.

"How are you doing, honey?" she asked softly. "Really and truly."

I sighed. "I'm great. I promise."

Her eyes examined me, sweeping over my features to check for cracks. "You've always been so resilient. No matter what happened to you, you brushed yourself off and kept moving. Even through my episodes, you've kept your chin up. I wish I had half your strength."

I wish you did too.

I let her statement lie. If I needed someone to hold me up, it would never be my mother. I'd accepted that a long time ago.

She sighed. "Oh, I forgot to mention Oliver is back from England. I saw him when I was having lunch with Patricia earlier in the week. He's looking so handsome and grown up, I just can't believe it."

I swallowed hard. I did any time the Bergen family was brought up. "Is he? Patricia and Nathaniel must be happy to have their son back on this side of the world."

"Definitely. They haven't been the same since Nate's accident. Nathaniel is so angry, and Patricia sometimes strikes me as a little lost. Hopefully with Oliver's presence, she'll feel more grounded."

Oliver was Nate Bergen's golden boy brother. Five years older than us, he'd graduated from Savage U two years ago and moved to London to work for the British branch of a US finance company. I'd encountered him plenty over the three years Nate and I had dated in high school. I couldn't say he ever came across as the grounding type. I didn't know if he had his brother's penchant for hurting women—there'd never been rumors alluding to it—but he hadn't been especially warm.

I made some humming sound, which was enough for my mother to go on.

"I told Oliver you're at Savage U now and gave him your phone number. I thought it might be nice for the two of you to connect. You could share memories of Nate and—"

"Mom, no." The rebuke came out sharper than intended, but what the fuck?

"Listen, I know you and Nate didn't end on a good note, but you had a lot of happy times. Shouldn't you focus on those instead of holding on to the bitterness?" She waved her hand in front of her face. "But what do I know? It was just a thought. Oliver seemed eager. Then again, he could have been humoring an old lady. Either way, the ball is in both of your courts now. Although, I would love for you to get together with him at least once if he calls."

The end she was referring to was the nuclear meltdown that had wiped our relationship off the map. There was cheating, property destruction, and a lot of erratic behavior. My mother would *never* know about what'd happened after the *for-old-times'-sake* dinner Nate and I had the week before I left for Berkely. She might survive it, but I was pretty certain her sanity wouldn't.

I exhaled a slow, heavy breath. "I doubt he'll call, but I'll be polite if he does."

She squeezed my hand. "I never doubted you, honey."

··········

I stayed through dinner, though, by the end, I was forcing myself not to leave. At home, I always had to be on. No one had told me that, I'd just known from a young age. Now that I didn't live like that full time, sliding back into that role was exhausting.

Helen had texted that a few people were going to be hanging on the boys' deck, drinking and smoking. I couldn't think of a more perfect way to spend the rest of my night. This girl needed to find her chill because it had definitely gone missing.

I arrived home to an empty house, so I assumed they were all next door already. Running up to my room first, I changed into a pair of boyfriend jeans and a slouchy Savage U T-shirt. My hair went into a braid draped over my shoulder, and my feet went into thick, fuzzy socks. Then I grabbed my new favorite hoodie in case it got cool. Not because it was *his*. Although, I wouldn't have minded rubbing it in his face that it was still in my possession.

Downstairs again, I grabbed a couple hard seltzers from the fridge and headed onto our back deck. I could always count on Helen for good weed, and *god* did I need it tonight.

It was pitch dark in our yard, and the motion sensor lights didn't click on right away. The circle of light coming from next door wasn't enough for me to see by, so I stood there like an idiot, waving my hands to get the lights to turn on.

Voices carried through the night sky. I recognized Helen, Marco—Amir's friend and housemate—and Zadie's dulcet tones.

"Is Elena coming?" Zadie asked.

"I texted. She should be here soon. My phone's inside, otherwise I'd check to see if she sent me a message," Helen replied.

Lachlan's baritone cracked the dark in half. "Elena's coming? Where has she been?"

My breath caught in my lungs. I gripped the deck rail, listening carefully.

"Why so curious?" Marco chuckled. "Are you into her? She's a pretty little thing. Kinda snobby, but some dudes are into that."

"Fuck off," Julien groused, which made me smile. First, because he'd defended me, but more importantly, that he was socializing. "You don't know what you're talking about."

"Not into her," Lachlan answered. "I'm just curious if I have to brace myself. That's all."

My skin itched, like it was pulled too taut over my bones. I should have gone back inside or yelled across the yard. Instead, I stayed rooted in my spot, my mind warring with my body about whether to move.

Skin slapped skin, then Helen spoke up. "Dude, uncool. That's my friend."

"Elena is sweet when you get to know her," Zadie said, fighting the good fight for me.

But Lachlan, beautifully dicked Lachlan, was having none of it. He'd formed his opinion of me at first sight, and nothing I or anyone else said could change it.

He chuckled dryly. "I wouldn't use that word to describe her."

"She's hilarious as hell," Theo added.

I always knew I liked that kid, even when I'd wanted to beat his head with a bat that one time he was an ass to Helen. Fortunately, he'd rectified it by worshiping the ground she walked on.

"I never said she wasn't," Lachlan said.

A few murmurs I couldn't hear, probably from Zadie, then Amir spoke up.

"My girl says she's sweet, then she's sweet."

Lachlan's deep hum resounded through the darkness. "Fair enough. I know the kind of sweet she is. Grew up with it. She's sweet like poison."

Three things happened at once—because the universe and our electricity grid fucking hated me: I gasped at a volume that wasn't the least bit discreet, the light flooded both me and the rest of the yard, and my sternum caved in from the force of Lachlan's judgment.

Sweet like poison.

...like poison.

Poison.

They were looking at me. What a picture we were, all of us too stunned to move. Time suspended. Lachlan's harsh words hung in the air like daggers poised to do serious damage.

Oh no, wait. Wrong metaphor. Lachlan's daggers were fucking embedded in my skin. I was surprised by how much it'd smarted to hear him say that.

I would never let it show, though. With a nod, I turned on my toes and slowly walked back into my house, not missing Lachlan rising to his feet. As soon as I closed the sliding door, the floodlights clicked off, but I knew they could all still see me inside the kitchen.

My purse was on the table, so I set down my seltzers, opened it up, and pulled out my favorite pale-pink lipstick. Using my phone's camera, I swiped it across my lips and smacked them together, then I slung my purse over my shoulder and headed toward the front door. Before I got there, it swung open, and Helen and Zadie crowded the doorway. Their faces were splashed with pity.

For me.

I could have screamed.

"Ele—" Zadie started.

I held up my hand. "I'm sorry I won't be able to make it to your cute little shindig. I'm sure I'm missing the party of the century. It's just that…well, I spent the day watching paint dry and I'd rather not have a repeat of that tonight. I'm going out."

Helen crossed her arms over her chest, pity sliding into annoyance. "You don't have to do that, act all tough like that didn't bother you."

I flipped my hair over my shoulder. "What would bother me about some overgrown, truck-driving lumberjack from god knows where calling me poison? It's not like he knows me. I couldn't give two shits about his opinion." I started toward them, needing them to move before my frayed edges tore apart. "If you'll excuse me, I have somewhere I'd rather be."

Zadie stepped aside, but Helen parked herself right in front of the doorway.

"Dude, I don't know what's up with Lock talking about you like that, but no one else thinks that. If you heard him, I suspect you heard the rest of us. You're not what he said, and I don't know why the fuck he said that, but he's categorically wrong."

I threw my hands up. "Are you going to let me leave or not?"

Helen shrugged. "Not."

Zadie moved next to her again. "You're not leaving. The three of us live together, but it's never just the three of us, is it? It's time for a girls' night."

Helen held up a fat little joint between two fingers. "Does this entice you? There's more where it came from."

"I don't want a pity party." Even though I was feeling like a pitiful bitch, I did not want anyone to feel sorry for me. That would make me absolutely vomit all over the place.

Helen scrunched her face. "Pshaw. How could I pity you? I grew up in a trailer with a drunk-ass mama. You were born with a silver spoon to two doting parents. And you look like a fucking Disney princess, have a disgustingly hot wardrobe, and a decently functioning brain on top of all that. Honestly, I want to punch you in the face sometimes."

Despite my foul mood, that made me laugh. "Just sometimes?"

Helen jerked her chin, the corners of her mouth tipping in amusement. "Used to be all the time. You were downgraded to sometimes when you bought us all matching bats."

I held up a hand. "Don't bring up the bats unless you're going to allow me to bust Lachlan's truck windows out."

Zadie covered up her laugh with her hand, and Helen closed the door firmly behind her.

"No busting windows, sorry." Helen waved the fatty at me. "But smoke this and you'll be too mellow to even think about vehicular murder and won't care about the crap he said."

Conceding, I sighed and held out my hand. "Give it to me, baby."

Helen was right and wrong. The mellow came over me quickly, and my desire to destroy was reduced to smoke. Even then, cushioned as they were in the very back of my mind, Lachlan's words stayed.

Sweet like poison.
...like poison.
Poison.

Chapter Ten

Elena

An iced coffee was set down on the small table beside me. Moments later, a big body overtook the rocking chair on the other side. Because that was what Lachlan did—he overtook.

Barely sparing the man or the coffee a glance, I continued reading my newspaper. My feet were kicked up, resting on the porch railing. In this position, and in my smallest sleep shorts, the bottom curve of my ass was on display.

I'd known he'd show. As soon as my head cleared from the copious amounts of weed I'd smoked last night, I was certain Lachlan would spoil my Sunday morning ritual.

That was when I'd decided to wear my skimpiest pajamas. If he was going to force his presence on me, I'd make it as painful for him as possible. He might not like me, but my ass was another story. The man definitely appreciated my ass.

"Elena." He rumbled my name impatiently, as if I owed him my attention. "I brought you coffee."

Curling the newspaper inward, I peered around the condensation-covered cup, nodded, and went back to reading. Lachlan's chest sounded like there was a rockslide going on inside it.

"Elena." This time, he barked my name, almost like a command. Goose bumps prickled my arms. All I could do was hope he didn't notice. I'd be damned if he knew the way his dominance affected me.

I repeated the action, curling my paper, peering at Lachlan this time, nodded, then went back to reading. A second later, the newspaper was snatched out of my hands.

"Stop ignoring me," he ordered. "I came to apologize to you."

I frowned at the paper crumpled in his fist. "This apology would be a lot more convincing if you weren't barking my name and snatching my newspaper."

His fingers slowly opened and he smoothed the crinkled paper, folding it neatly in half. He didn't give it back to me, though. He held it hostage in his lap instead.

"I'm sorry for what you heard last night. It was completely out of line."

I let his apology hang for a while as I stared at my toes. They were nice. My pinkie toes were just a little crooked, which I'd decided long ago gave my feet character. Sometimes, I thought about selling pictures of my feet to pervs online just to see how much I could get. But then I'd have to live with the knowledge that foot fetishists would have the privilege of masturbating to my adorable toes until the end of the world, and that was too much to even contemplate.

Enough time had gone by that Lachlan was shifting uncomfortably in his chair. I finally gave him my attention. There was a gash and a purple bruise under his eye.

I pointed to it. "What happened?"

He took his time answering me, letting his eyes trail over my bare legs and arms before landing on mine. His mouth curved at the corners.

Lachlan Kelly was smirking at me. I braced myself for what was to come.

"We don't talk about fight club, right?" He held up a thick finger. "First, and most important, rule."

Oh, balls.

He thought he was so clever, throwing my own quip back at me. I was unimpressed.

"You know, you're terrible at apologizing."

His exhale was heavy. His eyes trailed over my legs again. "Julien threw his half-full beer can at me last night."

"Did he? Oh, Julien is getting another free year of rent." Laughter tore out of me. I would have paid to see that. "What did you do to deserve that?"

Lachlan's fingers curled around the ends of the rocking chair armrests. "I spoke out of turn about his friend. Said something I shouldn't have. Something that wasn't deserved. I have no excuse, so I won't offer one. Nothing like that will happen again."

"It wasn't a surprise, you know." I dropped my legs from the rail and crossed them. Lachlan's eyes followed my movement before snapping back up to mine.

"What wasn't?" he gruffed.

"That you think of me that way. You made your opinion clear when you made me a dirty little secret, Lachlan." Elbow on my knee, I rested my chin on my fist. "I suppose I *was* surprised how comfortable you felt trashing me in front of our mutual friends. Do you think they keep me around for my stunning good looks? Or would it boggle your mind that they actually like me?"

"A lot of things about you boggle my mind, Elsa, but not that people like you." He rubbed his chin while perusing my legs without an ounce of shame. "What did you mean about Julien's rent?"

My smirk dropped. I hadn't meant to say that. I'd been hoping he'd let it slide. Of course, he didn't.

"That's between Julien and me. I shouldn't have said anything." I picked up the coffee, stabbing the straw through the lid. One sip was all I needed to know Lachlan had gotten my order right. I would have been surprised if he hadn't. I suspected he didn't do anything unless he was certain it was the right move—with the exception of sleeping with me, I supposed.

He hummed and rocked in his chair, stretching his long legs out in front of him. He wore his signature work boots, loosely laced and untied, worn-out jeans, and a plain black T-shirt. It worked on him in a way it wouldn't on most men. I checked him out the same way he had me, unabashedly and without shame.

His T-shirt stretched across his massive chest, hugged his thick, work-hewn biceps, and molded over the softness of his stomach. In another life, I would have laid my head there any chance I got. To tell the truth, I was tempted to do it now. But Lachlan would probably rocket out of his chair at light speed if I got anywhere near him.

Since I was *poison*.

"What's with the newspaper?" he asked.

"What do you mean?"

"I didn't think anyone read the paper anymore, much less anyone under fifty."

I flicked my fingers. "Clearly, you were wrong."

His head bobbed a few times in acknowledgment. "Is there a story there?"

I eyed him over my coffee cup. His head rested on the high back of the chair. His long fingers were clasped at his abdomen. Idly, I wondered if he ever got uptight. If he did, he never let it show.

"Do you really want to know, or do you feel obligated to sit here and make polite conversation to make up for calling me poison?"

He winced but turned to meet my inquiring eyes. "I have never once felt obligated to make polite conversation."

I huffed a short laugh. "That must be nice. I suppose, growing up in the woods, or wherever you came from, there wasn't a lot of social pressure."

That made him chuckle. "I have a feeling you and I didn't grow up so differently." He rubbed his chin again. "There was social pressure. Still never felt obligated. And once I got tall and big and rough, strangers tended to stay away from me."

I raised a brow. "Which suited you fine."

He inclined his chin. "Yeah. So, what's the story with the newspaper? I want to know."

Giving in, I told him. "There's not really a story. My mother likes to sleep in, but my dad and I are early risers. He's read the Sunday paper for as long as I can remember. One day, I decided I wanted to take part in his ritual too. It started when I was four with the comic section. As I learned to read, I moved on to Arts and Style. By middle school, I was devouring the whole newspaper every day instead of just Sundays. Dad used to tell me reading the newspaper armed him with knowledge. For me, it was a comfort. Because no matter how shitty things in my life were, I could pick up the newspaper and read in black and white how tiny I was in the grand scheme of things."

"Other people's bad news comforts you?"

I rolled my eyes. "Of course, you would think the worst of me. No, that's not what I meant at all. I'm talking about reading an article about advancements in HIV medication that make the virus undetectable. The underdog winning the World Series. A designer from an impoverished part of Tunisia showing her first collection in Paris during fashion week. There's so much more than *this*."

He nodded as I spoke, giving me his full attention. "I get that. I really fucking get that."

I took another sip of coffee, then put it down. "Sometimes it's vital to remind myself the world *isn't* the people I see on a daily basis."

His stare was so steady on me, it was almost disconcerting. It wasn't hard, but it was penetrating. My breath caught in my throat as I stared back.

Finally, he turned his attention to the porch ceiling. "When I need to get out of my head, I go for a drive. I caught the habit from my dad too. Whenever he needed to get out of the house, he'd go for a drive. A lot of the time, he'd take me if I asked. There was never a destination. That wasn't the goal. The driving was the ritual. When I turned sixteen and got my license, I took up the habit. Anytime I need to think, clear my head, I get in my truck and drive."

Lachlan's eyes were still fixed on the ceiling, so I studied his profile. He'd cracked a small part of himself open, matching the part of me I'd put on display for him, and that surprised me. This *entire* interaction surprised me. It was too gentle after the brutality of last night's words.

I had a hard time believing this man wanted to know anything about me. Not after his blunt rejection. Especially not after what I overheard. I couldn't understand what he was doing here this morning, other than smoothing things over with our friends by going through the motions of apologizing.

"How am I poison?" I asked.

Lachlan startled, bringing his narrowed eyes back to me. "Come on. There's no reason to go there."

"I think there is. I want to know why you think I'm poison."

He took a long time to answer, sweeping his gaze over me as he thought it through. Lachlan could peel my skin off with his stare, it was so hard and searching. If I didn't really want the answer to my question, I would have said *fuck it* and ran for the cover of my house. But I did, so I stayed, letting him flay me with his smooth, melted-chocolate eyes.

"That's not what I said, Ellie. I didn't call you poison." He shifted forward in his chair, elbows on his knees. "I said you were sweet like poison, and that had more to do with me than you. You're so fucking tempting, like a piece of candy laced with arsenic. Bad for me, but I want to pick it up and suck it down anyway. I won't, though."

I kept my facade icy calm. "You're not invited to suck on any part of me, Lachlan, so don't worry. I won't poison you again." I rose from my rocking chair, deciding to abandon my newspaper to the cause, and took two steps to stand in front of him. "Though I'm worried it might be too late for you. My poison may have already infected your blood since you can't seem to stay away from me."

Hands on his armrests, I leaned over him, giving him a clear view down my loose camisole. It was a power position if there ever was one. He could look all he wanted, weep at the perfection of my tits, but he didn't get to touch. Poor guy.

Unfortunately, this power position also gave those who were walking by on the sidewalk an even more clear shot of my ass. My misstep became clean when a cavalcade of male testosterone started launching a hundred bombs at my backside.

"Fuck, look at that! Daddy likes."

"Yeah, shake it, baby."

"No shame in that ass game. Fucking nice!"

It sounded like the entire fraternity population of Savage U chose that very moment to saunter down the sidewalk. It was early enough, I could believe they were just getting home from some cheesy, raucous party, and at least half were probably still drunk.

I started to whirl around, possibly grab the closest blunt object and brain a few of them—which, in this case, would be a misnomer since they're clearly lacking gray matter—but I was caught around the middle and hauled into Lachlan's arms before I could act. He had me off my feet and inside my house in another blink. The door slammed, and I was pressed against it, Lachlan's forearms caging my head, his warm breath ghosting over my lips.

"What did I tell you, Elsa? What the hell did I tell you?" he growled at me.

Remembering exactly what he said, I lifted my chin. He was so close, looming over me, our lips nearly brushed. "You want to be my keeper, Lachlan?"

He jerked his head back, adding inches between us, enough room for him to deliver a fierce scowl.

"I want you to give a shit about yourself. I want you to be smart enough to know you can't sit on your porch wearing almost nothing." His hand balled into a fist next to my head. "Use your damn brain, girl."

I shook my head, enraged he thought he could have any say over what I wore. He had no idea what he was talking about. None. And he definitely didn't have any right to open his big mouth.

"Do you think what I wear or don't wear will keep me safe? I could have been in a baggy sweat suit and those assholes would have catcalled me. Ask me how I know." I jabbed at the wall of his chest with my finger. "Layers and layers of clothing won't keep me safe. A cute summer dress and my ugliest underwear won't keep me safe. Ask. Me. How. I. Know."

He ground his jaw back and forth, leaning into me so his chest flattened mine. I expected him to bite back, to growl and command. The softness he gave me nearly knocked my knees out from under me.

"How do you know, Ellie?" Knuckles trailed down my cheek. "How the hell do you know?"

I shoved at his oversized chest. "Enough. You've proven your point." And I'd said way too much. "Go home now. You're forgiven. Don't worry. I'll tell everyone you were properly apologetic and all that."

At first, he didn't budge. And it alarmed me that I wasn't even tempted to knee him in the balls to get him out of my personal space. I just...waited. His rough fingertips skated over my cheek and jaw as he peered down at me.

"I built you a really nice deck. Nice and private. Why don't you sit out there? Wear your pretty little pajamas. Hell, go out there naked. You'll be safe." His scowl was so deep, he'd have permanent lines before he was thirty if he kept it up.

They'd probably look good on him too, the rat bastard.

"I'll put that in the suggestion box," I deadpanned.

Except it wasn't quite as dead as intended. His nearness clogged my throat in a way that made everything come out sounding like his big hand was wrapped around my neck.

With a heavy sigh, Lachlan threw up his hands and backed away from me. "I don't want to fight with you anymore. I said my piece. You know where I stand. I'd like for us to be civil to each other, and yeah, I'm including myself in that."

His fingers curled around my shoulders. They were warm and rough on my bare skin. A memory flashed behind my eyes. Of him dragging his fingertips down the length of my spine, tracing my hip bones, pressing his thumb between my lips.

Nothing was the same as it was before, though. Instead of twisting his fingers in the straps of my cami, Lachlan used his hold to move me aside and open the door for his quick escape.

He glanced back at me over his shoulder. "I want you to be safe. No one should be looking at you or talking to you the way those assholes did."

"Including you?"

He grunted, bowing his head. "Especially me."

He pulled the door shut behind him, his heavy, retreating steps on the porch stairs loud in the quiet early morning. Once his footsteps faded, I leaned against the front door.

My fluttering heart refused to calm for several more minutes. Fists flexing, one at my side, the other on my chest, I tipped my head back and sighed.

No man had ever made me feel like Lachlan did.

And I wasn't sure that was a good thing.

Chapter Eleven

Lock

It took Julien three days to confront me. After the beer can to my face, I'd been waiting for it, bracing myself to take what he had to give me.

I shouldn't have been surprised he'd been waiting too.

It was on the ride home from his physical therapy appointment, the first time we were truly alone since the weekend. He'd been silent on the ride there, and when he climbed into my truck afterward, sweat prickling his forehead, he asked me to go for a drive.

I had nowhere to be, and it was clear he didn't want to go home. We drove, the whoosh of my tires flying over pavement the only sound for long, drawn-out minutes. I pulled into the parking lot of the beachside burger joint I'd taken him to a couple weeks ago. His jaw flexed, mouth tense and tight through the hassle of getting out of the truck, wheeling across the parking lot, ordering, and settling in on the deck overlooking the ocean.

I waited for him to say his piece. Gave him the space for it. I was in no rush. Not with the sun warming my shoulders and the ocean crashing into the sand in front of me.

Julien cracked his knuckles one at a time. "I didn't take you for the type of dude who'd disrespect a woman after he got with her. I stand corrected."

Turning from the beach to peer at him, I sat up straight. "What are you talking about?"

He waved a dismissive hand. "Fuck off. You think I didn't notice her in the house, in your *bedroom*, when everyone else was away? My leg is jacked, not my eyes and ears. The kitchen will never be the same after the two of you spurted your fluids all over it."

That made me huff a laugh, but I sobered just as fast. "I'm going to have to ask that this stays between us."

Julien inclined his head. "I'm not about spreading rumors. Whatever the two of you do is between you. You disrespecting her in front of everyone? Nah, that won't stand."

I shoved my fingers through my hair. I'd gone too long without a cut. It could use one. Either that, or I'd have to start tying it back soon.

"I apologized to her," I told him. "It's squashed."

He shook his head. "All's well and good, but I gotta say, man, I think less of you these days. You did her dirty."

My eyes narrowed on him. "Did she talk to you?"

"Nope." His gaze turned to the beach. "She didn't have to. I know you were hitting it, then suddenly you weren't, then you were trashing her, saying shit that isn't true. If you took a minute to actually talk to the girl instead of bringing your preconceived notions along for the ride, you'd see that."

"Yeah, I don't need to talk to her. She's not going to be my girlfriend, and I have more than enough friends."

He sucked in air between his teeth. "Harsh, Lock. Why'd you even go there if you were going to be a dick to her? You have to live next door, hang out with the same people, see each other all the time."

He had a point. I obviously hadn't been thinking with my brain. I was usually a lot more levelheaded than that, but there was something about Elena—beyond the fact that she was one of the most beautiful women I'd ever laid eyes on. She got under my skin, made me forget myself. Those skimpy little lace and silk pajamas and slips she liked to parade around in didn't help matters. The whole week I'd been building her deck, my palms had itched to slide over the slick material that skated along her curves. The urge to touch her had driven me to distraction. I was lucky I'd walked away from that job with all my digits.

"I hadn't planned on being a dick to her. I never would've talked about her like that if I'd known she was listening." My excuses were weak at best. I didn't even know why I was making excuses. I owed Julien nothing. No explanations or apologies.

"Shouldn't have said it at all." He crossed his arms over his chest. "If I didn't need you for my ride, I'd throw another can at your face."

"One was all you get," I said lowly. "I got that you were pissed and I'd misstepped, so I took the hit. It's not going to happen again."

His head jerked in my direction. "Message received, captain. No one questions the almighty Lachlan."

My exhale was heavy as I rubbed the back of my neck. "I never said that."

"It was implied."

He gave a lazy shrug, but he wasn't as laid back as he was portraying. Whether it was pain from his PT session or something else, I couldn't tell, but the tendons in his neck were taut, and his arms were crossed so tight, the sinews in his forearms rippled beneath his skin.

"You pissed at me for more than bad-mouthing Elena? Or are you pissed I went there with her?" I leaned forward, getting closer to him. "Did *you* want to go there?"

Julien stilled, staring at me hard while his nostrils flared. "Let me tell you something, dude. That girl was a stranger to me until four or five months ago. She heard about my situation, met me, and offered me the room in your house. I asked her the catch, because there's always a catch. I figured the rent was astronomical. If you want to know the truth, *any* rent is astronomical to me since Amir never charged me a dime the whole time I was living with him. Elena wanted to know my financial situation, I gave it to her. I'm thinking she's going to go back on her offer since I clearly can't pay. You know what she did?"

He paused for my reaction. I shook my head. I had no idea what she did, but something deep in my stomach told me whatever it was, it had instilled Julien's deep sense of loyalty to her.

"Tell me," I said.

His jaw slid back and forth for a moment. "She told me I'd pay on a sliding scale, my rent in proportion to my income. And since I couldn't work because of the accident, my rent was zero dollars. Zero fucking dollars to live in a nice-ass house, my own private room and bathroom. This girl was a stranger, she had no reason to offer me this, but she did. She didn't ask for thanks or tell anyone what she was doing. In fact, she flipped me off when I tried to thank her. She told me I could repay her by uglying myself up a little more. She didn't want competition from a guy who was prettier than her."

I winced, but Julien laughed, his scarred mouth forming a crooked grin—one I didn't see very often.

"You don't understand, Lock. This was like a couple months after my accident. You think people tiptoe around me now? Back then, it was like they were ghosts, floating around me. No one wanted to upset me or hurt my feelings by telling me how goddamn fucked my face was...is. And then, here comes this gorgeous girl in her fancy clothes, openly making fun of me without hesitation. It was a breath of fresh air. It made me feel normal for a little while. Before all this? I was the biggest shit talker you'd ever meet. It's like Amir and Marco can't see past my fucked-up face to remember that. But Elena saw it. Maybe it was a kindred spirit thing, I don't know."

Our waitress dropped off our food, giving a chance for Julien's story to sink in. I doused my burger in ketchup and poured some over my fries. Julien took a big bite from his wrap, getting guacamole on the corners of his mouth. We fell back into silence, eating and watching the waves.

"You never answered my original question." I wiped my mouth with a paper napkin and stuffed it under my plate so it wouldn't blow away.

Julien talked with a half-full mouth. "It didn't deserve an answer."

"No?"

"Nah. If you think the only reason I could care about Elena is because I want inside her pussy, I don't think there's much to say."

I almost flinched at his words. And the idea. His rebuke was sharp, and the sting was felt, but the implication that he had a chance of knowing her like I did got my hackles up. I snapped.

"You care about her because she gives you a place to stay."

He tossed his half-eaten wrap down and wiped his fingers and mouth before turning his head to stare me down.

"Is that what you heard? In all I said, that's what you heard? Not the generosity of a stranger? The way she brought me back—keeps bringing me back—from the deep, deep abyss I'd kinda like to fall into? None of that registered for you, Lock?"

"I heard it all. You still didn't answer my question."

He sighed, looking me over like I was an unwanted stain. "No, I don't want her like that. I find her attractive as hell. If I wasn't in my current situation, no doubt I'd be hitting her up. Luck was on my side, though. I got to know her as a person instead of a good time for my dick. I'm not gonna try to fuck the one person who makes me feel human."

He turned his chair toward me, bumping the wheels against my shoes. "Sometimes, the ones who look like the good guys aren't so good. And sometimes, the ones viewed as the villain have the biggest hearts."

None of this had gone as I'd expected. The anger bubbling in the base of my gut was the most surprising part of it. I didn't like being told anything about Elena. I didn't enjoy sitting here, being schooled on the girl I'd already written off. Most of all, the seed of wrathful jealousy taking root in me was unwelcome and wouldn't be fed. I didn't have room for any of this, nor did I want it.

"I'm hearing you. I'm done running my mouth about her," I promised.

"Shouldn't have happened in the first place," Julien grumbled.

"You're right."

None of this should have.

But that was Elena. No matter my intentions, they seemed to always fly by the wayside around her.

Chapter Twelve

Elena

Once school was in full swing, things more or less settled. Honestly, I thought most people were too busy to concentrate on petty beefs—especially the assholes in New Ventures. There'd been a packet of ketchup left on my chair, but I hadn't been dumb enough to sit down without looking first. That had been their only weak effort at outwardly humiliating me.

Oh, they'd definitely spent plenty of time over the last two weeks calling me a bitch under their breath, and Kayleigh and Abby continued to sit beside me, which I could only presume was an attempt to make me uncomfortable.

What they didn't realize was I didn't give a damn. I'd been called a bitch since I first grew tits. I answered to it as readily as my own name. And the only thing that made me uncomfortable about Kayleigh and Abby were their bad dye jobs and atrocious choice in perfume.

My god, we were in our twenties now. Why were they still wearing Juicy Couture? It had barely been acceptable in high school.

Lachlan Kelly continued to be a thorn in my side the two days a week I couldn't avoid him in Spanish class. We didn't have assigned seats, yet he always plopped his big body down beside me.

At least he smelled good. Ridiculously good.

He was looking at me while we waited for the TA to pass out test packets. Yes, three weeks into the semester, and we were already taking an exam. Our Spanish teacher did not play.

"Are you ready for this?" he asked.

I lifted a shoulder. "Of course I am."

He huffed. "Of course you are."

I tipped my chin down. "Are you?"

"Of course I am."

That made me snort-laugh. "We should have a wager on who gets the higher score."

"Yeah?" He leaned over the side of his desk. "What's the wager?"

"Hmmm..." I tapped my chin. "If I win, you stop sitting next to me and forcing me to accept rides home from you."

He shot me a look that was unamused. "Sorry to burden you by driving you home."

"You should be."

Not that I truly minded it anymore. The ride, that was. The company, I could've done without.

"I win, you accept your ride without complaint and deliver me coffee every morning for a week."

My eyes rolled to the ceiling. "Why would I deliver you coffee?"

"I like coffee. I'd like it even more if it was delivered." He stretched his legs out in front of him, crossing his ankles.

I had no idea how a man that massive could look so utterly relaxed and comfortable with himself. He took up space unapologetically, like it was his due. The TA swerved around Lachlan's huge feet without complaining, handing him his test packet.

"Deal?" Lachlan asked.

"Fine. Deal."

But only because I had every confidence I'd beat him. I'd been taking Spanish since I was in preschool. I'd call myself fluent, though the business language I was learning in this class was mostly new to me. Still, I didn't anticipate this test to be a challenge.

The first two questions were short answer, then there would be a portion where we listened to a recording and wrote down a summary of what we heard. In this class, being able to write in Spanish was just as important as speaking, which made it different and frankly more interesting than the other Spanish classes I'd taken.

I took my time answering the questions, determined to best Lachlan. There was absolutely no way he was winning this. Not a chance I was going to be his coffee wench.

At first, I didn't understand what was casting the shadow over my test. Frowning, I looked up to find Lachlan standing there, clutching his test packet. What in the world was he doing?

He cleared his throat, then he...started reciting Shakespeare in a clear, booming voice.

"*¡Ser, o no ser, es la cuestión!*"

Hamlet? Lachlan had decided to give Hamlet's soliloquy in the middle of a test worth twenty-five percent of our grade? He'd lost his mind.

But why the hell was Dr. Garcia smiling like the cat who ate the canary at the front of the classroom? And why was no one tackling Lachlan with a straitjacket?

I didn't like this. It felt like an inside joke no one would explain to me. Except I wasn't the only one confused. There was more than one furrowed brow and gaping mouth.

Lachlan came to the end of the soliloquy and exchanged a glance with Dr. Garcia. The man nodded, and Lachlan gathered his things, shot me a smirk, then sauntered out of the classroom.

What? What had just happened?

· · · · • · • · · ·

I had to force myself not to rush through the rest of the test. Even if Lachlan had gotten a zero and wasn't competition anymore, my grades mattered to me. I wrote thoughtfully and with precision, and when I handed in my packet, I wasn't the last one finished, but almost. Only a couple stragglers remained.

Lachlan was waiting for me outside, parked on a bench, which he made look like doll furniture. His long arms were spread across the back, so he was essentially taking up the whole thing himself. Sun dappled his tanned skin. His face tilted up to the sky.

Did this man ever get tense?

I stopped in front of him, my knee hitting his. "You lost?"

He grinned at me. "Unless you got higher than a one-hundred, which is impossible, *you* lost."

I crossed my arms over my chest. "Are you demented? You didn't even finish half your test. I'd be surprised if Dr. Garcia even lets you back in the classroom."

He cocked his head. "Did you look on the back of the test?"

"Why would I?"

"If you had, you would have seen a bonus question."

I sank down on the bench next to him. "There was a bonus question?"

He scrubbed his jaw with his hand. "Not really a question. An activity."

I slapped his thick thigh with the back of my hand. "Out with it."

"I finished the first two short-answer questions, so I thumbed through the packet before I went on. On the back, it said the first person to stand up and loudly recite the included portion of *Hamlet* would automatically get a perfect score." He shrugged. "I guess I was the first one."

I stomped my feet. "That is absolute bullshit."

"Says the loser."

I flipped him off. He was lucky I didn't do worse to his smug face. "I don't think this qualifies as a win, Lachlan."

He dropped his arms and straightened, peering down at me from his perennial high horse. "Are you backing out of our wager? Is that what's happening?"

"Circumstances aren't what I agreed to."

His brown eyes narrowed. "Come on, Elsa. Admit you lost, fair and square."

I shoved his arm, not budging him a millimeter. "Stop calling me Elsa. I know you know my name, you ass."

He barked a laugh. "I always knew your name."

"Then why do you keep calling me the wrong one?"

His brow pulled together in the middle. "Are you ready to admit you lost?"

I shoved him again. "You didn't answer my question."

He caught my hands and lowered them to my thighs. "Stop hitting me. You keep doing it, I'll think you want to be hit back. And since the only place I'd ever hit a woman is on her ass after she begs for it, well..."

Heat flooded my core. Every time he threatened to spank me, I had the urge to present myself to him like a wild animal, ass up, face down.

"I would never beg you." At least I'd managed to say it with conviction, though I didn't feel it. Not in the least.

"We both know that's not true. But that's not what we're talking about, is it? We're talking about you backing out on our bet. I gotta admit, I'm disappointed in you. I thought you had a little more integrity than that."

"Oh, Lachlan." I shook my head. He wasn't going to get me with that. "Wrong button to push."

He exhaled and let go of my hands. "All right. How about this?" Rising from the bench, he slung his backpack over his shoulder and offered me a hand.

I hopped up on my own, scowling at him. If I didn't scowl, I'd laugh, because he looked so grumpy, and this was the most ridiculously fun argument I'd had in a long time.

And then, he had to go spoil it.

Bending his knees, he grabbed me by the back of my thighs and hoisted me over his shoulder. I shrieked, but he patted my butt and started walking with me hanging upside down.

"Quiet, Elsa." His bark was mocking. I could almost hear the laugh under it.

"You think this is funny, asshole?" I slapped at his back and butt and kicked my feet in protest. His arm was an iron bar around my legs.

"I told you not to hit me," he said calmly.

"You're kidnapping me. You don't get to have the moral high ground, buddy."

He walked so carefully, his steps a mile long, I was barely being jostled. If I cared what anyone on this campus thought of me, I would have been humiliated. I wasn't, though. What I was feeling came from the rage family.

"I'm walking you to my truck, which was part of the wager." He swatted my ass lightly. "You agreed to this. I'm just taking you at your word."

"The wager is null and void." I wiggled on his shoulder. "And you said you wouldn't spank me unless I begged."

His palm came down on my butt again, hardly more than a pat. "If you think this is spanking, you'll be in for a surprise."

God, how did he continually make my panties wet? This was a problem.

"I won't be in for a surprise because I'll never experience that. I don't beg."

Suddenly, my world went from upside down to right side up and my feet were on the ground again. Dizzy from the vantage change, I stumbled into Lachlan. He caught me under the elbows, holding me upright and steady.

Blinking, I blew my hair out of my face and took in my surroundings. We were in the student parking lot, next to Lachlan's old crusty truck.

"You good?" he rumbled.

"I'm fine now that I'm not being tossed around like a rag doll."

He laughed, and it was so deep and resonant, I felt it in my chest. His teeth were perfectly white and straight except for one eyetooth. It was slightly twisted, making it stick out from the others. I wondered about that tooth. Why did the rest of them line up while that one rebelled? Was it natural? Or a braces mishap?

I caught myself drifting closer to Lachlan, my head tipped back as I studied his slowly disappearing smile.

"Let's get you home." But he took another long moment to release his hold on me.

"I can buckle myself into the truck this time," I said.

He huffed lowly, ignoring me otherwise. The truck door creaked open, and he all but shoved me in. Then he strapped me in like he did every time, giving it a tug to ensure it was properly in place. I gasped as it tightened across my lap even though I'd been expecting it. His head swiveled to look at me, bringing us face to face. His eyes swept from my parted lips to meet my gaze.

"Okay?" he asked.

"I'm fine."

He stared at me for another moment, brow pinching as if he doubted my fineness. Then he closed me in his truck, rounded to the driver's side, got in, and drove me home. No other words about the wager. No other words at all, actually.

· · · · ● ● ● · · · ·

The sun had barely risen when I knocked on Lachlan's door. It took him less than thirty seconds to answer, like he'd been waiting for me. His eyes were sleepy, but amusement danced in the chocolate depths. His hair was messy, like he'd just been rolling around in bed.

Not with me. When he rolled around in bed with me, his hair had been damp with sweat from how hard he worked at getting me off.

Balls. That was ancient history. So last season. It hadn't even been that good.

I shoved his coffee at him. "Here. Don't say anything or I'll dump it on your head."

Instead of being a good sport by taking his coffee and letting me slink away with an ounce of pride intact, he cuffed my wrist and pulled me into the house. I started to protest, but he tapped my lips.

"Julien's sleeping," he said quietly.

He pulled me with him through the silent house to the sliding glass door that led to his deck. When we were outside again, he let go of my hand, took his coffee, and held it up in front of his face, like he had X-ray vision and could see the contents through the paper cup.

"It's a vanilla latte. I figured you were a black coffee kind of guy."

His grin was wide. The laugh that followed was new to me. Filled with genuine amusement, it sounded like it had originated from the depths of the Grand Canyon, echoing off ancient rock walls until it finally thundered to the surface. My ears tingled, and something low in my stomach squirmed. I'd never heard this man laugh. At least, not like this. So free. So unbothered.

To maintain my sanity, I hoped to never hear it again.

"So, you got me something entirely different than you thought I'd like?"

I shrugged. "You never said what kind of coffee I had to bring you."

He took a sip and made a show of smacking his lips. "Not bad." Another sip, and he hummed as he swallowed. "If this is supposed to be some kind of punishment for beating you, it isn't very good."

"Don't tell me you're a latte guy?"

He lowered his chin and reached out to tug on the ends of the strings hanging from my hoodie. "I'm not a latte guy, but maybe you've converted me." He gave another tug. "Am I ever getting this back?"

I shook my head. "Nope. You should know I'm an only child and very bad at sharing. Once something is in my possession, I never let go."

He sipped his latte and propped his butt on the deck railing. Relaxed, as always. Freaking Lock.

"Luckily, I'm used to dealing with an annoying little sister taking my things."

His expression was smooth, without any humor now. Which was fine, since I didn't really find being compared to his little sister very funny.

My eyes narrowed on him, patience running thin. "Why am I out here with you? I didn't know I had to include conversation with the coffee delivery."

He watched me over the top of the cup. "I knew you'd have something to say and I didn't want to wake up the house. You forgot to wear pants, so I pulled you back here."

I pulled up the hoodie to show him my running shorts. "I'm wearing pants. It just so happens I obtained this hoodie from a giant, so they're covered."

He raised one of his thick brows. "Obtained? Is that what we're calling theft now?"

"When you gave it to me, you never said you wanted it back. Honestly, I'm shocked you're so pressed for a sweatshirt. We both know I wear it better than you ever could."

"I'll get you one in your size."

I wrapped my arms around myself. "Face it, Lachlan, you're not getting it back. Now, may I be dismissed? I have things to do—"

"Small countries to take over?"

I finger gunned him. "You're catching on. Good job, you."

I had to leave right then and there. I scurried back to my house. Bringing Lachlan coffee was supposed to be a chore. A punishment for losing. It definitely shouldn't have involved banter. Who knew Lachlan Kelly gave such good banter?

Tomorrow's coffee drop-off would be quick and to the point.

·········

It took two coffee-drop-and-runs before Lachlan caught on and caught *me*. On Saturday, he was waiting for me on his porch, smug and grumpy rolled into one.

I thrust his coffee toward him from the base of the steps. "It's a Frappuccino, extra whip."

He chuckled, eyeing the cup in my hand like he didn't know what to make of it. "Straw?"

I held up my empty hand. "Nope. That wasn't part of the deal."

He trudged down the stairs, stopped right in front of me, and slid the cup from my hand, popping the top off. Mounds of whipped cream were piled on top of the frozen coffee. Truly, a ridiculous amount.

I held my breath, waiting to see what he'd do, if he would back down.

Lachlan opened his mouth wide, taking in a mouthful of cream. He got it all over his lips, not even attempting to stay clean, but it didn't gross me out. He had a way of eating that made me want to have a taste too.

He must have seen the want in my eyes, because he tipped the cup toward me and brought it to my lips. My tongue darted out, taking just a dollop on the tip. I hummed at the smooth, sweet flavor. He had rockslides in his chest again as he took another mouthful.

He offered me the cup again, brushing the cream against my lips. I licked it off my top lip. Lachlan watched the trail of my tongue. Wanting more than just a dollop this time, I opened my mouth and used my lips to take in more whipped cream.

"Good?" he rumbled.

"Mmm."

I didn't eat whipped cream. I had to fight the urge to bury my mouth in it and suck it all down my throat. What was this? Why did being around this man scramble my brain and make me want things I never had before? It certainly couldn't be a good thing.

He reached out and swiped his rough thumb along the side of my mouth. "You made a mess of yourself." He took his time sucking my mess right off his thumb.

"What are you doing?" I blurted. *No one* made me feel like this, like I wasn't in control of myself and my reactions. This guy didn't even have to try, and I was literally eating out of his hand.

"Collecting my prize," he said simply.

That raised my hackles. All of this did. I didn't like not knowing if I was coming or going with Lachlan. He pushed and pulled until I was dizzy. Some women might have been into his whiplash, but I was more of a solid ground kind of girl at this point in my life. I'd been jerked around enough for a thousand lifetimes. No one got to do that to me anymore.

"I think you're playing games." I crossed my arms over my chest. "You're not interested in me, but you keep finding reasons to be around me. I don't like games. I've always been a poor winner and a terribly sore loser, so I don't play."

He cocked his head, pinning me with an unwavering stare. "Do I look like I play games? That's not my style, Elsa. I don't deny I like having you at my beck and call. It's been fun, but it's not a game."

"Then what's the point of this? Why won't you let me drop the coffee on your porch and leave? Why were you waiting for me today?"

"You have a bad habit of putting a lot of words in my mouth that aren't there. You accused me of hating you. You say I'm not interested in you. You tell me you're not my type. I never said any of those things. As for this morning, I was waiting for you because, like I said, I've been enjoying this."

He put the frap down on the porch steps and wiped his mouth with the back of his hand. His eyes swept over me, my little pastel sundress, heels, hair I'd spent an hour molding into soft curls. My mother would approve of this outfit. It was far more her than me, though I was aware I looked good.

"Where are you off to?"

His swift change of topic caught me off guard. It shouldn't have. Lachlan was blunt and to the point. I supposed he figured he'd answered my question, so the topic was closed. Since I really didn't want to stand here all day going back and forth with him, I answered.

"I'm going to my parents' house for brunch, where I'll most likely be guilted into spending the day with my mom."

He lowered his chin. "There's someone out there who can make you do something you don't want to?"

I scoffed. "I have to keep up the perfect daughter image or the world will fall apart."

He nodded like he understood. Like he didn't question that sentiment. It made me curious about him, about the wilderness he emerged from. I wouldn't ask, though. This interaction had already gone on far longer than I'd meant for it to.

"Your parents live nearby?"

"Yes. I'm a Savage River townie."

He smirked. "That's right. You and Helen went to high school together."

"Yes. She knew me at my best."

His big shoulder went up. He must've heard stories. "People change."

I crossed my fingers. "Here's hoping. Anyway, that was my last coffee delivery, so—"

That snapped him out of his laid-back routine. "That's not how this works. I said a week. You agreed to it."

"This is the end of the week," I argued.

"Except the bet began on Tuesday. Wednesday was your first drop-off. I get seven coffees."

I shook my head. "No. This is the last day of the week. I'm all done."

His head tipped to the side as he scrutinized me from head to toe. "Are you really backing out of a bet? I didn't think that was your style." With a shake of his head, he turned to head for the porch. "See you later, Elsa."

Groaning, I kicked at a rock on the path. "I know what you're doing."

He waved at me over his shoulder before bending to pick up his frap. "I'm just going inside to drink my coffee monstrosity."

I flipped his back off. He chuckled like he knew what I had done.

"Fine. I'll be here tomorrow with your stupid coffee, and that's only because I don't want you holding anything over my head, *not* because you're right."

I swiveled on my toes before he could gloat. I went exactly three steps before I had to bite my tongue to stop myself from screaming. Why did this man continually get under my skin? All it took was a look, and I was acting like an imbecile.

No more.

I had to take control of the situation.

Lachlan might claim he's not playing games with me, but that was exactly what he was doing. Toying with the snooty rich girl next door for his own amusement.

I was no one's entertainment.

Chapter Thirteen

Lock

I had two weeks of relative peace before I had no choice but to make my mother aware of Saoirse's potential college plans. As expected by both my sister and me, all hell had broken loose in the form of Lily Smythe-Kelly.

State Senator Smythe-Kelly, I should've said, since that was how she preferred to be addressed—probably even by Saoirse and me, though she'd never spoken the desire out loud. It suited her a lot better than "mom."

"Your father is trying to steal my daughter."

My mother was blunt, to the point. Unlike her name, she wasn't flowery with her words. I took after her in that regard. We were both economical with what we said, never wasting a syllable.

"He's not," I answered.

We were FaceTiming, so I got to experience my mother's full range of emotion. Most of it hinged on righteous indignation, but there, peeking out from behind it, was fear.

"He already stole one of my children. He can't have Saoirse."

I scrubbed my face roughly. "He didn't steal me."

"Didn't he?" Her face pinched like she was sucking something bitter. I guessed that was how she felt about my dad. "Are you moving back home after school? No. You're disappearing to Wyoming. *Ranching*, Lachlan. Really."

"I'm not disappearing, and we're not talking about me."

We'd talked about my plans for after college until we'd exhausted all the words on the subject. As far as I was concerned, it was closed.

She must've heard the wall I dropped, so she changed tack again.

"Why would he suggest Saoirse go to UC Boulder? She doesn't know anyone in Colorado. She won't like it there. It's ridiculous."

Despite it being barely past sunrise, one of my mom's assistants approached her, speaking in a low voice about an upcoming phone call with another senator. They volleyed back and forth a few times, leaving me hanging. Resting my phone on my knee, I sank down to the top step of my porch, scanning the quiet street. It wouldn't be quiet for long. Soon, everyone would be dragging themselves to their Monday classes. For now, it was just me and the silence only broken by intermittent mumbles coming through my phone's speaker.

"Lachlan?"

I picked up my phone. "Yes?"

"Talk Saoirse out of this ludicrous notion."

"No. It's not ludicrous."

Her face pinched in consternation. "Of course you'd take your father's side."

I'd heard that plenty of times. It rolled right off my back these days, though I hadn't forgotten the burn it used to leave behind.

"I'm taking Saoirse's side." I kept calm, refusing to be baited into an argument.

When I spotted Elena speeding down the sidewalk, my coffee in her hand, I stopped listening altogether. I'd somehow missed her drop-off yesterday. Had it not been for my mother's early morning call, I probably would have missed this one too.

Her footsteps stuttered when she saw me on the porch, then she lowered her head, plowing forward with determination.

I was ready for her by the time she hit the base of the steps. Once she dropped the cup with the thick, green liquid in it, my hand darted out, cuffing her wrist and drawing her toward me until she plopped down beside me. I kept hold of her as I pointed my phone in her direction, cutting my mother off midword and stopping Elena's struggles to get away.

"Lachlan?" My mother straightened her spine and tipped her chin down. Game face on. Everyone was a potential constituent. "Who's this?"

"Mom, this is Elena Sanderson, my neighbor. Elena, this is my mother, Lily."

"Lovely to meet you." Without missing a single beat, Elena offered a smooth, easy smile she'd probably practiced a thousand times. If I didn't know better, I would have thought she'd dressed and prepared for the occasion. Her hair was tucked back in a loose braid. Silvery tendrils brushed the sides of her face, which was sort of sparkly at her cheeks, and her smiling lips shined with gloss. Her white top was feminine, cut close to her body and ruffled at the shoulders, and her skirt was short and flowery.

She made a pretty picture on my phone screen. In real life, I couldn't decide if I wanted to cover her up or lay her across my lap, flip her skirt up, and redden her perfect ass.

"You too, Elena. Tell me, how is my son as a neighbor?" My mother didn't miss a beat either, slipping into her affable, every-woman, mother-of-the-year mask. "Not too loud partying all the time, I hope."

Elena laughed politely. "Oh, not Lachlan. He's so quiet, I barely remember he's here." She elbowed my side. "He can be a pain, though. I lost a bet to him so I've been his coffee gopher for a week. He aced our Spanish exam. I'm sure he told you that, though."

Mom's eyebrow arched. "You *didn't* tell me that, Lachlan. Good for you. Though, it's not very gentlemanly to make a woman buy you coffee this early in the morning—or ever, for that matter."

Elena leaned into me, grasping my mom's attention again. "Oh, don't worry about me. A bet's a bet. I agreed to the terms. Besides, I've been torturing Lachlan by bringing him frilly coffee drinks all week. He's getting a matcha latte today."

The laugh that burst out of my mom was more genuine than I'd heard in a while. "Good for you, Elena. Hold his feet to the fire. That's how you have to handle Kelly men. Otherwise, they'll run right over you."

"I have no trouble holding my own with Lachlan," Elena assured her.

They chatted amiably for another minute, two women who were veterans of making small talk that didn't sound like small talk, then my mother had to go rule the world again.

"Lachlan, this discussion isn't finished," she warned.

"I didn't think it was."

She signed off with a cursory, "I love you. Talk soon." I dropped my phone on the porch, trading it for the green drink I'd been gifted.

"No straw again?" I turned to Elena, who was watching me with sharp eyes.

"Your mom's Senator Smythe-Kelly?"

I nodded, taking a sip of the drink. Too sweet, but not as offensive as it looked. "There's no coffee in this."

She flicked her fingers. "It's coffee adjacent. How is your mom a state senator? I thought you emerged from the backwoods or something."

"I never said that."

"You let me believe that."

"I told you we probably grew up similarly. My mom's been involved in state politics since she could breathe. Her father held the same position before her." Her huff was so indignant, I had to laugh. "You like to put words in my mouth. I'm getting a little tired of it."

The scowl she sent me was sharp and displeased. "Then you should probably say what you mean instead of grunting and frowning at me all the time. And maybe you should stop trying to be in my space every chance you get."

I gripped the base of her braid and tugged it, bending her head back so I could peer down at her face. The smooth column of her throat bobbed when she swallowed. Otherwise, she stayed perfectly still.

"I don't think you mind me being in your space. You're so used to getting your way with everyone, you like that you can't with me, even though you want to hate it."

She reached up and gripped my jaw, digging her nails into my scruff. "Do you want to know what I think?"

"Yes," I murmured.

"I think you need to get over yourself, Lachlan. You don't get to have me again."

"I don't believe that for a second. You can act like the ice queen all you want, but I know how warm and soft you get for me. I bet you're warm and soft right now, aren't you?"

"You wish," she whispered, pushing my face away.

I dropped my hold on her hair, and she shot to her feet and down the steps in a flash. She swiveled to face me, her hands on her hips.

"I liked you because you were straightforward and took what you wanted. This—" she pointed back and forth between us, "—teasing and taunting isn't cute to me. This is what all the assholes around here do. They play like timid little boys. If this was how you had been in the beginning, I would have been drier than the Sahara. I'm totally over these games, Lock."

With that parting shot, she flounced away, her tiny skirt riding dangerously high on the backs of her thighs. The only reason I didn't get up and follow was because she'd pinned me in place with the truth.

What the hell was I doing?

Elena was hot as hell in bed, but that was supposed to be where it began and ended. No connections. No commitments. Absolutely no promises. I'd walk away from Savage U clean and begin my real life in Wyoming after graduation.

But she was right. I kept coming back for more, even if it was just trading barbs and driving myself to distraction. I was the one pursuing her, forcing our interactions, not the other way around.

It wasn't fair to either of us, but especially not her. I never wanted to be the guy who jerked women around. That wasn't me.

Decisions had to be made, but first, it was time to get ready for class.

Chapter Fourteen

Elena

My last nerve was a fraying tightrope by the time I walked into New Ventures on Friday. And of course, it was all Lachlan's fault. He was the only human being who could rattle me. He'd done exactly as I'd asked and left me alone all week. But he was everywhere. *Everywhere.*

I walked outside, he was tinkering with his crusty truck in his driveway.

If I wanted sunshine on the deck, he was already on *his* deck, reading a book.

Our paths crossed incessantly on campus when they never had before.

And Spanish class was the absolute worst. He was just...there. So there. His presence was as massive as his shoulders and impossible to ignore.

There was no way I'd last an hour sitting between Kayleigh and Abby. Not that they were getting to me, but my fuse was so very short, they were liable to get a pencil to the eyeball if they looked at me wrong.

Therefore, I parked myself right beside my old buddy, Salvatore. He jumped in fright when I sat down and leaned as far away from me as possible without toppling over.

I pointed to his Leaning Tower of Pisa posture. "What's that about?"

"Um. You're sitting next to me. You never sit next to me." His nose twitched. "Are you going to mess with me or something?"

Shaking my head, I pursed my lips in consternation. What was the use of reforming if dudes like Sal still thought I was the bad guy? "What gave you that impression?"

His eyes shot to the front as the douchelord posse walked into class. "I thought you were friends with them. Any class I've ever had with those guys, they find some way to go after me."

I snarled. "That really sucks, Sal, but I'm definitely not friends with them. As far as they know, you have a horse cock and I'm pining to ride it again."

He sputtered, barely keeping his glasses on his face from jerking back so hard. "That was *you* who started that rumor? I thought Kayleigh was recording me or something when she asked if it was true."

I bit down on my bottom lip, sort of pleased with myself. "Well...did you confirm it for her?"

Sal turned bright red, and it was kind of cute. If I were into skinny, nerdy types, Sal would totally do it for me. His glasses were stylish. His hair had a charming flop to it when he brushed it. It'd taken me a few glances to notice, but Sal could get it. Not from me, but from a lot of other girls, for sure.

"Uh, no. My—" he waved his hand in the direction of his crotch, "—junk is private. You know, between me and the girl I'm with."

I nodded. "I respect that, but if I were you, I'd ride the horse cock wave, especially if it's even close to true. You might not get another chance like this."

He snapped open his laptop, sending me a glance out the side of his eyes. "I'm good how I am. I guess it was cool of you to say that, though."

I looked over my shoulder as the Pi Sig boys chest bumped each other, and Kayleigh and Abby simpered at their antics. The fact that I'd been part of their group until far too recently made me sick to my stomach. Even worse, my mother was pushing for me to hang out with Kayleigh again since her dad did business with mine. If my mom knew I'd slapped Kayleigh silly last semester, she'd undoubtedly need to be locked back up in her favorite padded room.

Professor Seavers started class, tearing my thoughts from vapid girls, stupid boys, horse cocks, and Lachlan freaking Kelly—who, unfortunately, could have been categorized with the horse cocks.

Toward the end of class, Professor Seavers introduced our midterm project, which would be worth fifty percent of our grade. We'd be working with a real startup company, forming a business plan, including marketing, budgeting, visions for expansion—basically, lassoing the moon for them. During homecoming, alumni judges would watch and score our presentations. The most exciting part was in the past, some alumni had invested in the startups they were introduced to during the presentations. That raised the stakes on the assignment significantly.

Damn, was I excited. My head was bubbling like a bottle of champagne, ready to burst with ideas, and I didn't even know which startup I'd be working with yet.

"Now"—Seavers braced her hands on her lectern—"you'll be working in either pairs or trios. I encourage you to choose who you work with wisely. Don't choose your buddy just because you have fun together. Imagine this is a real business—because it is—and pair up with someone who will be an asset."

The classroom door swung open, and everyone's head swiveled from the professor to the person entering the room. A sandy-blond head peeked in. When Seavers waved him in, the rest of him followed.

The bubbles in my head filled with lead, causing me to sink down in my chair.

Seavers grinned as wide as her no-nonsense style would allow. "Just in time. One of my former students agreed to come back and talk to you about his experience in this class. He also owns one of the startups a few of you will be working with. Give Oliver Bergen your attention."

Oliver and Nate could have been twins. From my vantage, Oliver and Nate had shared height and build—tall and lean—with features that were strikingly similar. Oliver had a smattering of light stubble on his jaw, but it only made me think this was what Nate would have looked like in a few years if he hadn't died. Sadness and fear twined in my belly, inextricably linked whenever I allowed my thoughts to turn to Nate.

Oliver grinned, the corners of his eyes crinkling. At least his smile was different from Nate's. It actually reached his eyes and wasn't rimmed with evil. Then again, he was older than Nate, so he could have had more experience hiding it.

He scanned the crowd, pausing on me for a moment before continuing. He spoke for several minutes, but I barely heard a word. I'd promised my mother I would text him, possibly meet for coffee, but I couldn't breathe sharing a classroom with him. Anything more wouldn't be happening. For once, I'd have to disappoint her.

Sal tapped my arm, startling me back to the present. From the humming conversation going on around me, I realized Oliver had stopped talking and people were discussing partnerships.

"What do you think?" Sal asked.

"About what?" I rubbed the center of my forehead, trying to clear my mind.

"About working together." He blinked at me from behind his thick glasses.

"You want to work with me?" I asked.

"Only if you do. I think we could make a dynamic team. Obviously, I don't know what our startup business will be, but between the two of us—"

"Yes. We'll work together."

I might've been out of it, but I wasn't stupid—and I would have to be to turn down working with Future Bill Gates. Besides, it wasn't like any of my other classmates were jumping to partner up with me. Not that I wanted them to. The Pi Sig hooligans probably couldn't even *spell* startup, much less create a business plan for one.

Sal grinned. "All right. That was easier than I thought it would be."

"Let's hope it's a sign of what's to come."

We packed up our things, my mind whirling with plans of escape. Oliver was talking to Seavers and her TA. I planned to slip by as quickly as I could, crossing my fingers I wouldn't be noticed.

The second I stood up, though, he raised his head and locked eyes with me. I nodded to him, hoping that would be enough, but he didn't take his eyes off me as I made my way down the steps, then started toward me before I could reach the door.

"Elena Sanderson," he called smoothly.

Sal paused beside me, his eyes darting back and forth between us. "You know him?" he asked.

"Acquaintance. It's okay. You don't have to stay with me," I murmured.

He hesitated for a few seconds before hustling out the door. I respected his hesitation, even though he left me in the end. He had probably sensed my unease, but since we were in a bright classroom, which was relatively safe in the grand scheme of things, he took me at my word.

Oliver stopped a comfortable distance away, tucking his hands in the pockets of his dress pants. They were cut slim on his long legs, and he'd gone sockless in his loafers. It was a good look on him. The Bergen fam had never lacked in style. Morals, on the other hand...

"Elena, how are you?" he asked.

"Great. I'm great." I gestured to the classroom behind him. "I see you're back from London taking Savage River by storm."

He chuckled, sending shivers down my spine at how similar it sounded to Nate's.

"And you're exactly like I remembered. No wonder my brother was obsessed."

Bile rose in my throat. Obsessed was probably the right word for what Nate had felt for me. Not in the romantic, bodice-ripper kind of way some women dream about either. His obsession was more of the *it rubs the lotion on its skin* variety.

"I don't know about that." I adjusted the strap on my bag. "It's great running into you, Oliver. I'm sure I'll see you around class, so—"

He raised a light eyebrow. "Are you in a hurry to escape, Elena?"

Yes. Yes, I am. I can't bear to look at you for one more second. You have his face.

"No, of course not, but I am meeting a friend, so..."

"Great." That word again. How many times would we say it in the span of a minute?

He grinned and tipped his chin toward the door. "I'm heading out too. We'll walk together and catch up."

Shit. Fuck. Balls.

"That would be wonderful." Except, I wasn't meeting anyone and there was no way in hell I'd be leading Oliver back to my house. My scrambled brain whirred to find a way out of this.

His hand landed on the small of my back, applying gentle pressure as we exited the classroom. It stayed there until we were outside, then he shifted to walk beside me, tucking his hands in his pockets again.

"Tell me how you're liking college. Is the social game still as cutthroat as I remember it being back in my day?" His tone was light, friendly, exactly as it should have been, yet it put me on edge. But maybe that was my guilt doing that.

"Your day wasn't that long ago, and no, things haven't changed. Fortunately for me, I've made a tight-knit group of friends, so I've retired from cutting throats for now."

He barked a laugh. "Really? The little Elena who used to hang around our house thought of cutting throats as a hobby, not a job."

I shrugged, though my shoulder felt like it weighed a thousand pounds. Good thing I could fake it with the best of them.

"What can I say? I grew up a little. That's not to say I won't cut a bitch if I have to, but it doesn't have the same panache as it used to."

I answered his polite inquiries about my parents and my major, all while stifling my blind panic. Sweat beaded at my hairline, and I had to hold my jaw tight to stop it from quivering. I was leading this man around campus like I was giving him a tour. Sooner or later, he'd catch on that I had no destination. That I'd lied. And then what? How would he react?

Like a mirage, hope dawned on the horizon. My feet had directed me to potential salvation in the form of the campus maintenance headquarters.

"That's where I'm going."

Oliver stopped midsentence, squinting at the square building with four wide garage doors taking up most of the front.

"You're kidding." He turned his head to frown at me. I blinked up at him, doing my best impersonation of guilelessness. "You're not kidding. What are you doing going to campus maintenance? Slumming with blue collars to get a taste for the real world?"

Oooh, yes. There's some of that Bergen venom. I knew it was nearby, lying in wait.

Before I could answer, my own personal mountain emerged from the building. I raised my hand to wave at him, trying to keep the frantic to a minimum.

"Hey, Lock. Sorry I'm late."

His head jerked in my direction, and even from a distance, I could make out the pinch in his brow. Still, he stood there, waiting for me expectantly. Taking off at a fast clip, I hurried toward him, and Oliver kept pace.

"That's your friend?" he asked.

"Yes. *Great* friend," I answered breathlessly.

By the time I made it to Lachlan, my heart was thrashing wildly in my chest, and I was having trouble hiding the wheeze every time I tried to take a full breath. I didn't have panic attacks. Only...I did sometimes. And this was the beginning of one of those times.

Lachlan placed his hand on my nape, giving it a squeeze, and gently pulled me into his space. He peered at me, frowning deeper as he took me in.

Oliver held out his hand. "Hey, I'm Oliver, Elena's old friend. I was just walking her to you."

Lachlan shook his offered hand. "Lock. She's here now. We're good," he gruffed.

Oliver chuckled. "I can see that. El, I look forward to seeing you again soon."

When he was out of earshot, Lachlan took both my shoulders in his hands and turned me to face him. He dipped his head, bringing us eye to eye. He didn't speak or ask me what'd happened. And that was good. Because I was crashing. Instead, he let me hear his breaths, long and slow, long and slow. His hands moved down my arms, then back up again, gently squeezing as he went. All of it was steady, rhythmic, bringing me back to the here and now.

After a minute or two, my breathing slowed, matching his. My eyes were glued to Lachlan's. He never took his gaze off mine.

"I'm okay," I rasped.

"You're not. I have time. There's no hurry."

Ripping my eyes from his, I took him in. He was wearing his work boots, laced this time, canvas pants stained with oil in a few spots, a Savage U T-shirt, and a maintenance worker jacket. I turned my head to examine one of his hands on my shoulder. It was dirty, black under his nails. If I looked closely, I could just make out his fingerprints on my maroon shirt.

"You got me dirty," I said.

"Are you mad about that?"

"No, not really."

"Are you ready for me to let you go?"

I sucked in a breath. "You can try."

The second he took his hands off me, I crumbled, falling into his chest. He caught me easily, bracing an arm around my upper back, the other across my butt.

"You weren't ready," he admonished.

"I thought I might be." My head rested on his chest, his heartbeat steady against my cheek. "I wasn't sure until you let me go."

If I'd been in a better place, I wouldn't have been melting into Lachlan's firm embrace. But I didn't think anyone could fault me for allowing myself this moment of indulgence. Being held by him blocked out the world until there was only the weight of his arms, the solid warmth of his chest, the soft cushion of his middle, and the scent of motor oil, the outdoors, and Lachlan. The last of my panic began to ebb in the cave Lachlan created for me with his body.

He sighed. "Don't take chances like that." His forehead came down on the top of my head for half a second before he straightened. "I'm driving you home."

"I can probably walk if you give me a minute or two for my legs to start functioning again."

Ignoring me, he hauled me over his shoulder like he'd done last week, except slightly more gentle. This time, I hung off him like a rag doll, since my mini panic attack had sapped all the energy and most of the fight out of me. I even let him tuck me into his truck without a fight.

He climbed in on the other side but didn't start the engine. His fingers strangled the steering wheel so hard it squeaked.

"Who was that guy?"

My head lolled toward him. "My high school boyfriend's brother."

"He hurt you?"

"Oliver? Or my ex?"

His jaw worked back and forth. "Either."

"Not Oliver."

"What's your ex's name?"

"Nate, but don't worry about righting the trespasses he committed against me. He's dead."

Lachlan's exhale was sharp and jagged. "Fuck. Dead? And his brother...what'd he want?"

My lips formed an obscenely sweet smile. "To catch up, of course. He and Nate could have been twins."

"And that sent you into a panic attack."

"It wasn't full-fledged."

His hands squeezed the wheel again. "I'd hate to see full-fledged if that wasn't it."

"You would. It's ugly." I reached out and patted his clenched hand. "Thank you for being there. I didn't think I knew where I was going, but maybe in the back of my mind I did. Maybe I went to you because I knew I'd be okay once I got there."

His hand opened to envelop mine as he released a heavy sigh. "You don't have to thank me, Elsa. *Don't* thank me."

"Fine. I take it back. You're unthanked." My mouth twitched.

His mouth twitched back. "Better. Are you ready to go home?"

My fingers wiggled in his hold. "If you're ready to let go of my hand."

He held on for another beat, then placed my hand in my lap carefully, as if he was handling fine china. I guessed it was sort of nice to be handled that way once in a while.

Halfway back to the house, I turned to him, studying his profile. Through his scruff, his jaw flexed like a heartbeat. He was going to ruin his teeth, grinding them that way.

"Are you mad I showed up?" I asked. "I mean, I told you to leave me alone, then—"

"Absolutely not," he grumbled. "I'm going to be pissed if you continue on that line of thinking."

"Okay." I stacked my hands together to hide the residual trembles. "Are you going to get in trouble for leaving work without telling anyone?"

He lifted a shoulder. "Maybe. Don't care."

"I'm not going to thank you."

"Good. I'd be pissed if you did. We covered that."

We went back to silence until Lachlan pulled up in front of my house, putting the truck in park. He stretched his arm across the back of my seat, lowering his eyes to mine.

"Is that guy going to be a problem?" he asked lowly.

"No. Honestly, it's my baggage that's the problem. He'll probably show up to my class another time for this assignment we're doing, but I think I'll be better prepared for that. This week has been a lot. Having to exchange niceties with Oliver just...tipped me over the edge."

He brought his hand down to my shoulder, encasing it in warmth. "Whatever is going on between you and me, I'm here, no questions asked. If he makes you uncomfortable, text or call me, and I'll be there. You were right to come to me today. Don't question that. All right?"

I blinked hard and bit down on the inside of my cheek while I nodded. *Fucking fuck*, this guy could not be sweet to me right now. Not when I was so incredibly vulnerable. I could only handle this side of him when I had my brass balls on.

"All right."

With more confidence than I had any right to have, considering my legs hadn't been working ten minutes ago, I scrambled out of the truck and away from all that was Lock. Fortunately, I didn't land on my face and managed to get inside my house in one piece.

Helen and Zadie looked up at me when I slammed the door shut and fell back against it. They were lounging on the sectional together. Zadie was reading. Helen was playing with her phone.

"Bad day?" Helen asked.

"The worst week. I need to commemorate the end of it." I dropped my backpack and trudged to the couch where I flung myself onto the cushions.

"We were just talking," Zadie started.

"Mmmhmm. We're all going to the beach tomorrow," Helen declared.

"All?" I asked.

"Us." Helen darted her finger between the three of us, then pointed to the side. "And the boys. All of us. Food, music, ocean, chill. Don't pretend like you don't want to go, Ms. Malibu."

All out of fight—and not *really* wanting to fight anyway—I agreed to the plan. The beach, my girls, food? Yes, please. Perfect ending to a fantastically shitty week.

Chapter Fifteen

Lock

A MAN MY SIZE wasn't made to spend long hours on a beach. I could've lived outside in the woods, among ancient trees and mountain breezes, or worked on the ranch's craggy, rolling fields. Sitting in sand with the sun burning my shoulders wasn't for me.

But here I was. Sand. Sun. Ocean. All of it. I came voluntarily when Theo mentioned the crew was headed to the beach for the day. The crew meant Elena, and since I hadn't been able to get her out of my mind—the lost, vulnerable look of her throwing herself at me for safekeeping—I threw on a hat, a pair of shorts, and a T-shirt, and came along for the ride.

It wasn't torture. Not even a fucking bit.

The sun was beating on me, but it was hard to notice when my dick had been at half-mast since the moment Elena divested herself of her little sundress to run into the ocean in a bikini that barely covered an inch of her body.

She'd been out there for a couple hours, vacillating between floating and boogie boarding. Even from where I sat on the sand, I could see she was content. She was a woman born to be in the sea. When she emerged, water dripping down her smooth skin, she looked like Aphrodite in her shell or something. Like art.

Helen flung herself down on the empty chair beside me, grabbing a water bottle out of the cooler. She guzzled half of it and sighed.

"Man, this was what I needed. This semester is *killing* me," she said.

"You're doing it to yourself. No sympathy from me."

She snorted a laugh. "Thanks, Lock. Whatta pep talk."

I pumped my fist. "You can do it."

That made her laugh harder, bending at the waist to let it all out. "Oh god. You're fucking terrible at being peppy. Don't do it again."

Stretching out my legs, I crossed my ankles, keeping my eyes on Elena showing Zadie how to boogie board while Amir stood by like his girl's bodyguard. There were a lot of big hand gestures and bending over, pointing her ass in my direction. It was distracting. I could've let myself sink into that sight, forgetting what was on my mind. I didn't, though.

"Did you know a guy named Nate? Elena's ex?" I asked.

Helen stilled. "Yeah. I knew him. He was a piece of shit. The world is a better place without him in it."

"He treated her bad?"

She made a hissing sound. "I don't know what went on between the two of them. Our school was so big, people could get lost, even the head cheerleader and her football captain boyfriend. All I know is they were toxic, and knowing Elena now, away from that guy, I'm going to lay the blame squarely on him."

I read between the venomous lines. Her ire toward this guy wasn't on behalf of what he did to her friend. This was a lot more personal than that. A lot closer to home.

"He treat you bad, Hells?"

She was wearing sunglasses, but I knew her well enough to recognize she was rolling her eyes.

"Nate was one of those privileged boys who thought the world belonged to him. He took and took and took, because he knew if he got caught, he'd get a slap on the wrist at worst."

I sucked in a deep breath before asking, "He took from you?"

"He got close. Really, really close." She scoffed, her mouth tipping into the smallest grin. "Actually, it was Elena's cousin, Penelope, who rescued me. That girl is the shit. She beat the hell out of Nate with a bag of books. Then, my bestie, Gabe, who's Pen's boyfriend, beat the hell out of Nate with his fists. That was my justice, and you know, it was pretty damn poetic."

A minute went by where I was struggling with being entirely useless. There was nothing I could do to fix what had happened to Helen, and fixing was what I did. If I couldn't find the break and repair it, I went crazy.

Helen lowered her sunglasses, peering at me over them. "Why're you asking about Nate?"

Groaning, I took off my hat and shoved a hand through my damp hair. "His older brother showed up on campus yesterday. He freaked Elena out enough for me to be concerned."

Concerned was the mildest term I could put to it. I'd been up late last night, picturing Elena's quivering chin. Never thought I'd call her fragile, but that was what she'd been while I'd held her—while she'd clung to me.

Helen flinched. "Shit. I didn't even know he had an older brother. I tried to know as little as possible about that asshole." She turned back to the ocean, finding Elena wading in up to her knees. "She was freaked out?"

"Yeah. Couldn't get away from him fast enough."

"Thanks for telling me, and for being there yesterday. I know she's not your favorite person but—"

"Never said that."

Her attention whipped back to me. "Uh...you kind of made it clear more than once, dude. It's a thing. Lock dislikes Elena. We all know it. Although, no one has a clue why."

I shook my head. "I never said that, Hells. Some people, it takes me a while to warm up to. I liked you right away. Theo, it took me longer."

"You called her poison, dude."

"Sweet like," I corrected.

"Same difference." She slapped my shoulder. "Whatever. Sort your complicated feelers. I'm going to cool off in the water. You should go play with the boys. There was talk of football—just don't smash my man into the sand if you play. I'd like to keep him in one piece."

Helen left me, running for the ocean. When she reached Elena, she hooked her arm around El's neck and took her underwater with her. They both splashed above the surface seconds later, screeching and laughing. Something that had been sharp and stabbing in my gut dulled at the sight of Elena's full-blown smile and the sound of her laughter. Warmth that wasn't from the sun settled over me in a disconcerting blanket.

It shouldn't have satisfied me so much that this girl was happy.

I shouldn't have been breathing a sigh of relief to see her smile again.

But it did.

And I was.

Shit.

I got up, kicking my way through the sand to where Theo and Marco were tossing a football around. Theo grinned at my approach.

"All right, Lock's here. Does that mean you're ready to play, big man?"

I caught the ball he threw me, lining up my fingers with the laces. "Only if you're ready to be beat."

Marco jogged over to my side. "I call Lock's team."

Theo glanced at the water where Amir was still standing guard over Zadie. "Great, now I have to pull him away from his girl and try to keep his attention on the game? I might as well forfeit." He cupped his hands around his mouth. "Amir, you're on my team. It's go time."

Amir barely glanced in his direction, crossing his arms over his chest. Zadie pushed him in our direction. When she wouldn't relent, he finally kissed her hard, smacked her butt, then started toward us.

Marco cackled at his boy's pointed reluctance, clapping me on the back. "We've got this in the bag, man. No sweat."

He was probably right. It'd be an easy game.

Right now, I needed something easy to remind me why I avoided complicated.

Elena's laugh cut through the ocean breeze and my sternum. That arsenic-laced candy was so very tempting, it was all I could do not to reach out and take it, damn the consequences.

Yeah, I really needed the reminder.

Chapter Sixteen

Elena

Helen and I were at war. One dunk, I could deal with. Two was pushing it. Three? Nope. She was going down.

"Zadie! Help me get Helen," I screamed, rushing through the waves.

Helen laughed, backing away while she splashed ocean water at me. "Never gonna happen, dude. You won't take me alive."

I lunged, barely missing her. "That sounds like a challenge."

Of course, Zadie didn't help me. She'd probably rather drown herself than dunk someone else. Freaking sweet little pacifist. If I didn't like her so much, I'd try to dunk her too.

Helen was in my sights. Lunging again, my fingers grazed her side at the same time a rogue wave crashed into both of us, sending us under. For a second, I let myself be carried by the tide and blocked out everything else. Then Helen found me and grabbed my hand, tugging me back to the surface.

We called truce after that, wading to the shoreline for a break. Zadie gave up on boogie boarding and sat with us on the wet sand. The three of us watched the boys' attempt at playing football. It was silly, since Lachlan barely had to move to block and his throws to Marco went for miles. And I was pretty sure he was taking it easy on them.

"It's too bad Julien couldn't be here," Zadie said.

"Yeah." Helen scooped up sand and passed it back and forth between her hands. "I mean, he could have. We would have made it work for him. Sand is probably tough, but—"

"He has pride. You think he wants his boys helping him hobble on the beach? Or worse, having to carry him?" I grimaced at the idea. Julien could walk, but he wasn't steady yet. There was no way he could be here without assistance, which would kill him.

"He would hate to know we were talking about him like this," I said. "Let's just acknowledge it sucks Jules isn't here and move on. All right?"

Zadie's bottom lip popped out a little but she nodded. Helen tossed the sand she was holding at the ocean.

"You wanna tell me about Nate's brother?" Helen asked.

Caught off guard, I stared at her, frowning. "Lock?"

She nodded. "Yeah. He said you were freaked out."

Zadie touched my arm. "Are you okay now?"

"Don't worry about me. I'm always fine." I flashed a big smile at her and winked like a dirty old man. They both kept staring, waiting for me to spill, leaving me no choice. "So, I ran into Oliver Bergen yesterday. He looks exactly like Nate, and yeah, it freaked me out."

Helen made swirly lines in the sand with her fingers. "Do you think he's...like Nate?"

"I don't really know him," I answered. "He's five years older, so we weren't in school together or anything."

Zadie hadn't grown up with Helen and me, but she'd been our roommate for over a year, so she'd heard stories. She knew who Nate was and what a shitty human being he'd been.

"Did he want to talk about his brother?" Zadie asked.

"Not really." I sucked in a breath. "*I* don't want to talk about his brother."

Helen punched her palm. "Sometimes, I'd like to dig up his corpse just to laugh in his face. Fucking loser. Thank god he was the one spoiled little rich boy who got what he deserved."

I turned to her. "You think he deserved to die like that?"

She leveled me with a hard look, her dark eyes scorching. "I think he deserved a hell of a lot worse. Not even for hurting me. I personally know two other girls who were victimized or almost victimized by that sicko. Who knows how many other girls he took from. Do you have some weird sense of loyalty? Some leftover love for your high school sweetheart?"

"No." My lips flattened in a hard line. "Just...from what I heard, it was a pretty terrible accident."

"Good. I hope he suffered. He sure as hell made a lot of girls suffer while he was alive." Helen crossed her arms and rounded on me. "Why does it sound to me like you're defending that asswipe? He's a rapist."

"I know. I know what he was."

I decided right then I wanted her and Zadie to know how well I understood. I didn't want to bite my tongue anymore. Except, I wasn't great with emotions, so it all came out as a sarcastic jumble.

"He raped me the summer after graduation. A week before I left for Berkeley, we had a farewell dinner. After, he walked me to his car, opened the door for me like a perfect gentleman, shoved me in the back seat, and raped me. Thankfully, he's always been a two-pump chump, so it only lasted a minute or two, but there is not a chance I'll ever forget who he was and what he did to me. I remember every little detail, down to the total on the receipt wadded up on the floor behind the driver's seat."

Zadie gasped and immediately got on her knees to hug me. Even though hugging didn't really come naturally to me, I liked hugging Zadie, so I leaned my head into her softness, taking the comfort I knew she had to give to make both of us feel better.

"Elena." Helen blinked at me, her lips parted.

"I don't want pity." I shook my head hard. "I will put stones in my pockets and walk into the ocean if you dare pity me. It happened, and I dealt. I'm dealing."

I had started going to therapy after Nate and I broke up in high school. My therapist had been the second person I called once I was ready to say the words—Pen was first. She had hooked me up with someone I went to daily for a while at Berkeley. I probably could have used some more therapy now, but hey, who couldn't?

Zadie sat back down, but she kept her arm linked with mine. And that was okay, because it wasn't pity, not from her. She was letting me know she was there in her own Zadie way.

"I don't pity you." Helen squeezed her eyes shut. "I'm pissed I can't kill Nate Bergen again."

And I'm pissed I feel even an ounce of guilt for the way he died.

Waves crashed. The boys yelled at each other as Lachlan threw another pass that went a mile long. Someone was playing music halfway down the beach. All that hung in the air with my confession.

"I've only told two people about that night."

Helen's eyes shot to mine. "Really? Why not go to the cops?"

"Why didn't *you*?" I shot back.

"My mom's a piece of shit, and cops don't take the word of girls who come from pieces of shit. You, on the other hand, come from a palace and sprinkle glitter when you walk. Why didn't you tell someone?"

She didn't sound angry at me, more confused. Most people would've been. If they knew anything about my family, it was that we were wealthy and my parents adored me. That was true, but it wasn't the whole story.

"I did. I told Pen and my therapist." I folded my arms around my middle. "Telling anyone else wasn't an option for me."

"Thank you for trusting us enough to tell us," Zadie said.

"I hate like hell that happened to you, El. Hate it so fucking much." Helen bit down on her bottom lip and turned away from me to face the ocean.

If I could have turned away, I would have. I understood Helen. We were girls who had been made to be tough. We'd grown up in different circumstances, but we'd been shaped by the same weight of the world.

"I hate it too." I pulled my legs to my chest and rested my chin on my knees. "Honestly, I thought I was supposed to feel lighter. I'm thinking I got ripped off. I feel exactly the same. I could have just held that in for eternity."

Zadie sputtered a laugh, then quickly covered her mouth. "I'm sorry, I shouldn't laugh."

"You absolutely should." I tugged on one of her curls. "If you stop laughing when I say ridiculous things, I'll have to tell Amir your secret."

Her nose scrunched. "What secret?"

I tilted my head. "Remember the other night when you admitted you don't like when he goes down on you? In fact, you hate having your clit touched and would rather sex be under five minutes?"

Her sweet little mouth morphed into an *O*. "You know I never said that. If you tell him that, I will kill you seven times!"

I threw my head back, cackling. "I will. You'll never get oral again. You know that man lives to please you. Quickies for the rest of your life, Z."

Helen shook her head, her smile returning. "You're truly evil."

I grinned at her. "I know."

"I love oral," Zadie said softly. "Amir's so good at it."

My gaze collided with Helen's, and it was all over. We fell into each other, laughing so hard, tears rolled down my cheeks. Zadie couldn't stop herself from joining in. I didn't think I'd ever laughed so hard in my life. My stomach ached, and I couldn't sit upright, and it was just...good. So, so good.

This. This was the moment the lightness came. It wasn't from the confession, the sadness, trading traumas with Helen. It was the after. When everything slipped back to normal. Except my new normal was better than it ever had been. I'd never had this, laughing freely with my girls. No jealousy or competition between us. We were just three girls thrown together, finding the randomness of *us* made the most sense.

And now, I knew I could probably tell them anything.

Maybe one day I would.

Chapter Seventeen

Elena

"Oh my god, I'm so hungry," Helen groaned.

We were in the parking lot, kicking sand off our feet, ready to head out. I was happily crisp and ready for a nap. But now that Helen mentioned hunger, my stomach let loose a growl so loud, all eyes fell on me.

I rubbed my belly. "The demon that lives within me needs to be fed."

"Makes sense," Marco muttered under his breath. I flipped him off. He drew a heart in the air.

We were becoming such great friends.

Everyone started checking their phones for nearby restaurants while Lachlan stood by his truck. He threw his hat down in the bed and ripped his T-shirt over his head, using it to wipe his sweaty hair. Then he poured water into his hands and splashed it on his face. My tongue almost rolled out of my mouth when he dumped the water over his head, streams sluicing down the sides of his face to his broad chest.

He opened his eyes, finding me staring. He cocked his head. I raised an eyebrow, biting my lip. God, why did I have to be so attracted to this man? It was annoying, considering I couldn't do a damn thing about it. We were done, done, done.

I walked over to him, leaning against the side of his truck. "I swore I just stepped into an eighties hair band video. Only, instead of a writhing woman with big hair, it's a big, sexy lumberjack."

He chuckled as he pulled a fresh T-shirt over his head. "Sexy, huh?" He touched the tip of my nose. "You have freckles."

"The sun always brings them out."

"You look like a California girl."

"Born and bred, baby."

He scanned me from bottom to top. "Are you thinking about covering up?"

I touched my bare stomach and batted my lashes at him. "Not really."

He pulled a T-shirt out of his bag and held it out to me. "Put this on."

I batted his hand away. "Why are you always trying to cover me up?"

Before he could answer, Theo called for him, asking for the name of the diner they'd gone to once. While Lachlan's attention was off me, I drank in my fill of his sun-kissed skin, wishing I could slide my hands under his tee to get to more of it. He turned back to me, finding me staring again. The look he gave me would have been stern if not for the heat behind it.

"You're riding with me," he announced.

"Why? Wait—where are we going?"

He chuckled, pushing me into the passenger seat. I was so used to it now, I went without much resistance. "While you were eye fucking me, everyone else decided where to go eat."

"You're smug. You can't be sure that's what I was doing."

He buckled my seat belt, then dragged his fingertips along my bare belly. My body betrayed me by shivering.

Lachlan smirked like he'd proven something. "I know what I know."

The drive to the beachside diner wasn't long. Once we were there, I hopped out of the truck and grabbed my sundress from Theo's car. I wasn't about to admit I liked riding in Lachlan's truck better than being crammed in the back of Theo's Toyota—but that was solely for the leg room.

Our group found a round corner booth that fit us all, and I ended up wedged between Marco and Lachlan. It wasn't bad, as far as man sandwiches went.

Lachlan was uncharacteristically twitchy, passing the laminated menu back and forth between his hands. I dug my nails into his thigh under the table.

"Stop moving. You're driving me crazy," I hissed.

When he stilled, I started to move my hand away, but he reached down and placed his on top of mine, keeping me there. I didn't have time to process the move before our bubbly, adorable brunette waitress approached the table, her pen and pad poised and ready for action.

"Hey, I'm Emily. Are you ready to or—" Her eyes swept the table and stopped on Lachlan. They went impossibly wide and incredibly bright. "Lachlan! I didn't know you were coming in."

"Em." He inclined his chin. "We're ready to order."

"Oh." Her cheeks went red as she scrambled to hold on to her pen. "Of course. I was just...surprised. It's been a little while, but that's okay, you're here now, and that's great."

As she stood there taking orders, inching closer and closer to Lachlan, her cheeks burned brighter. She kept casting him furtive glances, and when everyone had ordered, she touched his shoulder, whispering how happy she was to see him.

It was obvious to me, and probably everyone at the table, he had fucked her. Maybe he was still fucking her.

No one asked him. He was Lock, the impenetrable wall. If he wanted us to know something, he'd tell us. Otherwise, it was his.

I ripped my hand out from under his and placed it on the table. Jealousy surged from the black pit within me to the surface. It put me on edge with the desire to destroy. If he didn't leave me be, he'd be my first victim.

I took a long drink of my water, crunching a mouthful of ice. Conversation went on around me, but I was numb to it. My mind was too busy scheming, forming ideas of ways to hurt Lachlan, to humiliate poor, blushing Emily.

I could trip her, make her spill a tray of drinks.

Tell her manager I saw her spit in my food.

Inform her her precious *Lachlan* was fucking me too.

I could ruin her—I almost craved it—I didn't even know her.

"Elsa," Lachlan said under his breath. "I can hear you thinking. Stop."

I crunched on my ice and schemed. It was the only way I could stop myself from succumbing to the evil. While part of me wanted to lash out, a bigger part of me hated that this feeling still thrived in me.

I wasn't a kid anymore. I could feel this without acting. Besides, Lachlan wasn't mine, so why did it matter that he'd brought us to a restaurant where one of his hookups worked? It didn't. It was none of my business.

All my ice was gone, and the tension emanating from the giant beside me—who seemed insistent on keeping his bicep pressed against me—was too much for me to bear for even a second longer.

"Let me out," I said lowly.

"Don't," he murmured.

"I have to go to the bathroom," I said loud enough for the table to hear. "Please, let me out before I piss myself."

"Such a lady," Helen teased.

"Why thank you," I replied. "I think Lock must enjoy golden showers since he won't let me out to go to the bathroom."

That got him moving, grumbling in protest as he slid out of the booth. I made a break for it as soon as I was free, striding through the diner to the alcove where the restrooms were. I stayed in the ladies' room as long as I dared, fixing my hair and rubbing some of the sand out of my hairline. My mom wouldn't approve of me being out in public after getting *dirty* at the beach, but she wasn't here, and I looked cute.

Cuter than Emily.

Gah! Why was my brain such a damn twat?

I pulled open the door to leave the bathroom and almost ran smack into the object of my cat-scratch jealousy. Emily was standing just outside the alcove, worrying her bottom lip with her teeth.

"Hey." She shot me a smile. Her cheeks were still rosy, and only deepened as I took her in. She had nice tits. Bigger than mine, for sure. I bet he liked them, the asshole.

"Hi."

"So, you're friends with Lachlan?"

That was it. I was never calling him Lachlan again. She could have the name.

"I know him," I said.

"So...did he...do you know if he came here to see me?" She tucked a curl behind her ear. "I mean, did he mention me?"

My caustic reply was stopped in its tracks when a dark shadow fell over the two of us. We turned to the implacable man whose eyes were pinned on me in accusation. I'd only gone to the bathroom, so he had nothing to accuse me of. But since he always thought the worst of me, he'd probably come up with something.

"Ellie, time to go back to the table." He gripped my nape. "Come on."

"Lachlan, I—"

He cut Emily off with one look. She flinched backward, hitting the counter. I almost felt sorry for her, when moments before I'd been contemplating how to accidentally spill an entire bottle of ketchup on her head.

He led me away from an open-mouthed Emily so fast, I stumbled over my feet. That was the danger in wearing flip-flops. When being manhandled by large men, they became a tripping hazard.

"You're going to relax," he said in a smooth, sure tone, as if it were fact.

"Have you met me?" I uttered.

"*Relax.*"

"Stop trying to boss me."

He sighed heavily. "We're talking when we get home."

"There's nothing to say."

"I think there is. We're talking."

Our friends were staring as we approached the booth. I guessed me being led back to the table like a naughty puppy wasn't an everyday sight. He let me go so I could sit down, but instead of returning to my seat between him and Marco, I kept going, climbing over Marco's lap to squeeze myself between him and Zadie.

"Daddy scolded me for taking too long in the bathroom," I told our gawking friends. "I've learned my lesson and won't ever do it again."

"Oh my god," Zadie whispered.

"I know, right?" I whispered back. "That guy's a weirdo."

When Lachlan finally sat down, Marco scooted closer to me, draping his arm over the back of the booth. "Is your man going to kill me for this?" he murmured.

"No, but I will if you imply he's my man again," I replied, not bothering to keep my voice low. The jealousy monster down at the bottom of the darkest part of me was being fed a feast right now, loving that I'd allowed it to take over and act out, if only a little bit.

"Well, this isn't awkward at all." Helen rested her chin on her hand and pointed back and forth between me and Lock. "What's the deal here?"

I shrugged. "You'll have to ask Lock."

"No deal." His rough denial cut off any further comments.

I spent the rest of our meal ignoring Lock and the questioning looks from my friends. For their part, once the food came—delivered by a silent and contrite Emily—they moved on without further acknowledging the weirdness that had settled over us.

Not satisfied in the slightest from the few bites I'd managed to choke down, I hooked my arm through Marco's as we exited the cursed diner. At least I got some satisfaction out of this act of defiance.

It had felt that way, until I noticed Lock wasn't with us in the parking lot. Through the salt-smeared windows, I spotted Lock pulling Emily aside, their cloudy figures close together. His head was bent toward hers as he spoke to her. Her chin was raised as she stared up at him with hopeful eyes.

My stomach lurched. My destructive urges flowed through me like lava. If I didn't get out of here, fast, I'd give in to them. I hated Lock for making me revert to my old ways, powerless over my own brain.

Except, that wasn't true. I still had the power. I chose not to give in and destroy. Theo and Helen were already headed toward his car. I broke away from Marco, skittering after them through the parking lot.

"I'm riding with you guys," I called.

They stopped and waited for me. Theo opened the door, and I crammed myself into the back seat. When she got settled and Theo rolled out of the parking lot, Helen turned around, sweeping me over with narrowed eyes.

"You have a thing for Lock, huh?" She said it so bluntly, without emotion or pity, I didn't even think to deny it.

"I'll get over it." And I would. I got over things. I moved on. It was what I did these days.

She smacked my knee. "He's dumb if he doesn't recognize how hot and badass you are, dude."

I shrugged. "Silly me for crushing on yet another dumb boy."

Theo eyed me in the rearview mirror. "For what it's worth, he was pretty reluctant to tell me the name of the diner when we were trying to figure out where to eat after the beach. I don't think he wanted to run into her."

I met his gaze. "Do you know who she is?"

He hesitated. When Helen pinched his bicep, he answered. "He found the diner on one of his drives. He took me there once. Emily was working. I got the impression they had hooked up. But that was last year. I haven't heard anything about her since."

I leaned my head against the window. "It's fine. I don't even care."

They let me be after that.

Thankfully.

Lachlan: *Come out back. Let's talk.*

It wasn't late by college student standards, but I was already in bed. Days at the beach, confessing one of my darkest secrets, and battling back my base instincts always wiped me out.

I'd done my post-sun skin routine, lotioning myself until I was as slick as a baby seal. After it soaked in, I slid into my favorite satin nightgown and tucked myself into bed with a horror flick playing on my laptop.

Early 2000s murder porn always relaxed me.

One text from Lock ruined all of it—which reminded me to change his contact name on my phone. No more Lachlan. That was Emily's now.

Me: *Actually, I'm fine where I am. Have a nice weekend.*
Lock: *We need to talk.*
Me: *I don't want to talk.*
Lock: *Too damn bad. Your reaction today told me we definitely need to talk.*
Me: *Oh, go gloat to someone who cares. I'm not coming out there so you can let me down gently. I know where we stand. You don't need to apologize for not wanting me. I get it. You're off the hook.*

Sense came over me, and I deleted that text before I could send it. I would have never been able to show my face again if I had.

Lock: *I see you typing. Come out and talk. It's easier.*
Me: *No. Good night.*
Lock: *El, stop being stubborn. Let me settle you.*
Me: *That is...wow. The ego on you. I'm in bed, Lock. I was half asleep before you texted. I'm so settled. I'll say it again: good night.*

Minutes passed before my phone vibrated again. I made myself wait through a gory murder scene before I checked it.

Lock: *I'm glad you're settled, Ellie. Good night.*

Settled was the opposite of what I was feeling, but I'd always been good at pretending. If it meant Lock would give me space so I'd have a chance to get over him, I'd keep faking it for as long as I had to.

If he kept calling me Ellie and taking care of me like he had the day before, it was going to take a *lot* of faking it.

Good thing that was something I was an expert at—ask any of my ex-boyfriends.

Chapter Eighteen

Lock

I didn't get the talk I wanted, but on Tuesday, I *did* get woken up at three a.m. by a series of texts.

Ellie: *I need help.*

Ellie: *I need to borrow a wrench. One that will fit a water pipe.*

Ellie: *You can leave it on your porch. I'll be over in five minutes. If it's not there, I'll assume you don't have one.*

Ellie: *Or you could be sleeping. Either way, I'll form plan B.*

When she showed up five minutes later, her silver hair glinting like the moon against the midnight-black sky, I was sitting on my porch waiting for her, toolbox at my side.

"Not the tool I was looking for," she said dryly.

I patted my toolbox. "What do you need a wrench for?"

"Do you have one I can use?"

"I do. Tell me what it's for."

Through the dark, she leveled me with a glare. "Murder."

My lips twitched. "Then you'll need a shovel to bury the body."

She huffed, approaching the bottom step. Her hair was swept up in a braid that was tucked into the neck of my hoodie. If she had pants on, they were hidden. With her, it was fifty-fifty, pants or no pants.

She huffed with impatience. "It's kind of time sensitive. Just give me the wrench."

"If it's time sensitive, then you'll accept my help without arguing."

Arms folded, her foot tapped on the ground. One, two, three. "Fine. You're driving, though."

"Never doubted it."

I threw my toolbox in the back seat and climbed in. Normally, I would have gotten Elena secured first, but she buckled herself in faster than I could get to her. That bothered me more than I cared to admit.

She directed me to an address two streets over. "It's one of my rentals. A pipe under a bathroom sink is spraying water. I want to try to fix it myself before shelling out for an emergency plumber."

I glanced at her as I drove. We were the only ones on the street. "You know how to fix leaky pipes?"

"I've watched YouTube videos. I take my job as property manager seriously. I wanted to be able to do the basics for cases like this, I just don't have all the tools I need. That was my mistake."

"Good thing I'm here."

"I could've done it."

That made me grin. "I don't doubt it. I'm glad to help, though."

We pulled up to a house similar to mine. A red-haired girl opened the door before we even made it up the walk.

"Thank you for coming so fast," she called.

As soon as we were inside the door, she led us through the house and upstairs into the hall bathroom. There were towels everywhere and a steady stream of water coming from under the sink.

I sank down on my haunches, and El joined me on her knees, sticking her head under the counter. She looked good like that, her sweet ass in the air. I tried not to stare for long. That wasn't what she needed from me, and it definitely wasn't what I should've been doing.

I waited to see what she'd do first, giving her the chance to have the independence she craved. When she twisted the shut-off valve without a second's hesitation, I grinned.

As if sensing it, her head turned sharply in my direction. "What? Don't smile. I'm not a complete imbecile."

I had to hold back a laugh. Even when she was spitting venom, she got to me. That was an unexpected as hell turn of events.

The redhead hovered at the door, wringing her hands. "My roommate's girlfriend has a bladder the size of a walnut. Thank goodness. She walked in here to use the bathroom and got blasted. We would have had a flood if she hadn't been up in the middle of the night. But I guess we weren't thinking. We should have shut off the water before we called. I'm sorry."

Elena glanced back at her, offering a practiced smile. "I should have told you to do that over the phone. That's my fault."

"We'll fix it," I assured her. "We'll let you know when we're done."

Elena opened my toolbox like it was hers and searched through it. She might've watched some YouTube videos, and if I wasn't here, she would have figured it out. I *was* here, though, and I wasn't going to let her struggle.

Reaching around her, I picked up the wrench I needed. Elena tried to snatch it from me, but I held it by my side. She scowled, a tiny wrinkle forming between her light eyebrows. If she had any idea how adorable she looked when she was pissed off at me, she'd probably make it her goal to be sweet to spite me.

"Watch me this time. Let me show you, then next time, you can do it."

Her lips pursed. "Why do you think you get a say?"

"My tools, I get a say. Should we do this or waste more time arguing?"

With a heavy sigh, she waved me on. I worked, and she watched. If I was being honest, I took my time, because I was enjoying her attention. She lowered her head close to mine, studying my hands like she was memorizing my movements.

"Is this your first middle-of-the-night call?" I asked.

"Mmmhmm."

"Your dad expects you to do repairs?"

"I asked him to make me the property manager. It's a real job to me, so it doesn't matter what he expects. As property manager, repairs are my responsibility."

"He probably wouldn't like knowing you were out in the middle of the night like this."

The idea of her doing this without me drove a spike through my temple. Maybe I didn't want to teach her so she'd have to call me. It didn't sit well with me to allow her to enter strangers' houses on her own.

"My dad doesn't need to know," she answered.

I nodded as I turned the wrench. "You could hire someone. Nothing says you have to get your hands dirty."

"I told you, I don't mind getting my hands dirty. And when it comes to my properties, I'm not going to waste money on something I can do myself. Besides, I want to count on as few people as possible. I'll be buying my own set of wrenches after this."

My eyes slid to her. Her bottom lip was tucked between her teeth while she concentrated on my hands. "So you don't have to count on me."

This side of her sent me into a tailspin. It wasn't that I didn't like when she was in her silky pj's or feminine sundresses with perfect hair and makeup. Being attracted to Elena had never been in question—not since the second I'd laid eyes on her. I could walk away from attraction, not think anything of it. But when she shared how her mind worked, the dichotomy of her personality, the parts of her that resonated strongly with me—that made it almost impossible not to take her face in my hands and kiss the living hell out of her.

"Mmmhmm. So I don't have to count on you." Yeah, I'd burned a lot of bridges with her. No surprise there. It wasn't like I hadn't seen the flames.

"How does a senator's son know his way around pipes and power tools?"

I shrugged. "My dad's like you—he does as much as he can on his own. As for me, I've been fixing things for as long as I can remember. I like to know how things work, how machines run, and if they're broken, what it'll take to make them right again. My dad showed me what he knew, and I learned the rest by doing."

I tossed the wrench in my toolbox and wiped my hands on my legs. The water on the floor had soaked through my sweatpants, but it didn't bother me much.

"The coupling came loose. No reason that I can see. Turn the water on and see if it sprays. If it doesn't, I think you might have been lucky and had an easy fix."

Elena stretched under the sink, ducking her head beneath the counter. Like an asshole, I didn't move, so the side of her was pressed against the front of me. Her muscles flexed as she twisted the valve, turning the water back on. The pipes clanked, but no spray.

"It's fixed?" she asked.

"Looks like it." I wrapped my fingers around her arm and placed a hand on top of her head, helping her slide out from under the counter without bumping.

"Thank you." Her eyes flicked up to the hand on top of her head, and something indiscernible passed over her features before they flattened out. "We should go. Maybe you can go back to sleep."

I didn't tell her once I was up, there was no going back to sleep. I just packed up my tools and followed her downstairs.

The redhead was in the living room, sitting on the couch, her chin on her chest. Her eyes were closed, so she must've dozed off. I cleared my throat, startling her awake.

"Sorry." I rubbed the back of my neck. "We're all done. You should be good."

"Oh, god, thank you so much." She hopped up, pressing her hands together under her chin, flashing a happy smile directly at me. "You have no idea how much I appreciate you coming out here in the middle of the night. You saved me."

Elena stepped forward, putting herself between me and the redhead. "That's my job. Let me know if you have any other problems."

Redhead's brow furrowed. Her eyes darted around Elena's face like she was trying to place her. Then she shook it off and smiled brightly. "Ah—okay. Thanks so much."

One precise nod of her head, then Elena swiveled on her toes, marching for the front door. I tipped my chin and followed.

It was still dark out, maybe four in the morning at the latest. The roads were silent, houses pitch black.

I followed Elena to the passenger side of my truck, putting my toolbox on the ground before opening her door. She climbed up herself, but again, I put my hand on top of her head and the other on her lower back until she was seated. Reaching across her, I belted her in, catching her warm, summer-lemon scent.

She let her head fall back on the rest, staring up at me, unreadable as ever. "Are you going to make me talk to you?"

"I don't want to make you do anything. I'd like you to listen, and since you're being stubborn, I'm going to talk while I have you as a captive audience."

"Then talk." She tucked her hands in her pockets, turning her head to look out her window.

With a sigh, I put the truck in gear, slowly pulling onto the road. "Yesterday shouldn't have happened. If I thought for a second Emily still worked there, I wouldn't have given Theo the name. You've accused me of playing games with you, and though I don't think I have, I admit to my signals not being as clear as they should be. That's because nothing is clear to me when it comes to you. But one thing you can be certain of is I would never put you in a position where you have to share space with a woman I've been with. Not purposely."

"Poor Emily was so sad, Lock." No inflection. The sass had drained right out of her. It could've been because of the hour, but I didn't like it, whatever the cause.

"We don't need to talk about her. I settled things with her—things that were already settled—and that's done. I need to settle things with you. I'm not going to assume you were jealous, but I know you weren't comfortable. I'm sorry for that."

"Forgiven." It came out so rote, there was no telling if she meant it or not.

Probably not, if I was a betting man.

"Ellie...fuck." I knocked my fist to my forehead. "I keep making missteps with you and it's driving me crazy. I don't know which way is up or down."

"You should work on that." Our houses came into view. She sucked in a deep breath and slowly exhaled. "Thanks for your help, Lock."

"Lachlan," I grunted, pulling into my driveway.

"Hmmm?"

My hand shot out, covering hers to stop her from unbuckling. "You call me Lachlan."

"*She* called you Lachlan. That's her name. I relinquish it."

I pressed the button on her buckle, releasing her. Instead of letting her go, I caught her by the nape and hauled her across the bench seat into my lap. She was wedged against the steering wheel, hissing and slapping at me.

"You're so...so...infuriating," she cried. "Just because you can put me wherever you want doesn't mean you get to do it *whenever* you want."

Catching her wrists in one hand, I lowered them to her lap and brought my free hand up to cup her warm cheek. Her lip curled in a snarl, even as her head leaned into my palm. I didn't think she even realized she was doing it.

"Listen to me, Ellie. Every damn time that girl called me Lachlan, I corrected her. I'm Lock. That's what everyone calls me. I didn't give her that name."

She twisted her arms, trying to break free, but I held her steady. "If you hate it so much, why didn't you correct me?"

"Would you have stopped if I'd asked you to?"

Her lips parted, then pressed together. She shook her head.

"I didn't think so." My thumb stroked along the side of her nose and cheekbone. "But here's the thing: I never wanted you to stop. I like how it sounds coming out of your mouth. If you're not going to give me that because you think it belongs to someone else, then I'm going to have to convince you otherwise."

Her eyes dragged from my mouth up to meet mine. "Why are you doing this? Why do you care what I call you?"

I slowly shook my head. "You think I know? I told you, up is down with you. The only thing that makes sense is keeping you close and my name coming from your pretty mouth."

"You think my mouth is pretty, Lock?"

"It's Lachlan to you." My thumb went to her lips, pressing on the full, rosy bottom one. "You know your mouth is pretty."

"What do you want?" she asked on a sigh.

"Right now?"

"Sure, if that's the only answer you have."

I dipped my head, grazing my nose against hers. "Right now, I want to move my hand and replace it with my mouth. I want to take some of that sweet out of you and suck it down. I want you to give it to me."

She caught my thumb, biting me just hard enough to pinch. Her tongue darted out to soothe the rough pad. She might as well have been tonguing my dick for all the blood that surged below my waist.

"Even though I'm bad for you?"

She didn't require an answer. Her lips met mine in a slow, teasing kiss. I let her lead and explore. She sucked on my bottom lip, using her teeth to nip and taste.

"Let go of my hands," she murmured.

"I didn't remember I was holding them."

As soon as her hands were free, they were under my shirt, sliding from my stomach to my chest. She rubbed along the width of my shoulders, kneading lightly. Her hands were so damn soft and fine, but they weren't shy. She went where she wanted, without asking permission.

Her mouth was on my neck, sucking at the corner of my jaw. It was all I could do to sit there, running the silk of her braid between my fingers. I wanted her straddling me, pressing the heat between her thighs against me. But there was something about *not* doing that, about Elena taking, me giving, in the dark of my truck, that satisfied the rabid beast inside me.

Her lips caressed the underside of my jaw, moving in a line to my chin, before finally finding mine again. I cupped the back of her head and opened my eyes to find her already staring at me.

"Do you want to come inside?" she asked.

"Yeah, I do, but I'm not going to." I patted her thigh. "Open, baby."

"Why?"

"Because I'm going to get you off then send you to bed."

She sucked in a breath. "That easy?"

Palm on her inner thigh, I pressed. She let her legs fall open for me and pulled her hoodie up so I could get to her skin.

I couldn't stop the smugness from showing on my face, but she was watching my hands anyway. I slipped one into the elastic band of her loose running shorts, finding her bare and hot. Equal parts alarm and desire shot through me.

Cupping her, I nudged her face back with my chin. "You were going to walk into that house, alone, without underwear? Do you know how crazy that makes me?"

She tugged on my bottom lip with her teeth, a delicate growl vibrating her throat. "Don't tease me, Lock."

My answering growl was anything but delicate. "It's Lachlan to you."

"Make me come and I'll think about it."

My middle finger nudged her clit. "Is this where you want me? Or do you want my fingers inside you, fucking you until you're shaking in my arms?"

She gripped my wrist, holding me against her. "My clit. I want you to rub it with that rough finger. I still remember how it felt—"

The calloused pad of my finger swirled over her swollen little bud. Her mouth fell open, sucking in a sharp breath. I took my opportunity to sweep my tongue between her lips, taking the taste of sweet I'd been craving since I walked away from her. Elena moaned into my mouth, going so pliant, it was only me holding her up. Not that I minded. Not even a little. Causing this prickly girl to go docile from pleasure could be an addiction.

Her mouth broke from mine. She stared at me with a creased brow, panting lightly.

"What, Ellie? Tell me what you need from me." I was too gruff, but holding back took a lot of effort, too much to be worried about being nice.

"Kiss me. Kiss me, kiss me, kiss me, Lachlan."

Her mouth crashed into mine, fingers tangling in my hair, tugging me down to her level. Her tongue coaxed mine out to battle, clashing with wet slides and whimpers until she gave in and I took over. I fucked her mouth, plunged a finger into her pussy, and rolled her sweet, needy clit under my fingertip. She clung, her elbows on my shoulders, hands and fingers digging in my hair.

She rode my hand until her inner walls tightened, fluttering around me. Her plush ass rose and fell on my lap. My cock was in agony. The denial I was forcing on myself wasn't making much sense, not with my sweet girl writhing in my arms, holding on to me like she had no plans of ever letting go.

"Beautiful." My lips grazed hers. My movements slowed, but she still held on to me. "So fucking beautiful."

Her head crashed into my chest and stayed as her breathing slowed. "How do you do that?"

"Do what?"

"Get me off so easily? You have a gift."

"What do you mean, baby?" I was still cupping her between her legs, in no rush to part from her in any way. "Your body lights up the second I get my hands on you. That part has never been a challenge between us."

She blew out a breath, warming my chest through my T-shirt. "Never mind." She knocked her forehead into me a few times. "I'm going to go back to bed now. I'm pretty sure I'll be able to sleep, you know, if I can make it up the stairs."

"Want me to carry you?"

I felt her smile before she shook her head. "What would my roommates think if they saw? No, I can make it. I'll crash on the porch if I'm too weak for the steps."

At my entire body stiffening, she snickered. She'd been messing with me.

I tugged on her braid. "You think you're funny?"

Raising her head, she shot me a sassy-as-hell grin. "I know I am." She nodded toward my hand down her pants. "Do you think you've made friends with her? Can you let her go?"

"I'm just getting started on making friends with her, but I'll let both of you go for now." One last swipe on her clit, earning me a tremble and a whine, I released her.

Elena slid off my lap and across the bench seat. She wasn't moving fast, too pleasure drunk and lethargic—exactly how I liked her. I was able to make it around the truck to help her out. She raised a brow at me, then shot a pointed glance at the bulge in my pants.

"What are you going to do with that?" she asked.

"Ignore it. If you keep looking at it like that, it won't go away."

"You're not going to tell me to drop to my knees?"

The genuine confusion in her question was a knife to my skull. It told me a lot about the men Elena had let into her life before me. That ended here and now.

I dragged her into me, tipping her chin to meet her wide eyes. "I'm never going to tell you to do something with your body unless we're both on board with playing that kind of game. If you're going to drop to your knees, it'll be because you want to. *That's* what gets me hard and gets me off."

She reached out, palming the ridge of my cock. "So, *if* I went down on my knees right here in the driveway, you'd turn me down? No one will see, Lachlan. There's no one around."

It was as easy as breathing for me to drag her hand off me. Not that I didn't want her touching me, sucking me, swallowing me whole. I did. *Fuck*, I did.

But not like this.

And not now.

I pressed a kiss to the center of her palm. "Come on. Let's get you inside. You look tired."

I knew what I'd said when I'd said it. Instead of getting pissed at being turned down, she was pissed I said she looked tired. Living with my mom and Saoirse, I'd learned a thing or two about women, and they really didn't fucking like being told they looked tired.

Elena stomped across the grass just ahead of me. I followed her onto her porch, crowding her as she unlocked her door. Before she stepped inside, I spun her around and pressed her back into the jamb.

"Are you going to bed?" I asked.

"Maybe."

"Are you pissed at me?"

Her nose wrinkled. "I'm not sure."

"You're not. Are you going to let me give you a ride after Spanish without fighting me?"

"We'll see."

"You will." Stooping, I touched my mouth to hers, holding there for a long beat before letting go. Then I took her by her shoulders and pushed her into the house. "Good night, Ellie."

She closed the door harder than necessary. I stayed until I heard all the locks click. Rubbing the back of my neck, I trudged back home.

I should have been pissed at myself for going there with Elena again.

I should have been troubled.

I should have been forming a way to tell her it was all a mistake.

The only thing on my mind was how perfect she was when she went soft with me and how I'd denied both of us long enough. No more of that.

I pulled my truck in the garage and replaced my toolbox, then I popped the hood. The truck was good, but my hands needed something to do to calm down, so I got to work checking over everything.

There was always something to fix.

CHAPTER NINETEEN

ELENA

THERE WAS GUM IN my hair. Not at the bottom either. A huge wad of gum was lodged in the very center of the back of my head. I was fuckity fucked.

Throwing open the front door of my house, I screamed. "My hair! They fucked with my hair!"

No one was home, so I was screaming to the walls, because of course. It was probably for the best that Zadie and Helen missed my tantrum anyway. They would laugh at me forever if they saw me throwing all the pillows off the couch and kicking them around the living room.

I was just about to let loose another scream of fury when the door burst open. Lachlan filled the doorway. His head swiveled until he found me, surrounded by a pile of throw pillows, probably looking as manic as I felt.

"I heard screaming." He prowled toward me, his focus so intent, I was pinned in place. "Are you hurt? What happened?"

Oh no. This was worse than Zadie and Helen witnessing my fit. Far worse. I wanted this man to fuck me, not put a pacifier in my mouth.

But dammit, I was pissed off, and if I didn't destroy a few things, I'd explode.

"I'm not hurt, I'm furious." I kicked another pillow, sending it flying at Lachlan. He caught it with one hand, putting it gently on the couch. When had he rounded the sectional? How had I not noticed him moving?

"Come here," he commanded.

I crossed my arms and shook my head. "I'm not done destroying things."

He beckoned me closer, his arm outstretched. "Get over here, Elsa."

"I'm too angry to come there. Go away so I can let out my anger in private. You don't need to see this."

He jabbed at the floor in front of him. "I'm not arguing. If I have to come get you, I'll make good on my promise."

"What promise?"

His brow lowered. His eyes went impossibly dark, giving him a menacing air that sent a thrill down my spine. "Gonna light that defiant ass up, El. Spank all the sass and venom out of you."

My toes curled into the hardwood below him. My entire body listed in his direction. I would have gone to him, let him set me straight, but then I remembered the gum in my hair—and there was nothing sexy about that.

"I can't," I whined.

"You can. Let me make it better."

I took a step. Then another. "You can't spank me right now. I'm not up for that."

His chin dipped as he tracked me crossing the room. "Then I won't. You need to come here anyway and tell me what's making you murder pillows."

This man. This man, this man, this man. He made it really hard to hate him, even though I sort of wanted to. I thought for sure he'd follow me inside when he drove me home after Spanish yesterday—especially when he kept his hand high on my thigh the whole ride.

But Lachlan Kelly wasn't easy.

He'd pulled up in front of my house, opened the door for me, and pecked my nose.

Pecked my motherflipping nose. And wouldn't you know it, my dumb ass nearly swooned, it was so adorable.

Since when did I do adorable?

Since this big, beautiful man gave it to me, that's when.

What he didn't give me was the D. After that peck, he informed me he had to go back to campus to work. I'd had to hold myself back from slapping him.

Yes, Lachlan turned me into a maniac.

No, I would not let him see how much of a maniac.

Well, that had been the plan until he'd walked in on me kicking pillows, my hair sticking out in all directions. He was catching quite the vivid glimpse of maniacal me.

I pressed myself to his chest, and his arms closed around me. His mouth touched the top of my head, and suddenly, I didn't give a shit about the gum or my hair. That was how good his hugs were.

"Who am I killing?" he asked.

A surprised giggle slipped out. "What?"

"Like when you laugh like that, all sweet and soft." He tipped my chin with his knuckle. "Who fucked with you? Did someone touch you? Give me names."

I took his hand from my chin and moved it to the back of my head. He stilled when he felt it, frowning in confusion. Gently gripping my shoulders, he turned me around.

"Is there...gum in your hair?" Confusion laced his voice. He hadn't yet come to the conclusion that I wouldn't possibly put gum in my own hair.

"There is."

"Wha—?" He spun me back around, scowling now. "Are you telling me—did someone do this to you?"

I nodded. "I don't even know how they did it, but yeah, the sneaky little bitches in my class are responsible for this. If I don't murder pillows, I'll murder people."

Everyone had been leaving class at once. Abby had positioned herself in front of me with Kayleigh and the Pi Sig boys behind. Something touched my hair, but I hadn't really thought much of it since we were bumping elbows and shoulders at the same time. When I got outside and absently ran a hand over my hair, I knew exactly what had happened.

Those petty ass bitches had hit me right where it hurt the most. They couldn't embarrass me, and Professor Seavers wouldn't stand by while they hurt me again, so they'd found my soft underbelly and a-fucking-ttacked.

I wasn't too proud to admit to being a vain little lamb. My hair was my precious. My Prada could burn—god forbid—but I'd recover as long as I had my hair. I spent several fortunes on highlights four times yearly and could feed a small country with the products I used to keep it healthy and thick. Kayleigh and Abby knew that. When we'd been "friends" last year, I'd told those twats which products to use on their skanky hair and brassy highlights.

"What the fuck, Elena!" Lachlan's ruddy cheeks reddened. "Someone purposely did this to you?"

"Girls who don't like me." I reached behind my head to touch the tangled mess. "Shit. I can't cut this. I'll have a bald patch."

My head fell into his chest. He squeezed me tight, rumbling so low, it felt like he was purring. Strangely, I found it soothing, so I stayed there, letting him hug me and rumble at me when I should have been solving my problem.

"I'll get it out for you," he said. "You have peanut butter?"

I smirked into his T-shirt. "You need a sandwich before getting to work?"

Chuckling low, he patted my butt. "No, sweet girl. I'm going to use it to get the gum out of your hair."

Pulling back, I arched a brow. "Sweet girl now? Really?"

He dragged his thumb along my brow. "You're being sweet now, all snuggled up to me."

I didn't know what to do with that, so I ignored it. "How do you know how to remove gum from hair?"

"I have a little sister. Saoirse has gotten a number of things stuck in her hair in her lifetime. My mom never had the patience to try to get it out, so I took over the job." He lifted a shoulder like it was no big deal. "Are you going to let me fix you?"

I nodded. "If you can."

We ended up on the deck, me on a cushion on the ground, Lachlan in a chair. He positioned me facing away from him between his spread legs. He was working through my hair with incredible patience, using a comb and peanut butter to remove the gum bit by bit.

"I'm never going to be able to explain how grateful I am that you're doing this," I said.

"You don't have to explain. You have pretty hair. You don't want it ruined. I get that."

I tried to look back at him, but he cupped the sides of my head and turned me back around.

"You think my hair is pretty?"

"Mmm." He combed in silence for a minute, maybe two, before really giving me an answer. "When I first laid eyes on you, I was in your old dorm, hanging with Helen. You'd charged into the room, and the first thing I'd noticed was your silver-blonde braid. It was like a fucking rope over your shoulder. You looked like Elsa, you know, from *Frozen*. That was my first thought."

I wanted to turn to look at him again, but he was having none of it. That was okay, though. Now, I knew he never thought my name was Elsa. He just thought I looked like her—which honestly, was adorable.

Gah, again with the adorable!

"You took off like a rocket," I said.

"Mmm. Didn't think I liked you."

"Nice."

"I'm sitting here, removing gum from your hair, baby. I think it's obvious I was wrong."

"Now you like me?" I was fishing, but I wanted him to say it, especially after admitting to *not* liking me at first glance—which, damn, smarted more than it should have.

"Again, I'm removing gum from your hair. Yeah, I like you."

I leaned my head against his knee and closed my eyes. I probably should have been riding my fury or plotting my revenge, but that was the last thing on my mind. Lachlan's gentle hands in my hair and his steady combing went a long way to working me out of my anger.

He settled me. He had that way about him, something I was missing, and seemed more than willing to freely give to me.

"Tell me who did this to you." His tenor was low and smooth, but the violence that burned at the edges was unmissable.

I sighed, lifting my head. "There are a few people in my New Ventures course who don't like me very much. Pi Sig boys and their girlies. They don't scare me, and now I'll know better than to let them anywhere near me."

His hands stopped moving in my hair. "Is that the class where you got hurt a few weeks ago?"

"Um." I really didn't want to answer him. He didn't need to be my white knight. This bitch was packing her very own pink bat.

"It is. Did they push you?"

"Lock, babe, you don't have to worry about me. I've got it covered."

His hand came around my jaw, tilting my head back to look up at him. "I don't mind you calling me babe, but if you say Lock again, I'm not going to be happy."

"You're very particular for a rugged, lumberjack mechanic. I never would have guessed."

The corners of his mouth quirked. "Just when it comes to you."

"Good," I whispered.

He'd put me back in a trance, combing and combing that massive piece of gum away. He was so careful with my hair, rarely even pulling it. I was going to smell like peanut butter forever, but at least I wouldn't have a bald spot.

"I'm not really a lumberjack," he said.

"No? A mountain man then."

He chuckled. "That might be more accurate."

"How did you end up at Savage U? You don't—"

"Fit?"

I nodded. There was no denying Lachlan stuck out like a sore thumb. A very hot sore thumb I wanted to ride until I passed out...

"My parents went here. They liked it, and I didn't have a strong affinity for any other school, so I applied, got accepted, here I am."

"I never wanted to come here. I wanted out of this town," I told him.

"I have a hard time believing you couldn't find your way out. What happened?"

There was no way I was confessing everything to him. No way. Telling Zadie and Helen had been bad enough. I'd caught them giving me sad eyes a couple times since the beach. If Lachlan looked at me any different, I wouldn't be able to deal. There'd be murder pillows, murder walls, maybe even murder dick.

I shrugged like my mind wasn't full of chaotic murder plots. "I went to Berkeley for a year. Turned out, it wasn't my vibe."

"You're a beach girl. Freckles on your nose, salt on your skin," he murmured.

"It's true. I missed the beach. I missed my family. My dad had to actually give my mother his full attention the year I was gone. I don't know if he'll ever let me leave again."

"Townie for life, huh?"

Grinning, I tucked my head against his knee again. "Definitely not for life. That's extreme. We'll see where I wind up when I graduate. What about you? Not a beach boy, huh?"

"Nah, not a beach boy. I'll be in Wyoming, working my family ranch with my dad."

My nose wrinkled. "A ranch? I don't even know what that means. Do you grow crops?"

"We have livestock. Cattle." His knuckles smoothed along my cheek. "It means a thirty-thousand-acre ranch where we have two large herds of cattle and a couple hundred horses."

"A *ranch*." The concept was so foreign, I didn't even know how to respond.

"I can't wait to get back there."

"What's so good about ranching? And Wyoming? Until this moment, I wasn't certain it was a real state. Actually, I'm still having trouble believing it."

His chuckle was thunderous and rich. "What else would it be, you loon?"

"A vast conspiracy, obviously."

He tipped my head back again, giving me a look that was unreadable. When his mouth twitched then curved, I was pretty sure that meant he liked me.

"It's real. More real than a lot of places I've been. The part I like most is that every day is different, but there's enough of the same to make it feel like home. The air is fresh, the skies are clear, the land is honest."

"Do you ride a horse?" I asked.

"Yeah, I have a horse I always ride when I'm there. His name's Ramses."

"Ramses must be massive."

Lachlan burst out laughing. "You're right. He's a goddamn beast."

I nuzzled into his leg, trying to picture this giant man on his giant horse. I couldn't quite see it. Maybe he'd send me a picture one day when he was in all his ranching glory.

It was absolutely insane that my stomach twinged. Lachlan would be leaving and never looking back, but that was almost two years away, and we weren't even really...anything.

"I can't see you ever being happy working in an office."

"No, never," he said softly. "I have to be outside, or at least fixing things with my hands."

"You're fixing me."

And that was why I was having twinges. I was attached to him because of reasons that had more to do with me than him.

He gave my hair a gentle tug. "Do you know how good it makes me feel to take your problem into my hands and make it right? Damn good, Ellie."

More twinges.

The sliding glass door whooshed open behind us. "Oh my god, what in the peanut butter is going on out here?" Helen appeared in front of us, sweeping her eyes from Lock to me. "This is a very unsettling tableau."

I waggled my brows at her, thanking all that was Prada for Helen's well-timed intrusion. I needed to be a bitch after being sweet for too long.

"Oooh, *tableau*. Was that your word of the day on your calendar this morning?"

She shook her head, the corners of her red mouth curling with evil. "No, it was twatwaffle. It was kind of funny, because the illustration next to the definition bore an uncanny resemblance to you. I'd sue if I were you. But I guess you don't really have grounds for defamation because everyone knows you're a—"

I kicked her in the shin. "Shut up, floozy, or I'll have Lachlan throw peanut butter at you."

"I'm not throwing anything," he intoned.

Her hands went to her hips. "Care to explain?"

I waved my hand around my head. "I have gum in my hair. Lachlan was kind enough to offer his expertise in removing it. The end."

Her hip cocked. "Last I heard, there was tension. All better?"

"All better," Lachlan replied.

"He let me borrow his wrench, so I forgave him. I think I got the short end of the stick, but who's counting?"

Helen pointed to Lachlan's knee, which was currently the resting place of my head. "This looks cozy."

"It is." In truth, I'd been concentrating on the twinges and had completely forgotten how we were sitting. Snuggling Lachlan's knee was most likely suspicious, but I was hoping Helen would be the cool girl she was and let it slide.

"So..." She pulled up a chair and parked herself in it. Right in front of us. "What is happening here? I'm invested."

I flicked my nails in an attempt to drive her away with my indifference. "Lachlan was just telling me about his family ranch. There's cattle. Two different types. I didn't even know—"

"Yooo!" Marco leaned over the railing of the deck next door. "No one told me the party's at the girls' house." He jogged over in that way guys do that was actually slower than walking. He made it look good, though.

Marco pinched his nose when he arrived. "Holy shit. I'm about to go into anaphylaxis. What is happening?"

Helen looked up at him. "You're not actually allergic, are you? Because you're in the splash zone. I've already been threatened."

I lifted my head off Lachlan's knee. Cozy time was over. "Where's Phantom?"

Marco's face was blank for a moment before he realized I was referring to Julien. I forgot not everyone knew my nickname for him.

Marco cocked his head toward the other house. "Jules is doing some homework like a good, boring boy. The kid isn't the most entertaining company."

"Well, we're making peanut butter and hair sandwiches over here," Helen said dryly. "By the way, how in the hell did you get gum in the back of your hair? Did you fall asleep with it in your mouth or something?"

"She didn't do it to herself." Lachlan's tone was menacing. Shivers raced up my spine. "People in one of her classes have been bothering her. She's trying to act like it's not a big deal, but it very much is."

Helen winced. "Are you kidding me? Pardon me while I go get my bat. When I get back, point me in the direction of the little bitches who need to be taught a lesson."

I rolled my eyes, even though deep down—and maybe not so deep down—her anger and protectiveness on my behalf gave life to a part of me I hadn't even realized was dead.

"Give me names," Marco gritted out. "All I need are names."

I tried to shake my head, but Lachlan held it still in his big hands. "I'm disappointed you guys doubt I can fight my own battles. The Pi Sig boys are angry because I helped ruin them. Their weak little displays of revenge don't faze me."

Lachlan cleared his throat.

"Okay, until now, they didn't faze me. But I'm not going to show them I care. Instead, I'll find a way to obliterate them before the semester is over." My eyes slid to Helen's. "Besides, what would Theo think if you beat up his ex-girlfriend?"

She stiffened, her jaw going tight. "Abby's one of the gumball hos?"

"Mmmhmm." I liked that name. Kayleigh and Abby were now officially Gumball Hos.

She clicked her tongue on her teeth. "Can't believe Theodore ever went there with that chick. She's like slime. It fits in anywhere it's placed, but it doesn't have a shape of its own. There's nothing there. Just gelatinous goo."

Marco crouched down in front of me. "They touch you again, you tell me."

Lachlan's chest made that rockslide sound it sometimes did, but this time, it was more like boulders crashing. "I've got her."

Marco's head jerked up to the man behind me. His brow furrowed as they stared at each other, but something in Lachlan's expression must've put him at ease. The creases in his face relaxed, and he turned a grin back to me.

"I guess he's got you," Marco cooed. "That's cool with me, as long as someone does."

"I've got her," Lachlan repeated.

Helen laughed, patting his shoulder. "We get it, big guy. No one's going to take your pretty away from you."

Lachlan patted the top of my head. "I got it all."

I gasped, swiveling around. "You did? Really?"

He nodded, his eyes so warm as they swept over me, my chest went tingly.

So many twinges.

I climbed to my feet and flung myself at him, wrapping my arms around his thick neck. "Thank you, thank you, thank you. You saved my life, Lachlan Kelly."

He pulled me firmly into his lap, locking his arms around me. "You don't have to thank me. *Don't* thank me."

"I am, and I will."

He took my face in his hands, giving me a hard, invasive stare. A stare that melted my bones and burrowed deep, deep, deep. He took a breath, his chest rising. I held mine, anticipating.

"You stink."

A delighted laugh burst out of me. "Fuck you."

He leaned forward and touched his lips to mine. In front of everyone. "You're welcome."

Helen pulled a chuckling Marco with her into the house, sliding the door shut, but not before I heard him say, "Yeah, he's definitely got her."

I couldn't even deny it.

Even if he didn't want me, Lachlan had me.

CHAPTER TWENTY

ELENA

OH, TODAY WAS A good day. A really good day. My walk home from campus was all sunshine and butterflies. I felt like a Disney princess—*not* that one. More like Aurora, except if some strange man tried to kiss me while I was sleeping, he'd be the one taking a long, long nap.

So, maybe I wasn't exactly princess material. That didn't make today any less wonderful.

"You should have seen them, Pen. They were practically frothing at the mouth."

Penelope threw her head back and laughed. What would I do without FaceTime? I needed Pen's face like a drug.

"Only you would be excited about getting bullied," she said.

"Bullied is a state of mind. Besides, I'm still *pissed* about the gum. But showing up to class with my hair down and curled made it worth it. I'm pretty sure one of them peed her pants."

If there'd been any doubt about who'd stuck gum in my hair, it had been erased by the bright-red faces on the Gumball Hos when they saw my hair cascading down my back, no worse for wear—except the lingering scent of peanut butter.

"And that's your revenge, right? Living well? They say that's the best kind."

"We'll see."

She frowned. "Why does that sound so ominous coming from you?"

My brow arched. "Because you know me so well."

She started to laugh, but her shoulders rolled forward and she slumped instead. "I don't like this, you know? You shouldn't have to watch your back in class. Not in college."

I wrinkled my nose at her optimistic outlook. "It's obvious you don't go to Savage U. Here, when dealing with a certain crowd, watching your back is a necessity. I'm just lucky I didn't end up rooming with them like they originally wanted. I would have woken up without eyebrows or—"

"Or next to a horse head?" Pen guessed.

"If they were feeling particularly *Godfather-y*, sure. Although, something tells me Kayleigh and Abby aren't well versed in classic movie references. It's *Mean Girls* or bust for them, and they watch it as a how-to guide rather than a social commentary."

Pen tilted her head to the side. "Can you believe you chose to live with Helen instead? If I'd told you back in high school this was your future, you—"

"Would have stuck my head in an oven—but only *after* locking you in a padded cell."

She was trying not to laugh, pressing her lips together in a flat line. Pen didn't like joking about mental health, but *I* was the one with the mother who had a depressive disorder. I lived my entire life trying to keep her sane, so I felt I was entitled to jokes as compensation.

"Laugh, Penelope," I whispered.

She let out the faintest little guffaw. If she hadn't been on camera, I would have missed it. I loved corrupting my sweet cousin.

"Speaking of people you love, did you see the soccer schedule I texted you?"

I shook my head. "You know my eyes glaze over when you tell me things about Gabe."

"Well, this was about me too. He's playing at Savage U next month. I'm coming up, and I was *hoping* you'd come to the game. Helen and Theo will be there. Maybe you could bring Lock too?"

I stopped at the intersection before my block, checking both ways before running across the street. "We could hang out after," I suggested.

"Nope. You're coming to the game. Gabe is basically family, and I know how important family is to you..."

Huffing, I had to quell the urge to throw Penelope, and consequently my phone, down on the sidewalk.

"How dare you," I said. "You're right, but how dare you?"

"So, you'll be there?"

"Probably, but I won't like it, you lovely, lovely woman."

Almost home, I raised my head from the phone to check if Lachlan's truck was parked in his driveway.

It was, and Lachlan was standing right behind it, casually leaning against the tailgate. He wasn't alone, though. He was having a chat that looked super friendly with a girl who wasn't one of my roommates.

"What's wrong?" Pen asked.

I tore my eyes from the visage of the man who was sort of mine but not really to look at my cousin.

"Lachlan's next to his truck, talking to a girl."

Pen hissed. "Don't go crazy. He's allowed to talk to girls."

"I know that. Of course he is. But when I'm talking to you, *I'm* allowed to tell you seeing him even acknowledge another girl's existence—at least one outside of my tight circle—makes me homicidal, right?"

"You can definitely tell me that. Feelings are one thing. Acting on them, when you know they're irrational, is another. Point the cam toward him so I can assess the situation."

I did as she asked, letting her see Lachlan laughing with the cute redhead in running shorts and a tank top.

"Okay, spin me back around." When Pen could see me again, she grinned. "Look at their body language. Lock's arms are crossed and he's leaning away from her. They're at least three feet apart, and she looks like she's telling a funny story, not seducing your man."

I snarled at her. "Don't be so smart."

"Can't help it."

It seemed I'd been standing in the same place too long. The girl, who was facing my way, spotted me. She rose on her tiptoes, waving.

"She's waving at me," I said.

"Did you wave back?" Pen asked.

"Nope. If I lift my hand, it won't be to wave."

Pen tsked. "She could just be asking Lock for directions. The poor girl could be innocent and you want to claw her eyes out."

The poor girl in question started my way, jogging with a whole lot of pep in her step. What was she so happy about? Suspicious.

"She's coming," I murmured.

Pen laughed. "Don't hang up. I want to hear this."

As the redhead approached, it hit me that I knew who she was—the renter with the leaky sink. Wow, I thought she'd been eyeing Lachlan and his big toolbox. I guessed it was confirmed.

"Hey," she called breathlessly. "You're here."

The girl stopped in front of me, smiling wide. There wasn't anything threatening about her, but I really wanted to hate her.

I smiled back. I hoped Pen would be proud. "Hey, I'm here. Is your sink okay?"

"Oh, yes. You guys fixed it perfectly." She ran her hand over her thick, curly ponytail. "I was out for a run and saw Lock coming home. He let me wait for you with him."

My forehead crinkled. "You were waiting for me?"

"Yeah, so"—she glanced to the side—"when you were at my house, I thought I recognized you. I racked my brain, and then I remembered—you're the girl from the *T*. That night, I was there with Nate and—"

"What's your name?" I asked sharply.

"Sera. Well, Seraphina, but everyone calls me Sera."

Blood drained from my face. My phone slipped from my hand, dropping to the sidewalk with a muted clatter. Sera bent, picking it up. Noticing Pen on the screen, her eyes widened.

"Is she okay?" Pen asked.

Sera looked at me, then Pen. "Here, I'll give you back to her."

She handed me my phone. I barely saw Pen on the screen. "I'll call you later, okay?"

She agreed, and I ended the call, sliding my phone in the back pocket of my cutoffs.

"What do you want?" I asked.

Her head tilted, her eyes pinching slightly. "I wanted to thank you."

"Thank me?"

"Yes. Thank you. That was my second date with Nate and he...I don't know, he was so charming, but in a way that was so intense, it kind of scared me. And then you came over, and what you said—I'm sorry he did that to you. I hate that it happened, but I guess, I really feel like you saved me. It could have been me too."

I sucked in a breath. This wasn't what I'd expected when she said she'd been with Nate. I thought maybe she was going to threaten to turn me in or yell at me for killing him. Not this. Definitely not this.

"I don't know what to say." I opened my mouth, but nothing else came out. I truly was at a loss for words.

Sera touched my forearm lightly. "After he died, I never told anyone what you said. I thought...well, I thought you wouldn't want that information to be public. I just told the police he'd been upset after he saw you at the diner, stormed out, and left me there."

I swallowed hard. "For the last two years, I've wondered why no one ever questioned me. It was you."

She nodded. "It was me. Whatever happened to Nate, whatever the reason he crashed, he deserved it. I know it wasn't only you he hurt. Since he died, I've heard things, and I just know...well, I hope he suffered."

This freckle-faced girl, with her pretty auburn hair and bright smile, had a soul for vengeance. I was pretty certain I fell in love with her on the spot.

"I hope he did too." I meant it. I hoped he died drowning in his own blood, picturing all the evil acts he'd committed. "Thank you for keeping me out of it. Thank you for keeping my secret."

"You don't have to thank me." Her eyes met mine. "I would have told you sooner, but I didn't know how to get in touch with you. I didn't try as hard as I could have, I guess, because I wasn't sure if you'd even want to hear from me. Then I recognized you the other night, and I knew I had to tell you."

I let out a slightly caustic laugh. "I thought you were here to hit on Lock."

Her eyes bugged. "No, I have a boyfriend and—wait, aren't you together? I just assumed..."

"We're something, not really defined, but—"

"But you don't want some rando girl making a pass at him?" she supplied.

My laugh was less caustic, more sincere. "You're cute as hell, so no, keep your adorable little hands off him."

She held her hands up, which were surprisingly calloused. "I'm a drummer. There's nothing adorable about these things."

I huffed. "Really? I'm going to throw you in a river. You're cool and pretty? Nope."

She leaned in, cupping her mouth like she was telling me a secret. "I'm in the marching band."

"Oh." I pressed my lips together. "That's...nice for you."

She shrugged. "I love it, but yeah, nerd alert!" Snickering to herself, she lifted her wrist and frowned at her smartwatch. "Shit. I need to run. Literally. But maybe we could hang out again? Like, not in the middle of the sidewalk?"

Was I making a friend? Pen would be so, so proud of me.

"Let's do that. You have my number. Text me when you're free."

When she disappeared down the sidewalk, I texted Pen I was fine and I'd call her back later as I walked to where Lachlan had been waiting. I propped my butt on the bumper beside him, releasing a long exhale.

"All good?" he asked.

"I think so. We dated the same guy."

His chin lowered. "The toxic ex?"

"That one. I warned her off him a couple years ago, and she was just thanking me."

"Good. I wish someone had done that for you, but I'm glad you did it for her. She seems like a ni—"

I held my finger up. "I don't want to know what she seems like to you."

His eyebrows drew together. "What's this? Are you thinking things you shouldn't be thinking?" His hand shot out, grabbing my nape to pull me to him. Trapped between his legs, my chest was flush with his. One thick finger dragged down my nose, then he leaned in and kissed the tip.

I met his gaze and gave it to him straight. "You know how most people are sixty percent water? I'm sixty percent jealousy. It's what fuels me. It's irrational and vexing as hell, but my mind is bright green and glowy."

He blinked once. Twice. "You were jealous when you saw me talking to her?"

"Yes. And if you say something nice about her right now, I might give in to the irrational urges in my head."

His mouth twitched. One of his hands slid down my back, cupping my butt. "I'm going to revel in this just once. You getting worked up over me talking to another girl does something to my primordial brain."

My eyes narrowed. "Don't toy with me, Lachlan. That toxic ex? He used to flirt, fondle, fuck other girls to make me jealous because he knew I'd try harder to keep him—that I'd do all manner of crazy things to make him want me. It was ugly, not sexy or cute."

He squeezed my ass and followed with a light swat. "Look at me, El. I like knowing you care. That does it for me, but that doesn't mean I'm going to be anything less than straight with you. I won't play games or make you feel crazy—not on purpose. I'm with you now. As long as I'm with you, I won't flirt, fondle, or fuck anyone else. That's not who I am. You don't know that yet, but you will."

"That's a big promise for someone who doesn't do commitment."

His head jerked back. "I don't think I ever said that. If I did, I meant I'm not looking to get into something deep with anyone, not when I'll have to walk away. I'm not interested in fucking around." He yanked me deeper into his body. "I'd like to fuck you, though. A lot, in every way we can think of. I think you want that too. As long as both of us keep wanting that, then you have nothing to worry about with me. Do I have anything to worry about with you?"

"Are you asking me to sneak around with you and only you?"

He huffed a laugh. "Does this look like sneaking? Did me kissing you in front of our friends look like sneaking?"

"No, it didn't."

"I'm asking you to have fun and keep it light with me and only me." He palmed the back of my head, tipping it back. Soft brown eyes searched mine. "Do you want that?"

I did want that. The connection I felt to my body when I was with Lachlan and the connection pulsing between *us* was powerfully alluring. If he took it all away again without warning, I'd be pissed. Trusting him to do right by me would be a big step. I didn't trust easily, especially not men.

"When it's over, give me a warning, okay?"

His smile was gentle. "That, I can do. I think we'll both know when it's time to walk, but I won't assume we're on the same wavelength this time. I'll talk to you."

A sardonic laugh slipped out of me. "I've never talked about the end at the beginning."

"Neither have I, but now that we are, it makes sense. I'm always up front, and I am who I am. Nothing's going to change that or what I want." He captured my gaze. "You get me on that? No surprises."

Twinge.

"No surprises," I agreed. "Can the talking part be over now?"

"Soon. You never answered if I have to worry about you. Are you with me and only me?"

I nodded slowly. "I don't like most men, Lachlan. Unless Tom Holland comes strolling up to me and offers me a ride on his spiderwebs, you don't have to worry about me. Even then, I might take the ride, but not *the ride*."

He cracked an amused grin. "How is Tom Holland your type but you're all over me? Elsa, we are not the same."

Reaching up, I brushed his hair down across his forehead. God, he was cute and fuck hot. This man just did it for me. "I don't know. I need to see you in spandex, then I can make an educated decision."

He slapped my butt with his wide palm. "Never gonna happen, sweet girl." Then he kissed the tip of my nose. "I need to get going."

"What?"

"Work. I have to go to work." He straightened, setting me aside. If I had less control of myself, I would have stomped and whined. But I wasn't that girl. I'd never beg and plead with a man to give me attention.

"Okay. See you later." I turned toward my house, but Lachlan spun me back around before I could take a step. "I thought you had to work?"

He held my shoulders, keeping me in place in front of him. I stared back at him, hiding my disappointment.

"I do, but I'm wondering why you went from liking me to giving me the cold shoulder in the blink of an eye."

"I don't like being kissed on the nose."

He blinked. "Okay. I won't do it if it bothers you."

"That was a lie. I don't want you to stop." I folded my arms across my chest. "It only bothers me when that's the only kiss I'm getting—especially after we just talked about fucking each other for the last ten minutes."

His confusion morphed into something hot. Yanking me into his body, he dipped down and covered my mouth with his. Clinging to his shoulders, I tried to climb him, to get closer. His arm banded beneath my ass, lifting me so I could wrap my legs around his middle. He turned, pressing me to the back of his truck, his thick erection hitting my center.

I whimpered, sliding my tongue along his. My hands tangled in his hair, pulling him closer, closer, marveling at how well his mouth fit with mine, how delicious his taste was to me, how exactly we aligned with each other.

His kisses slowed, turning languid. These were just as good as the first crushing ones. I grinned into his mouth, and his lips tipped against mine. I kissed the smile off him, licking the edges of it.

"Okay. That was a much better goodbye." My forehead rested on his. My legs were still locked around him. He'd go. He wouldn't stay here and miss work to fuck me. But I'd keep him here for as long as he allowed.

Which wasn't long. "You're gonna have to let me go, sweet girl." His lips brushed over mine. "You're making me forget it's broad daylight. Making me want to open the tailgate and fuck you in the bed of my truck."

"Let's do that. I've never done that before."

He chuckled. "We can do that, but it's not going to be when there are people walking by every two minutes."

I lowered my legs, taking special care to rub myself against the thick ridge bulging behind his zipper. He groaned, giving my butt a hard squeeze. I liked knowing he was as affected as I was.

"Have a nice day at work, babe." I patted his erection.

He fisted the back of my hair, jerking me into him again. The rumble that came from his chest was so close to a purr, I almost melted into him.

"You're going to drive me mad, aren't you?" His jaw was tight, but he didn't look the least bit mad about it.

"Yep. And you're going to enjoy every second of it."

I couldn't wait to find out what Lachlan's limits were. It would be a fun challenge.

But I was really kind of hoping he was strong enough to handle me.

Chapter Twenty-One

Elena

All I'd gotten the rest of the week were some really good make-out sessions. Lachlan had been edging me, and it was driving me bananas. I could've taken care of my own business, but I had the memory of his fingers on my clit and how much better the orgasms he gave me were than the ones I gave myself.

I craved it.

If he wasn't going to give in, I'd drive him out of his mind too.

Saturday morning, I parked my butt on my front porch in a satin pajama set that would surely make Lachlan go caveman if he saw it. The black satin shorts stopped just below the curve of my butt, with sheer, white lace panels on the sides. The racerback top was flowy, with more sheer lace panels between my breasts and down the back. A healthy amount of side boob was on display too.

I'd been a good girl over the past couple weeks, acting out my morning ritual in the privacy of my back deck. I assumed Lachlan was aware I'd acquiesced, just as I assumed he'd figure out sooner than later I hadn't this morning.

Now, all I could do was wait. I kicked up my feet on the railing and opened my newspaper to the arts section. I wasn't quite ready for hard-hitting international news yet.

I lost track of time, sinking into my ritual like a warm blanket. The sound of Lachlan's soothing voice coming from the opposite direction of his house pulled me back to the present.

"I know, baby girl. I'm here. I'm always here. All you have to do is call me. I'll always answer."

Oh, shit. Oh, fuck. Really? He's that guy already?

I popped up from my seat, tossing my newspaper aside. There he was, taking his time meandering down the street, his eyes on his phone, carrying a tray of drinks in his other hand.

"I get it. I hate that I can't be there with you. I hate that they're pulling this shit on you while I'm down here. You don't deserve to be put in the middle. I'll talk to them."

He must've felt the laser beams shooting from my eyes because he looked up, finding me immediately. He had the audacity to smile at me and quicken his pace like he was coming for me.

"Saoirse, calm, baby girl. I want you to say hi to Elena," he cooed into the phone.

What the fuckity fuck? I know this man has big balls, but this is beyond the pale. Introducing me to his other woman...or am I the other woman?

Lachlan climbed the porch steps, setting the tray of coffee down on the table beside my chair. He wrapped his arm around my stiff shoulder and pressed his mouth to my ear.

"When I hang up with my sister, we're going to talk about you sitting out here in these pajamas. I thought we had an understanding."

Shivers racked my body as his low murmur set in.

"Lock? Where is she? Show me!" A young, excited female voice burst out of the phone.

Lachlan held up the screen so we were both on it. Excellent—video chats with family members while I was practically naked.

The girl on the screen couldn't have been more surprising if she'd tried. She was the antithesis of Lachlan. I never would have pegged them as siblings. Her hair was honey blonde, her features delicate. From what I could see of her, she was thin, almost waifish.

When she smiled, though, that was when I saw it. Her chocolate eyes lit the same way her brother's did, and they shared the same perfect, white teeth and wide mouth.

"Hi!" She waved at the camera. "I'm Saoirse."

"Well, hello." I tilted my head to glance at Lachlan, finding him already staring down at me, watching somewhat warily. I turned back to the screen. "I'm Elena, Lachlan's neighbor."

She giggled. "Oh, I know who you are. He's told me all about everyone there, but especially you. I accused him of having a crush a few months ago when he mentioned you at least three times in one conversation and—"

"I was complaining about her," he grumbled.

I snorted, and so did Saoirse. She leaned closer to the camera, lowering her voice conspiratorially. "He's been saying sweet things about you lately. When I called him out about it a few days ago, he didn't deny it. So, tell me, what's my brother like as a boyfriend?"

Lachlan groaned. "Stop. You're only supposed to be saying hi."

She rolled her eyes. "I've been begging him to let me look at you. Holy crap, are you pretty. And your pajamas are sexy as hell. Does Lock let you sit outside in those? He'd flip out if I tried to wear anything like that at all, let alone in public."

I raised a brow, pressing my lips together so I didn't burst out laughing at her excitement. She was so cute, as different from her brother in personality as she was in looks.

"He doesn't like it, but sometimes doing things I know he doesn't like is the only way to grab his attention," I told her.

Lachlan's arm tightened around me, his face lowering to the side of my head.

Saoirse gasped. "Are you kidding me? My brother's not giving you enough attention? Has he seen you? Dude, bro, if you don't pay attention to your girl, someone else will take the job. What are you even thinking?"

Lachlan pulled the phone away from me, snarling at his sister. "All right. Enough. I will call you later."

She giggled. "If I didn't make trouble, what would be my purpose?"

The transformation from grumpy older brother to indulgent sibling was swift and complete. Lachlan's eyes and smile went soft.

"Love you, baby girl."

She sniffed once. "Love you too. Bye, Elena."

"Bye, Saoirse," I said softly.

Lachlan hung up, tucking his phone away, and turned to me. He dragged a finger along the bare skin under my arm, tracing the side of my breast, slipping under the fabric to tease my nipple.

"Is this for me?" he asked.

"It's for me."

He pinched my nipple a little harder than I liked. "You're trying to get my attention."

"Yes," I admitted.

"Are you trying to get someone else's attention?"

"Just yours."

He squeezed my breasts, rubbing his thumb over the taut peak. "Then send me a picture. Knock on my door. Wear this on your deck. If this is for me, then only give it to me. You want my attention, you have it now. But I think I warned you what would happen if you came out here half naked again."

I leaned into him, already slick between my thighs. "I'm in trouble."

"Yes." He slid his hand out of my tank, gripping my nape. "Take me to your room."

I never would have let anyone else tell me what to do, but it came naturally with Lachlan. Besides, weren't these the results I'd been craving? I knew I'd be punished for acting out. I'd been looking forward to it.

Inside my bedroom, Lachlan closed the door and twisted the lock. I stood beside my bed, doing my level best to look contrite, even as my stomach brimmed with anticipation.

I wasn't the least bit sorry. Maybe I would be when he was finished with me, but something told me I wouldn't be.

Lachlan kicked his boots off and took a seat on the edge of my bed, patting his lap. I started to sit, but he caught me, turning me around.

"Head and shoulders on the bed, stomach on my legs, ass in the air." There was nothing hard about his orders, nothing scary or mean. He used his regular, rugged tone and looked at me like he wanted me, not like he wanted to hurt me.

That had me scrambling to comply, trying to position myself just right. His groan when I was in place told me he liked me this way, spread out on him, helpless to his mercy.

He pushed my top up, exposing my back. Rough fingers trailed down my spine to the waistband of my shorts. Hooking his fingers, he pulled my bottoms down in slow motion, giving me ample opportunity to protest. Or maybe he was doing what he did best: edging me to the point of insanity.

"No panties, Ellie? Goddamn, are you a bad, bad girl. Showing off *my* tits, *my* ass, *my* pussy to every undeserving little shit who walks by." He gave my butt a light swat. "You want my attention, I'll give it to you. But you have to ask for it the right way."

"I always want your attention."

He smoothed his palm down the length of my back to the swell of my ass, gripping a cheek and giving it a jiggle. My mind was whirring, deciding if I liked that, when the first real slap rained down on my right cheek. Jerking from surprise more than pain, it took me a moment to relax again. When I did, I was gifted with a slap on my other cheek.

"If you don't like this, tell me and I'll stop." He soothed my burning butt cheeks with soft caresses.

"I'm not sure if I like it yet, but don't stop."

Taking me at my word, his hand dropped down three more times, hitting a different spot each spank. I whimpered, and my head reared back so I could see him. His eyes were on my bottom, looking at me like a starving man. One finger trailed along the valley between my thighs, from my clit to my ass. He brought his finger to his mouth and sucked my flavor, his eyes closing as he groaned.

"I think you do like it," he said. "How can this be a punishment if it makes your pussy this wet?"

I wiggled my hips back and forth. "I've been wet all week. You keep kissing me and kissing me, leaving me on the edge. You could blow on my pussy and I'd come."

"Hmmm." Using two fingers, he parted the lips between my legs and blew cool air on my pulsing, swollen folds. I didn't come, but my spine bowed hard while I mewled and clawed at my blankets. "Close. So close. But not enough."

Lachlan continued my punishment, spanking my butt and thighs while he told me how pretty my pussy was, that he hadn't stopped thinking about it since he first slid into me, how he jerked off to the thought of me. Every word he said, punctuated by the never-ending slap of his palm against my flesh, sank into the places in my mind that had been worried he didn't want me like I wanted him. That was when I gave in, fully relaxing, almost melting across his thighs.

He gripped my butt cheek, giving it a jiggle again. "So pretty and red for me. Are you going to be my sweet girl and listen now? Or do I need to keep going?"

"I'll listen, I promise."

He cupped my face, leaning down to look at me. "Are you smiling, Ellie?"

"I think I am," I whispered.

"Fuck, sweet girl. *Fuck.*" He slid out from under me, rearranging my body so my feet were on the floor and my upper torso folded over the mattress. Lachlan stood behind me, one hand gripping my hip, the other exploring my slick folds. "I need you now. Tell me you're ready."

I pushed my butt back, seeking him out. "I'm ridiculously ready. So, so read—"

He plunged into me in one brutal thrust. If I'd been smiling before, I was absolutely euphoric when he didn't give me a single moment to get used to him. As soon as his hips met my ass, he pulled out and slammed back in, over and over. He was relentless, fucking me hard, desperate. Showing me he'd been missing this as much as I had. It was exactly how I needed him to take me, to erase the last of my doubts. The voices in my head were quiet as I gave myself over to this man, this experience.

Without warning, my inner walls clamped down on him. I was coming so hard, I saw stars behind my eyelids. I cried his name, and nearly sobbed with relief. I'd needed this, from him, more than I could explain or understand.

"Such a good girl. So naughty, but I like that. I like when you're naughty for me because you want me to get you in line."

I couldn't bring myself to speak with any kind of coherence, so I reached back, wrapping my fingers around his wrist, needing that anchor. Lachlan grunted, plunging into me harder.

"So sweet. That's my sweet. Only mine. You give it all to me. Even when you gave me poison, I always knew there was sweet under there. It's all mine, Ellie. Every ounce of this sweet is mine."

It was. It was his. No one else had ever called me sweet or brought that out of me. Any sweet he saw was because of him.

He leaned over me, blanketing me with his body, touching his lips to my shoulders, my nape, my spine. Giving me soft with the unforgiving rhythm of his hips colliding with my ass.

His face was beside mine, peering into my glassy eyes. "So fucking pretty, El. Pretty when you're sassy. Pretty when you're obeying. Can't get enough of that mouth, this tight pussy, those blue eyes. Can't look away from you."

"I can't look away from you," I slurred.

"Fuck, Elena." His lips trailed over my face, kissing me everywhere he could reach before he lifted off my back, gripped both of my hips, and powered into me.

Raising one of my knees on the bed, I angled my hips so my clit hit the edge of the mattress each time Lachlan thrust into me. It was all I could do not to scream the house down as my next orgasm flooded through me. I was lost to it, floating and being pulled under again and again.

"Oh, fuck, Ellie. Your perfect little pussy is rippling around my cock. I'm gonna fill you up with my cum until it drips down your thighs. I want to make a mess of you." He braced one hand on my nape, the other on the base of my spine, flattening me into the bed. "Tell me if I need to pull out. Gotta tell me now."

I shook my head. If he pulled out, I'd murder him. "Come in me. Give it to me."

Lachlan released a low roar as he vibrated behind me. His strokes became shorter, stronger, until I could barely breathe. The slap of his skin on mine filled the room, soon replaced by his deep, pained groans as he pushed into me one more time, stilling when he was as deep as he could get. Warmth from his release heated me from the inside out.

He stayed inside me, kissing my back and rubbing my shoulders for long, breathtakingly precious moments. When he pulled out, I was a limp noodle, barely able to roll myself the rest of the way onto the bed. Lachlan was moving around, but to see what he was doing would have required me lifting my head, and I wasn't into doing that.

I didn't even move when he touched my burning bottom, spread my legs, and cleaned me with a warm cloth. I thought I was stunned into paralysis. And that was...well, unprecedented.

"I'll be right back. Don't move," he said. My door opened and closed, followed by the faint sound of Lachlan clomping down the stairs.

If he didn't come back, I'd get mad later. For now, I'd probably nap.

My eyes were drifting shut when my door opened and closed again. Lachlan crouched beside me, moving my hair off my face. He grinned and leaned in to kiss the tip of my nose.

"I brought you coffee. The ice is a little melted now, but I think it's still drinkable. Want to try it?"

Rolling to my back, I pushed myself upright. I was super naked while Lachlan was back in his clothes. I didn't usually mind being naked, but I felt the need to cover up after being so vulnerable.

I held my hand out. "Can you grab my pajamas please?"

He rose, finding my discarded clothes, and handed them to me. I slipped them on while he watched unabashedly. I crinkled my nose at him. He laughed and picked up the coffee he'd brought to my room.

The ice was mostly melted, but I still drank it because the gesture had been so unexpected. Plus, I needed to do something with my mouth while I thought of what to say.

Lachlan settled on the other side of the bed with his own drink. The distinct green color made me smile. I'd hooked him on matcha apparently.

"You okay?" he asked.

I nodded, playing with my straw. "My butt is sore."

"Poor baby."

I snorted. "You don't sound sorry at all."

He smirked at me. "As long as you're okay and you liked it, then no, I'm not sorry. Are you sorry it happened?"

I lifted a shoulder. "I don't know if I learned my lesson, but I don't regret any of it."

Blowing out a heavy breath, he shoved his fingers through his messy hair. "I'm going to have to take you across my lap a lot, aren't I?"

Biting down on my lip, I raised my delighted eyes to his. "I bet it'll be a real hardship for you."

His hand shot out, grabbed my nape, and yanked me in for a hard kiss. "If I didn't want a challenge, I wouldn't be here."

He was so damn good at this. No wonder poor Emily had looked so lost. It wasn't just sex he was incredible at. The way Lachlan spoke, the things he said, were tailor made for me. I couldn't help wondering if he'd been like this with other women or if we just happened to click.

No. I didn't want to know. Thinking about Lachlan with other women threatened to burst my sex bubble, and I wasn't ready to leave it behind just yet.

I changed the subject.

"You were out getting me coffee this morning?"

"I was. I thought I'd find you on your deck and maybe you'd invite me to stay."

"One thing you should know about me is I'm terrible at waiting for things to happen."

"Noted."

I took another sip of my watery iced coffee. Kind of gross, but I liked the man and gesture enough to power through.

"By the way, when I heard you talking to your sister, it sounded like you were talking to a girlfriend. I was seconds away from eviscerating you."

He put his matcha down on the bedside table. "Damn. I guess I should feel thankful I'm still walking around with my guts intact. It never crossed my mind that it would sound like that to you."

"To be fair, you didn't know I was listening, but I did warn you I'm irrationally jealous." Giving up on my drink, I set it down and twisted to face Lachlan. He looked really, really good in my bed. "Your conversation sounded intense."

"All my conversations with Saoirse are intense. I think that's how seventeen-year-old girls are."

My eyes widened, and I blew out a breath. "Consider yourself lucky you didn't know me at seventeen. But Saoirse doesn't seem anything like the bloodthirsty cheerleader I used to be."

"She's a good girl. A little rebellious, but nothing to worry about. Hell, I'd be worried if she wasn't rebelling in some way." He shook his head. "Our parents had a shitty divorce and put us in the middle of it. My mom is bitter. My dad is lovesick. When I was at home, I shielded her from the worst of it. It was me passing messages and listening to my mom lament on my father ruining her life and my dad crying over the loss of the love of his life."

Fascinated with this glimpse inside Lachlan's life, I climbed on top of him, sprawled out on his chest, and propped my chin on my fists. His hands gravitated to my ass, pushing my shorts up to get at my bare skin.

"How long have they been divorced?" I asked.

"Five years. You'd think that would be enough time to let it all go, but my mom is still angry, and my dad is just as devastated as the day he left her."

"Wait." I flattened my palm on his stubbly cheek. "Your dad left your mother and he's devastated?"

He studied me, his soft eyes sweeping over me. "You really want to hear this?"

"Yes!" I instantly realized my enthusiasm might not have been appropriate given the topic, so I tried to temper it. "I mean, only if you want to tell me. If it upsets you, we can just drink our coffee until we're ready to have sex again."

That made him rumble with laughter, which sent my belly fluttering. Lachlan gave the best laughs. They were thunderstorms on a summer night, bursting into a black sky, shaking roofs for miles.

"I'm good. The sex will happen, but I'll answer your questions first." He tucked my hair behind my ear. "When they got together, my dad told my mom he was only in California for college and his goal had always been to move to Wyoming and take over the family ranch. But they fell in love. The big kind of love you don't walk away from."

I sighed. "This is going to be heartbreaking, isn't it?"

He pushed up and claimed my mouth in a hard kiss before he lay back against my pillows. "It doesn't have a happy ending, no. Mom has a legacy too, and that legacy is in California. They agreed to stay until they turned forty. They would raise their kids, Mom would have her political career, then they would move to Wyoming. I guess forty sounded fair to them back then—twenty years, you know? But forty came, and Mom had no intention of moving. Dad started commuting back and forth to Wyoming. He did that for five years until his dad got sick and he had to make a decision. Dad had given my mom five extra years, but she wouldn't go, and he couldn't stay. She went back on their agreement after keeping my dad from his dream for twenty-five years. And that was it. That was the end of their marriage. She knew it, but she refused to compromise."

I'd never been one to cry over sad movies or books. Broken love stories rolled off my back like water. But there was something about Lachlan's telling of his parents' shattered dreams that really struck me deep.

I sucked in a shaky breath. "It sounds like you're on your dad's side."

"No, I'm not. My dad knew who he was marrying. It would be ludicrous to expect a politician like my mother to just scrap it all to live on a ranch. That isn't who she is. I wish she could have been honest with him before they ever got married, but maybe she thought she would change. I don't know what she was thinking, but I do know there was no malicious intent."

I knocked my chin against his chest. "I don't even know your parents, and I'm kind of heartbroken over their marriage ending."

He scoffed and let go of my butt to palm the top of my head. "Told you you were all sweetness under that venom."

"Shush." I slapped his mouth with my fingertips. "You told me a sad story, so I'm having feelings."

"I have a lot of feelings too. I'm pissed off two adults are guilting a teenage girl. I'm angry they can't get their shit together after five years." He hauled me up his chest so he could bury his face in my neck. "I'm not mad I'm in Elena Sanderson's bed, having coffee, and getting ready to have sex with her for the second time before nine a.m."

"Oh, is that what you're getting ready to do?"

He nipped his way up my throat and jaw to find my lips. "That's exactly what I'm getting ready to do."

It didn't take long for Lachlan to kiss away the sad and replace it with all that was good and dirty and so damn addictive, I wondered how much I'd be willing to give up to keep it.

CHAPTER TWENTY-TWO

ELENA

"Slut."

"Fish cunt."

"Whorebag."

"Cheep prostatoot."

I was really worried by the spelling errors in that last one. The standards for admission at Savage U were obviously slipping. Then again, only a child would deface a chair to express their dislike of a classmate. I could forgive a small child for misspelling "prostitute."

From the snickering originating from Kayleigh and Dickweed, it hadn't been a child who'd taken Sharpie to my regular chair in New Ventures. They'd scrawled all manner of insults over the seat and back. I could only guess Abby had been tasked to distract Professor Seavers while they got their graffiti on.

It had been a week since the gum incident. They'd laid relatively low, only resorting to name-calling and frowny faces. When I told Kayleigh she was going to have terrible wrinkles from all that scowling, she immediately halted her facial intimidation campaign. Abby wasn't so easily thwarted, but I suspected she was already on a bi-yearly regimen of Botox anyway.

I took a picture of their *clever* insults and calmly switched chairs for the one beside it. I didn't trust that whatever they'd used to write with was actually Sharpie and wouldn't rub off on my clothes.

As soon as I sat down in my replacement chair, their true plan became apparent. I'd fallen for a red herring, immediately followed by falling on my ass. My chair gave way, and I splatted on the ground, but not before hitting my chin on the table in front of me.

That smarted.

Sal was right there, crouching down and taking my hand. I was seeing stars, so I needed a minute for my head to clear.

"Elena? Are you okay? You smacked your chin really hard."

My laugh was dry and weak to my ears. "I know. I was there."

Soon, most of the class was gathering around me, including Professor Seavers. I wasn't embarrassed at falling, but being fussed over like I was a victim wasn't my jam. They probably would have stopped if I'd gotten up, but each time I tried, my head went foggy.

"Shit." I clutched my jaw and crown. "I'm fine. I just need a minute. Please."

Sal took my arm. "Let me help you into my chair. I tested it for you. It's safe."

Seavers took my other arm, and I hated every second of her kindness. This wasn't her job. She should have been enriching our minds, not scraping a girl off her classroom floor.

Once I was securely seated in Sal's chair, he tipped my water bottle into my mouth. God, this kid was the real deal. He never hit on me, and once he'd gotten comfortable with me, he talked to me like a fellow human and not a walking vagina. Sitting beside him was one of the wisest decisions I'd made in a long time.

My jaw still hurt, but after a minute or two, the fog started clearing out of my brain.

One of my classmates pointed to my chin and hissed. "There's some blood there. You should probably clean that up."

I swiped at the underside of my face. My hand came away streaked with red. If I scarred from this, I was going to riot. I'd gotten through competitive cheerleading without so much as a sprained ankle, but in one college course, I'd gotten my face smashed twice and my shoulder practically dislocated. This was for the ugly, raggedy, feather-bare birds.

Fortunately our TA had a fully equipped first aid kit with everything my injured heart could desire. I bandaged my little chinny-chin up and held an ice pack there, giving everyone a big smile.

"I'm fine now, I promise," I told them. "I'm sorry for interrupting class."

Seavers's flinty gaze swept over the Pi Sig boys, who'd been suspiciously quiet during my ordeal, stopping on Kayleigh and Abby, who'd been suspiciously solicitous.

"Surely all of you are aware this classroom comes equipped with security cameras." That was all she said, and it was more than enough. If these buffoons thought they'd get away with blatant sabotage of my chair, they were even dumber than they looked.

Class went on, a thick tension hanging in the air, especially from the boys behind me. I wondered which of them had been the one to hold the screwdriver. I had a feeling Dickweed might've been the mastermind, but one of his minions had most likely done the dirty work. I just wasn't lucky enough for it to have been him.

At the end of class, Sal and I stayed in our seats after everyone else filed out, checking our calendars for times we could meet to work on our midterm project. We'd been assigned a startup that would provide a luxury summer camp experience for adults and use their profits to send underprivileged children to summer camp. We had set up a meeting with the founder for the end of the week.

"Are you okay?" he asked for the hundredth time as we packed up our stuff.

"I am, I promise. The ice helped the pain, I stopped bleeding, and I didn't crack a tooth. It's like my lucky day or something."

I slid my laptop into my bag. When I looked up, two maintenance workers had entered the classroom and were talking to Professor Seavers. My heart stuttered at the sight of Lachlan in his uniform. I'd never been a uniform girl until him. Or maybe I was simply a Lachlan girl.

I had a crush on my lovah. It was so bad.

Lachlan traversed the stairs in seconds, displeasure pinching his brow. "Are you hurt?"

"Hello, you." I grinned up at my towering man. "I'm just fine."

Sal cleared his throat. "She knocked her chin into the table. She was bleeding."

I slapped his arm. "Snitches get stitches."

His mouth pulled down. "So do women whose classmates think it's funny to mess with their chairs."

Lachlan pulled me to my feet, raking his gaze over me. When he landed on my bandage, he practically vibrated. "What. Happened?" His jaw was clenched in anger, but he touched me with nothing but gentleness, cupping my cheeks and running his thumb over my chin.

"Like the little snitch said, my classmates messed with my chair. Bam! Down I went." I pressed my palms to his rapidly rising and falling chest, dropping my tone to soothing. "You won't have to worry, Lachlan. There are cameras in here. They won't be my classmates for long."

"How can you tell me not to worry?" he bit out. "Someone deliberately hurt you."

"I think humiliation was more the goal." I rose on my toes, kissing his chin. "Don't be mad. I'm fine. I'm just going to go home and bond with a bag of frozen veggies."

He jerked back, staring at me like I had three heads. "I'm not finding this funny." He tugged me into his side, his arm banding around my shoulders. "I'll drive you home."

"You're working," I protested. "I can walk."

"If you argue with me, I'll sling you over my shoulder. I don't want to do that with you injured, but I will if you think for another second you're not going with me."

He hadn't calmed since seeing me injured. His body had turned into one taut muscle, poised for war. Under my hand, his heart thundered like a thousand horses stampeding across an open plain.

I leaned into him, nuzzling my nose into his shoulder. "Okay, you can drive me." It didn't cost me anything to give him that, and it smoothed one of the angry lines slashing his forehead.

He said a few words to his coworker, I waved goodbye to Sal, and a few minutes later, he tucked me into his truck. As soon as he climbed in beside me, he yanked me into his lap and tipped my face back so he could kiss my chin.

With a heaving sigh, he brought his forehead to mine.

"We got a call to replace a broken chair. I knew it was your class. I was just hoping I'd catch you before you left so I could feel you up in a dark corner. Instead, I walk in and see you like this. It felt like I'd been hit by a truck out of nowhere. You might think I overreacted, but it physically pains me to see you hurt. I fucking hate it."

Weaving my fingers in the sides of his hair, I held him steady. "Listen to me, Lachlan. I'm pissed those idiots got one over on me. My pride is definitely injured, and my chin is sore. I'm not afraid, though. My injuries aren't permanent. I'm okay."

He pulled back, reading my face for the truth. After a minute or two, he exhaled, shaking his head. "You're really unbothered, aren't you? You're being actively bullied, and you don't give a shit. How is that?"

"I would have to care about those people to be bothered. I like Sal. I'd be disappointed if Sal turned on me. The rest? It's pretty much par for the course for that set. *They're* bothered that they can't get to me. I refuse to be bullied."

"You can refuse all you want, but hurting you is crossing so many lines, Elena."

"And they'll be punished. What use is it for me to cry about it? I'll go on with my life while they're bogged down by trivialities that mean nothing in the real world."

He stared at me like I was an alien, and maybe I was to him. We'd led extremely different lives, whether he wanted to believe it or not. He might have grown up privileged, but I had a feeling he'd always been kind and easygoing. Lachlan had never boiled with rage over someone having something he wanted. He'd never dug his nails into his palms so hard it drew blood because a teacher complimented his best friend's English paper but not his. He'd never slashed tires or exposed naked pics or pushed a random girl in a pool for being too hot.

Lachlan would never understand what it was to waste away in the mire of jealousy and petty grudges. I was intimate with the muck, which was why I knew letting the Pi Sig boys fester in the excrement of their broken dreams was the worst punishment I could inflict.

"Sometimes I don't know what to do with you," Lachlan admitted.

"Join the club. I don't know what to do with myself a lot of the time."

His lips touched mine. "Let me take you home."

"That means I have to get off your lap?"

He chuckled, but it was dry, humorless. "That's what it means."

"Are you mad at me?"

He shoved his fingers through his hair. "No. I don't know what I am, but I'm not mad at you."

That didn't sound good, and we'd been *so* good over the last week. Nose kisses and spankings and coffee delivery and dick riding. It had been natural and easy, barely any fighting.

I crawled off his lap, pulling on my buckle. He held on to my thigh as he drove me home, but we lapsed into silence. Normally, that would be okay. Lachlan wasn't a big talker, and silence with him was always comfortable. Now, it might have been my sore chin and the strange circumstances, but by the time he pulled up to the curb in front of my house, I was on edge. He circled the truck like always, helping me out, then carried my bag to the door. He kissed me hard and waited for me to go inside before he walked away.

What he didn't do was promise to text or see me later.

And it was a good thing since I didn't see or hear from him that night.

Not once.

Not even to check in.

That smarted.

Chapter Twenty-three

Lock

It was rare that I didn't know my own mind. My mom used to tell me I left the womb with so much confidence, the doctor barely had to guide me out. I knew where I was going and how to get there. Always had.

Until Elena Sanderson.

She sent me spinning. It wasn't something she did on purpose. The person she was took all I knew for certain and turned it on its head.

Leaving her alone yesterday wasn't me, but I couldn't get myself to understand and reconcile my hurt girl shrugging it off like it was nothing. So, I took some time—time that wasn't mine to take—and got lost in my head.

I messed up.

Elena walked down her porch steps, eyeing me warily when she spotted me waiting for her on the sidewalk. My mouth went dry at her long legs in her short skirt. There was a small bandage on the underside of her chin, but otherwise, she looked none the worse for wear. She looked stunning. Maybe even more so than usual.

"You okay?" I asked.

"Dandy," she chirped, halting in front of me. "You?"

"Pissed off."

"Oh? At me?"

"Myself." I shoved her iced coffee into her hand. "The ice hasn't melted yet."

She brought the cup up and gave the liquid inside a swirl. "Thanks. Did it take you all night to fetch this for me?"

I winced. "It took me all night to get over myself."

Her head tipped to the side. "What does that mean?"

Unable to stand the foot of distance between us, I hooked her around the waist and pulled her against me. She placed a hand on my chest, keeping herself upright instead of sinking into me like she normally did. I guessed I wasn't the only one pissed off.

"It means I'm a protector. It comes as naturally to me as breathing. When I found you hurt yesterday, my instincts roared to life. I wanted to care for you, to soothe you, to solve your problems for you, but you didn't need that, and I didn't know how to handle it."

"I won't apologize for not being like the other women in your life." She met my gaze with her crystalline eyes. They weren't hard like I'd had been expecting. Underneath the impassiveness of her expression was a hint of vulnerability in the pretty depths. "I don't know if I needed you yesterday, but I certainly wanted you."

"Ellie..." That had to have cost her something to admit, but she'd done it without flinching. "You don't need to apologize, I do. There's no way in hell I should have left you. I'm sorry I let you down and allowed my ego to get in the way of taking care of you. It won't happen again."

"'Kay." She turned her head, staring down the sidewalk. I hadn't won her over yet.

"Come on. Let me drive you to class."

"I'll walk."

"Then I'll walk with you."

Taking her hand in mine, I wove our fingers together and started toward campus. She didn't resist, drinking her coffee in silence while we walked.

"Did you hear from your professor?" I asked.

"Yes. She wasn't really allowed to tell me anything officially, but she did mention the names of two guys, who, coincidentally, are no longer enrolled in her class. She doesn't know what will happen as far as punishment, but she'll pull for them to be expelled."

It took all my willpower to keep my hold on her loose and gentle. "Do you know the guys?"

"Not really. They were in Pi Sig, so there's a grudge there. I'm glad they're gone, and I'm crossing my fingers this puts an end to their campaign of terror, since I'd like to be able to fully enjoy that class without keeping my guard up constantly."

I would tear them apart limb from limb if I could. I knew nothing about them except they were harassing my girl, and that was enough. They didn't deserve to breathe the same air much less lay eyes on her.

She stopped walking, swiveling to face me. "This is strange for me, Lachlan. We're keeping things light and easy, so I don't know how much I can lean on you. I don't know if I'm allowed to be mad at you for letting me down, or if I'm even supposed to *be* let down. Maybe your absence was part of the 'light and easy' relationship you want with me. And that's okay if it is. We'll find our footing and set boundaries, but for now, I'm somewhat lost about how I should be feeling."

"You are allowed to feel however you feel. You're definitely allowed to be pissed off at me. I screwed up and let you down. Light and easy doesn't mean I'm going to blow you off when someone assaults you. Jesus."

I tugged her into me, wrapping her in my arms. She squirmed against me at first, but as I held her, the tightness in her limbs seeped out until she finally gave me that melt. She sank into me, curling her arms around my middle.

"My chin hurts." She had her face pressed into my chest, whining pitifully. It was damn cute and made something in my deep, dark wells light up.

"I'm sorry, sweet girl. Want me to take you home and get an ice pack?"

She shook her head, plunging deeper into the cocoon of my arms. "No, I just want this."

Oh yes, I was lighting up all right.

Fuck.

How could I have thought she hadn't needed me yesterday? Maybe I didn't need to stand in front of her to fight her dragons like I did for Saoirse, and even my mom. I wasn't going to be Elena Sanderson's knight. Instead, I'd be her castle—the place she retreated when the battles were done. I'd be there to protect her too, but only when she came to me for it. That would take some getting used to, but now that I understood my role, I'd take it by the neck and make it mine.

After long minutes of hugging my girl in the middle of the sidewalk, she raised her head, pushed up on her toes, and kissed me hard and fast.

"Okay. I'm good now. Let's go to class."

I took her hand in mine, gave it a gentle squeeze, and walked my girl to class.

・・・・・・・・・・

Being Elena's castle did not mean I was standing down. She could handle herself, that I didn't doubt, but she didn't have to. When she went to New Ventures on Friday, I was there with her, escorting her to her seat.

The skinny guy with big glasses was already there. He took my offered hand and gave it a solid shake.

"I'm Lock, Elena's boyfriend. I wanted to thank you for being here for her when she needed it."

He shoved his glasses up his nose, glancing from Elena to me. "Salvatore. Sal. And no problem. What those idiots get away with isn't right. I wish I could do more."

Elena narrowed her eyes at her friend. "You should go by Salvatore." Okay, that wasn't what I had expected her to say.

"Yeah?" He shoved his hands in the pockets of his khaki shorts. "I could, I guess. That's what my mom calls me. I just thought it was easier to tell people to call me Sal."

"Easier on whom? Salvatore's a cool guy. Sal sells insurance. Be Salvatore." She pressed her hand to my chest. "My *boyfriend's* leaving now. Say bye to Lock, Salvatore."

The kid's mouth opened and closed, his head clearly spinning. I chuckled, knowing exactly what he was going through. Glad to know it wasn't just me.

On my way out of the classroom, a couple guys entered, and I knew without a doubt they were part of the contingent harassing Elena. I couldn't do anything to them here, but as I made my way through the doorway, my shoulders just happened to check both of theirs. Hard.

I fucking hoped they bruised like Elena had. That was the least they deserved.

⋯⋯●●●●●⋯⋯

I was back to collect Elena when her class was over. As soon as the professor was finished teaching, I stepped into the room, giving all the assholes the eye on my way up the steps. Two blonde girls giggled and poked at each other from the other end of Elena's aisle.

Elena shot out of her seat, squaring off on them. "You have something to say?"

One of the blondes went pink. The other pushed her shoulders back and made a nasty, pinched face.

"Are you actually slumming it with a maintenance man now?" She scoffed. "First the dork, now a glorified janitor? How low can you sink, girl?"

I hadn't considered changing out of my work uniform to pick her up. Maybe I should have. The last thing I wanted was to embarrass her. It was the exact opposite reason I was here.

Elena leaned her back against my chest, pulling my arms around her. "First, you're a classist idiot. Second, I'd rather be with a glorified janitor who knows how to use his big—no, *huge* tools than an ex-frat boy who can only get it up when his girl is so drunk, she's barely conscious. Scurry along, little Abigail, you're not wanted here."

The girl's mouth flailed for a beat before contorting into a sneer. "At least I don't have to dumpster dive for boyfriends."

Elena shrugged and blew on her nails. "You'd know about dumpster diving since that's where you got your extensions, right?" She straightened in my arms and lowered her voice to a menacing whisper. "Remember the party at Jacob's beach house? I do. If you *ever* talk shit about my man again, everyone else will suddenly remember what went down there. Or should I say who? Are your knees still sore? Is that why you're such a cranky bitch?"

The girl huffed and whirled away, taking her blushing friend with her.

Sal snorted when they were gone, and I was trying like hell not to get hard in the middle of this fucking classroom. I'd seen Elena in action a couple times, but I'd never truly appreciated it until that moment.

"We have to go," I murmured into her ear.

"I could go a few more rounds with her," she protested.

"Come on, Rocky. I'm taking you home."

As soon as we were outside, I had her over my shoulder as I strode through campus. My truck was parked in one of the maintenance garages. By the time I shut us inside the empty space, my dick was threatening to punch a hole through my pants.

"Take off your underwear," I barked as I shoved my seat back, making room for her.

"What?"

"Need you on my dick, sweet girl."

In the dim light, her white teeth shined when she grinned. "You're hot for me?"

"No games, Elena. Come here."

With her eyes on me, she lifted her skirt and wiggled out of her panties, then she crawled across the bench seat. When she was close enough, I grabbed her arms and placed her in my lap, her knees on either side of my legs.

"Take out my cock."

One eyebrow popped, but she didn't argue, going to work on my button and zipper. I raised my hips enough for her to push my pants and underwear down, freeing my length into her smooth, warm palm. Her fingers wrapped around it, gliding from root to tip.

I pulled her tank and bra down, exposing her breasts and the sweet, dark-pink nipples in the center. Leaning forward, I held both of her perfect tits and took a nipple between my lips, sucking it deep. Her skin tasted like the first whiff of fresh air after a lifetime of living in smog. So clean and pure, I couldn't get enough of it.

Elena sighed as she worked my cock against her clit, rubbing the sensitive ridge at the top. Her arousal spread along my length.

"My boyfriend is so deliciously hard right now. I think my boyfriend really needs to come." She pressed her pussy down on my cock, trapping it between my stomach and her slick folds. "Does that feel good, boyfriend?"

Giving her nipple one last suck, I detached and took her head in my hands. "Does my girlfriend want this hard cock in her soaking wet, greedy little pussy?"

"Oh, I'm your girlfriend?" She gripped my base, angling me toward her opening.

"You know that." I nipped at her jaw, her chin, then covered her mouth with mine for a hard kiss. She bit me back, sucking my bottom lip between hers.

"You never said it," she breathed.

She lowered herself an inch, taking in the head of my cock.

"You're my girlfriend." I arched up, getting another inch inside her. She exhaled sharply, letting her head fall forward to rest on mine. "I'm your boyfriend. Now, they all know."

Nodding, she lowered herself another inch or two, pulling me halfway in. I fucking needed her, and she was teasing me. Even though I couldn't think of a reason why, I probably deserved this torture.

"Now, they all know," she repeated. "And you need to fuck me because of it?"

My hands slid down her ribs to the flare of her hips. "I need to fuck you because you standing up for me was the hottest thing I've ever seen. I need to fuck you because I *always* need to."

"Lachlan," she moaned.

She flooded with heat, and the inside of her softened with the rest of her. Pushing herself down my length, she took me all the way in, grinding herself at my base. I groaned so loud, it rattled my windows, but *fuck*, this girl was made to fit me. I was big, but she managed to take all of me, holding me in her tight, perfect channel, wrapping around me like a custom-made glove.

Our mouths clashed, hands clawed and caressed. There was nothing careful or slow. We were acting out a need that, for me, was incredibly visceral. Getting as deep and fully inside my girl was imperative for surviving to the next second, then the next.

Her chest was plastered to mine, fingers tangled in my hair, her ass slapping on my thighs as she bounced up and down on my cock. Rising and slamming, again and again, she went hard, fucking me back with all her might.

"That's my girl," I groaned. "So perfect, taking my cock so damn sweet. That's my fucking girl."

"I can't get enough of it," she breathed in my ear. "I can't get enough of what you do to me, Lachlan. How you make me come. Only you."

My cock swelled inside her at that proclamation. Knowing it was only me who could make her this wild. It damn sure was only Elena who drove me this far out of my mind.

"Need you to come, sweet girl. Tell me what you need to get you there."

"Kiss me."

I took her mouth, sweeping my tongue inside her puffy lips. Her tongue curled around mine, offering me her moans with it. We kissed hard and wet, pushing our lips together until we were locked as tightly there as we were below.

Elena slid her hand between her thighs, rubbing herself and touching where we were joined. Her fingers made a *V* around my thrusting cock, giving it added friction, as if I needed anything else to drive me closer to the edge.

She'd come first. I'd hold out until she was ready. My orgasm would be unsatisfying if she didn't get hers first.

Kissing down her jaw to her throat, I sucked on the crook of her neck. She shuddered, then trembled all over. Yeah, that was her spot. I kept sucking, gently enough not to leave a mark.

All she needed was gentle.

Her inner walls flexed and rippled around me, coating me with her slick arousal. I wasn't ready for this to end, but I had no choice. Her body spoke to mine, commanding me to fill her, soak her with my own arousal until we were coated in each other. My arms wrapped around her, holding her to me as I rutted into her from below, fully emptying myself.

When it was over, when we were panting and limp, Elena laid her head on my shoulder and sighed. I held her there, stroking her hair and the length of her spine.

"Where are we?" she whispered.

Chuckling, I gave her butt a soft smack. "Maintenance garage. I park here sometimes. There's rarely anyone else in here or I wouldn't have taken the chance, no matter how desperate I was to get inside you."

She pressed up on my shoulders. "I'm not complaining. Not even a little bit."

Using my thumb, I traced the elegant slope of her nose and the fine arch of her brow. "Did you ever think you'd fuck a glorified janitor in his truck?"

A laugh sputtered out of her. "I did not, but I can now say I had one of the best orgasms of my life with a glorified janitor in his truck."

I slapped her butt. "Damn right you did."

With a squeal, she rolled off me, leaving my cock out in the cold. I tucked it away and helped her into her panties after she cleaned up with a couple tissues. Then I drove her home, like I'd been supposed to do in the first place.

Chapter Twenty-four

Elena

It was too early to wake up. Way too early, even for me. But my mind wouldn't let me stay asleep, even though I was all snuggled up in my own personal heated blanket.

I wondered if Lachlan knew how cute he was when he was sleeping. He looked his age, maybe even younger, with the extra pink in his cheeks and softness of his mouth.

Oh, the twinges were coming hard and fast. I had to get out of bed or he'd catch me getting gooey over him—and that wasn't part of our light and fun agreement.

Or maybe it was. Who the hell knew what constituted as light and fun?

Slipping my stolen hoodie over my short nightie, I quietly left my sleeping man in bed. After I made coffee, I sat on the deck with my laptop, going over my notes from my and Sal's meeting with our startup owner, Shana Dade.

At first, I hadn't been very thrilled about creating a business plan for this particular project. The only summer camp I'd done as a child was going house to house with my nanny to where her nanny friends worked so I could swim in a different pool while they socialized. Most summers, I hung out at Pen's house or with my ex-bestie, Grace. Until high school. Then there was cheer camp, but that wasn't *camp* camp.

Camping outdoors? Making s'mores and crafts out of sticks? That was as foreign to me as my summers were to Shana Dade.

By the time Sal and I had walked out of the meeting with Shana, I'd been sold. She made luxury adult summer camp enticing, and, on the flip side, she had sold me on the importance of kids getting back to nature, especially underprivileged city kids. Her business model was solid, and her plan to use existing resorts to launch the adult portion would be especially attractive to investors.

She was already running her program at a wilderness resort in California and had her sights set on a luxury ranch resort in southern Wyoming. The pictures she showed us of the property were stunning. I was teeming with ideas to expand on what she had already implemented, and Sal was all over working out the numbers.

I clicked on the website for Shana's dream resort, Sweet Brush River Ranch. Two former presidents' children had been married there. There was an expansive lodge as well as cabins. There was a Michelin-starred, farm-to-table restaurant, and a spa that used indigenous ingredients and offered every service under the sun.

I'd meant to ask Lachlan if he was familiar with this place, but when he'd stepped into my room last night and given me *that look*, all my thoughts had been wiped out.

There was a knock on the front door, startling me out of my research. Judging by my empty coffee cup, a good amount of time had passed, but I had no idea how much. Setting my laptop on the kitchen counter, I went to answer the front door.

Through the blurred panes of glass on each side of the door, I made out the shape of my parents and came to a halt. I hadn't been expecting them. They hadn't called. Why the hell were they here?

My mother was waving at me, so there was no chance of me hiding and pretending I didn't know they were here.

Balls.

I opened the door, a bright smile plastered to my face. "What a surprise!"

Dad gave me a kiss on the cheek and pushed by me into the house. Mom air-kissed both cheeks and held up her full hands.

"We brought breakfast for everyone," she announced.

I gestured around the empty living room. "Unfortunately, everyone's still asleep. I'm not even sure if they're here or with their boyfriends."

I followed my parents into the kitchen, took one of the bags my mother was carrying, and set it on the island. Dad was in inspection mode, opening and closing cabinets, running his finger along surfaces. Seeing him like that in *my* house raised my hackles.

I cocked my hip. "Aren't landlords supposed to give twenty-four-hour notice before entering the property?"

He scoffed. "You're taking care of the place. What do you need notice for?"

My mother hugged me from the side. "It looks great in here, honey. You girls are keeping up the place so well. Don't let your father get to you. When he was in college, he lived in a cesspit."

Dad tucked his hands in his trousers, leaning his backside against the counter. "It was only a cesspit between our weekly maid service."

Mom tutted. "That isn't something to be proud of, Gil."

He waved her off. "What do you expect from four men who'd never been expected to pick up after themselves a day in their lives?"

Mom mimed cracking a whip. "At least I was able to whip you into shape a little. No more socks everywhere around the house."

He rolled his eyes. "I've always hated wearing socks."

She giggled, moving around the island to pat his chest. "I know, which is why you rip them off wherever you're standing."

He caught her hand, pressing a kiss to her knuckles. "Good thing I married you and you can't get away from me."

When my parents were good, they were wonderful. The model of a perfect, adoring couple. And my dad did adore my mother. He did. It was just...he was a self-centered, power-hungry bastard who put work before his mentally fragile wife time and time again. It was hard for me to see them like this when I knew the flip side all too well.

I cleared my throat before they started making out in my kitchen. "Can I ask what prompted the surprise visit?"

"We missed you. Is it a crime to want to see our daughter in her element?" Mom asked.

Dad's eyes flicked to the space over my shoulder. I turned, my stomach dropping at the sight of my big, brutally beautiful boyfriend lumbering down the stairs, raking his fingers through his hair.

"Who's that?" my mother whispered.

Lachlan's head turned, first finding me, then my parents behind me. His brow furrowed, but he didn't hesitate to join us in the kitchen.

"Good morning," he rumbled to me, kissing the side of my head.

If meeting my parents qualified as fun and light, I didn't know, but there was no avoiding it now.

"Good morning," I replied, brushing my hand along his arm. "My parents decided to stop by with breakfast. Lachlan, this is my mom, Diedre, and my dad, Gil."

Lachlan didn't hesitate to step forward with his hand out to my dad. "Nice to meet you, Mr. Sanderson. I'm Lachlan Kelly, Elena's boyfriend."

Dad's gaze snapped from Lachlan to me before he shook his hand. "Nice to meet you too, young man. I recognize your name."

Lachlan's shoulder went tight. "Oh?"

"You're one of Elena's tenants, are you not?"

He nodded. "That's right. You have an impressive memory."

Dad did one of his business chuckles. "It's a small part of my success." He placed a hand on Lachlan's shoulder. "Meet my wife, Diedre."

From the other side of the kitchen, I observed my boyfriend meeting my parents and doing a damn good job of it. It was obvious in his mannerisms and the things he said that he'd been bred in the same kind of world I lived in. He knew how to properly shake hands with a powerful man and that powerful man's wife. He may have been dressed in athletic shorts and a Savage U T-shirt, but Lachlan Kelly was every bit the society kid I was. He could eschew that life now, but it didn't change the way he'd been brought up.

My mother invited Lachlan to stay for breakfast, which he accepted without hesitation. While she and I got to work setting things up, he and my father talked about Savage U professors.

My mom tipped her head next to mine as she counted plates. "You didn't tell me you're seeing anyone."

"It's pretty new," I murmured.

"But committed? I should hope so since he woke up in your bed."

I sighed. "Yes, we're committed."

She sighed back. "I guess this means no more setups."

I bumped her shoulder. "Yes. Please, no more setups."

"He's not anything like the boys you've dated."

"No, he isn't."

"He seems nice."

I turned my head, meeting her eyes. There was nothing judgmental there. If anything, there was a layer of hope in her gaze.

"He's actually wonderful," I whispered.

Her lips pressed together in a tight line as she sucked in a sharp breath through her nose. Sometimes, I wondered if my mom knew more than she let on. If she'd been aware of the things I'd gone through with Nate or had at least had an inkling. I wouldn't ask, and perhaps she would never be in a place where she could offer me words or gestures of support. Then again, she'd been shoving me toward Oliver just a few weeks ago, so I hoped she *didn't* know.

Breakfast was made easier when Helen and Theo emerged from upstairs, taking some of the spotlight off Lachlan and me. Under the table, he took my hand and squeezed. I mouthed, "Sorry," and he shook his head.

"I don't mind," he murmured.

He may have meant that...before my dad launched right into his inquisition as soon as it appeared we'd gotten comfortable. Gil Sanderson didn't have any chill.

"So, Lachlan, what are your plans after graduation?" he asked.

He wiped his mouth with his napkin and bundled it up in his fist. "I'll be going to work on my family's cattle ranch in Wyoming."

My father couldn't hide the surprise at his answer. "Ranching? Really? That's...unexpected."

I rubbed Lachlan's back, leaning into him. "California only gets to borrow him. He's biding his time until he can get back to the wide-open plains and mountains. I plan to take him to the beach as much as possible so he'll have something to miss when he leaves."

Twinge.

"I'll miss a lot of things," he said. "I don't know if the beach is one of them."

"Well, you don't know that because it's easily accessible now. When you're gone, though...you're going to wish you'd built more sandcastles."

Everyone at the table laughed, then Helen took the conversational reins, telling my parents about this sandcastle art show she and Theo had seen at Venice Beach a couple weeks ago.

They stayed until my father couldn't bear being away from his computer and office a second longer. After a flurry of hugs and promises to visit soon, they left. Theo and Helen promptly went back to bed. My parents were *that* exhausting. Plus, it was only ten a.m.

Lachlan picked me up and took me to the sectional, stretching out with me on top of him.

"I'm surprised you're not running away. That was neither light nor fun."

He gave me one of his soft, indulgent smiles that told me he liked me. "I've met him. As strapping and Scandinavian as he is, I still can't see your dad wielding an axe."

It took me a moment to catch up, remembering one of our many, *many* fights while he built my deck.

"Screw you. My dad could beat up your dad."

That made him boom with laughter, jiggling me around on his chest. I liked it. This was what I imagined it was like lying on a vibrating mattress in a seedy motel. Well, minus the seedy motel.

"Too bad they'll never meet. We could test that theory," he teased.

"Yes. Too bad."

・・・・・・・・・

Lachlan and I spent most of the day together, but I made him go home and sleep in his own bed. I still didn't know how to do light and fun, but I kind of thought it meant we couldn't spend every night together.

I regretted it as I starfished in the center of my mattress and picked up my phone to tell him to come back.

Before I could, I read a text from my dad.

Dad: *I looked into your boyfriend. I assume you're aware he's the son of Senator Smythe-Kelly.*

I had all sorts of sarcasm locked and loaded, but my father didn't respond well to my brand of humor, so I tucked it away.

Me: *Of course I'm aware of that. You didn't need to look into Lachlan. I know him and who he is. He's a good guy.*

Dad: *That may be all that's important to you, but I need to know exactly who's in my daughter's life. I'm going to also assume you're aware the "ranch" Lachlan is going to work on is a world-famous ranch resort, Sweet Brush River Ranch. The Kelly family has owned the land for generations.*

I dropped my fucking phone on my nose, sending sparks of pain through my bones. I barely registered the injury to my face as my dad's words pummeled my chest from the inside.

Thank Prada we were speaking over text. I could get away with not admitting I very much didn't know Lachlan's family was anything more than simple ranchers.

Me: *Of course I know that too. I do talk to my boyfriend, you know.*

Dad: *Good. I'm glad for you. Lachlan comes from a solid family with their own wealth. We don't have to worry about him being with you for the wrong reasons. Having a connection to Senator Smythe-Kelly could be very useful to us.*

Me: *Absolutely not. This is a new relationship, and it is MINE. You won't go anywhere near Lachlan's mother or throw around her name for your own gain. That is never going to happen.*

I stared at the text I'd just typed out, but there was no way I could press send. My father would lose his mind if I spoke to him like that, so I deleted it all and typed something much more diplomatic.

Me: *Sure, but Lachlan and I are new, so that's something to think about for the future. Thanks for looking out for me. I'm going to sleep now. Tell Mom I love her. Xoxo.*

Dad: *Good night, Elena.*

I stared up at the ceiling, trying to wrap my head around this new information. In the grand scheme of things, it didn't matter. Since I'd already read about Sweet Brush River Ranch, I knew it *was* a working ranch with two herds of cattle and hundreds of horses, just like Lachlan had told me. He had just left out some major details.

I had to wonder why, and if I should've been angry. As it was, I wasn't certain what I was feeling. Confused, for sure. Possibly a little hurt. But mad? No, I didn't think so.

It wasn't like Lachlan was hiding a secret girlfriend or something. Knowing him, how humble and down to earth he was, he probably didn't love putting his family's true wealth on blast. Not that *just* thirty-thousand acres was anything to sneeze at, but for a girl like me, a world-famous luxury resort was what really made an impression.

The old me would have been blowing up Lachlan's phone with texts, demanding answers and an invitation to his resort. The newer me, who'd been through almost two years of therapy resulting in a marginally less impetuous Elena, plugged in my phone on the far side of my room and climbed into bed with a book.

I would not react.

I'd trust there was a reason he chose not to tell me about the resort yet, and I'd trust when he was ready, he would.

Chapter Twenty-five

Elena

Things were going well. So smooth, I was coasting. It troubled me.

My therapist would have told me it was because I'd spent so much of my life looking for a fight—and finding it—I'd walked around with my dukes up, detonating at the slightest sign of being crossed or someone having something I felt I deserved.

There was no one to fight, not even the assholes in New Ventures. They'd left me alone all week for the most part—which might have had something to do with Lachlan escorting me to and from class. *Or* it could have been due to the fact that two of the boneheads had been placed on disciplinary probation and booted from the class for tampering with my chair. Either way, their absence made it a lot easier for me and Sal to get some meaningful work done for our startup project.

The last week of calm led me to my current need for storming. Luck would have it, it was Saturday night, and I was in the stands with Lachlan on one side of me and my cousin Pen on the other while her boyfriend, Gabe, tore up the soccer field. Helen and Theo were a couple rows down with Zadie and Amir. The whole gang was here. Rah, rah, rah.

Maybe I'd accepted Gabe in Pen's life, but he was still my nemesis. A good-natured nemesis these days, but I was looking forward to sparring with him when the game was over.

Hopefully he'd lose.

I would never tell Pen I thought that. She knew I was thinking it, but we had a "don't ask, don't tell" agreement when it came to Gabe. And it wasn't like I wanted him to get hurt or anything. Just...you know, knocked down a peg so he was grumpy enough to tangle with me.

Lachlan pulled me into his side. "He's got major talent."

I touched my forehead to his. "That is my nemesis you're talking about. Watch it."

The grin he gave me was indulgent, like I was this adorable little thing. "Tell me again what he did to become your nemesis."

"He stole my cousin." I drew a circle in the air in front of my face. "There's nothing rational about my feelings toward Gabriel Fuller. I have grudgingly accepted his existence."

Pen leaned around me. "She loves him. He loves her. They just won't admit it. But they're nice to each other because they love me."

I shook my head adamantly. "That isn't true. Stop spreading vicious lies."

She tugged on my T-shirt. "You wearing Gabe's number says otherwise."

Lachlan swiped his thumb over my cheek. "And painting his school's colors here."

I would have covered my cheeks, but I didn't want the stripes to smear. "Once a cheerleader, always a cheerleader. It means nothing."

Pen smiled at Lachlan. "She loves him, but we can pretend we don't know."

Penelope and Lachlan had met in passing a time or two last year when she and Gabe had visited Helen and me, but this was their first *real* meeting. My cousin was the opposite of me in a lot of ways—science minded and unfailingly kind, serious but friendly, Pen had never cared about popularity and the things that came with it. She did her thing, confident in who she was, not giving two shits about others' opinions of her. She was more like Lachlan than me, and though there'd been a faint twinge of jealousy at their immediate camaraderie, I squashed it like a grotesque bug.

Something exciting happened on the field because everyone around me started screaming and standing. I hopped to my feet, zeroing in on Gabriel fucking Fuller flying down the grass like he was floating, winding around other players without so much as a stutter in his movements. His feet moved so fast, it should have been illegal. Come to think of it, it probably was. This was Gabe.

He made it to the goal, throttling the ball into the net. I guess it was impressive or whatever. I might have screamed his name and clapped so hard my hands tingled. And maybe I hugged Penelope and told her her boyfriend had mad skills.

He was still my nemesis.

·· · · •·• · · ·

After the game, we met Gabe outside the locker room. He ran up the ramp, a madman grin on his face, and scooped Penelope into his arms. When he'd committed enough PDA to last a decade, he moved around the group, shaking hands with Amir, smiling at Zadie, and high-fiving Theo and Helen.

Gabe stopped by Lachlan and me. His curls were damp and wild. He needed a haircut.

I pumped my fist. "Good job, mister. You really showed that ball who's best."

He took my fist and bumped his against it. "Thanks for the enthusiasm, but you know, you don't have to cheer so loud. I was a little embarrassed for you."

"Oh no, those were screeches of horror at how terrible you look in blue. Can you convince your team to switch colors?" I took Lachlan's hand in mine. "Also, this is my boyfriend, Lock. Be nice to him."

Gabe and Lachlan shook hands and patted backs in that way guys seemed to come out of the womb knowing how to do.

"Nice game," Lachlan said. "We spent at least half of it on our feet cheering."

"Thanks, dude." Gabe's arm shot out, hooking around my neck to pull me in. "I'll say this once, and only once. Treat my second-best girl right. You might be able to pound me into the ground with your giant fists, but I have some crazy friends who don't give any shits about committing random acts of violence—"

I ducked out from under his arm and got between him and Lachlan. "Nope. No threatening my boyfriend."

Pen tried to cover her snicker with her hands. I shushed her too.

Lachlan brushed my hair aside to cup my nape. "It's all right, El. I heard him, and it doesn't bother me. I have no intentions of hurting you. I'm glad even your nemesis is looking out for you."

Gabe's job dropped. He threw his arms out. "You told big man I'm your nemesis? I thought we'd moved past that! I'm hurt." He spun to Penelope. "I'm hurt, Lucky-luck."

She patted his chest. "You'll be fine."

"I will if you buy me a milkshake." Gabe cupped his mouth. "To the *T*!"

Pen glanced at me. She knew. I knew. The *T* wasn't a good place for me.

But what could I say? My heart thudded with the beginnings of panic, but we were in a group of friends who didn't know the truth about the night Nate died or what had led to it. There wasn't time to find a way out anyway. We were swept up, cramming into cars to caravan to the diner. Pen and Gabe went with us.

On the drive there, Gabe talked and talked, making Lachlan and Pen laugh. I made myself stay present, snarking back at him like everything was fine.

And maybe it was. The *T* was just a building. It didn't hold ghosts, only memories. I'd had plenty of good ones there. I could make more tonight.

Lachlan reached across the bench seat and caught my hand in his. He gave me a glance, warmth filling his chocolate eyes, and that was all it took for me to start believing the story I was weaving in my head.

Chapter Twenty-six

Lock

Jealousy wasn't a problem for me the way it was for Elena. As long as my girl knew who she belonged to and everyone she encountered did too, I was laid back. Watchful, but relaxed.

Seeing Elena interact with Penelope set off an unfamiliar wave of jealousy in me, though. She was different with her cousin. Before tonight, I thought she'd cracked her barriers for me, but when it was just her and Pen speaking to each other, I saw I was wrong. Like a flipped switch, her walls went down for Pen and right back up when she turned away.

They'd stayed cuddled up the entire time we were at the *T*. I got words, jokes, but not the full force of Elena Sanderson. It drove me crazy not knowing if that was due to her being with her cousin or if something else was off.

But I let it go.

We were back at the house. The girls were inside grabbing drinks. Amir, Gabe, Theo, Julien, and I were out on the deck. Amir, Theo, and Julien were smoking blunts while Gabe stared longingly and I passed.

Gabe rubbed his jaw. "Man, they never tell you the things you have to give up to play sports."

I chuckled. "I've never done it. It's probably better I don't know what I'm missing."

His eyebrows shot up. "For real? You've never smoked?"

"Never interested. I'd rather sit around a fire with some beers."

His fingers slid through his curls as he leaned back in his chair. "I feel that. Back in high school, we used to have some sick beach bonfires. Crazy shit never failed to go down at them. Of course, there was always a copious supply of weed, so maybe I don't quite feel you."

Tipping my beer to my lips, I watched the cherry at the end of the blunts burn bright as the guys inhaled. There was nothing tempting about it to me.

"I'm thinking of fires in the woods anyway. Different vibe."

"Mmm." Gabe took a long pull of his beer. "So, Elena, huh?"

"Mmm. Elena."

He swung his beer back and forth between two fingers. "You seem pretty chill."

I lowered my chin. "Pretty chill, yeah."

"She's not."

"Not usually, no."

His head cocked. "How'd that happen?"

I shrugged. That was a good question. "I like her." Simple answer.

Gabe nodded a few times. "Yeah, I see that. She's pretty rad in her own *I'll cut you if you cross me or wear my Chanel without asking* kind of way. And I know we do the whole mortal enemy thing, but she's basically family, so I gotta keep on the lookout. Now that she's not around, I have to ask: are you serious with her?"

"We're keeping it light," I explained.

Some of the humor faded from his face, suspicion replacing it. "What's that mean?"

"Means I'm not in California for the long haul. I don't want to hurt anyone when I leave, and I don't want a reason that makes me regret going."

My scalp suddenly felt too tight on my head. I yanked at my hair, but it did nothing to alleviate it. Fucking weird.

"So, you have plans to dip on my cousin-in-law?" Gabe pressed.

"Not gonna dip," I bit out. "We're on the same page, having fun."

But that didn't sound quite true, even to my own ears. This was more than that. It probably always had been.

"Until it's not fun? Then you get to bolt and not have to deal with the serious stuff? Nice."

I shook my head. "That isn't me, and that's not what's happening here, I can promise you that."

He winked. "Got it, buddy."

He turned away from me, sliding into the smokers' conversation. Something had told me I'd lost Gabe's respect, but he didn't get it. I was up front about who I was and what I wanted. Elena understood.

I didn't get lost in my head. My girl came out and took a seat on my lap, where she belonged. She was brighter now. Her laugh went all the way through her, and she leaned into me instead of her cousin. Yeah, I liked that.

"Is Gabe being nice to you?" she murmured beside my ear.

"He thumped his chest a little, but it's all good."

She pulled back, frowning. "Again? Why?"

With two fingers, I pushed her pretty lips up. "Nemesis or not, he's looking out for you. That's a good thing. Don't forget you have that."

"Hmmm." She nuzzled her way back into the crook of my neck. "That's fine and all, but why would I need my nemesis when I have you to look out for me?"

I palmed her ass, giving it a squeeze. "You've got me now, Ellie."

· · · • • • • • · · ·

I was behind her, my chest flush with her back, her breasts pressed against the headboard. We were on our knees, my cock sank deep inside her, gliding in and out of her at an agonizingly slow pace.

Her head rolled back on my shoulders. Her lips tipped into a sexy little smile. "God, you feel good. You just…ahhh, I can't get enough of this."

It was good. Incredible. I couldn't get enough either. But I needed more.

"Need to see your eyes, sweet girl." I growled at her like a bear. I felt like one. Like a bear, finding his mate, mindless with the need to rut into her.

It'd been a long, long night of feeling Elena in my lap. Sneaky touches in the shadows. Her teasing me with her little round butt rocking on my dick. Nipping at her earlobes, her jaw, her neck. Working both of us into a swirl of shaking need.

I had her. I was as deep as I could get inside her, but it wasn't enough. I had to go hard. Lose myself in her. Too many hours of behaving meant I was ready to unleash.

Pulling out, I spun her around and pressed her into the mattress. I took a second to look at her. Those round, pink-tipped tits. Her sexy stomach with tan lines at her hips and a thin trail of blonde peach fuzz leading from her belly button to a trimmed triangle of slightly darker curls.

"Look at you."

Her eyes were feasting on me just the same. I was nothing pretty. Not like her. But from her cloudy, lust-filled eyes, I didn't doubt for a second she liked what she saw as much as I did.

Falling over her, I pressed her thighs open wide, and in one smooth thrust, I was fully seated inside her again. Her neck arched back as her mouth fell open on a sigh.

Craving control over her, I cuffed her wrists and held them above her head. She moaned as I went harder, losing myself in her tight heat. There was nothing like this. Nothing better. There couldn't be.

Her arms writhed, but I held on, pushing them down on the mattress. She moaned again, higher now, and I thrust into her with more force.

Her face contorted in a way I'd never seen. Her eyes were wide, panicked.

"Hands," she panted. "I need my hands. Please, please, let me have my hands."

It took me a beat to register what she was saying. As soon as I did, I released her. Her palms came to my shoulders, and her fingers curled around the top, holding on tight.

I stopped moving, sweeping my eyes over her. "You okay?"

She nodded, her eyes abnormally bright. "I'm good. I just didn't want to be held down. But I'm good. You feel so good. Keep going, babe. I want you."

Raising her hips, she drew me in. Her tight heat was too hard to resist, even as worry seeped into the back of my mind. But Elena didn't hide her feelings. If she said she wanted this, I'd give it to her.

Those blue eyes stayed on me, pinned to my face the whole time. It was impossible to look away from her. Even as she came, she fought to keep her eyes open, to stay fully with me. I whispered her name, so when she had to give in and squeeze them shut, she'd never forget who was fucking her. The more I said her name, told her how perfect she was, how beautiful, what a precious little treasure I found her to be, the more she trembled and mewled.

It was sweet and desperate, and pulled me over with her. Shoving my face in her neck, I groaned as I filled her inner walls. Her arms and legs were around me. I slid my arms under her and rolled us to the side so I could hold her without crushing her.

Neither of us said a word. Something had happened there. I wasn't sure what or if it was good or bad. For now, I held Elena until her shaking stopped, and then, because maybe I still needed it, I held her for a little longer.

•••••••••

My back was against the headboard when Elena came out of the bathroom. She'd scrubbed her face and slipped into one of my shirts. It was late, time to sleep, but it didn't look like that was what was on her mind.

She sat down facing me, crisscrossing her legs. "I'm going to tell you something. I don't want it to be a big thing, but I know you're probably wondering about why I freaked out a little."

I straightened, leaning forward. "I'd like to know so I don't do something you don't like again."

"Well, that's because you're the best. Honestly, the best. You know you're the only man who's made me come."

I blinked. "What the fuck? No. How can that be?"

"That wasn't even what I wanted to tell you." She shook her head like that wasn't a massive fucking deal. Damn, men had been failing this girl. "Again, I don't want this to be a big thing."

"Whatever you say can be as big or small as you want."

The breath she inhaled was shallow and ragged. Her eyes were on a spot over my shoulder. My gut sank. This was going to be a big thing. Something I didn't want to hear. Nevertheless, I would listen as intently as possible.

"A little over two years ago, my ex-boyfriend—we'd been broken up for about nine or ten months by then—took me out to dinner before we went away to college. It was a mistake. We didn't have anything to say to each other. Nate taunted me about all the girls he'd banged after he'd dumped me, that sort of thing. I didn't care, which I guess was what made him mad. I don't know. It doesn't matter."

She flicked the thought away with her hand and took another, slightly deeper breath.

"After dinner, he pinned me down in the back of his car and raped me. He drove me home when he was finished, kissed me on the forehead, and told me to have fun at Berkeley. So, that's why I freaked out about my hands being pinned. I didn't know I'd be triggered, but I was already off tonight—"

"I'm sorry." I dug my fingers through my hair, remorse and guilt cramming into every one of my empty crevices. "Shit, I'm sorry, Ellie. I've been really rough with you—"

She touched my knee. "Stop it right now." Wrath lashed her words. "If you treat me like I'm damaged, I'll *feel* damaged. I can come with you because I know you want me more than your next breath. You want me, and you want me to find the same pleasure you do. My body isn't a commodity when we're having sex. It's just us, taking and giving. If that stops, if you're afraid to take what I'm freely offering you, I might as well go lie down with Nate's corpse, because he'll have ruined me."

She had me spinning again. This time, it was like a fucking fun house where everything was warped, and I was *sick*. Sick for her. Sick she went through that. Sick something I'd done tonight had brought her back to that place.

"I'm hearing you." Reaching out, I gripped her chin, bringing her eyes to mine. "I don't know the right thing to say."

"Say you won't treat me like glass."

"I won't treat you like glass." I rubbed at my chest. "You have to give me a minute to process this utter fury. I don't know what the fuck to do with it. This guy is dead, right? Like, really fucking dead?"

That brought a short laugh out of her. Her fingers wrapped around my wrist, drawing my hand from her chin to her cheek. She leaned into my palm, letting her eyes drift shut.

"He's really fucking dead. I killed him."

I jerked forward. "What?"

Her eyes snapped open. "Thanksgiving break, I went to the *T* for a milkshake. Nate was there with a girl—the girl from the leaky house, Sera—and something in me snapped. I went to their booth, told the girl her date was a rapist, dumped my shake on Nate, and booked it out of there."

"You don't like going to the *T*."

That was why she'd been leaning into Pen. Fuck, if she'd told me, I would've gotten her out of there. As it was, she'd never set foot in that diner again. I'd burn it the fuck down if she asked.

"I don't like the *T*." She closed her eyes again. "I got in my car. Nate followed me in his. He chased me. It was raining that night. It never rains, but it was that night. He was driving so crazy. I didn't know what he'd do if he caught me, but I was terrified. I'm not a girl who gets scared like that, but Nate had that effect on me."

Raining... Thanksgiving break... Something was hitting me.

"Did he crash into a boulder? Was he driving a white Mercedes? Nate Bergen?" I asked.

Her eyes were on me again, the space between her brows pinched as she frowned. "Did you read the articles?"

"Why do you think you killed him?"

"He was chasing me, and I lost him when I took a sharp turn, but I knew. God, I knew. I turned around and saw his car all smashed up. I didn't stop. I was going to, but someone else did, so I drove past. I left him there, and I didn't tell anyone. I didn't even call 9-1-1. I just drove away."

Every word she said hit me like a rubber bullet to the sternum. *Bam-bam-bam.* Knocking my breath away and making my heart pound.

I took her hand in mine, kissing the palm, then I pulled her until she was in my lap, turned to face me. I wanted to make sure she heard what I had to say. She had to understand.

"I had to work, so I came back to Savage River early after Thanksgiving. I couldn't sleep, so I went for a late drive. It was raining, so it was going to be a short one."

Elena went deathly still, but I kept going, telling her my version of that night.

"There was a white car on the opposite side of the road, crumpled into a boulder. I parked, called 9-1-1, and approached the vehicle. The window was down. Immediately, I realized the airbag hadn't deployed. The driver was alive, but he was in a really bad way. I talked to him the whole time. Felt like hours but was probably ten minutes."

The bedroom filled with the sounds of our breath. Mine calm and steady, steadier than I'd ever been. Answers to questions I'd had for two years gave me a peace I didn't know I'd been seeking.

Elena's breaths were rapid. Her eyes were wide, darting all over me. There was no peace there, but I could be the one to give it to her.

"I can't believe you were the person who stopped. The man in the truck." She started shaking, so I pulled her against my chest, gently stroking her hair. Slowly, her breathing evened out to match mine. Now, I could give her some of the peace she'd just given me.

"I used to be thankful I'd been there so he didn't have to die alone." It had been gruesome, brutal. Watching that kid die haunted me for a long time. Sometimes, I still had nightmares about his last gurgling breaths.

I touched my lips to her hair, inhaling her scent, which was mingled with mine now.

"I'm still thankful I was there, Ellie. But the reason has changed. Now, I'm thankful I was there to see him suffer."

Her head tilted back so she could look at me. I touched her lips, her chin. She kissed my fingertip. "He really suffered?"

"Mmmhmm. His chest was crushed by the steering wheel, and he drowned in his own blood. It had to be horrific to go through. And he went with the knowledge that you saw him crash. You got to witness his demise. That piece of shit lost, Ellie baby, and he knew it."

Her eyes were clear when they met mine. There were no tears there. She wasn't breaking down, although it would be more than understandable.

"Promise you're not traumatized?" she said.

"Damn, sweet girl, you don't have to worry about me." I pecked her nose. "It wasn't a good night, but I got over it a long time ago, promise."

I'd never tell her about the nightmares. That would go to my grave with me.

She kissed the side of my neck. "Thank you for telling me he suffered. I hope it hurt like hell and his last moments were spent being scared."

"I think they were."

Maybe it was twisted, dirty, bad, wrong, but when we eventually laid down to go to sleep, Elena snuggled against my chest, sighing contentedly, and I closed my eyes, peaceful with the knowledge that I'd watched my girl's tormentor and rapist fade away to nothing. Abso-fucking-lutely nothing.

If that was wrong, I'd stay wrong for my sweet girl.

Chapter Twenty-Seven

Elena

My body was overheated. I tried to toss my blankets off but grabbed empty air. My eyes refused to open, too heavy with sleep and relaxation. Because despite being fevered, I felt languid and loose, like I could melt into the mattress.

The most fiery part was between my thighs. Wet and so, so hot, the feeling was pulling me downward. It was the roughness against my skin that woke me. Before I opened my eyes, I threaded my fingers through Lachlan's hair as he buried his face between my thighs.

"Mmm." My spine arched, and I stretched like a cat after a nap. "Good morning."

He kissed the crease of my thigh. "Morning, sweet girl." He peered up at me, giving me a scorching look. "This okay?"

Biting my lip, I nodded. "Please." It was more than okay, and he knew it. Weeks ago, I'd given him carte blanche permission to wake me up this way. If I could have chosen, I'd start every morning like this.

Lachlan cradled me in his huge hands, holding me to his mouth and licking me everywhere. His tongue was hot and precise, trailing along my center then rimming my entrance. I wove my fingers through his hair as he caressed me with his mouth, lovingly bringing me higher and higher with each stroke of his tongue.

"Oh, that's so good," I cooed. "Don't stop."

He pressed his lips to my clit, sucking lightly. My hips rose, and he held me like that, his fingers digging into my flesh. My arms and hands were free, but my pussy was prisoner to Lachlan Kelly, and it didn't scare me in the least. He ate me like he loved me and couldn't get enough of me. Like I was the most precious person in the world, undamaged and pure. I knew it wasn't true, but I was going to shroud myself in this feeling until it faded.

I came with a whimper, and Lachlan groaned, keeping his lips over me the whole way through. When I started to come down, he kept working me, laving me with attention and endless strokes of his tongue.

I probably should have told him to stop when I lost count of how many times he made me come, but I didn't want him to. After last night and everything we'd uncovered and revealed, I desperately needed to know Lachlan would still want me with the same fervor he had before. If he was just doing this for me as a consolation, I'd shrivel up and blow away.

As if he could hear my worries, he held me tighter to his mouth. The sound rumbling from his chest could only be described as pure pleasure. He was grunting and rasping from my flavor on his tongue. This wasn't a consolation. This was Lachlan giving us both what we craved.

"I need you." I tugged at his hair, but he was stubborn, licking me harder. I shook all over as he took my sensitive, swollen clit between his lips, tears welling in my eyes. It was too much, too good, just right. "Please, babe, come here. Please, I need you."

He peered at me from between my legs, and my heart cracked. His eyes were filled with passionate determination and pure, raw desire.

"Come here," I whispered. "Come fuck me, Lachlan."

He crawled up my sweaty body, licking trails over my heated flesh along the way. And then, he was sinking into me while he held me in his arms. He went slowly at first, rocking into me while peppering my shoulders and neck with wet kisses. My nails dug into his arms and back to keep him close to me.

"I want to take my time with you, Ellie," he husked against my ear.

I had no idea what time it was, and I really couldn't remember the day of the week. We might have been in that bed for a thousand years or an hour.

"Take your time with me then."

"Let me see you ride me." He rolled us like he always had, before he knew my secrets. He handled me with care, but that was Lachlan. Even when he was spanking the sass out of me, he always took care.

My knees dug into his sides as I found my rhythm, taking his thick length even deeper into me. He held my hips, moving me over him. I was tender and so slick, every movement and thrust lit me on fire.

Lachlan's broad chest was shiny with sweat. Some of his hair was plastered to his forehead. When he helped lift me up and shove me back down, his biceps and neck flexed. So, so strong, my man was. He was watching me, my face and tits and stomach and pussy, with intensity and so much want, I had to close my eyes to escape it for just a moment. He took my breath away, plunged white-hot lasers into my chest.

"Look at me, Ellie. I need to see your eyes."

I gave him his wish, and my breath caught when we connected. "Lachlan," I moaned.

"Yeah, that's my girl," he crooned at me. "Love you riding me. I could look at you forever like this."

I slid my palm up the center of his sweaty chest. "You're so sexy. So beautiful. Do you know that?"

He grunted, pushing into me from below. "Know you think that, and that's all that matters."

After long minutes of staring at him, mostly in disbelief that he was mine, I fell forward, tucking my head in his throat. Lachlan released a long groan and rolled us again to our sides. Pulling one of my legs up, he draped it over his arm so he could go deeper, harder. We held each other as we fucked, sweet mixed with pure filth. And it was perfect. Exactly what I needed. More than what I needed. So much more. That was Lachlan and what he kept giving me.

More.

·········

Lachlan dunked his fingers into the bowl of water without complaint. He was humoring me, but that was because I'd made him a sandwich followed by an epic blow job, if I did say so myself.

"Do you do this to yourself?" he asked.

A laugh popped out of me. "No, sir, I don't do my own nails."

His mouth twitched. "Then why should I trust you with mine?"

I pulled his fingers out of the milky water and picked up my mini scrub brush. "Because I've been getting manis and pedis since I could walk. And because I think you know how well I can take care of your body—that includes your hands."

Lachlan's nails were stained from working on engines. It didn't bother me. I barely even noticed anymore. And I loved how rough his fingers were. God, did I love it. But I also had this strong urge to take care of him, possibly since it seemed like he was always taking care of me.

And maybe I was still a little off-kilter with everything we'd both revealed last night. Lachlan had shown me we were okay through the hours we'd spent in bed this morning. This was me trying to find my own form of normalcy.

I still couldn't believe he'd been there when Nate died. What were the chances? I didn't know if it was fate or the universe balancing itself, but I couldn't deny there was an element of inevitability that drew us together.

Helen walked through the kitchen, heading to the fridge. Her footsteps stopped, and she backtracked, raising an eyebrow at Lachlan.

"What's happening here?"

"A manicure," he said. "My girl is cleaning me up."

Helen's eyes met mine. They were filled with glee. "Okay, no shame in that game. Think Theo would be down? This is cute."

I scrubbed at Lachlan's nails, laughing. "It took some special convincing."

Lachlan cleared his throat and shifted in his chair. Helen snorted.

"I'll remember that." She grabbed a drink from the fridge and wandered out, leaving us alone.

Lachlan relaxed after a minute or two, kicking back in his chair. A warmth settled in my stomach seeing him like that after everything.

"I think you like this," I said.

He cocked a grin. "I don't deny it. There isn't much you could do to me I wouldn't like."

My eyes darted up to his. "No other girlfriends ever tried to give you a manicure?"

He chuckled. "Nope. The last girlfriend I had was back in high school. Manicures were the last thing on either of our minds."

I wrinkled my nose. "Ew, I don't want to hear that."

That made him laugh harder. "No, that's not what I meant. I'm just saying, high school kids aren't too concerned about their nails. We spent more time thinking about where to find alcohol for our next field party."

"Field party? I love it."

He jerked his chin. "Gabe mentioned bonfires. You go to those?"

I rolled my eyes. "Yes. Everyone did. And the alcohol just seemed to magically appear. I certainly never spent any time worrying about where it was acquired. But let's circle back to these high school girlfriends."

"Don't even remember names," he rumbled.

I picked up his clean hand and brought it to my mouth. "That is a very good answer." I kissed each of his fingertips. "I love your hands."

"Even when they're filthy?"

"Even then, but only because they're yours."

"That's sweet, Ellie."

I shrugged, self-conscious. "You bring it out in me."

"Only me?"

I waved the nail brush at him. "You've known me for a year now. I think you know the answer to that."

Lachlan rocked back in his chair, his mouth curving. "Yeah, only me."

When I finished with Lachlan's hands, he picked me up and tucked me into his lap to watch a movie. He never mentioned going home or leaving me, and I was glad for it. Otherwise, I might have clung to his neck like a monkey.

After last night, then the beautiful day Lachlan had given me today, it was going to be difficult to let go of this man.

Ever.

Chapter Twenty-eight

Lock

A YEAR AGO, ELENA stormed into my awareness. Back then, I never would've believed how easy it was to be with her. Even a couple months ago, I wouldn't have believed it.

I hadn't known her then, not the way I did now. Last week, she gave me her closest held secrets, and I'd given her a new one of mine in return. I'd been worried things might've been shaky after that, that we'd slide into a dark place and not be able to find our way back to the light, but that hadn't happened. All Elena needed to be happy was a steady dose of my attention, orgasms, coffee, and snuggles, which I was more than fucking willing and pleased to provide. We'd spent every night together since then, chasing more and more of the light. In the back of my mind, I knew I was getting to the place where I wasn't going to want to let her go, but I had no desire to stop.

It was Friday afternoon, and we were stretched out on her sectional, her legs over mine, my feet resting on the coffee table. I picked up her ankle to kiss the delicate bone. Goose bumps instantly appeared on her calves.

"Let's go for a drive," I said.

She perked up. "I get to go on a famous Lachlan Kelly drive?"

I ran my palm along the front of her smooth calf. "It's not that I haven't been taking you. I haven't been going on drives at all lately. Haven't been antsy."

"Are you antsy now?"

"Little bit. I want to go see some stars, but I want to do that with you, if you're willing."

She sat up, her feet on the ground. "I'm ready *and* willing. Let's go."

"All right. Grab a sweatshirt and whatever else you need to sleep with me tonight. I'm gonna run home and take care of something. I'll meet you by my truck in ten minutes."

Her eyes narrowed. "Why do I feel like this drive is more than a drive?" She gasped. "Are you going to propose? No, wait, it's way too soon for that." She gasped again. "Are you going to drive me to a remote location and murder me?"

Grabbing her arm, I yanked her over my lap and spanked her sassy little ass. She screeched with laughter, wiggling her butt at me, taunting me.

"That's all you have for me, big man?"

I smacked her cheek. "That's all you're getting from me, sweet girl. I need this butt sitting in my truck. Can't light it up too red." One more swat, then I lifted her into a sitting position and pressed my lips to hers. "You're a madwoman."

"I know." She grinned into another kiss. "Does this mean no murder?"

"Nah. No proposals either. Sometimes a drive is just a drive."

··········

With the windows rolled down, we drove down the Pacific Coast Highway. Late Friday afternoon traffic sucked, but we weren't in a rush. The scenery was stunning, the music Elena chose was tolerable, and the girl was handsy. I could've sat in bumper-to-bumper traffic with her all day.

Her feet were propped on the dash, toenails painted the palest pink. I knew she'd gotten her nails done a couple days ago so they were shiny and fresh. It was rare they weren't finely polished and perfectly filed. She never gave me shit about the oil under my own nails. Last week, when she'd asked if she could give me a manicure,

I'd said yes. This was following the best blow job of my life. I would have agreed to a lot I normally wouldn't have.

I was glad I had. She took her time, scrubbing away the stains that she could, kissing each of my fingertips when she was finished with them. That had been a fucking awesome night. I was thinking this one might top it.

"What is the best place you ever ended up on a drive?" she asked.

"Hmmm...down here?"

"Sure."

"I don't know. I like when I discover something I never would have if I hadn't gone off the beaten path. There was this cove filled with tide pools I happened upon at low tide—one of the prettiest places I've ever been. I'll take you. Another time, I drove around Venice Beach and wound up a few miles away at this burger shack. Best burger of my life. I took Theo and Helen there under the promise they'd never tell another soul about it."

"Will you take me there?"

I glanced at her, taking her hand in mine to rub my thumb over her smooth nails. "Will you make the same promise?"

"Of course. I'm really good with secrets, and if I'm being honest, I'm having a jealousy flare that Helen's been somewhere with you I haven't."

Traffic came to a standstill, so I turned my head, taking her in. She wasn't joking.

"You know I don't have feelings like that for Hells," I said.

She made a circle over her head. "The things that go on in here aren't rational. I know you aren't into her like that. Believe me, I would've chopped off her gorgeous hair if I thought that was happening. I just want to go on your favorite drives with you to the places that made you happy. That's what the jealousy is about."

Jesus. If we weren't sitting in traffic, I would have taken her over my lap and spanked the living hell out of her for saying something so damn sweet. For making me feel like a little kid who wanted to drag the pretty girl around to show her all his toys. For making me want things that weren't going to be possible.

"I'll take you to all my places. And we'll find some new ones."

"Good." She squeezed my hand, then took hers back to pull her hair into a braid. I watched her crisscross the three sections, completely forgetting we were on the road until the car behind me honked.

"We should play Twenty Questions," she announced when she was finished.

"I'm in. You want to start?"

"You go. Think of something and I'll ask the questions."

I tapped my head, instantly picturing her pajamas. No idea why they'd popped into my mind, other than I always had a steady rotation of Elena images passing through: naked, pajamas, sundresses, more naked.

"Go," I said.

She hummed. "Is it an animal?"

"No."

"Food?"

"Nope."

"My tits?"

I barked a laugh. "It wasn't, but now it is."

She smacked my arm, laughing too. "Shut up. Is it a vehicle?"

"No."

"A person?"

I shook my head.

She chewed on her bottom lip.

"Are you out of questions?"

She shushed me. "I'm trying to get in my Lachlan Kelly headspace. It's full of engines and cattle and power tools, so—"

"Don't forget your tits. My headspace is covered in your tits."

She smacked me again. "We're playing a game here. Stop trying to distract me so you can win. Is it something in my house?"

"Yes."

She clapped. "Look at me. I'm the boss at this game."

"You still have fourteen questions."

"Oh, I won't need them." She ran the end of her braid along her lips. "Is it furniture?"

"No."

"Is it in my bedroom?"

"Yes."

"My vibrator?"

I shook my head. "Nope."

"Lube?"

I grinned at her. "You have a one-track mind."

"You're the one thinking about something in my bedroom." She poked my bicep. "Is it my sheets?"

"No."

"Hmmm...is it...clothing?"

"Yes."

"Panties?"

"No."

She snapped her fingers. "It has to be bras."

My lips tipped at her confidence. "Nah. I don't like when you wear a bra, so I definitely wouldn't be thinking about them."

"Perv," she cooed. "Let me think. Well, if I'm to trust your mind went to something you like, then...my pajamas?"

I nodded. "That's right. Ding, ding, ding. Damn, Elsa, you're good at this game."

She kicked her pretty feet and squealed. "Holy shit, I got it with five questions to spare. Wow, I'm gifted."

My shoulders shook with laughter. After this drive with this girl, I'd never look at traffic jams the same.

And I could say, without a single doubt, nothing would ever top this one.

···●●··●···

An hour later, we reached our destination. Elena had been right. This drive wasn't just a drive—I'd always known exactly where we'd end up.

Her face was plastered to her window, taking in the bumpy, dirt road we were on, winding through Topanga Canyon to the campground spot I'd reserved for us.

"Are we...staying here?"

I couldn't get a read on her, if she was interested or horrified. I figured the only way I'd get her sleeping under the stars was to spring it on her, but we wouldn't be exactly roughing it.

"We are." I pulled to a stop in front of the campground, which didn't resemble any form of camping I'd ever done.

Elena hopped out of the truck, charging onto the site, which was more of an outdoor hotel room built in the middle of two massive trees. There were lights strung up around the perimeter, and lanterns scattered throughout the area.

"You brought me to"—she spun around, her hands pressed together under her chin—"a treehouse? We're really staying here?"

"Up to you. We can hang out, have dinner, and go home when we're ready to go to bed. Or we can sleep here. Whatever you want."

She slowly crossed the packed-earth floor. When she reached me, she leaned into my chest. "You found this place for me?"

She didn't have to say it was obvious this place wasn't something I would've chosen for myself. From the oversized claw-foot tub for open-air baths, to the round bed hanging from one of the thick tree branches, to the candles on every surface, this was where a man took his woman.

"I did. Thought you might like it, but it's okay with me if you don't."

"I do like it. I'm not sure if I'm sold on sleeping outside, but I could be convinced."

Cupping her crown, I pulled her into me, giving her a long, wet kiss. With Elena, I could never predict her reaction. So far, this was better than I'd hoped.

·········

"So, this is camping."

"It's not the kind of camping I've done in the past, but I guess it qualifies." I had the tail end of her braid in my fist, stroking the silky threads with my thumb, content as hell.

We'd made dinner in the open-air kitchen and eaten it in the back of my truck, where I'd spread out some blankets. Now, we lay gazing up at the stars—exactly what I'd been wanting to do with my girl.

She rolled into me, curling her arm around my middle, propping her chin on my chest.

"Are you trying to turn me into an outdoor girl?" she asked.

"Not trying to turn you into anything. This is something I like to do, so I'm sharing. If you don't like it, that's okay."

"But if I don't like it, then I don't get to count the stars with you. You'll do that with someone else."

"I'm not gonna go stargazing with Theo, but next time I want to spend some quality time outdoors, I'd go with him."

Her mouth twisted. "I like it so far. I'm not one-hundred-percent sure I could get on board with more than a night of this, but with you, maybe."

She settled against me, and we got quiet, watching the shifting sky. Or were we shifting? Sometimes it was hard to tell.

"What's the sky like in Wyoming?" she asked.

I sucked in a breath, hit hard and sudden with a wave of homesickness. "During the day, the sky is pure blue, and the air is crisp. You know, they call it Big Sky Country because the sky seems like it goes on forever."

She shivered, pressing herself deeper into me. "I don't know why, but that gives me the creeps. I think I'm too much of a city girl."

I chuckled. "I get that. It makes you realize how small you are when you're there. Especially at night, when it's just you and space. You can see the Milky Way like you're looking through a telescope. There's nothing like it."

She groaned and gently scratched my scruff. "You're going to go back there and never leave. We won't even get to have you for a visit."

I took her hand, kissing her palm. "If you still like me enough in a year and a half to want me to visit, then I will. That'll be my life, but

I'm not gonna forget everything that came before it. Maybe you'll come out to the ranch and I'll get your fancy ass on a horse."

She took her hand away from me, scoffing. "I've been on a horse. I took riding lessons through middle school."

I reared back so I could look at her. "You never told me that."

"I don't show you all my cards. I have to keep you coming back for more."

"That's never going to be a problem." I touched my lips to the top of her head. "Did you like it?"

"It was my mother's thing. I don't have a problem with horses. Some of them are sweet. But riding wasn't my hobby of choice. My mom always dreamed of having a whole dressage team, but she only got me."

"Why didn't they have more kids?"

Her sigh was heavy, and it said a lot without any words.

"You really want to hear this?"

"I do."

"My mother was pregnant once before me, and it ended in a late-term miscarriage. I don't know what that was like for her, but I can only imagine it was terribly sad. Then she had me, and my parents were hopeful that meant her body was capable of carrying more children. That the first one was just a fluke. That wasn't the case, though. She got pregnant again when I was three. That was a brother, Jonathan. He was stillborn. I have memories of her round belly. They're vague, but I can remember kissing it and talking to the baby. There were two more after that, but no happy endings. I was ten during her final pregnancy, so those memories are pretty clear. After she came home from the hospital the last time, our house was like a tomb."

My chest constricted like it was being squeezed from all sides with a vise. I didn't know Elena's mom well enough for this reaction to be for her. This was all for my girl, thinking of her living through that turmoil, the confusion when the brother she'd been expecting didn't come home. Fuck, I hated that for her.

"That must've been tough to live through."

"It wasn't easy, that's for damn sure." She fiddled with the collar of my T-shirt, hooking her fingers around it. "I don't know what my mom was like before that, but she went black each time she lost a baby. That's what I called it when I was a kid. I still think of it that way, even though I know her diagnosis now. She's been institutionalized a few times, and it's helped, but she still struggles. My dad tries to keep her insulated from everything ugly, but what she really needs is him, and he's not there enough. From the time I was little, I was expected to pick up his slack."

Taking her chin in my hand, I tipped her head back. "What's that mean?" I sure as hell didn't like the sound of it.

"It means I am The One Who Lived. All my mom's hopes and dreams were pinned on me. I haven't spent a minute of my life without the pressure to be as perfect as I can be for her. To make up for all she lost. That's why I rode horses for so long. It's why I dated boys my parents wanted me to, made the right friends, took the classes they thought I should. It's why I visit my mother when my father asks me to, even though *he* should be there. It's why I didn't tell them about the horror show that was Nate. It's why, by the time I got to high school, I was a bitter, jealous, angry girl."

She raised her head, staring down at me like she'd been cracked open and was spilling all her secrets over me. I'd take them and keep them if it relieved some of that pressure she lived with.

"Ellie…" Cupping her cheek, I tried to think of something to say, but I had nothing. Except, I understood her more than I had a few minutes ago.

"I love my mother, Lachlan. My father too. For my whole life, we were a trio of brokenhearted people who expressed that in vastly different ways. My mother has never gotten over it, and I'm not sure my father has either."

"Seems like a hard thing to get over, I'll give you that. But you're here. They have you, and they're lucky because you're something special. Not because you're The One Who Lived. It's because you're you."

Her nose wrinkled, and she pushed at my face. "Don't say incredibly sweet things like that to me. I'll have to bite you or destroy property to tilt the world back to where it belongs."

Grinning, I pulled her on top of me and took her face in my hands. "You deserve sweet things said to you, only because they're true. You don't need to go destructive."

She balled her hands into fists and lightly pounded my chest. "Smash, smash."

"You're so fucking cute."

"Even though I have a tragic backstory?"

"Yep. Still cute. And I feel like I get you more now. You're a caregiver, the protector of your family. So am I. We didn't get there the same way, and our methods are different, but we're more alike than not."

And just like me, she'd never leave her family. They were her responsibility, and she'd be here for them. I saw it more clearly than I ever had.

"Lachlan," she sighed.

"Yeah. I have you, Ellie."

She laid her head in the crook of my neck, pressing her lips to my pulse. "I trust you."

"I want you to."

When I walked away from all this, I'd take this moment with me. The ice queen melting for me and showing me more of her damage inside. Trusting me not to damage her further. And I wouldn't.

I don't break things. I fix them.

I looked up at the stars, promising myself I'd do anything not to add another wound—even if it hurt.

CHAPTER TWENTY-NINE

ELENA

I woke up in the dark, the kind of warm I only got from being near Lachlan. My mind clicked on, and I remembered where I was, though I found it almost impossible to believe I'd fallen asleep in the bed of his truck, out in the open.

Lachlan Kelly made me do crazy things, like spilling my guts and camping.

Peering up at him, I found him awake, watching me.

"What time is it?" I asked.

"Around midnight. You didn't sleep for long, but I couldn't bring myself to wake you up."

"Was I being cute?"

He laughed softly. "You're cute, always. You were being serene. And I like having you spread out on me. Don't think I can get enough of it."

Now that I was awake and he was looking at me, I had to fight the urge to shove my face in his neck so he wouldn't see the rawness I'd uncovered. I should have known he wouldn't allow it. He hadn't last weekend when I'd revealed the truth about Nate, and each day since, he batted away any shit I tried to pile between us. Lachlan took my face in his big, rough, safe hands and brought my lips to his. Kissing me slowly, but so damn thoroughly, he smoothed away my jagged edges.

I brought my knees up, straddling his hips, and tucked my hands under his shirt. This was easier. When we reached for each other, what came next was as natural as breathing. So we were in the bed of his truck under a starry sky, that didn't matter. What mattered was getting closer to Lachlan in a way I understood.

He tugged my shorts off and yanked my hoodie over my head. His shirt came next, and I grappled with his shorts until they were under his hips and his cock was nestled in my folds.

I'd been so afraid the way he touched me would change after he found out about my assault. And maybe it had, but how couldn't it? We knew things about each other and were bonded in a way that was unbreakable. He hadn't pulled away from me, though. If anything, his touches came more frequently, kisses lingered longer, and the way he fucked me became tinged with an edge of greed.

I liked it very much. I liked *him* very much.

Tugging me down to his mouth, he sucked on my nipples and kissed my chest. His lips traced the undercurve of one of my breasts while he palmed the other, teasing the taut peak with his thumb.

I rocked my hips slowly, little movements so the head of him brushed my clit. It didn't take long for me to feel my own arousal coating him. It went without saying, even in my own head, no man had ever made me this wet. Every single time we were together, I wanted him inside me with a desperation singular to him.

Lifting up, I angled him to my opening and took him in. He stopped moving, my nipple captured in his lips, as I lowered myself to the hilt. His groan vibrated my flesh, sending shivers through me.

"Damn, sweet girl." He nuzzled into my chest, his arms banded around me. I fell over him, my breasts flattened against him, letting him hold me.

Lachlan rolled us to our sides so we were face to face with my leg draped over his hip. He rocked into me, taking it easy, but going so deep, it made my heart pound. He held my braid, which was partially unraveled, and rubbed it on his lips and cheek. It was sweet. So sweet, I whimpered. How did I handle this?

I tried to hide, but as I dove for his neck, he caught my chin and kissed me. Okay, I could do that. I wasn't so exposed when we were kissing.

Except I was. He opened my mouth to his, and I had no choice but to let him in.

Breeze from the valley blew across my burning skin. I tucked myself closer to Lachlan, the hairs on his chest rubbing against my budded nipples, tight and sensitive from his attention.

He held me as our bodies glided, unhurried. There was something incredibly peaceful about being in each other's arms under the midnight sky. We had nowhere else to be, no one else to be with. It was just us, taking and giving.

It was a lot. The emotions stirring with his gentle, sweet caresses were unfamiliar and altogether frightening for a girl like me from a man like him. I was already attached, but I could see myself getting to a place where he'd have to pry me off with a crowbar if he kept treating me like he saw beneath my pretty venom and loved every ugly, mottled, scarred bit of me.

"Make me come," I whispered, even though there was no one around. It just seemed wrong to interrupt the serenity of the moment with loud demands—and I needed to feel something other than my heartstrings going taut.

He wedged his arm between us, cupping my pussy. The pad of his fingertip rolled my swollen clit until I was trembling and quietly moaning. With his other hand, he held my throat, keeping me in place so he could watch me. My eyes were closed, but his gaze was so heavy and intense, it was a tangible thing, stroking over me and delving into me.

When he got close, he pressed me onto my back and fucked me with long, powerful strokes. His lips were on my face, kissing me like feathers. I couldn't stop shaking, coming around him. It was all I could do to hold on tight so I didn't get taken up by the gentle wind.

He finished with a pained groan next to my ear. I tucked my face in his shoulder, my limbs circling him to keep him anchored to me. I needed that moment to put my game face on. If he saw me now, he'd know I was sliding into dangerous, unlight, unfun territory.

It was his fault, really. This was what he got for being so fucking wonderful and thoughtful, and making me come with his big dick and magic fingers. What did he expect? For me not to fall for this shit? I might have presented as some wily, untouchable cheer-bot, but underneath my very poor facade, I was just a woman with a fragile heart and lovelorn vagina.

We lay in the truck for a while, but it wasn't so comfortable anymore. The blankets only provided so much padding underneath us. I could've slept like a baby on top of Lachlan, but my man needed a mattress.

"You want to sleep in the bed or drive home?" Lachlan asked.

"We can stay. So far, I like this version of camping," I told him. "Don't even think about getting me into a tent, though. And I refuse to use an outhouse."

He chuckled, pulling me out of the truck to my feet. "I never thought you would."

•••••••••••

I was wearing satin pajamas. My adorable turquoise ones with the black lace trim. The sun had risen an hour, maybe two, ago. Snuggled up in Lachlan's hoodie, I tucked my legs inside with me. It would be hot in the canyon later, but this early, it was barely above sixty. Yet, here I was, outside, sipping a cup of coffee from a mug that said "Glamping: Camping for bougie people." The floor under my chair was dirt. The ceiling was a clear blue sky. I'd spent a night outside, but that wasn't the strangest part.

The strangest part was the sense of contentment settling inside me. There was no question most of that was due to the man sleeping in our treehouse bed. The rugged, overgrown man who knew most of my ugly and still looked at me like I was something precious.

Twinge.

Ugh, I was so stupid for him. Thank Prada he couldn't see how gooey I got at the very thought of him. I couldn't even look at him sleeping now, with his tree trunk arm slung above his head, or I'd blush. *Me,* blushing over my own boyfriend.

This was probably love. I didn't twinge or blush for anything less.

He'd said only light and fun, but things had changed. We'd gone through heavy and dark, and he was still here. As far as I was concerned, the promises we'd made at the beginning were null and void due to lack of information at the time of the agreement. Lachlan had to feel it too.

I wasn't worried.

How could I be when my beautiful man had climbed out of bed and was stalking across the dirt to get to me with a look on his face a lot like hunger.

"You look good out here, Elsa," he rasped.

"You do too."

I set my mug down and popped my legs out of the hoodie. When he got to me, I was ready for him. Sweeping me in his arms, he buried his face in my neck, and I wrapped my arms and legs around him.

"My outdoors girl," he rumbled against my skin.

"Only for you," I murmured back.

With a groan, he reached into his pocket and slipped out his phone, frowning at the screen. "Shit, looks like my mom went off in my texts last night."

"Is there an emergency?"

He stuffed it back in his pocket and pressed his cheek to mine. "Not anything that can't wait. We've got another hour here. I'm not going to think about anything but this."

With my ass in his hands, he strode across the dirt floor to our treehouse bed and tossed me down on it. He stood over me, looking at me. His eyes were soft as they trailed along my limbs and hair. When our eyes met, the corners of his mouth curved with satisfaction. I didn't know what he was thinking, but in that moment, I felt like I was his favorite everything.

No, I wasn't worried at all.

・・・・・・・・・・

The drive home was quiet. Without traffic this time, it went a lot faster. Lachlan's phone vibrated a few times. Each time he read the texts from his sister, he frowned. His parents were putting her in the middle again.

"Do you want to stop so you can call her?" I asked.

He shook his head. "Nah. Let's just get home. I'll deal with it then."

"Okay."

Our hands were clasped in the middle of the bench seat the rest of the trip. He let go when he pulled into his driveway, then he was around the truck, opening my door before I could miss him. He had me out, pressing me into the side of the truck, kissing the hell out of me.

His body leaning into mine, his thick erection digging into my stomach, his mouth feasting on mine like there was no tomorrow. He took my breath away. Knocked my knees out from under me. Held me close and let me soar.

If he had expected me not to fall for him when he did things like *this*, then he was really, really dumb. And Lachlan wasn't dumb. I suspected he was falling along with me.

Forehead against mine, he exhaled a shuddering breath. "I need to go home, take care of this family shit."

"I should go take care of family shit too."

He pecked my nose. "You're a good daughter, you know?"

"Thank you for saying so."

He gave me one more hard kiss. "I'll see you later." Backing away, his eyes stayed on mine as I pried myself off his truck. With a sharp nod, he carried my bag to my house, dropped it on my porch, and gave me one more kiss. "Thank you, Elsa. For camping with me. For all of it."

He strode down the steps, back to his house before I could respond.

I touched my tingling lips and whispered, "Thank you for taking me. I might be totally in love with you."

Then I went inside to shower and change into my good-daughter costume. It was time to face what I couldn't avoid.

Chapter Thirty

Lock

I crossed the grass between our houses, the condensation from Elena's coffee cup dripping down my fingers. I'd taken my time getting back here with it.

Hearing my boots crunching the dead grass, Elena folded her newspaper, revealing her black nightgown. I knew that one. It was made from the softest cotton and slid over her body like a second skin.

Fuck.

I hated that I had to do this. But I'd let it carry on too long. I hadn't been thinking of her feelings when I hadn't ended this before we got too deep. That had been all me. Somewhere along the way, I fell in love with Elena, and I couldn't convince myself to let her go, even though there was no question I had to. It was all because of my greed for her, my own selfishness.

She was mine, but I couldn't keep her. It wouldn't be right. I'd ruin us both if I tried.

"Good morning," she chirped. "Is that for me?"

"It is." I climbed onto the deck and set the coffee down in front of her. Bending over, I cupped her nape, drawing her mouth to mine. She gripped my shirt, making a high, almost keening sound as I kissed her long and deep for the last time. Fuck, I just needed to memorize this, to take some of this sweet with me. After today, this morning, I wasn't going to get any more of it. Not even a taste.

Settling into the seat across from her, I waited for my heart to stop thundering. My stomach was sick, filled with dread. I was doing the right thing. I knew that. I didn't want to, but there was no choice. Not for her. Not for me.

"How was your mom?"

I hadn't seen her since I'd dropped her off on her porch yesterday. I'd been dealing with my family turmoil, making long phone calls to my mom and dad. Reality had hit me square in the face.

She sighed. "She was in bed when I got there. It took me half the day to coax her out. My dad didn't answer my calls for hours. He had no idea his wife was wasting her day away. She wouldn't say, but I'm pretty sure she spent Friday in bed too. Naturally, I'm worried, and I'm pissed my dad isn't paying attention."

"Did he come home when you called?"

"Yes, he did." She drew shapes in the condensation coating her cup with her fingertip. "By the time he was home, she had rallied. She's good at faking it."

"I'm sorry."

She shrugged, turning to me. She brought her feet up to my legs, resting them on my thighs. "I'm used to it. Nothing changes."

It was time. I was putting this off because I didn't want to do it but I had to.

Elena rubbed her feet along my thighs, giving me an easy kind of smile I'd never get again from her. "What should we do today? Can we go to the burger place? Or to see the tide pools? I'm going to be so busy the next two weeks getting ready for my New Ventures presentation, we need to make today count."

My fingers circled her delicate ankles, stilling her movements. This was it.

"We have to talk, Ellie."

Her hand flew to her braid, holding on to it like a rope. Her feet dropped to the ground. "I thought we *were* talking."

"About us. This thing we're doing. It's been fun. Great, actually. But it's time. I'm calling it."

Fire burned low in my gut. The right thing didn't always feel good, but that didn't make it any less right. I had to keep reminding myself of that. This was for her. To save her from more pain. To not add another wound. This was for Elena.

"Speak clearly," she intoned. "Say exactly what you mean, Lock."

I wanted to correct her, to tell her it was Lachlan, but I was giving up that right, and it pissed me off. Not at her, but at the impossible circumstances. My anger and frustration over it all made my next words come out harsher than intended.

"I said from the beginning what I wanted and didn't want. I was up front with you. It shouldn't come as a surprise. This was only supposed to be fun, short term. That's what we said. I'm standing by our agreement."

"You were supposed to warn me." She folded her arms over her chest. "You promised you'd warn me. You said I wouldn't be blindsided. You lied to me."

I shook my head. My mouth opened, but no sound came out. She was right. Exactly right. But things had changed so rapidly, I had to do it now.

"You're right. I messed up. But this"—I gestured back and forth between us—"I don't want this. It's going past the point of what I'm looking for...what I told you from the beginning I was looking for."

She turned away from me just as her chin started to quiver. That one glimpse was enough to punch me in the solar plexus. Her sadness winded me, took me down to my knees. Her back moved as she filled her lungs with air.

When she faced me again, her jaw was solid stone. "I'm too much for you. That's what you're saying. You asked, so I thought you wanted to know me, but I guess you realized I'm a lot more than you're willing to handle. It's not *light and fun* to be with a girl with all this baggage. I hear you loud and clear."

I started to reach for her out of pure instinct, but she flinched away like I was a stranger.

"Elsa, don't be like that."

Her lip curled. "Don't ever call me that again, *Lock*." She rose from her chair, regal as she held her chin high. "You aren't who I thought you were."

Standing, needing her to hear, to understand this was for her own good, not mine, I got in front of her, blocking out everything around us.

"This has nothing to do with your baggage. There was no future here. I'm doing you a favor leaving now. It was only going to get harder, because this was always going to end. We never should have started, and I'm sorry for that. I'm really sorry. That's on me. I'm making it right now, though."

She held herself so still, her limbs vibrated. "Oh, should I thank you? Is that what you expect?"

With a heavy sigh, I shoved my fingers into my hair. "No, of course not. But it doesn't have to be this way. We can still be friends. I'm right next door. I'll be here when—"

"We were never friends," she hissed.

I leveled my gaze on her. Her blue eyes blazed back at me. So mad. So untouchably beautiful. "You had to know this was coming. You knew what I was about. I never hid it from you."

Again, I reached out for her out of pure instinct. She stumbled back, hitting against the table. I grabbed her shoulders to steady her, but she wrenched out of my grasp, her chest heaving.

Her pretty lips turned down in a deep frown, accusation pouring off her in waves as she glared at me. My hands were extended, holding on to thin air when all the fuck I wanted to do was hold on to her and never let go.

But keeping her was impossible. This hurt now. The way she was looking at me killed me, but it would have been worse months or years down the line.

"Ele—"

"Get the fuck off my deck."

It staggered me, to get that poison from her when I'd uncovered her sweet. I knew it was there, had fallen in love with it, with *her*, but I'd never have it again.

"I never wanted to hurt you," I told her.

She was steel when her eyes met mine. Colder, harder, more impenetrable than I'd ever seen her. If she was in pain, if she hated me, if she wanted to rip off my head and eat her cereal out of it, she didn't let me see it.

"I won't ask you again. Get off my deck and do not come back. You aren't welcome."

With that, she spun on the ball of her foot, calmly opened her sliding glass door, stepped inside, and closed it behind her, disappearing into her house.

Bending at the waist, I heaved a ragged breath. Why the fuck didn't doing the right thing feel better? It should have been a relief. Maybe that was coming. When I saw she was okay, moving on from this, then it would come.

The melting iced coffee sat abandoned on the table, her folded newspaper beside it. Goddammit, I was going to miss this. Miss her.

With one last look at the deck that had been both the start and end of us, I walked down the steps, crossed the dying grass, and went home.

Chapter Thirty-one

Elena

I didn't say a word to anyone. The utter humiliation of being left almost superseded the devastation of losing the first person I'd been wholly open with.

I avoided Pen's calls. Brushed off Helen and Zadie. Folded into myself like an old, discarded newspaper for two solid days.

A spark of fury burned in my belly, but it had yet to grow. I seemed to be stuck in shock, unsure how I'd gotten here.

Deep down, I knew it was me. Lachlan might have painted him dumping me into a lovely picture of selflessness—he'd done it for *me*—but behind it was the real shit show: I wasn't worth taking a chance on. My baggage was too heavy for that big, strong man to carry.

Who could blame him, really? I was just a girl with a crazy mother, a rapist ex-boyfriend, and a streak of jealousy wider than a city block. Sure, I'd put out, but he hadn't even been able to pin me down like he'd wanted to without me freaking out.

When Nate had broken up with me the final time our senior year of high school, it had been a relief. I'd gone through a minor destructive phase to soothe my bruised ego, but that had been a massive turning point for me. He'd freed me from that madness.

Lock letting me go didn't feel like freedom at all.

This was being locked out in the cold. Rejection bound my lungs, making it difficult to breathe. I had no idea how to move on from this.

Zadie tapped my arm. "Hey."

I looked up from my phone, surprised to see her and Amir sitting beside me. We were in accounting, so it made sense, but my head was stuffed with cotton, so it was taking me some time to process…well, everything.

"Sorry." I rubbed my forehead in an effort to wake myself up. "Hello, you."

She peered at me, concern etching into her soft features. "Are you sick? You look tired."

I flicked her knuckles lightly. "Thanks, lovely. You're beautiful too."

She giggled. "You know you're stunning, El, but Amir and I were here for two minutes before you even realized it." She pushed a blueberry muffin toward me. "Eat this. I think you might need it."

"Thank you." I took it, but I didn't eat any. My stomach was rolling too violently to even attempt it.

Zadie stared at me. When I didn't touch the muffin, she sighed. "Are you okay?"

"Lock broke up with me." I shrugged. "Give me a week or two, and I'll rally." I was my mother's daughter, after all. Us Sanderson girls were really good at faking it until we were breaking. That might not have been the exact saying, but it fit. It didn't feel true, but one day, it might.

"Shit," Amir hissed. "Sucks, girl."

I snorted. "Understatement. That salt-of-the-earth, nice-guy routine really fooled me."

Zadie shook her head hard. "What happened? I mean, was there a fight? Did he say why? He seemed to like you *so* much."

I recited his little speech for her, and the spark inside me grew. It still wasn't big, but if I tended to it, maybe my anger would overtake this blinding, aching sadness.

Anger had been my near-constant companion in the past. It was an old, familiar friend. If I invited it inside, it would be like a sweet little reunion.

"I don't really want to talk about it anymore. If you could tell Helen...and, I guess, everyone else, that would be great."

She rubbed the top of my hand. "He'll realize what a big mistake he made."

"Thanks for saying so, Z. He won't, but I appreciate you'd think that."

The biggest sucker punch was I couldn't summon anymore anger. I wanted so badly to be furious, to blind myself with rage, but it wasn't happening. This melancholy weighing me down was for emo kids and terrible poets, not girls in adorable pink Free People slip dresses. It clung to me like an ill-fitting second skin, or a disgusting leech, sucking me dry. I couldn't shrug it off or replace it. It was with me until it was done with me.

After accounting, I dragged my feet getting to my next class. I hadn't seen Lock since he'd *set me free,* but I couldn't avoid him when we shared a class—especially not when our seats were right beside each other.

I stalled in the bathroom for as long as I could, swiping lip gloss on my lips and a little on my cheeks so I didn't look like a dead girl. At least I was good at dress-up.

Who am I, thinking thoughts like that? Jesus, next I'll be piercing my lip, dying my hair black, and carrying around a beat-up notebook to write down my innermost thoughts.

It was marginally easier to laugh at myself than admit I was heartbroken.

I'd *camped* for that man. I'd ridden everywhere in a truck and eaten hamburgers in the back of it. And I'd been happy to do it because I'd been with *him.*

Stupid, stupid, stupid.

Sucking in a ragged breath, I quietly walked into Spanish, my gaze automatically zeroing in on Lock's spot, except he wasn't there. Someone shifting in their desk drew my eyes to the opposite side of the room. My stomach heaved. Bile rose in my throat. He'd changed seats, moving his as far from mine as possible.

Spinning on my toes, I walked right back out of the classroom.

It was too late to drop this class, so I'd have to take an incomplete. Or fail. I didn't know what would happen, but there was no way I could attend that class for the rest of the semester. The room was far too small to share it with him. So what if my GPA was just recovering from my atrocious first year at Berkeley? It would recover again. My dad would give me shit, but he'd get over it.

Clutching my stomach, I hurtled down the hallway toward the front of the building.

"Elena!"

Oh, no way was he chasing me down. I must have been hearing things. He couldn't possibly be doing that. Not after he dumped me. Not after he went to great pains to be nowhere near me. He wouldn't do that.

"Elena, stop," he barked from right behind me.

Hot, rough fingers wrapped around my bicep, holding me with a gentle firmness that stopped me in my tracks. He spun me around so fast, I smacked into his chest. Catching his clean, summer scent sent me scrambling back, but I could only go so far in his grip.

"Take your hand off me."

He immediately let go, but he didn't stop crowding my space. "Go back to class."

I shook my head. "No. I'm dropping it."

Eyebrows contracting, he frowned at me. "You're not dropping the class. Get your ass back in there."

"Whoa." I pushed off his chest, giving me a foot of space. "You don't get to talk to me like that anymore, and you certainly have no say in what I do, Lock."

The tendons in his neck stood out, but at least he was wise enough not to correct his name.

"We can share a class. I moved my seat so—"

"How magnanimous of you. Whatever makes your life easier." Oh boy, I guessed I'd found my anger. Damn, that felt a lot better than melancholy.

He practically growled at me. "I'm trying to make you more comfortable. This has nothing to do with me."

"That isn't true. I chose to leave the class, but *you* chose to chase me down." I blew out a hot breath. "I don't want to do this."

"Do what?" He looked at me with a gentleness that should have been incongruous with his size and unruly ruggedness, but it was so natural, it reminded me of all he'd taken away from me. That gentleness had been directed at me a few days ago.

"Any of this," I answered.

"What can I do to make this easier?" he asked.

Easier? He could go back in time and never have given me a taste of something I'd never have. He could try to love me even though I was difficult. He could find me worth the effort.

None of those things would happen. And being near him wouldn't get easier. Not anytime soon. Maybe never. So, I asked for all I could.

"I want you to disappear and not exist. Can you at least give me that? Let me pretend you don't exist. If I want to drop Spanish, let me do it. Don't make me stand here, talking to you, feeling your hand on my skin, touching me. It's mean, Lock."

His head dropped, and he scrubbed at his jaw. "This isn't what I wanted."

"You wanted to walk away, and you did. Don't circle back. It isn't fair to me."

Fuck me if I didn't have tears in my eyes. I was so close to throwing up and crying and making a complete fool of myself.

"Don't drop the class, Elsa." Firm, bossy, he commanded me like he had the right to.

"Disappear, Lock."

For the second time in the span of ten minutes, I spun on my toes and walked away.

At least this time he didn't chase me.

· · · · • • • • · · ·

I went through the motions. I had to. Sal and I had a lot to do to prepare our presentation, and although I'd let myself down time and time again, I couldn't do it to him. We worked together every spare minute we had, which was such a goddamn blessing, I could've gotten down on my knees.

By Friday night, we were done. We'd be presenting to the class on Monday, then to the alumni next weekend. I was proud of our business plan. We'd worked our asses off for our little startup.

The problem was, now I was at loose ends, and that meant thinking. Thinking meant more melancholy because I hadn't been able to hang on to more than a couple minutes of anger at a time.

Helen and Zadie offered to hang out, to have a girls' night or go out dancing, but they'd been shooting me pitying glances all week. I had to escape.

The destructive side of me wanted to stir up trouble. I scrolled through my phone, rolling my eyes at all the phone numbers of people I barely remembered.

I stopped on Sera's. Maybe band geeks could be fun.

Me: *Hey, it's Elena.*

Sera: *Hey, girl! I'm so excited to hear from you!*

Me: *I was thinking we should hang out. Is there anything going on tonight?*

Sera: *Absolutely. My roommates and I are getting ready to go to the bars. Want to come over and pregame with us? We'd love to have you.*

Me: *Perfect. I'll be there in twenty.*

Sera: *We're going to have so much fun!*

I honestly didn't care if we had fun. As long as I did something I'd regret tomorrow, something that would take my focus off the hollowness in my chest, I'd be satisfied.

Digging in the back of my closet, I chose my smallest sundress that barely hit me midthigh. I'd only worn it once because of how minuscule it was, but since I was all for making bad decisions, it seemed like the time to throw it on.

A pair of heels and swipe of lip gloss later, and I was ready, heading out the door. My timing was a wreck. Lock's truck pulled into his driveway at the same time, with Julien in the passenger seat.

Or maybe my timing was perfect, given the slamming of his door and furious charge across the grass. Julien was a lot slower, but I was pleased to see him using his crutches instead of his chair.

"Get back in the house," Lock ordered.

Sputtering a laugh, I shook my head and turned to go in the opposite direction. His brick wall of a chest stopped me as he maneuvered himself in front of me.

"Where are you going in that dress?" he demanded.

"Not cool, Lock," Julien said from behind me. "Let her go."

I laughed harder, trying to dodge around him. Of course he wouldn't let me.

"This isn't disappearing." I drew a circle in the air around him with my fingertip. "It's the opposite of that."

He ignored me and carried on with his caveman ways. "You can't go out like that."

Julien sidled up beside his friend, bringing his shoulder in front. "Back off," he muttered.

"Untrue. I'm going. You can watch me leave, but that's the *only* thing you can do."

Lock brought his hands up like he was going to put them on me, then dropped them to his sides, balling them into fists.

"You're pissed at me, I get it. But that doesn't mean I'm going to stand by and let you do something dangerous."

I rolled my eyes even though his concern was a sharp knife to the gut. "I'm going to Sera's house. Remember her? Leaky sink? I won't be alone, so you can stop worrying your pretty little head about me and disappear again."

His eyes were darker, harder. As they swept over me, I had to suppress a shiver. They still affected me the same.

"I'll drive you," he said.

I turned my attention to Julien. "Babe, get your bear under control. He's saying crazy things that don't make sense. I think he might be rabid."

Julien tipped his chin at me and subtly shifted his body in front of Lock's. It was a joke. If Lock wanted to, he could knock Julien over as easy as a bowling pin.

"Go. Have fun but be safe. Call me if you need a ride home," Julien said.

I winked at him, but it was all show. This was gutting me. All of it. If I didn't fill myself up with bad decisions, I'd be a dried-up husk.

"Oh, I don't think I'll need a ride." I shimmed my hips, and the obscene hem of my dress kicked up to the tops of my thighs. "I'll be just fine."

Lock's chest cracked like thunder. He reached for me, but Julien was there, keeping him at bay while I made my escape. I couldn't fool myself into believing Lock was jealous I might catch the attention of another man. After all, he'd gotten what he'd wanted from me. No, that show he'd put on was some possessive, knuckle-dragging shit. He may have discarded me, but that didn't mean he wanted another man to have a go at me.

The only thing that kept my chin up on my way to Sera's house was the knowledge that Lock would never find out the very idea of someone else's hands on me made me want to rip my skin off.

·········

My first thought when I woke up was that the chest my head was resting on was all wrong. It wasn't even close to broad enough. The arm resting loosely on my back was nice, but it was no tree trunk. It didn't anchor me to the mattress like it was supposed to.

Eyes flying open in panic, it took me far too long to focus on the man sleeping beside me. I almost sighed with relief when I realized he wasn't a stranger, then another wave of panic flattened me to my back at being in bed with Julien.

I racked my brain to remember the night before, but it was spotty. I'd taken shots with Sera and her band geek friends. By the time we got to the bar, I'd been more than tipsy. Flashes of me dancing on the bar, throwing darts at boys instead of the target, taking body shots off random girls, and flirting with ugly boys hit me like a nauseating brick.

My phone was on the table beside the bed with five percent left in the battery. It was only six. I couldn't have slept more than a few hours. No wonder I was dizzy. My messy ass was still a little drunk.

There was a series of texts from Sera. I clicked on her name to read them through bleary eyes.

Sera: *I'm sorry. You told me to leave you there.*

Sera: *An angry guy with a hood over his head answered the door. He yelled at me for letting you get so drunk.*

Sera: *I cried a little. I cry when I'm drunk. I'm sorry!*

Sera: *You seemed to know him and were happy to be with him, so I left. Well, he slammed the door in my face, so I didn't have a choice.*

Sera: *Please text me that you're okay! I feel awful.*

I had no memory of any of that, but I shot her off a quick text before my phone died so she wouldn't call the police on Julien for kidnapping me or something.

"I'm surprised you're awake."

Julien's low voice startled me into dropping my phone on my face. It hit my forehead with a clunk. Nice. Why not have yet another injury on my face?

"Did we have sex?" I asked, though I was almost certain we didn't.

He burst out laughing, which was pretty fucking rude. "You could barely stand when your friend dumped you on me. You're hot, but I'm not into that. Plus, you were snoring on my pillow before I could even get into bed."

"I don't snore." I sighed in relief. "We were snuggled up when I woke up, so I got concerned."

"That was all you. You're like an octopus when you sleep." He pushed himself up on his pillows. "You feel like shit?"

"Still a little drunk. I'll feel like shit soon, I'm sure."

He brushed my hair off my face, giving me a tender, pitying look I hated. "Why are you doing this?"

"I'm brokenhearted. I just wanted to feel something other than sad." I covered my face with my hands, groaning at myself.

"Did it help?"

"I can't remember much of last night, so probably, temporarily, it did."

"And now?"

"Still brokenhearted." I peeked at him from between my fingers. "What is the point of this? Are you trying to make me feel worse?"

"I'm trying to help you not self-destruct."

"Can't I be sad?"

"Sure, but do you want him to see you like this? Will that make you feel better or worse?"

My heart skipped a beat or two. "I don't want to see him at all."

He put his palm on the top of my head. The weight of it was surprisingly comforting.

"Sorry, buddy, but that's not a choice. You're going to see him, he's probably going to chest thump because he's Lock, and even if he doesn't say it, he regrets letting you go."

"He doesn't."

"If he didn't, do you think he'd be concerned about where you were going and what you were wearing? That show he put on last night was a man living in a world of regret who doesn't know what to do with himself. So, make him sorry. Let him see you being okay, moving right along with shit. The last thing you should be doing is wallowing like a sad little guppy."

I shoved at him, but there was no real force behind it. "He doesn't want me, and I'm not a guppy, Phantom. Don't call me that."

He gave me one of his crooked grins. "Yeah...well, we're gonna have to agree to disagree there. But let's say you're right. You're still coming out on top. You're not wallowing and making yourself feel worse. You're going to fake moving on until you really *do* it. And if I'm right, let him eat shit while you shine."

All of what he was saying sounded so damn daunting. I rolled into him, groaning. Julien caught me, patting my back and letting me stay there a minute or two.

"Think you should go home," he murmured. "Take a shower and brush your teeth."

"You're kicking me out?" I peered up at him, scowling. "After all I've done for you?"

"Yeah...well, you're surprisingly smelly for someone who's so hot."

Gasping, I smacked his arm and flung my body out of his bed. "I hate you from the very bottom of my heart."

"I got you up, didn't I? And I told you you were hot." Julien climbed out of bed and stood with his crutches. "I'll walk you out. Make sure you leave."

I snorted. This boy was rude, but he also knew how to make me feel a hell of a lot better. When I was sober, his tough love might not resonate as much as it did now, but I'd take what I could get.

After grabbing my stuff, I opened his bedroom door, and Julien followed me out. I'd almost made it to the front door when it opened. Lachlan Kelly filled the doorway, eclipsing everything else.

He froze at the sight of Julien in his pajamas and me...well, also in Julien's pajamas, my dress and shoes dangling from my fingers.

"Excuse me." I nodded to the door. "I'm leaving."

Lock stepped into the house, sweeping a thunderous gaze from me to Julien.

"What's this?" he asked.

Something occurred to me then, with the three of us standing there. In my drunken state, I'd asked Sera to bring me here, but I really doubted I'd come looking for Julien. I turned to him, and he grimaced before I even got the words out.

"Why were you the one to take care of me?" I whispered.

He shook his head. He didn't want to say it, but reality was plain as day. He'd taken care of me because Lock hadn't been here. That was made all the more evident by his appearance at a little after six in the morning. He was just coming home.

"Oh," I breathed, nodding to myself. "I see."

"Someone want to fill me in? Why the fuck is Elena wearing your clothes?" Lock had the au-freaking-dacity to sound like he'd been wronged. For the thousandth time, I begged for my anger to insulate me from this agony, but I was on my own.

Reality speared into me. We weren't fated or inevitable. Lock was just another man who took and took until he stripped my bones clean. I was too smart for this to be a surprise, but Lock had been convincing.

All I had left was my pride. My heart was gone. Dust. I lifted my chin just like my mother had shown me when I was a little girl and walked by the man who'd done this to me with my head high, like he didn't mean a single thing.

Chapter Thirty-two

Lock

The door slammed in my face. I swung around to Julien, who wore a satisfied smirk.

"Why was my girl coming from your bed, wearing your clothes?" I demanded.

He shrugged. "Not your girl. She can do as she pleases."

I stepped into my house—*my fucking house*—and stared down a man I considered a friend who wasn't looking like much of a friend right now.

"Care to change your answer? That one wasn't acceptable."

He leaned against the wall behind him, taking some weight off his crutches. "Was there something untrue about what I said?"

I hit my chest. "There's no loyalty? Is that what's happening here?"

Julien straightened, giving me a withering glare. "If that's what Elena and I wanted to happen, you'd have no say. You willingly gave up those rights, remember?"

My hands went to my hips as I paced back and forth in the entry. If I got closer to him, I'd lay hands on him. If he'd been more able-bodied, I might not have been holding back. This was beyond the pale. I couldn't believe what he was saying to me. After months of driving him places, talking, living together, he did this?

And *she* did this?

"Are you telling me you slept with *my girl*?" My heart was thrashing. My body craved violence. "You fucked my girl?"

"That's not a question you get to ask."

I saw red at his refusal to deny it. "The second I'm done, you come and pick up my castoffs? Can't walk out of here and find your own?"

I didn't see it coming. One second, Julien was using his crutches for support. The next, his fist flew in my face, connecting with my jaw. My head snapped back, a bell chiming in my skull.

"You're *such* an idiot," he seethed. "Of course I didn't do anything with her. But if you refer to her as a castoff again, we're gonna have huge problems, big man. It's not gonna be just me you're facing with that shit."

"*Fuuuck*," I bellowed, which only sharpened the pain in my jaw. "All you had to do was answer."

"All *you* had to do was not disrespect Elena. She doesn't deserve that, and, you little shit, neither do I. So, fuck you for that too."

Bending at my waist, I cupped my aching head. How the fuck was this saving me pain? How was this better? This last week had been miserable. Couldn't sleep. Couldn't eat. Couldn't concentrate. I continually questioned whether I'd done the right thing. None of this felt right.

I looked up at Julien. "What I said to you was uncalled for. I'm sorry. I need answers, though."

His mouth puckered like sharing the room with me was making him bitter. "Even if I wanted to get with her, do you honestly think *she'd* do that? You should know her better than I do."

He was right, but his answer did nothing to cool the fire in my head.

"So, you deny she was coming from your bed?"

"I don't deny it. She slept in my bed for a few hours."

I yanked at my hair, disgusted, panicked, manic from his admission. I wasn't disgusted at her, but at myself for allowing this situation to bloom. This was my fault. All of it.

"You wanna ask me why?"

Stopping, I took a few deep breaths to calm myself down. It didn't do much good, but it was something.

"Why, Julien?" I gritted out.

His face was perfectly serene when he dropped the bomb on me. "You weren't here."

"What's that mean?"

"Am I wrong? Didn't you just stumble in after being out all night?"

As he said it, Elena's stricken, whiplashed expression became clear. She saw me coming home at sunrise and assumed...*fuck*.

"She came here looking for me?"

He shrugged like it didn't matter. "She asked her friend to bring her drunk ass to our house. She was crying your name when she was sleeping. So, yeah, I think she came here to see you. I held her for you, you fucking dick." He hit my boot with his crutch. "What you're doing to her is weak. I thought you were better than this, but I misjudged. Going out fucking when you had to know there was a high chance of her finding out is honestly some of the shittiest behavior—"

"I wasn't fucking anyone. I wasn't *with* anyone."

His jaw squared as he considered the veracity in my claim. I could admit it was pretty hard to swallow on the surface, but weak as I might've been in his eyes, he had to know I wasn't cruel.

"Where were you, then?" he asked.

"Driving." I exhaled, rubbing some of the grit out of my eye. "I went up the coast, stopped at Pismo Beach, and turned back. I couldn't sleep, and I had to get out."

"Couldn't sleep, huh? Guilt keeping you awake?"

He sounded far too gleeful about that.

"Something like that," I muttered.

"You made a mistake." He didn't form it as a question. He was telling me, and the hell of it was, he might've been right.

But nothing had changed. There was no taking back my decision. We were still impossible.

I lowered my chin. "I'll talk to her. Tell her where I was."

"Don't be a dick."

I pushed out a dry laugh. "I'll try. Seems like all I'm capable of being lately, but I'll try."

·•••••••••

I found her the next morning. It was déjà vu, crossing the grass to her deck. As soon as I took the first step, her head popped up from her newspaper. When I'd made this same walk a week ago, I'd been greeted with a smile. The wariness with which she watched me now was entirely different.

My hands were empty, but I didn't expect she'd want anything from me this time.

"Good morning." I hovered at the bottom of the stairs.

"Good morning."

I nodded to the empty chair beside her. "Can I sit for a minute?"

"Have at it."

She wasn't wearing my hoodie. That had been left neatly folded in the back of my truck last week. I'd wanted to return it, especially when I realized she'd washed her scent out of it, but I knew she wouldn't take it back.

The other thing that changed from last week was her clothes, and not just the lack of hoodie. Elena had gotten fully dressed in shorts and a tee, with shoes on her feet. I'd never once seen her reading the paper in anything other than her pretty pajamas. I realized she'd been expecting me and had gotten dressed to face me.

Newspaper neatly folded on the table, she waited for me to talk. I swallowed down my daily dose of glass, filling my belly with it.

"I'm doing a shit job of not hurting you." I rubbed the sore spot on my jaw. "I'm sorry I wasn't there for you last night. I was driving all night. I didn't intend to be gone that long, but once I was on the road, I kept going and going. When you saw me yesterday morning, I hadn't slept in a solid thirty-six hours. That's my only excuse for barking at you the way I did, but really, there's no excuse."

She finally looked at me, taking in the bruise on the side of my face. "Did Julien punch you?"

I scoffed, rubbing the bruise again. "He did."

She nodded. "Good."

"I get that it's hard—"

"No, you don't. If you got that it's hard, you wouldn't keep showing up, insisting I talk to you. You wouldn't still be trying to act like my boyfriend when you're *not* that anymore. You chose this, now you have to live with it."

Leaning forward, I hung my head in my hands. "I'll leave you alone after this. I just needed to tell you I'm not with anyone else. I didn't want you to think that's why I ended us."

She exhaled slowly, but that was the only sign she'd taken in what I'd told her. I couldn't tell if she was relieved or didn't give a shit. "And now, I know. You did your duty, assuaged your guilt, now you can disappear like I asked you to."

"Elena—"

"You know what, Lock? You're a coward."

My brow dropped low. "What makes you say that?"

"You are. I know I'm a lot, but you knew that when this thing started. You pursued *me*. But it was all a little too real, huh?" She shook her head. "I look at you, and I see this pillar. You're so strong, I thought maybe you could hold me up when I needed it."

"I could've. I still will if you need it."

She shook her head even harder. She was so damn mad at me. "You can't. You walked away because I was too much."

"You weren't too much. Don't think that for even a second. The problem was—" I broke off, dragging my fingers through my shaggy hair.

"What? Just tell me."

I dropped my hand, giving her the raw, honest truth.

"You weren't too much. To me, you're just right. That's why I had to walk."

A delirious laugh burst out of her. "Oh, that's hilarious. That makes perfect sense."

This couldn't keep going on. For either of us. I'd make her see, then she'd be okay. She'd get why this couldn't work.

"Last week, when I dropped you off after our camping trip, I walked into a family shitstorm. My mother was enraged Saoirse decided to go to college close to my father in Colorado. She's hurt, we all know that, but it's coming out as anger, and she's on a tear. Saoirse is so miserable, she wants to move in with my dad and finish her senior year in Wyoming—which is, yeah, really extreme for her considering she kind of hates the ranch. And my dad—El, he's like me. He's a big, taciturn man, and it takes a lot to rile him. He always found my mom's spurts of temper endearing."

"Why are you telling me this?" Elena asked with the sharpness of a razor.

"My family is broken because my parents made a selfish choice a long time ago. My dad—Jesus, I don't know if he's ever going to be the same. Last weekend, he cried while we were on the phone. It's been five years since the divorce and he's still devastated at the way everything has devolved."

Every crack of his voice had been a lash of a whip. My dad didn't cry. He rarely raised his voice. He was mellow and thoughtful, and his family had been the cornerstone of his identity. And it all fell apart because it was based on ephemeral hopes and dreams instead of reality.

Listening to my dad's tears was when I knew. After we slept under the stars, I wanted to keep Elena forever. My mind had jumped years ahead, to me on Ramses, her on the back of one of the gentle mares—Calliope would've suited her—riding trails around the ranch together. Her blonde hair streaming against the endless sky, me so fucking proud to call her mine.

But that had been a dream, just like my parents'. The reality was Elena's obligations were here, and mine were more than a thousand miles away. Right now, we were running parallel, but I'd veer off on a different course, and there was no taking her with me. Ending things with her had been eviscerating, but it had been the right thing to do for her—*and* for me. I didn't want to wind up like my dad, pining for the woman he'd never have again.

"That's awful, and I'm sorry your family is going through that, but I still don't know why you're telling me this." Some of the coldness had melted from her. She was looking at me now. Not meeting my eyes, but her gaze was on me.

"I'm telling you I could never do that to you. I care about you too much to take this further. We could stay together until graduation, but then what? I'm leaving, El, and you're staying here with your family. There's no future, even if—"

Before I could finish my thought, her phone rang, cutting me off. She hesitated, then grabbed it, frowning at the screen.

"Hello?" Twisting in her seat, she gave me her back. "What? When?"

Alarm straightened her spine. Her shoulders shot up.

"How could you not know? Where were you?"

Her voice broke, thick with anger and unshed tears. I was out of my seat, crouching by hers in an instant. Glassy eyes lifted to mine, hitting me like a sheet of ice. The person on the other end of the line wasn't delivering good news.

"Okay, I'm coming. If she wakes up, tell her I'll be there soon."

Elena ended the call, but she didn't move. She stared through me, her chest hitching. I'd seen her like this before, when Oliver Bergen had followed her to the maintenance building.

"Look at me," I ordered, rubbing up and down her arms. Her eyes focused on mine. "Breathe with me, Ellie. Slow and steady."

Her fingers gripped my arms, digging into my skin. It took a minute, but finally, some of the panic bled from her, and her breathing started to align with mine. Her chin wobbled, but she clamped her jaw tight.

"My mom—I have to go to the hospital," she rasped.

"Okay." I pulled her upright. "I'll drive you. Don't worry about anything other than getting to your mom."

Being here for her like this was so natural, I couldn't help myself. I'd have to respect her wishes, for both our fucking sakes, but that wasn't going to start now.

Elena leaned into me, letting me take her weight and help her into the truck. She sat still as I buckled her in. Placing my palm on her chest, I captured her eyes again.

"Breathe, sweet girl. I'll get you there as fast as I can."

She nodded, shifting her gaze away from mine. By the time I had climbed into my side of the truck, she was typing on her phone, her head down, hair curtaining her face. She stayed like that as I drove.

"Is your mom hurt?" I asked carefully.

"My dad found her in the bathtub, and I—" She shuddered. "Thank you for driving me, but I don't want to talk."

"Of course. Anything, El."

A pit of vipers writhed in my gut, but I'd let her be. I had to. It was better that way.

· · · • • • • · ·

I'd been in the waiting room alone for an hour, maybe two, when the cavalry arrived. Gabe Fuller stood in front of my chair, kicking the toes of my shoes.

"Oh, fuck no. You are not sitting here."

I raised my head to peer up at him. "I drove Elena here." And I hadn't seen her since she'd walked into her mother's hospital room. I still had no idea what was going on, how serious it was, how long she'd be here, but I'd wait to find out more.

"Gabe, stop." Penelope pressed her hand to his chest, pushing him back. He allowed himself to be moved a couple steps, then he stood his ground.

"This fool is showing his face, at a time like this? I warned him," Gabe seethed.

Unfolding myself from my chair, I stood, keeping my hands in my pockets. I didn't want to fight him. He had every right to be pissed. I was relieved Elena had so many people in her corner. People willing to take me down to defend her honor.

"I'm here for her. She wants me to leave, I will."

Gabe swiveled his head to his girl, then back to me. "She doesn't want you here. You already dipped out on her once, go ahead and do it again."

Pen put her chin on Gabe's shoulder. "Lock, Gabe and I are here to take care of Elena and my aunt. It was kind of you to bring Elena to the hospital. I'm sure she appreciates it, but it would probably be better if you leave now."

Pen made it sound so easy, like I could just walk away. But she was right. Elena probably wouldn't want to see me when she left her mom's side. I didn't even know what I was doing here. I shouldn't have stayed. This wasn't my job anymore. But I couldn't figure out how to get myself to leave, not when I knew she might need someone to lean on. A pillar.

"If she comes out, if she asks, I'll be down in my truck for the next couple hours. She can text if she wants me to grab something from home." I ground my molars together in frustration at how goddamn useless I was. "Just...let her know I'm there."

Gabe clucked his tongue. "She's not gonna ask. Anything she needs, her family will provide."

Pen sighed. "Thanks, Lock. We're good here, but I'll let her know if she asks."

··········

It was another hour or two before the passenger door of my truck opened and Elena hopped in. She let her head flop back on the rest and sighed, her eyes fluttering closed.

"You okay?"

She held her hand up. "Let me sit here. I need a minute. I thought maybe you'd give it to me."

I nodded, not that she could see me. It had only been a few hours since I'd found her sitting in the sun on her deck, but that seemed like a year ago.

"I ran away," she said.

"You did?"

"After I yelled at my dad."

"Did he deserve it?"

"He did." Her eyes opened, and I didn't pretend I hadn't been looking at her. "My mom has hypothermia. He found her in the bathtub this morning, but she'd been in there for hours and hours. My father worked all day yesterday and into the night, and he was so tired, he didn't even notice his wife wasn't in their bed."

The level of calm she exuded worried me. Elena wasn't calm by nature, and from what she was saying, she should have been raging up a storm. But she was almost placid as she sat beside me.

"Yeah, he deserved it," I said.

"That's not why I yelled." She huffed a short laugh. "Would you believe my father tried to blame *me*? He said if I'd gone to visit her yesterday, this wouldn't have happened. He said if I spent more time with my mother, she would be happier. This man makes million-dollar real estate deals and he is *that* obtuse. He tried to blame me for his nearly catatonic wife—the one he ignores like it's his job."

"What the fuck?" I bit out.

"I've never yelled at my father before." The corners of her mouth tipped.

"Did it feel good?"

"Great. He's going to be mad, but I don't care right now. He needed to hear it, and I refuse to accept the blame this time. That's on him."

She turned her head, sweeping over me with her tired gaze. "I think I might yell at you next."

If she needed to yell, I'd take it. I told her I'd be her friend, so it was time for me to stand by my word.

Even if it hurt.

Chapter Thirty-three

Elena

I'd pretty much run out of fucks.

Last weekend, I'd warned my father that my mom was going dark. I'd told him to make an appointment with her psychiatrist. I'd asked him not to work so much, at least while her mental health was on a razor's edge.

I was his daughter, his *child*, yet I'd been thrust into the role of my mother's caretaker. I'd never once questioned it, though I'd resented it plenty.

I was done with men who couldn't take care of my heart.

"I'm so mad at you." I didn't even know why I was in Lock's truck, other than I had needed an escape and he was here. God, why was he here?

"I know." He had the audacity to sound sad.

"Are you hanging around the hospital to prove me wrong? Is that what this is?"

"I'm here because despite us not working, I told you I'd be here for you when you need me."

"Nice of you to start keeping promises now."

"El, I'm trying to protect you from something worse than *this*. Do you remember what I told you about my parents? My family?"

"Sure I do. You don't want to wind up like your mom and dad. Who does?"

He pinched the bridge of his nose. "I feel like you're not hearing me."

"That's funny, because you haven't been listening to my wishes for the last week. If you don't want to be with me, then you need to go away. Stop getting in my face, and stop *being* here."

"It's not about what I want."

If I thought my hands had any hope of fitting around his neck, I would have strangled him. But I honestly didn't have the energy to try.

"I think it's completely about what you want. If it wasn't, you would have had a conversation with me instead of climbing onto my deck and unilaterally breaking my fucking heart."

I hated the way my voice cracked. I hated that I couldn't disguise my sorrow. I hated that I still loved this big, stupid man, and it was going to take me a long, long time to get over him.

"Elena," he breathed. "Fuck, sweet girl, I'm *sorry*. I'm so fucking sorry. I'm flying blind here, trying to do the right thing, but I'm screwing it all up."

"You never asked me, you know."

"Asked what?" His fingertips touched mine. In a moment of weakness, I almost let him continue, but I couldn't. I just couldn't. Balling my fists tight, my nails cut crescents into my palms.

"My plans after I graduate. You never asked."

He gestured to the hospital. "I didn't think I had to."

"Your mind was so made up, *you* didn't hear *me*. I was desperate to leave after high school. I couldn't wait to get out of here."

"But you came back."

I threw my hands out, wanting to scream in frustration. "I was *raped*, Lock! My rapist died in front of my eyes. I couldn't hack Berkely because I was fucking traumatized, not homesick. The worst things that have ever happened to me are in Savage River. I hate this town."

"I—you're right. I didn't ask. But you have your mom, your family. Even if you leave Savage River, you'll stay close."

This was how I knew his excuses were just that. If he wanted me, if he really desired to maybe, possibly have a future with me, he'd stop telling me what he thought I wanted and actually listen to the words coming out of my mouth.

"Do you think I want to spend the rest of my life as my mother's keeper? Because I don't. She has a husband who needs to step up. It can't be me anymore, and I told my dad that. As soon as I graduate, I'm gone. I can't stay here anymore. Everything bad happens here."

Lock would just be another tick on the list.

He sat statue still. His bruised jaw clenched. Maybe he didn't know what to say, but I did.

"It wasn't the phone call from your dad that ended us." My hand went to the door. I was done with this. "I was letting myself fall in love with you, giving you *everything*, while you were holding back from the very start. I told you about my darkest moments, but you couldn't even tell me you don't just own a ranch, you own a luxury resort where presidents' children have gotten married. It isn't some backwoods chunk of land where a girl like me could never be happy. Sweet Brush River Ranch isn't in the middle of nowhere. You never told me because you never wanted more from me than what you got, did you? Your foot had always been out the door, I was just too stupid and love drunk to notice."

I flung open the door and jumped out of the truck. He called my name, roared it, but I shut the door. He could go fuck himself with his conciliatory offers of friendship. I had more than enough friends.

I am done with Lachlan Kelly.

Chapter Thirty-four

Elena

Being done with Lachlan Kelly would have been a lot easier if I hadn't woken up to a text from him. And because I hated myself enough, I'd checked it instead of blocking him like I really should have.

He'd sent me a picture of a tween boy on a big, midnight-black horse. I double-checked, making certain it was from him. It was. Then I stared at the picture, zooming in and out, trying to decipher his message.

I came to the conclusion the boy was him, but that was only because, despite his young face, his hands were the size of baseball mitts as he clutched the reins, and he still had the same shaggy haircut.

Twinge, twinge, BOOM!

I closed the text, unwilling to put another ounce of mental energy into trying to figure Lock out. We were done. If he thought sending me adorable pictures of him in his youth would somehow endear him to me, he was clearly delusional.

Helen and Zadie were in the kitchen eating breakfast. I grabbed a banana and a gallon of coffee, needing to mainline it to get through the day. This was a big one. When I sat down at my usual spot, there was a Frappuccino topped with piles of whipped cream already there.

"What's this?"

Helen pointed to it with her fork. "Lock just dropped it off. I told him, next time, he better bring me a drink too. He's already on my shit list, he should know better."

"Did he spit in it?" I pushed it with my fingertip, my stomach flipping over and over. What was he up to? And more importantly, why wouldn't he leave me alone?

"Of course he didn't," Zadie admonished.

"Then why is he bringing me coffee?" I looked back and forth between them. Helen shrugged. Zadie smiled. I knew what Zadie thought, and it was *not* correct. I wouldn't even be entertaining it.

"Is it an apology frap?" Helen asked.

"I don't want his apologies. He needs to disappear so I can pretend he never happened."

Helen pushed my frap with the tip of her finger. "Don't think that's happening."

"Perfect. I absolutely needed another complication right now."

"Any word on your mom?" Zadie asked gently.

Giving in, I scooped whipped cream into my mouth with my straw. "When I left the hospital last night, she was talking, but still really out of it. She'll probably be in the hospital for another day or two, then possibly inpatient treatment for her depression."

Helen shook her head. "Dude, this really sucks."

I had to laugh at Helen's eloquence. "No kidding. She'll recover, but I don't know if my dad will. The asshole is actually taking the day off to be with her. I know he's going out of his mind, but I refused. Even if I didn't have my big midterm presentation today, I would have refused."

Zadie's eyes bugged. "Your dad didn't want to stay?"

"I think it's more that he doesn't know how to stay. He's going to have to figure it out." I scooped up more whipped cream. "I hate that he got this for me."

Helen let out a long sigh and cocked her head in the direction of the house next door. "All I know is he screwed up in a big way, but I still think he's a good guy. It might be deep down. *Way* deep down, but it's there."

I held my hand out. "Do you think that helps?"

She twisted her red lips. "Yeah, no. I guess not. My mistake."

I ate one more scoop of whipped cream then dumped the frap in the trash. My stomach was churning too much to even contemplate finishing it.

Tossing my banana peel in the trash too, I said goodbye, grabbed my backpack and phone, and headed to class. On the way there, Lock sent another picture. This one was of him and a man who had to be his father standing in front of a crystalline blue lake. Lock was taller than his dad, but still young. Maybe fifteen or sixteen. He was cute—of course he was—but I still didn't get what he was doing.

I crammed my phone into one of the inside pockets of my backpack. I *really* didn't have time for this.

·········

A post-class drink turned into a party on my deck. All the boys came, even Julien. Zadie was cooking, and Sal was just trying to keep up with everyone.

I wrapped my arm around his bony shoulders and clinked my glass with his. "Our TA said Professor Seavers had never once asked so many questions during a presentation."

"And she smiled," Sal added. "Seavers smiled at us."

I help up my glass. "That's right, bitches. Seavers smiled at me and Sal—guaranteed *A*."

The last week had been dismal, but finally, *finally* there was light. Our business proposal had been so solid, it had stood up to both Seavers and our classmates' brutal interrogation. Dickwad Pi Sig boys had been so smug at the start, like they planned to poke holes in the work Salvatore and I spent countless hours on, but they couldn't find any. They had almost looked defeated when they left.

That just made this day all the better.

Zadie brought out piles of pasta, salad, bread, and antipasto. I had no idea how she'd managed to cook all of it on such short notice, but I wasn't looking a gift horse in the mouth. I filled two plates and joined Julien in his spot in the shadows.

"What's shaking, Phantom?" I handed him his food. He grunted as he took it. I knew he didn't like me doing things for him, but it wasn't exactly easy to carry a plate while on crutches.

"You look happy," he said.

"I'm happy about the project," I hedged.

I'd received two more pictures from Lock. One of the sun rising over a range of mountains. The other, a close up of a steer. I wasn't stupid. He was obviously sending me pictures of his family's ranch, but I couldn't figure out why. It felt like another one of his games.

"Your mom?" he asked.

"I'm letting my dad handle it. Or forcing him to. She was lucid enough to talk to me on the phone, so that's an improvement. How are you?"

He chuckled. "Just dandy, as always. My knuckles are still smarting."

"Well, you shouldn't have punched a brick wall. I could have told you that."

He rubbed the top of his hand, shooting me a half smile. "He deserved it."

"Thank you for defending my honor."

He leaned back in his chair and rubbed his chest. "What can I say? I'm a gentleman."

Heavy, clunking steps on the other side of the deck drew my attention. Lock had arrived, uninvited, and his attention was squarely on me. Rolling my eyes, I gave him my back.

"Are you kidding me?" I mumbled.

"Told you he was in a world of hurt. He can't even stay away for a day." Julien made this sound like a good thing.

"That's because he's an ass. I have asked him over and over to give me space."

Behind me, Lock greeted everyone. The fact that none of my friends were kicking him off the deck grated my nerves. They had to know I didn't want him here, and yet...

Obviously, of the two of us, Lock was the favorite, but this was *my* deck. If I had more energy, I'd tell him to go, but I didn't, so I'd just stay in the shadows with Phantom.

That worked for a while, but like all good things, nothing lasted forever.

"Elena, tell us about your project," Theo called out. "Tell us what we're celebrating."

Swiveling in my chair to face the rest of the crowd, I tipped my drink toward Sal, who had found himself between Amir and Marco, looking like he was going to either bolt or faint.

"I think my partner should explain," I said.

He cleared his throat. "Uh...it's actually really interesting. This woman, Shana, brings an adult summer camp to resorts—"

As Salvatore explained the idea, my friends' eyes were on him. Lock wasn't my friend, and his eyes were on me. His head was canted toward Sal, so he was listening, but he was watching me.

At least, until Sal got to the part about Sugar Brush River Ranch. That caught Lock's full attention.

"You should see this place. I'm not the outdoors type, but I put myself in a kid's shoes who doesn't have access to wide open outdoor space, and it would be paradise. To spend a week on a working ranch, riding horses, stargazing, making s'mores around a fire—" he broke off, chuckling self-consciously. "Shana is really convincing and passionate. She made Elena and me want to fly out to Wyoming to check out this ranch ourselves."

Theo slapped Lock's arm. "You know that place? It's your stomping ground."

Lock's eyes hit mine again. "I'm familiar."

"You should hook Elena's girl up with a connection. It sounds like a cool program," Theo said.

Lock inclined his head ever so slightly. "It does."

After a few minutes, the subject shifted to Salvatore's dating life, which had picked up significantly since I'd started the rumor about his giant schlong. I hoped he was doing me proud.

I went inside to grab another hard seltzer and get some space from the massive weight of Lock's stare, but that was an incredibly stupid move. As soon as I turned around from the refrigerator, he was stepping into the kitchen, closing the sliding door behind him.

Shaking my head, I started around the other side of the island, hoping he'd let me go, but that was stupid too. Of course he didn't.

He blocked my path, not caging me in, but making it clear I wasn't going to get past him. I didn't feel unsafe, just frustrated out of my mind.

"Is that how you knew about the ranch? From the project?" he asked.

"No. Well, I didn't know it was yours. Not until my dad checked up on you. I had to pretend he wasn't dropping a bomb on me."

"I should have told you."

"You should have." I flicked my fingers. "It doesn't matter anymore."

"I think it does."

Sighing, I put my drink down on the counter and clasped my hands at my chest. "You have to stop this, Lock. You're making this so much harder for me. Why do you keep coming around? Why are you sending me pictures?"

"So, you did look at them. What did you think?"

Naturally, he would ignore everything but what he wanted to hear.

"I thought you were an adorable kid and the ranch is as pretty as the pictures online. I hope Shana is able to find a way to bring kids there, because I think a place like that should be shared with people who will appreciate it."

"It's prettier in person. I've never seen a place that tops it."

"Okay. Well, thanks for sharing, but it's enough. I really can't take anymore, and I don't know why you're sending me pictures, but it needs to stop."

He ignored me once again. "I should have asked. I'd made up my mind—had things a certain way in my head. I didn't think we had a chance because I never once asked if you'd *give* me a chance. So, I'm going to sell you on it."

"On what?"

"On what it would look like if you decided on me."

My mouth fell open. He'd obviously lost his mind. Either that or he got off on torturing me.

I shoved at his chest, and immediately regretted it. I liked the way he felt far too much. It stung that I couldn't lay my head on what had been my spot. He'd taken that from me without any warning.

"I don't trust a word you say, Lock."

He nodded, but he didn't back off. If anything, my declaration seemed to make him even more resolved. "I understand that. I went back on my word and broke it. The thing about me is, when something is broken, I fix it, no matter how long it takes."

"Some things can't be fixed. My trust was always tenuous, but you were really good at convincing me I should hand it over to you. I won't ever make that mistake again, no matter how many pretty pictures you send me. We should give each other a break and end this charade."

"Did you enjoy the coffee this morning?"

I threw my head back and screamed at the ceiling, then I pushed around him, storming back outside. He let me go, but not before quietly laughing in my wake.

·····•·····

There were more pictures Tuesday. A house with an enormous wraparound porch. A coop with chickens and roosters. The Milky Way in an endless midnight sky. A herd of horses grazing on craggy, rolling hills.

I looked at every single one, hating both of us for it. I wasn't a ranch girl, so why the hell did these beautiful pictures fill me with a sense of longing?

Because *he* was going to be there.

Amir and Zadie walked with me out of accounting and lingered, which was a little strange. Zadie kept asking me questions, delaying my escape home when I should have been heading to Spanish.

When a rough, warm hand cupped my elbow, I shot Zadie an accusing look. She just smiled, and Amir nodded to the man looming behind me.

Lock was close. Too close. When he spoke next to my ear, my knees trembled. "Come on, El. It's time for Spanish."

"I dropped it."

He chuckled, low and deep. "No you didn't. Let's go. We're gonna be late."

Zadie and Amir casually strolled off like they weren't seconds from being murdered. Was there really no loyalty?

"Chicks before dicks, Zadie!" I cried.

Lock laughed again and scooped me up like the old days. I was upside down before I knew it, being carried across campus against my will.

"This isn't cute, and it's not going to make me like you," I seethed, bumping along on his back.

"Right now, I want your ass in class so you don't fail. We'll work on you liking me later."

"After this, I like you *less* than I did this morning, and I really didn't like you then." I slapped his back as hard as I could. His steps didn't even stutter. "Put me down. This isn't cute."

"Will you walk the rest of the way? Or are you going to run away and hide?"

"Fuck you, Lock. Put me down. I'll go to class."

He swung me around and set me on my feet, holding on to me as the blood rushed out of my head into my limbs. I pushed off him as soon as I was steady, giving him a burning glare before turning around to find we were already in front of the building. He hadn't put me down because I'd asked, we'd simply reached our destination.

In class, he sat beside me, and when we had to practice interviewing for a job in Spanish with a partner, I was stuck with him.

Fortunately, I'd found my anger, so it didn't hurt to sit so close. I didn't want to cry hearing his rough but gentle voice.

Speaking Spanish, Lock asked me about my past job experiences. "*Te odio.*"

He laughed at my vow of hate, then pressed on, asking about my greatest strength.

I narrowed my eyes. "*Te desprecio.*"

His eyes twinkled. This was amusing him while I wanted to crawl out of my skin. The hour trudged by so slowly, I fought the urge to scream. Finally, we were dismissed, and I bolted. Lock wasn't as nimble, but his stride was long, so he had no problem keeping up with me and steering me toward his truck like I was a wild horse he was corralling.

"Are you going to lasso me next?"

He cocked an eyebrow. "Now, there's an idea."

Groaning, I threw myself into his truck and buckled in before he got the chance to do it for me. He climbed in beside me and pulled into campus traffic.

"You really need to stop this."

He glanced at me. "I'm not going to. I *can't*. I panicked and messed up in a massive way, but it was never because I didn't want you. The opposite is true. I wanted you. I *want* you so fucking badly, I got scared."

I snorted derisively, not believing anything that came out of his mouth.

He reached across the space between us, stroking the side of my leg. "I'm not going anywhere."

I shoved his hand off me, though I was bereft when it was gone. "You should. I won't ever trust you again."

He hummed and turned on the radio. "You can pick the station if you want."

"You're unbelievable," I bit out.

"Pick the station, Elena."

I turned the music off and pressed my face against my window. Lachlan Kelly could suffer the rest of this ride in silence. He didn't deserve music.

As soon as he pulled into his driveway, I flew out of the truck and nearly face-planted. Righting myself, I ran up the steps to my porch. Lock followed me. As I fumbled with my keys, he came up behind me and took them, calmly inserting the right one and unlocking my door.

"You forgot this." He handed me my backpack, his lips curving.

"Don't look at me like that."

"I'm not going to stop, Ellie. As far as I'm concerned, you're mine. You never stopped being mine. But I need you to decide on me too. I'm not going to stop until you do."

I rose on my toes so I could look him square in the eye. "I. Don't. Believe. You."

Then I closed the door, hoping he'd do like I asked for once and go away.

Chapter Thirty-five

Elena

Lock was waiting outside my house on Wednesday when I left for class. I walked by him quickly, ignoring him, but he easily fell into step with me.

"Good morning. You look beautiful, Ellie."

I gave him a sidelong glance, keeping my face implacable while worms filled my insides. I wanted to tell him to take his compliment and go straight to hell, but it was easier not saying anything at all.

"How's your mom?"

"Better. My dad's taking her for inpatient treatment today to get her meds under control. What she was taking before wasn't working."

Okay, now leave me alone. Go away!

"How long will she stay?"

Ugh.

"Probably two weeks, if it's anything like the past. It's a nice place, she likes it, so I know she'll be fine. I'm not worried."

He was looking at me. I could feel it, heavy and light all at once.

"You can be, you know. You can give it to me. I'll carry it for you."

I rolled my eyes at that. "That's nice. I don't believe you."

"I know that. I've given you every reason not to, but I won't again."

He didn't sound frustrated or defeated, simply matter of fact. It drove me nuts. Every steady, unshakable part of this man made me want to scream. Because I needed him. I needed someone who would be an unmovable boulder when I was a landslide. And he couldn't be that for me. Not now.

"What do you want me to say? Do you want me to tell you that you being near me *all the time* is the worst kind of torture? Do you want me to lay out how pissed off I am that you were even capable of dumping me? Should I tell you I feel like the worst person in the world for being relieved my mother is going to be locked up so I don't have to worry about her for two solid weeks? Or how about that I wish she *wasn't* going to be hospitalized so I could spend my time worrying about her instead of being heartbroken over you? Which part are you going to carry?"

He brushed my hair behind my neck and leaned down, his lips skating over my ear. "All of it. I'll carry it all. And I'll keep the heartbreak. It's not yours anymore, and you're never going to get it back."

The urge to lean into him and let his words trickle through my blood like the sweetest poison was strong, but I couldn't do it. Not after the way he'd broken me out of nowhere.

"Pretty words. I don't believe them." I marched on toward my first class, and Lock stayed beside me the whole way.

・・・・・・・・・・

He was there to escort me to my next class as well, apparently skipping his own. And while I was in my classes, he sent me more pictures. This time, he was hitting me hard with pictures of the spa and the ruggedly beautiful gardens.

As I slung my bag over my shoulder, my phone alerted me to yet another text. This time, instead of a picture, Lock had sent me an address. As soon as I spotted him lurking in the hall, I held up my phone.

"What is this?"

His mouth curved. "Now you know my secret. You could expose it, maybe post it on Twitter, or you can keep it between us. I'm trusting you to make the right decision."

"Don't give me riddles, Lock." Pushing past him, I headed in the direction of New Ventures.

"It's not a riddle. That's the address to the burger place I told you I discovered. I'm not going to make you promise to keep it secret too. Now, it's yours."

I had no idea what he expected me to say to that. It seemed ridiculous on the surface, but knowing Lock and the way he valued certain things, giving me the address to one of the treasures he'd discovered was big for him.

More than confusing, it made me mad. I'd never go to this place without him. The way things were, I'd never go with him either.

"I'll send it to my favorite influencers. They'll adore it," I told him.

"If that's what you think is right. It's up to you." So calm and sure, probably because he was pretty certain I was only being mean and absolutely *wouldn't* be doing that.

I clamped my mouth shut for the rest of the walk and disappeared into my class before he could say anything else to devastate me.

Abby, Kayleigh, and the D-named Pi Sig douche were at the front of the class setting up for their presentation. Since birds of a feather tended to flock together, the startup they were assigned was Oliver Bergen's. Thankfully, he'd only been in the classroom that one time, but no doubt he'd be lurking around on Saturday during the alumni presentations.

I slipped into my seat beside Salvatore and elbowed him. "What are the chances this is a shit show?"

He snorted. "Compared to ours or the average project?"

I flipped my hair behind my shoulder. "Obviously, average. No one can compare to ours."

He rubbed his chin like he was thinking about it then cocked his head. "By my calculations, the chance of this utterly sucking is seventy-three percent."

I slapped him on the back. "Yes, Salvatore, I'm so proud of how I've corrupted you."

He burst out laughing, earning us glares from D-douche and a catty little smirk from Abby. They could go fuck themselves on a rusty nail. Class hadn't started yet. We were allowed to laugh. *Humorless goats.*

We did quiet down when class started, and Professor Seavers invited Abby, Kayleigh, and Dylan—I *knew* it started with a *D*—to present. I wasn't interested in Oliver's business or anything the three of them had to say, so my mind drifted where it always went these days: Lachlan Kelly. A part of me wished I could forgive him and let myself be with him, but the part of me that had been hurt too many times just couldn't do it. I refused to hurt myself again and again because I stupidly loved a man.

Sal made a strangled noise beside me, catching my attention.

"What's up?" I whispered.

He nodded toward the screen at the front of the room. "It's all wrong. Their projections for the business are based on a faulty formula."

Narrowing my eyes, I peered at the numbers on the screen. At first glance, it was impressive. Oliver was doing well for himself with his real estate app startup, and he was projected to grow like gangbusters over the next five years.

Except...

I gasped. "Holy shit."

"You see it too?" Salvatore leaned in closer to point out the faulty formula. The numbers didn't make any sense. All their work was wrong, and it started at the beginning.

A heavy book slammed in the front of the classroom. I jerked upright. Professor Seavers had stopped the presentation and was glowering at Salvatore.

"Mr. Fox, would you care to share with the class what was so important you couldn't give your classmates the courtesy of your attention?"

Salvatore's face drained of color, and he croaked, but no words came out. I couldn't stand seeing him like that, so I pressed my hand on his arm and threw myself under the bus.

"Actually, I was pointing something out to Salvatore about the math in the projections," I said.

Seavers' sharp gaze hit me like a laser. "Oh? I'd like to hear your observations, Ms. Sanderson."

The trio of idiots tried to protest, but one hiss from Seavers cut them off, and all eyes were back on me.

To be honest, I didn't understand exactly what Sal had explained to me—because math—but I had a steel-trap memory, so I recited his words as if they were my own. As I did, Dylan typed furiously on his computer, his brow pinched tight. Kayleigh looked like she was going to faint. Abby was over Dylan's shoulder, jabbing her finger at the screen.

Professor Seavers folded her arms on her chest as she stared up at the screen, checking out the validity of Salvatore's finding. After a minute, she turned to the presenters.

"It seems Ms. Sanderson is correct. Your projections are way off," she said flatly.

Dylan shot to his feet. "We were given the numbers we based our projections on. That comes directly from Oliver Bergen."

So, I wasn't the only one being thrown under the bus. Either Oliver was shady as hell or Dylan had found a handy scapegoat for his incompetence.

"Be that as it may, I can't allow you to be part of the event on Saturday unless you're able to have this fully resolved and I have the new projections in my hands within the next twenty-four hours," Professor Seavers told them. "Do you think that's possible?"

Abby nodded vigorously. "We'll take care of it."

They were so distracted by their crisis, they didn't even bother to shoot me or Sal dirty looks. When class ended, they booked it out of there, presumably for an emergency meeting with Oliver.

Lock walked me home after class, and I'd been in too good of a mood to fight him. He asked me why I was smiling to myself, and I just shrugged. He didn't get to hear about my triumphs anymore. He'd lost that privilege.

Lock was there the next morning. And the next. He walked me to classes and sent me pictures. He told me how to get to his favorite tidepools and the exact time of day to go. I thought he was trying to be sweet, but the idea of going to the tidepools without him just made me sad.

The one thing he didn't do was falter. No matter how many times I told him to go away, he stayed. He didn't get mad at me for rejecting him. He didn't try to touch me without my consent. Well...okay, except for a few hair brushes. But I'd consented to those in my mind. And he hadn't pressured me. He had just been there. He was always, always there.

After class Friday, Sal and I had to set up our presentation for the alumni showing up in the morning as judges and potential investors. Sal was the numbers guy, while I had taken the reins of the marketing. And...well, as with most parts of my life, I was extra.

Each group was given an empty classroom to set up in. When Lock told us he'd help, I didn't deny him. Because of said extraness, we needed all the help we could get. We had tents and a mock campfire. All around the room were blown-up photos of kids and adults camping. There was a hammock in one corner, an archery board in another. On the ceiling, we meticulously taped up constellations.

This was all to set the ambience and get our investors in the mood. Shana would be here in the morning to help sell her idea while Sal and I would share the nitty-gritty of profits, tax deductions, and the general projections of growth.

When everything was set up, Sal, Lock, and I stood back to check out our work.

"This is incredible." Lock's palm grazed my back, but he dropped it as quickly as it came.

"This is all Elena," Sal said. "She came up with everything you see. If it were up to me, it would have been a plain room and a projector. She made it special."

Lock looked down at me. "Yeah, she does that."

My cheeks heated. Goddammit, he had me blushing again.

"Thanks, Salvatore. You're the best partner a girl could ask for."

We walked out and carefully closed the door. Voices at the end of the hall had all three of us turning our heads. Professor Seavers, Oliver, and Dylan were standing in a cluster, tension rising from their group. From what I'd gathered, Oliver had not been able to provide the appropriate numbers on time, and by the way he kept shaking his head and throwing his arms up, things weren't looking so great.

Too bad, so sad, and all that jazz.

Oliver's head turned, and his eyes zeroed in on me. I froze as he shot a vicious glare my way. I guess he knew who'd pointed out the flaw in his numbers. My chest rattled as his waves of fury pummeled into me.

Lock cupped the back of my neck. "He can't do anything to you," he murmured. "You're safe. Breathe."

"He's mad."

He hummed in agreement. "He can stay mad, but he can't do a thing to you. Not while I'm here—and I *am* here, Elena."

"Eff that guy," Sal said. "He's running a shady business. The only person he should be mad at is himself."

"Yeah, eff that guy." Shaking away my fear, I looked up at Lock, whose jaw was tight with tension. "I'm ready to go now. I'm good."

I let Lock drive me home, and when he pulled into his driveway, I didn't immediately jump out. He left the engine idling and the AC cooling the cab while we sat for a minute or two before I turned on the bench, pulling my leg up so I could fully face him. Of course, he was already looking at me.

I sucked in a breath, then went for it. "I don't understand how it is so easy for you to flip a switch. We're sleeping together, and it's so good, but you send me packing. Then we're together for real and—even if you don't admit it, we both know we were falling in love—and you send me packing again. Now, you've flipped it yet again, deciding you want me back. If I forgive you, how can I trust you won't do it again? How do I do that?"

This time, when his hand touched mine, I allowed it. I wasn't proud, but after a solid week of Lock being close and denying myself contact, I gave in. Just a little. His fingertips were as light as feathers, brushing along my knuckles. When I didn't pull away, he caught my hand in his and held on, rubbing his thumb along the back of it.

Tension flowed out of my body so quickly, I fell against the seat and sighed. I would have been embarrassed, but Lock didn't react. His focus was on our joined hands.

"I do admit it." His eyes flicked to mine.

"What?"

"That I was falling in love with you."

I jerked back like he'd shot me, but he kept my hand in his. "What?"

"When it comes to you, there's no switch. I never turned anything off because I can't. I'm not capable of doing that. Not with you, Ellie." He scoffed, lowering his eyes to our hands again. "I stayed away from you for exactly forty-eight hours, and I was only able to do that because I knew I'd see you in Spanish class. I had to replay my dad's tears in my head so I didn't follow you inside that first day."

I wondered if it was too late for me to hear him. Maybe I'd gotten too hard to let what he was saying really penetrate.

"Pretty, pretty words, Lock, but the fact remains, you *did* walk away. You didn't follow me inside. You told me you were done with me. How can I know you won't do that again?"

Lifting my hand, he rubbed it against his stubbled cheek. "Because I know what it feels like. I know what I did to you, and I know what I did to myself. That's not happening again. It can't. We'll figure out the future together, Wyoming, all of it. I don't see myself going there without you. I can't see much of anything without you."

No. No, that sank in. His lovely promises had found the cracks and wormed their way through them.

"You're going to keep selling me on it?"

He looked at me from under his lashes, as if he could read my mind and was fully aware of what his pretty eyes had always done to me. "Until you love it like I do, yeah. I'm going to keep selling you on me too."

His lips touched my hand, and the contact, after almost two weeks of *nothing,* sent a ripple of little tremors through me. I lunged across the seat, straddling his lap so fast, I surprised even myself.

I kissed him hungrily, biting his lips and shoving my fingers through his hair. Groaning, he cradled the back of my hair and palmed my ass, pulling me into his chest. I slipped my hand under his shirt, soaking up his warmth as I sucked on his tongue and went feral for his kisses.

It was messy and wet, but we exchanged need and frustration in those kisses. All I could think about was how right it was to be back here, in my place. His arms were strong, his chest was warm, his middle was soft, and my body fit around him like a snake slithering back into my perfect den.

"Elena," he growled against my lips, tugging at the bottom one with another groan. "Fuck, Ellie, I love you."

I pressed into him harder, drowning out his voice. I *couldn't* hear those words right now. I wasn't ready for them. This was what I wanted: his mouth, his touch—not promises I wasn't sure I should believe.

We kissed until I ran out of breath and my head went fuzzy. I sucked in air, then dove in for more. He gave me as much as I wanted, holding me flush, keeping me as close as I could be. It wasn't enough. I wanted to claw off his clothes and skin to fit myself inside his skeleton so I could always, always have him around me. I'd never be afraid he'd leave me. He'd be mine. More importantly, I'd be his.

That whacked-out desire broke me out of my stupor. I tore my mouth from his. He leaned his head back on the rest, watching me from under hooded eyes. I touched my fingertips to his wet, swollen lips, doing the same to my lips with my other hand.

He patted my butt and rubbed his big hand up and down my spine, soothing me, calming me down with a simple touch. He couldn't have known the insanity going through my mind, but he could tell I needed what he was giving me without me saying a single word.

"I do love you," he murmured. "I won't hurt you."

"I want to believe you. I *really* do." I cupped his cheeks and sighed. It would be so easy if I could let myself fall into this blindly, but part of me was still too injured to let go. "I need more time."

He didn't flinch or let his expression change. "Then you'll have more time. I'm not going anywhere."

"What if it takes a year for me to get there?"

"Then I'll wait a year." *Steady as he goes...*

With all the reluctance in the world, I climbed off him and gathered my bag. By the time I reached for the door, Lachlan was there, holding it open for me. He walked me through the grass to my porch and unlocked my door. I cracked it open but turned back.

"Thank you for all your help. Sal and I would still be there setting up if not for you."

He stepped forward, dipped down, and pecked my nose. "Anything, Ellie. I'll do anything you need, and you never have to thank me." Then he gave my butt a light smack. "Go get some rest. You have a big day tomorrow."

He pushed me inside and shut the door before I could say another word. I leaned my forehead against it and sighed. If I could figure out how to do it, I would forgive him.

I pressed my hand against the wood and whispered the truth. "I love you too."

Chapter Thirty-six

Elena

I slept that night, and I did it well.

Normally, before something big and important, I'd have been up pacing, checking and double-checking the details. The perfectionist in me did not allow for rest. But when I walked inside after Lachlan had dropped me off, my knees had been weak—and not just from his soul-destroying kisses. I went directly to my bed. The past couple weeks had come crashing down on me all at once, sweeping me under.

I woke in a panic, obviously. All the double-checking I should have done last night would have to happen this morning. Despite my panic, for the first time in weeks, I wasn't angry. That had been swept away too.

Zadie was in the kitchen when I padded in. She was in the middle of stirring something in a big bowl at the island. She chirped a greeting at me, to which I grunted, and went directly to the coffee maker.

"I'm making lemon poppy muffins. They'll be ready in thirty minutes, if you have time to wait," Zadie said.

I grunted again. "I have the presentation today."

"No kidding. That's why I'm up at the crack of dawn, making you your favorite muffins."

My heart was like a little flower, turning in the direction of Zadie's sun to soak up her warmth and thoughtfulness.

"Holy shit, girlie." I circled my arms around her shoulders. "You're making muffins for me? What did I do to deserve this?"

She leaned into my embrace, grinning. "Bitch-slapped a girl in my honor and bought me a pink bat."

I preened. Those were some of my proudest moments. "You're easy, you hussy."

She choked out a laugh. "Only for my best girls and my man." Turning her head, she peered at me with narrowed eyes. "Can I just say that despite your caveman grunting, you seem like maybe, possibly, you're in a better mood this morning?"

"You can say that." I tapped her nose before letting her go to slurp down more coffee. "I think I slept ten hours straight last night."

Her mouth formed a cute little *O*. "Really? Did you just pass out, or did something happen to lighten your mind?"

I rubbed my lips together, flashing back to the truck, the kisses, the desire to insert myself inside Lachlan's skeleton.

"I made out with Lachlan and he told me he loves me."

Zadie dropped her spoon, squealing. "Of course he does. Any idiot could see that. He just got lost there for a bit. And that I understand, because you're you."

"What does that mean?" If anyone else had said that, I would have prepared for a fight. But this was Zadie, whose capacity for kindness continued to boggle my mind. I was safe with her.

"It means that a man like Lachlan, who is the kind of guy who knows exactly what he wants and has his path planned out, would be thrown off by a woman like you. You're unexpected, El. I'm certain he never saw you coming. He probably had to recalibrate once he realized *you* are his path. But I knew he would get himself together sooner than later."

I fought the urge to hug her again. Twice in the span of five minutes would be going overboard.

"I don't know if that's true or not, but I want to believe that," I admitted.

"Then believe it." She picked up her spoon. "Now, go get dressed while I make your muffins. You're wasting time with me when you could be pacing and worrying."

I rolled my eyes at her. Damn, this girl knew me too well.

••••••••••

I handed Sal a warm lemon poppy muffin. "For you, Salvatore."

He jumped, like I'd handed him a bomb. "Oh. Uh, thanks."

"I had nothing to do with the making of this muffin. My roommate, Zadie, is responsible, and since she's an absolute angel, trust that it's not loaded with poison."

His shoulders relaxed, and he started to unpeel the wrapper as we walked inside the building to our classroom. Apparently, I had a little more work to do with Salvatore since he trusted a stranger over me. What had I done to give him the idea I'd poison him?

Was it wrong that I was amused?

"You look nice today, Salvatore."

His eyes took a quick perusal of me as he chewed a big bite of muffin. He swallowed hard, giving me a wobbly smile. "You do too. And you can tell your roommate her muffin is delicious."

"Oh, I will." I winked and Sal sputtered, his cheeks flaming bright red.

Sal and I were both dressed to the nines in suits, ready to meet with potential investors. We were early, so we had time to double and triple-check that everything was in order. Shana would be here in an hour or so, then we had another half hour before showtime. I was finally feeling good about how things were going to go.

I should have known better. Optimism wasn't my friend. Things couldn't look up for long before the pendulum swung the other way.

The first sign that today wouldn't be going how I expected was the open door. It was only cracked, but it should have been firmly shut and locked. The second sign was when I pushed the door open, it met resistance. Something was on the floor that shouldn't have been.

"Sal," I quivered. "I can't look."

He placed his hand on my shoulder. "I'll go first. I'm sure it's fine."

Stepping aside, I closed my eyes and let him take the lead. His strangled cry had my eyes flying open to meet a horror show.

Destroyed. All our hard work was utterly destroyed. The hours we'd spent setting everything up had gone to waste.

My knees gave out, but Sal caught me, guiding me to a chair.

"It's okay, Elena, we'll figure it out."

I didn't see how we could. There wasn't enough time. Even if there was, defeat weighed me down so much, I couldn't seem to get myself to move.

This was too much.

My fight had run out.

I'm done.

Chapter Thirty-seven

Lock

I walked into chaos. Pictures were on the ground, the tent on its side, missing parts, constellations crumpled on the conference table. Sal was scurrying around, picking things up, but Elena was sitting in a chair, staring unblinking at a wall as tears rolled down her cheeks.

I pulled a chair in front of her, sat down, and took her hands in mine. "What happened?"

She gestured around her, sniffling. "They win."

"You know who did this?"

She blinked slowly, sending more tears cascading over the brim of her eyes. "I have a guess."

The idiots from her class. Who else would have done this?

I swiped the tears away with my thumbs, aching at the sight of them. Whoever had made my girl cry would pay. They'd be crying before the end of this.

I kept the riot of fury out of my voice and offered her the calm she needed. "We'll fix it. I'm here now, I know where everything goes. Get up. We'll make it right."

She shook her head. "There's not enough time. It won't...I can't. This is too much."

I'd never once seen her like this. Elena had gone through getting gum in her hair, a bump on her head, bloody chin, been called every nasty name, and probably a whole hell of a lot more she hadn't shared with me, and she hadn't missed a step. I couldn't help thinking I'd done this. I'd started the break, and this was the last straw that had snapped her in two.

I rubbed her arms, needing to bring her back. "Listen to me, Ellie. You're strong. I've never known anyone stronger than you. You've got this."

Her mouth pinched. Her chin quivered. "I hate that. I don't want to be told how strong I am. That's just an excuse the patriarchy uses so they keep piling shit on women. '*Oh, she's so strong. Look how she handles all that horror without breaking. Let's give her more. She can take it!*' Well, I don't want to anymore. Fuck being strong. Fuck the patriarchy. This is too much, and I am not strong enough to handle it. I won't be ashamed to say that."

Anger was washing away her tears. She was right. I'd done this to her, the pressure from her parents, the bullies, Nate, Oliver, the goddamn patriarchy—it was all coming to a head, and she shouldn't have had to handle it.

Leaning forward, I kissed her nose, then her forehead. "Sal and I have got you. We'll fix this, then we'll tear apart the ones responsible. I've got you, Elena."

Climbing to my feet, I stepped outside, called a few guys from maintenance, including Theo, then got to work with Sal. Within twenty minutes, five other guys showed up, all of them pitching in.

Elena stayed in her seat for a while, and everyone let her be. Once, I'd turned around from hanging up the constellations, and she hadn't been in the room. The next time I'd checked, she'd come back, makeup fixed, hair smooth, and was directing Theo where to hang pictures.

The timing was tight, but we got the job done. Everything was back in its place, and Elena had found her inner reserves to pull herself together. When the guys filed out, she thanked each of them. I went last, carrying a ladder with me.

"We did it," I murmured.

"You did. Tha—"

I tapped her lips. "Don't thank me. I'm happy as hell I can be here for you."

"I'm happy you were here for me too."

"We should talk, after all this."

She nodded. "Okay."

I hesitated, not wanting to leave. "I should go, let you do your thing."

"You should."

"Okay."

Her mouth twitched, and she placed her hands on my chest. I dipped down, giving her my mouth. Her lips were soft, sweet, and far too fast. She backed away, taking my sweet with her.

"Good luck," I gruffed, my chest filled with her. Everything was her.

"Thank you—and don't you dare tell me not to say it."

Chuckling, I shook my head. I gave Sal a wave, took one last look at my girl, and headed out. She was going to be okay. I had a good feeling about it.

·····•·····

I put away my ladder in a maintenance closet on the floor up from Elena's presentation and locked up. A group of three guys were headed in my direction, and something about them was familiar. As they approached, I recognized them from Elena's class. Specifically, one from last night. He'd been in the hall when we'd left the room. He'd known it was unguarded and held a grudge a mile wide.

"Hey, asshole," I barked.

All three of them looked my way, but my attention was focused squarely on the one. I strode up to him, getting in his space.

"You think you're funny?"

He stepped back. "I don't know you."

"Oh, I think you do. I think you know my girl too." I bumped him with my chest, backing him into a wall. "You think you're going to get away with what you did?"

"Is this about the chair? It's been proven I didn't touch her chair," he stammered.

One of his friends grabbed my arm, telling me to back off, but I shrugged him away. I'd deal with him later.

"So, you do know me."

He glanced left and right, but he wasn't going to get any help from his friends. "You're Elena's boyfriend, yeah. But I don't know why you're accosting me in the hall."

"You're pissed at her, aren't you? You screwed up your project and have somehow made it her fault. Isn't that right?"

He clicked his tongue. "She didn't have to be a bitch and point it out in front of the whole class."

I brought my arm up, pressing into his chest. "What the fuck did you just say?"

Shaking his head, he squeezed his eyes shut. "Nothing. It slipped out. I didn't mean it. It's just—fuck, I'm gonna fail the midterm, which means I'm gonna fail the class, and I'm pissed, but I get it's not her fault. Oliver Bergen is the little bitch who screwed us over."

"You know that, so why'd you go after Elena? You had to go out as a petty little boy? Destroy her work?"

His eyes met mine. "I don't know what you're talking about. I didn't destroy anything."

"No? Why not? Didn't want to get your hands dirty? Did you send one of your friends in to take apart her presentation?"

"Man, he didn't do shit," one of the guys claimed. "No one would be dumb enough to do something in front of the cameras."

I pressed my arm harder into his chest. "Is that right? Where were you last night?"

"Uh...fuck, I was out to dinner with my parents and grandparents—both sets. I'm sure you could call the restaurant if you're that concerned. Then I went out to the bars and got toasted. The last thing I was thinking about was fucking with Elena. I'm telling you, dude, I have no idea what you're talking about."

I turned my head to his friend. "There are cameras in the classroom?"

The guy nodded vigorously. "Yeah, of course. Dylan knows that now. That's how Tre and Andrew got caught messing with the chair. You think Dylan would be dumb enough to pull the same thing?"

With a breath of frustration, I backed off Dylan and pointed a finger at him. "If I find out you're lying, I'm coming for you. If you so much as look in Elena's direction, you'll see me there. If you try to talk to her, you'll find yourself short a tongue. She doesn't exist to you anymore. That's the same for all your friends who might hold a grudge. It's over. Move on with your lives while you have them. You get me?"

"Sure." Dylan straightened his collar. "Whatever. I get you."

The three of them shot me looks like I was the villain, but it didn't bother me. If it kept them away from Elena, they could believe I was the biggest villain around.

Now, I had to find out who was responsible for sabotaging Elena and Sal's project. And I had a feeling I already knew.

CHAPTER THIRTY-EIGHT

ELENA

I'D PULLED MY SHIT together and made magic happen. Well, some help was involved, like Lachlan and all his big, manly worker bees. Salvatore was impressing both me and the alumni he talked numbers with, Shana was charming the pants off everyone with her enthusiasm, and I gave in-depth explanations about our marketing plan.

There was a lot of nodding, smiling, and questions. So many questions.

I'd just gotten through a conversation with a pair of enthusiastic alumni when a tall man in dark jeans and a button-up approached me. His smile was friendly, and the way he looked at me made me wonder if we'd met.

I reached out to shake, and my hand was encased in his huge, warm mitt. My eyes flicked to his, and that was when the familiarity made sense.

"It's nice to finally meet you, Elena. I'm Connell Kelly."

My heart flipped in my chest. What was happening? "It's nice to meet you too. Lachlan didn't tell me you were coming."

He chuckled and gently released my hand. "My boy told me about this project, and I was so intrigued, I couldn't stay away." He ducked his head to create intimacy between us without invading my personal space. "To tell you the truth, I'd been looking for an excuse to fly down here to meet you. I've heard a lot about you since the two of you met. Of course, there've been more mentions over the last few months. It takes something special to turn Lock's head, so curiosity got the best of me."

"Did he know you were planning to be here?" I asked.

Connell winked. "He had an idea. Now, why don't you tell me about this program? I've read the brochure, but I'd like to hear it from you."

In a surreal turn of events, I took Lachlan's dad around the room, explaining Shana's vision as well as I could. Then I introduced the two of them, and I swore she nearly fainted. She quickly collected herself, but not without telling Connell Sugar Brush River Ranch was her absolute dream location for her summer camp.

The room eventually cleared out, but the two of them were still deep in conversation while Sal and I stood by like proud parents. Movement at the door caught my eye. Lachlan entered, and right behind him was a beautiful blonde girl I instantly recognized as his sister.

Saoirse's eyes landed on me, and she threw her arms out. I wasn't a hugger, but this girl was so happy to see me, I walked straight into her arms and let her go to town, squeezing me tight. Over her shoulder, Lachlan watched his sister and me with a soft expression, even as he shook his head at her antics.

"Hi," she whispered. "Surprise! We're here!"

She let go of me, and Lachlan immediately pulled me into his side, tipping my chin up with his finger to examine me.

"How'd it go?" he asked.

"Really, really well. Did you know they were coming?"

He cocked his head. "Are you mad?"

I shook my head. "Surprised."

"I knew they were coming. I told my dad about the startup. He liked the sound of it, so I asked him if he could fly in for this. I didn't want to make you nervous or I would have told you."

"That was incredibly thoughtful." And so very Lachlan.

He tapped my lips. "Later. We'll talk later."

"Okay."

Lachlan's family stayed behind to help break down the room, despite my many, *many* protests, which I should have known would fall on deaf ears. Saoirse made Sal blush just by talking to him, and watching Lachlan with his dad gave me all sorts of twinges. I was only a tiny bit jealous of how functional the three of them were together. But mostly, I was resolved.

I would've been a complete imbecile not to take the leap and give Lachlan my trust after he'd proven himself to me again and again. I would be punishing myself if I didn't take one more chance on him, and masochism just wasn't my kink.

And when we could be alone, I'd tell him that.

··········

I'd been home for an hour or so when someone knocked on my door. It couldn't have been Lachlan since he was spending time with his family. I was surprised to find Saoirse standing on my porch.

"Hi." She waved, and it was so enthusiastic and cute.

"Hey. What's up?"

She rolled her eyes. "Dad and Lock are talking about ranch stuff. They're going over numbers and talking about ordering equipment. It's super boring, so I told them I was coming to see what you were up to. I ran out before my brother could stop me. So, can I come in?"

"Oh, yeah." I stepped back, giving her room to enter. "I'm not doing anything interesting either. I needed a mind break after today."

"That makes sense." She glanced around the living room and bounced on her toes. "Your house is really pretty. Not what I pictured a college house to be like. Lock said your dad owns it and you're, like, the property manager or something. That's really cool."

"That's true, but I don't know if it's cool. It is an incentive to keep the place nice, though. Did your brother tell you he rebuilt our deck?"

Her eyes bugged. "He didn't, but I'm not surprised. I mean, he can build anything. He's so into you, he'd probably build you a castle if you wanted one."

Oh, balls. That was a jab to the heart, because I truly believed her. Lock had brought his dad here for me. He'd done so, so much for me. Because that's who he was. At least, who he was with me. I touched my chest where it was pinching. She must have seen the change in me, because she rushed forward, clutching my arms.

"He told me how badly he messed up. If I'd been here, I would have punched him. Instead, I yelled at my mom and dad. Told them to look at what they had done to Lock. Because they can't get their shit together and act like adults—don't tell my brother I cussed—they made him give up the girl he loves. And you know what? For once, my mom had nothing to say. And my dad...well, he's here, you know. I have a feeling now that I'm at your place, he's probably giving Lock a fatherly heart-to-heart."

"That's..."

Saoirse gasped. "I'm sticking my nose in your business and you barely know me. Let me just say Lock won't mess up again. He's really the best man I know, even better than my dad. So, if you give him a second chance, he'll treat you right. And then we'll get to be sisters—which may be a deterrent for you. I promise, I'm not always this extra, I'm just so excited to meet you."

I had to laugh. "I'm happy to meet you too, Saoirse. And I'll tell you a secret: I'm going to give him another chance. It's the last one he's getting, though."

She did a victory dance, but quickly sobered and looked me square in the eye. "If he screws up again, I'll help you bury the body. There are lots of places at the ranch. No one would ever uncover him."

Strangely warmed by her homicidal threats, I pulled her onto the sectional with me and made her spill about the ranch. Then she asked me millions of questions about college life. I gave her the best advice I could think of: avoid frat boys, make friends with the smart kids, and work your ass off while having as much fun as possible because real life will come too fast.

SWEET LIKE POISON

Saoirse and her dad were going to a football game later, so I told her she could borrow some of my Savage U gear and ran upstairs to grab a couple shirts for her to choose from. While I was rummaging around, the doorbell rang. My ears perked up, listening to Saoirse answer it in her friendly way, speaking to someone with a male voice who definitely wasn't Lachlan.

The door slammed, and Saoirse made something of a panicked squeal. I shot to my feet, poised to run to help her, when I heard *him*.

"Elena...come out, come out, wherever you are," Oliver Bergen cooed from downstairs. "I want to chat for a minute."

Oh, no, he did not. If I had hesitated, I would have panicked, but I flew into action, dropping the T-shirts and grabbing my pink bat from beside my bed. Whatever Oliver wanted, it couldn't be good, and I was ready for him this time.

I raced down the stairs, my bat resting on my shoulder. Oliver and Saoirse were standing in the middle of the living room, his arm around her shoulders. Her body was stiff, her eyes wide, petrified. As for Oliver, his forehead was shiny with sweat, his hair disheveled in a way that seemed like he'd been clawing at it. His eyes were unblinking. His smile was manic. He'd never looked more like his brother.

"You need to get your hands off her, Oliver."

He snorted a laugh. "You don't get to tell me what to do, Elena. This is *my* time to talk."

"Fine, I'll listen, but not until you let her go."

He jiggled Saoirse, making her yelp. "Nah, I don't think I'll be letting this sweet little girl go. I think I like her."

"Well, she doesn't like you." I cocked my bat. "Take your hands off her, Oliver. Do it right now."

"No." He stroked her cheek with the back of his hand. "I don't think I will. I don't think I'll do anything you want me to do, Elena. I'm going to talk about you destroying my life, and you're going to apologize. That's what's going to happen."

"I didn't do anything to you." I met Saoirse's gaze, willing her to break away and run, but she was frozen with fear. Oliver was bigger than her, stronger, and he had crazy on his side. If I weren't so mad, I'd be afraid too, but I wasn't going to allow fear to seep in. Not until I bashed his head in and saved Saoirse.

Oliver guffawed. "Didn't do anything to me? That's fucking rich, cunt. You took my little brother, jerked him around for years, and ruined him." Saliva flew from his mouth as he spit accusations so off base, they were laughable. "I've always believed you had something to do with him dying. The circumstances never made sense to me. Did you somehow tamper with his airbag? You can tell me the truth, Elena. It's not like you'll get in trouble. Who punishes pretty blonde girls?"

"Oliver—"

He reached into his pocket and pulled out a switchblade. "Oh, that's right, *I'm* the one who's going to punish this pretty blonde girl." He gestured from me to Saoirse. "Maybe both pretty blonde girls. I don't know if I'll be satisfied with just one. I might have been, had you gone down this morning. You *should* have. That room was a wreck. There was no way you should've had enough time to put it back together. But *somehow*, some-fucking-how, you did. And that's not right, Elena! You deserve everything you've done to me. You deserve to hurt. You deserve pain. You deserve to be ruined."

"Oliver," I yelled. "This isn't going to happen."

I couldn't hesitate, not with the knife in his hand. It was closed, but the madness glazing his eyes warned me his intentions were more than a threat. He wanted blood.

"Fuck you, cu—"

I swung my bat, colliding with his chest. He made an *oof* sound and bent forward, dropping his arm from Saoirse.

"Run!" I screamed, winding up to hit him again. "Go get Lock!"

Once Oliver wasn't touching her, she woke up and scrambled away from him. He howled as she darted toward the door, lunging for her. I swung my bat, catching him in the arm and spinning him around to face me. Saoirse yanked open the door and ran, yelling for her brother.

Oliver didn't let her escape deter him from his mission of destruction. If he'd been mad before, now he was furious. He flicked open the knife, swinging the blade around in front of him.

"Stay away from me," I warned. "Don't make me break your dick."

"Why not? You broke my business. You made a fool out of me and stole my chance to find investors. Why not break my dick too?" He scratched his head with the knife. "No, no, that won't do. I think I'd rather break you. You're not going to take another fucking thing from my family. Taking my brother and my business is too much, Elena. I can't let you get away with it."

"Fuck you, Oliver. Nate was a monster, and so are you."

With the speed of a man who'd given up all pretenses of sanity, he grabbed the end of my bat and yanked it out of my hands, tossing it aside. He took one step, then another, and I had nothing to defend myself from him.

I tried to break for the door, but he was there, blocking my path. Lock would be here soon. Lock would stop him. I just needed to give myself time. A door between Oliver and me. If I couldn't leave, I'd hide.

Swiveling around, I ran for the stairs, scampering up them as fast as I could. I felt Oliver behind me, his breath practically on my neck. There was screaming, and it might have been from me, but I didn't know if it was happening in my head.

I crested the last step, only to crash onto my face when Oliver caught my ankle. I kicked at him, connecting with something solid, but my feet were bare, and he was too crazed to feel pain, so he kept coming, crawling up my legs.

A boom rang out from the front door. *Lachlan!* Oliver must have locked it, because the banging continued.

"Just stay still," Oliver gritted out. "You slippery little bitch, stay still and take your punishment."

"Never! I'll never stay still."

I bucked and clawed at the ground, pulling myself away from him. Oliver might have had crazy on his side, but I had the strength of a woman who refused to become a victim yet again. I kicked out again, hitting what felt distinctly like a nose, then again and again, until Oliver loosened his grip and I slid on my belly out of his hold.

"You have to be punished," he yelled with the righteous passion only a rich, overprivileged mama's boy could summon.

I flung myself into my bedroom, slamming the door closed just as Oliver reached out to grab me again. He roared on the other side, driving his body into it over and over. All I wanted to do was curl into a ball and cover my ears until this was all over, but I made myself stand there, waiting, watching, ready to fight if I had to.

"You ruined me, Elena. Everything is ruined. All because of you. My family, my brother—it's all destroyed, because of you. Why couldn't you just let it go? Why'd you have to stick your nose in it?" The door handle rattled, but the lock held.

"Elena!" My heart flipped in my chest. Lachlan was here.

"He has a knife," I screamed. "Lachlan, he has a knife!"

The next five minutes were the longest of my life. I had no idea what was going on out there. There was scuffling, the sounds of fists meeting flesh, but I couldn't tell who was winning. If Oliver hurt Lachlan, if he stabbed or cut him, I'd rip his heart out and bind him with his intestines.

The doorknob jiggled, and I shrieked, jumping away from it.

"Elena, it's okay, sweet girl. It's me. I want you to stay there until I come back. The cops are outside. Tell me you're okay."

I pressed my hand to the door. "Are *you* okay?"

His exhale was heavy and ragged. "I'm doing fine. Now that I know you're good, I can handle what I need to."

"Lachlan, Lock," I called in a panic.

"Yeah?"

"I love you."

A pause, then a light clunk on the door. "I love you too, El. So fucking much. Stay there. I'll be right back and tell you to your face."

I believed him. I trusted him. So, I sank down to my butt and waited for the man I loved to come back to me.

Chapter Thirty-nine

Lock

A HUNDRED YEARS PASSED before I got back to Elena's bedroom. As soon as I knocked on her door, it flung open, and she leaped at me, wrapping her arms and legs around me. Shivers racked her entire body. Her breath was hot and frantic against my throat.

I was supposed to be bringing her downstairs to be checked out by a paramedic, but fuck that. Kicking the door shut, I walked her to her bed and sat down, my shaking girl clinging to me.

After the scene I'd walked in on, I needed to hold her just as badly. I'd never forget Saoirse's screams, her panicked attempts at telling me there was a man with a knife and Elena was alone with him, the quicksand holding my feet down, not allowing me to get to her fast enough.

When I'd thrown Oliver down on the ground, I'd done it with all the power and fury of a man in love with a girl who'd changed him irrevocably. That was a mighty thing Oliver would be feeling for some time. Still, it wasn't enough. Nothing short of death would have been, and I couldn't do it—not when it meant I'd be taken away from Elena.

Not when I was just getting her back.

"You're okay," I murmured. "He's gone. You're safe."

"I'm okay," she repeated. "I'm safe with you."

"That's right."

Pulling her gently away from my throat, I cupped her face in my hands, sweeping over her to check for injuries. Her chin quivered.

Her cheeks were flushed. Otherwise, she was none the worse for wear—at least on the outside.

"Beautiful, sweet girl. So brave. So, so brave."

She blinked at me, sucking in a ragged breath. "Saoirse?"

"She's fine." I stroked her cheek in a slow, lazy pattern. "She's not hurt. She's with my dad next door."

"Okay." Her chin quivered harder. She was trying with all her might to keep it together. "I couldn't let him hurt her. Not your sister."

"And you didn't, El. You saved both of you." I pressed my forehead to hers. "I've got you now. You don't have to be brave anymore. I'm not letting you go. I won't let anyone get to you."

She nodded against my forehead, taking shaky breath after shaky breath. "I was going to forgive you before this."

I pushed back from her again, frowning in confusion. "What?"

"I didn't tell you I love you because I almost died. I'd already decided to let you back in before Oliver showed up and...you know, tried to kill me." She shivered at her own words, then her eyes flicked to mine and she gave me the smallest smile. "I just want you to know I'm not forgiving you because of Oliver. I want to be with you because I can't stand *not* being with you. I hope you still want me even though my baggage put Saoirse in danger. Do you?"

"No question. Don't even think that. You are not responsible for the failures of men. Don't take that on." I took her hand in mine and balled it into a little fist, raising it in the air. "Fuck the patriarchy, right?"

She gave me another little smile. "Fuck the patriarchy."

I kissed her fist then the tip of her nose. "I love the hell out of you."

She leaned in and kissed the tip of *my* nose. "I love the hell out of you too."

The reality of what we'd just endured would come, but for now, all I wanted to do was bury my face in her moonlit hair and hold my girl.

Elena was sprawled on my chest, not sleeping, but finally calm.

The last two days had been the longest of my life. Now that my dad and Saoirse were home, Oliver was locked snug in a jail cell, and my girl was back in my arms, I could finally breathe. I couldn't seem to relax, though. It might be a long time before that happened.

Before Saoirse had come running to tell me about Oliver, my dad and I had had a talk. *The* talk that cemented everything I knew and shifted my way of thinking about things I hadn't understood.

"I'm not proud of myself," my dad said.

I blinked at him. "Why not?"

He scrubbed his scruffy jaw, a move I'd inherited from him when I was thinking.

"This situation between Elena and you was caused by my and your mother's carelessness. There was a time when we loved each other so much, it seemed like that would conquer everything. But neither of us had ever faced any challenges. We didn't know what kind of people we'd be when the vise of life tightened on us. I'm not saying we never should have married, but I am saying the promises we made were fool's gold."

My brow furrowed. "I know all this."

"You do, in a way. But you don't know it was me who broke your mother's heart first. Long before the divorce, I did something I'm ashamed of. I broke her trust, and we never recovered from it. Before that, we'd been making plans to move to Wyoming as a family, but I ruined it. She couldn't get over her anger, and I couldn't let her go. I still can't, but I don't have a choice."

"You let us think Mom was the bad guy."

He shook his head. "She wanted it that way. She never wanted you two to know about my—"

I held my hand up. "You don't need to say it. I don't want to know. I get it well enough."

"Yeah." His head hung low. "I'm telling you this because I don't want to be the reason you stop yourself from being with the woman you love. From what you've told me and what I know, the two of you are nothing like your mom and me."

"We're not." I could now say that with absolute certainty. *I'd never be my father, but if I somehow lost my mind and did what he was confessing to have done, Elena wouldn't stay quiet. No, she'd string me up by the balls and ring the shame bell so people from far and wide could come see me like that.*

I couldn't help smiling at that. Fuck, but I loved that girl.

"Your mom and I talked. Things are going to change. No more putting you and Saoirse in the middle," he said.

"It's about time."

Elena's fingernails trailed over my bare chest.

"Are you tired?" she asked.

"Exhausted."

She huffed a laugh. "Me too, but I don't think I can sleep."

"Too much on your mind, sweet girl?"

"I don't know." She propped her chin on her hands. "I'm happy you and I are back, but I hate that I can't…I don't know, celebrate it because of that asshole."

"Yeah." I stroked a piece of her silvery hair then tucked it behind her ear. "And I can't stop thinking if I hadn't fucked up in the first place, that guy would have never had the opportunity to get to you. You would have been with me."

Gabe had said the same thing to me when he and Pen had showed up here two days ago. Then he'd hugged me and thanked me for saving her. All it'd had taken was facing down a crazy guy with a knife to get Gabe back on my side. It was worth it, since that was her family.

She touched my mouth with her fingertips. "We can't do this. I won't allow another Bergen in my bed."

Exhaling, I nodded. "Then we won't. What's done is done. All we can do is move forward now."

"God, can we? I don't want to fight anyone. I just want to drink coffee with my hot boyfriend, go for drives, have lots and lots of sex, and maybe study once in a while. Can the rest of college be like that?"

"Am I the hot boyfriend?"

She poked my chin. "You know you are, Lachlan Kelly. Don't be coy."

Rolling to my side to face her, I tucked her flush against me, her head on my bicep. After wasting weeks not holding her, I couldn't get enough of having her in my arms. She fit there. Belonged right next to me.

"Then, yeah, the rest of college can be like that. Maybe we can throw some ranch trips in there so I can turn my city girl into a cowgirl."

Her hand covered my mouth. "You hush your filthy mouth. If you convince me to come with you when we graduate, it will be with the understanding that I will never touch a drop of cow shit, nor will I muck stalls or mend fences. My nails will remain pristine at all times."

I grinned behind her hand. "Will you ride with me?" My question came out muffled, but she heard and slid her hand down to my chest.

She bit down on her lip but couldn't hide the rosiness in her cheeks. She liked that idea. "That's a possibility."

"Good. I've got this fantasy—"

Her eyebrows shot up. "Oh, do tell…"

I smacked her ass. "Dirty girl. This particular fantasy involves us riding around the ranch together."

She snuggled in closer, sighing, and it was so fucking nice. If she could read my mind, see my level of contentment now that I truly had her back, she'd never doubt me again. Since she couldn't, I'd gladly keep showing her.

"We should spend the summer there," I said.

She tipped her head back, frowning. "Are you really trying to make plans with me for next summer? Really?"

"We'll be together. I want you with me. Always. So why not?"

Her next breath was shaky, but her frown melted away. "I think it's going to take me a while to be convinced you mean that. I love you, Lachlan, and I want that too, but I don't quite know how to be loved this way."

I slowly stroked her back as I listened and held her close. "Do you trust me?"

"I do. I trust you."

"Then trust that I'll be solid for you, even when you're shaky. Trust that we've got time, and I'll get you to a place where you don't have to second-guess my promises. Trust that I'm not going anywhere, no matter how long it takes. I've got you, Ellie."

She nuzzled into my throat, touching her lips to my Adam's apple. Her silky hair brushed the underside of my chin as she nodded.

"Lachlan," she sighed. I held my breath, waiting for her answer. "Okay. Let's do this thing."

My next breath was the sweetest I'd ever taken. The following one, even sweeter still. Elena was in my veins, my lungs, my head, my heart. Whether she was venom or the antidote, I didn't care, not when she was in my arms, sliding into sleep. Elena was my sweet, my poison, my fantasy, my beautiful reality. She was everything I didn't think I wanted, and more than I could have asked for. I knew what walking away from her was like, and that would never happen again.

As I'd told her a hundred times and would keep telling her until she believed it, I wasn't going anywhere.

Epilogue

Elena

Five Years Later

"Holy shit, this is disgusting, I love it so much."

Lachlan laughed without looking at me. He, along with two ranch hands, were focused on the calf halfway out of its mother. He didn't typically get involved in the births of calves, but his wife had begged to watch, so he'd arranged it.

His wife was somewhat demanding, but he never had a problem with meeting every one of her demands.

And by her, I meant me. I was the wife demanding to witness a calf being born. What was the point of living on a ranch if I didn't get to see babies?

There were a lot of fluids involved in this birth, and the poor mother was stretched beyond recognition. But there was a cute little baby emerging, with its tongue hanging out, looking like a tiny little cow, so maybe it was worth it.

Finally, one more push and lots and lots of bleating, the baby was fully out and lay in the hay. The mother nonchalantly turned around, looked at the being that had emerged from her body, and started licking it.

My heart did a little flutter.

Lachlan strode over to where I was standing on the outside of the pen and kissed the tip of my nose. "Was it all you'd been expecting?" he asked.

"So much more. Look how cute the baby is. Is it a boy or girl?"

One of the ranch hands—Miguel—yelled the baby was a *chica*. I answered him back in Spanish, telling him to name her Esmerelda because she looked like an Esmerelda.

Miguel laughed, and my husband swooped me up in his arms, carrying me out of the barn. People who worked on the ranch were used to seeing me being hauled about, so no one batted an eye.

Lachlan plopped me in his truck and buckled me in, then he placed a long, wet kiss on my mouth.

"What'd you really think?" he murmured.

"What do you mean?"

I knew what he meant. We'd been married for over three years now. Our wedding had taken place right here on the ranch, a month after we graduated college. When Lachlan made promises, he kept them.

The ceremony had been in a field of wildflowers, the reception under a tent near his dad's house. It hadn't been anything like the pictures on the resort's website. When the time came to get married, I hadn't wanted a big, elaborate affair, and...well, Lachlan wanted what I wanted. My parents had walked me down the aisle, Gabe and Pen had stood by me while Helen and Theo had been on Lachlan's side, and Julien officiated the whole thing. A little nontraditional, but that was us.

On our third wedding anniversary, my husband brought up having a baby. He wanted one. I did too, but I had been unsure on when to start trying. I still had all the memories of my mother's losses, and while my doctor assured me there was no physical reason I couldn't carry a baby to term, the doubts were in the back of my mind.

"Come on, Elsa, don't play games," he growled.

Oh, I didn't get Elsa a lot anymore. Only when I was in trouble.

"Are you asking if watching that cow give birth inspired me to want to do the same?"

He shook his head and closed my door, rounding the truck. I didn't like disappointing him. He did everything for me, treated me thoughtfully and with so much love, I never, ever doubted him.

When he got in the truck, I reached over and squeezed his hand.

"I love you, you know."

He glanced at me, his mouth curving. "I know you do, sweet girl. I love you too."

The ride back to our house was bumpy but smoothed out as we got closer. We'd built our house together during our first year in Wyoming—and by together, I meant I'd told Lachlan what I wanted, and he'd made it happen. He'd even built a mother-in-law suite in case we ever had to take my mom in permanently. I didn't foresee that happening since my dad had switched up his work-life balance and prioritized his wife. I'd given him no choice on the matter. Still, it was nice to have a place for them to stay when they visited, which was every other month.

I waved at a few camper kids riding by on horses. Seeing those kids enjoying a week at the ranch in the summer was a true highlight for me, especially since I'd been part of bringing Shana's program here.

I'd been working in the resort's marketing department since we moved here. It took a *lot* to run a place like Sugar Brush, well beyond the mechanics of the ranch. Actually, most days, I didn't go near a cow or horse. I worked in a beautiful office inside a world-class resort, the type of place I'd always envisioned for myself. It just so happened the world-class resort was in Wyoming, which had grown on me more quickly than I'd imagined. It helped that Saoirse was nearby in Colorado and we saw each other regularly. It doubly helped that my marketing team was four women around my age I had a lot in common with.

Life in Wyoming was good. Outstanding. And I was madly in love with my husband. Really, truly, madly, deeply.

When he helped me out of the truck, I took his hand in mine. "I want to show you something."

He sighed. I could tell he was a little disappointed I'd laughed off his attempt to discuss having a baby, but he'd get over it. I'd make sure he did.

"All right. Let's see it."

Inside, we both kicked off our boots, and I led him upstairs to our master bath. On the counter was a gift bag with his name scrawled on the outside.

"Open that. I think you'll like it," I said, pressing a hand to my chest.

He took my chin in his hand. "What did you do?"

"Open the bag, Lock."

That made him growl and bring his forehead down to mine. "Don't do that. Not right now."

I cupped his cheeks. "Please, babe. Open the bag. Then you can be mad at me if you're still in the mood."

Slowly, he let go and reached into the gift bag. His brow furrowed when he grasped the contents and yanked his fisted hand out. His fingers uncurled, and he stared at the two sticks in his palm.

"What did you do?" he repeated.

I leaned into his arm, butterflies flapping hard in my nervous stomach. "I thought it would take a month for the pills to wear off. I stopped them a few weeks ago and had no idea it would happen so fast. I also didn't tell you I stopped because I didn't want it to be a big thing. I know I should have, but—"

He wrapped me in his arms and pressed his face into my hair. "This is real?"

Tears welled in my eyes from the intensity of his reaction. "It's real."

"You really want this?"

"Do I ever do things I don't want?"

Bringing his head up, his shiny brown eyes met mine. "You want my baby?"

"I do. It's already in there, growing giant as we speak."

Chuckling, he swiped at his eyes, then peered at the two positive pregnancy tests. "Fuck, Ellie. *Fuck*. Between your height and my everything, you're going to give me some *giant* babies."

That made me laugh and fall into him. "No kidding. Why do you think I was nervous about getting knocked up? I'm going to be like that cow, all stretched out and disfigured. Are you ready for that?"

"You've been my girl for over five years, you've prepared me to be ready for anything." He shook his head, grinning at me. "God, sweet girl, I love you so fucking much. Do you know that? Do you believe it?"

"I do. I believe it. I love you too, daddy."

He groaned. "No, that's not going to be a thing."

"I can't call you 'daddy'?" I pressed into him, biting back a grin. "Are you sure, daddy?"

He backed away from me, laughing so hard, his shoulders were shaking. "No, Elsa. No more or your ass is going to be on fire."

I batted my eyes at him. "I'll be good, daddy, I promise."

And then I ran. I only made it as far as the bedroom before he captured me and turned me over on his lap, but let's be real, I wasn't trying to get away.

Why would I want to? Lachlan Kelly gave me beautiful days and hot, hot nights. He was my unshakable foundation, my calm in the storm. My husband was one of the good ones, and I knew it from the tips of my toes to the very depths of my soul. The life we were building wasn't anything like what I'd pictured before I met him—it was light-years better.

Lachlan had patiently uncovered my sweet and willingly gave me his in return. I knew how good I had it. There was no one else like this man. No better life than this. Not for me.

I wasn't going anywhere.

Playlist

"I'm not a good person" Pat the Bunny
"Sorry" Halsey
"Cool Girl" Tove Lo
"Confident" Demi Lovato
"Trouble" Cage the Elephant
"Lie" NF
"Cough Syrup" Melanie Martinez
"Baggage" Rare Americans
"Girls Your Age" Transviolet
"Brighter Than Sunshine" Aqualung
"Heavy in Your Arms" Florence + The Machine
"1965" Zella Day
"Muscle Memory" Lights
"Seventeen Going Under" Sam Fender
"Sweater Weather" The Neighbourhood
"The Emotion" Borns
"Love Brand New" Bob Moses
"Sweetest Thing" Allman Brown
"Two" Sleeping At Last
"Love Like This" Kodaline
"Unsteady" X Ambassadors
https://open.spotify.com/playlist/36AI34mc1Wd9RjhhHkWGsL?si=b9f6f3a9dab246ee

Keep in Touch

I'd love for you to join my reader group on Facebook. That's where you can ask questions, find out book news first, and discuss my books with other readers.

https://www.facebook.com/groups/JuliaWolfReaders

Acknowledgements

THIS BOOK WAS A long time coming. When I first wrote Elena Sanderson in Start a Fire, I honestly didn't envision her ever having her own happily ever after. But as the series progressed and she showed up more often, I kind of fell for her. More surprising to me, readers fell for her too.

Who was this girl who played nice with Grace in front of her mom?

Who was this girl who backed off Asher and Bex when Asher threatened to tell her parents what she was up to?

Who was this girl who had a loving, sweet relationship with her cousin Penelope?

I had a brilliant time answering those questions. I hope Elena is everything you wished for and more.

And for everyone who thought Nate Bergen got off a little too easily in the Savage Crew: I knew what I was doing. Trust the process.

Thank you to my beta goddesses: Jenny Dicks, Jenn, and Alley Ciz. Your notes and encouragement are invaluable to me.

Thank you Amber for holding down the fort in my reader group. It would be crickets without you.

Thank you to Kate Farlow and Regina Wamba for the beautiful cover design and photo. You really brought Lachlan Kelly to life.

To every single woman who has known a Nate Bergen or felt like an Elena Sanderson, I hope I did this story justice. "You are not responsible for the failures of men. Don't take that on. Fuck the patriarchy, right?"

JULIA WOLF'S BOOKS

The Seasons Change

Falling in Reverse

Stone Cold Notes

Faded in Bloom
Savage U

Soft Like Thunder

Bright Like Midnight
The Savage Crew

Start a Fire

Through the Ashes

Burn it Down
Standalones

Built to Fall

Rocked

The Unrequited Series

Unrequited

Misconception

Dissonance
Blue is the Color

Times Like These

Watch Me Unravel

Such Great Heights

Under the Bridge
The Never Blue Duet

Never Lasting

Never Again
The Sublime

One Day Guy

The Very Worst

Want You Bad

Fix Her Up

Eight Cozy Nights

About Julia

Julia Wolf is a bestselling contemporary romance author. She writes bad boys with big hearts and strong, independent heroines. Julia enjoys reading romance just as much as she loves writing it. Whether reading or writing, she likes the emotions to run high and the heat to be scorching.

Julia lives in Maryland with her three crazy, beautiful kids and her patient husband who she's slowly converting to a romance reader, one book at a time.

Visit my website:

http://www.juliawolfwrites.com